Fair Exchange

To My Big Bro
"Street" I luv ya!!

Keep At Movin'

Brenn

Fair Exchange

Brennan Pearl, Jr.

2006

This book is dedicated to:
My Grandmother Elizabeth Stone
My Mother Elaine Pearl
My Aunt Sandra West
and my Uncle Edward Isome Jr.

ACKNOWLEDGMENTS

I must give the following people my sincerest thank you for the contributions they made in helping my career as a writer. I appreciate everything you've done. My brother Tab Perry, Taylor Perry, Belinda Pearl, Alisa Shamel, Noel DeNoyer, Tracey Allumbaugh, Doug Schock, Sherry Holt, Rob and Georgia Bailey and a very special thank you to Penny Reynolds for the excellent editing she did on *Fair Exchange*.

A few shout outs to friends and family who helped along the way and stayed true. My cousin Steven (Destro) McClendon, Brandie Mills, Tab Perry II, LaTonya Daniels, Karen Nelson, Cheryle Heard, Robin Isome, Lonnie Gow, Yolanda Smith, Brennan Pearl Sr., Lafara Carter, Akilah Smith, Requel King, Tonya Houston, Christopher Cuben-Tatum, and Clinton Johnson who's always been on my team.

Thanks for believing in my vision

Fair Exchange

Contents

Chapter 1

The 90's were special for some and not so special for others in Cincinnati. The Woodward Riders won two state football championships. Cincinnati elected their first black mayor and Ray Whitehead, a twelve-year veteran of the Cincinnati police force, had his hands full trying to keep the streets clean from corruption and gang violence. Things looked rather promising for the New Year coming around the corner. Everybody knew the year would bring about changes, good for some, and possibly worse for others.

New kinds of drugs hit the streets. High school attendance and the percentage of kids graduating dropped at an alarming rate. The number of crimes committed had quadrupled compared to the figures of past years and gang violence was on the rise. The police department was short handed and Ray had requested more officers on several occasions.

Sergeant Ray Whitehead was in charge of training and preparing new officers with the knowledge they needed to enhance their street smarts while dealing with today's criminal element. Ray took pride in training and breaking in new rookies because as a taxpayer and policeman, he believed everyone deserved quality officers to serve and protect the community.

Ray and Hazel, his wife of over twenty years, arrived at work at their usual time 7AM Hazel worked at the front desk. Holding the door open to the lobby of the police precinct so his wife could enter, Ray gave her a quick kiss. "Honey, I have to see Captain Safeway, I'll pick you up around four o'clock. Is that okay?"

"Sure honey, don't forget that today is payday and we have to cash our checks."

"Oh yeah, that's right.

"So that means don't try to work a bunch of overtime today," Hazel said as she headed down the hallway towards her work station. Okay honey, Ray said as he went in the opposite direction toward Capt. Tom Safeway's office. Tom was not only Ray's supervisor, but he and his wife Debra were very good friends of the Whitehead family. Every other Sunday the Safeway and Whitehead families got together for football and dinner. From time to time Hazel cooked soul food for the Safeways during these Sunday visits. The Safeway's were a conservative white couple, so they called it "soul food Sunday" because of their close family ties. Tom looked up from his paperwork to see that it was his soul brother rapping at the door and got up to shake Ray's hand.

"Come on in Ray, I've got something to lay on you." Tom shut the door behind Ray. "I've got good news and I've got some bad news. Which would you prefer first partner?" Tom jokingly asked. Ray relaxed in his chair. "Give me the bad news first, but take it easy on me."

"Okay, you know we're short handed. I've got the chief breathing down my neck about the department working closer with the community to try and slow some of this gang activity. It seems we're losing the battle on the streets. The chief thinks this department should get involved in the D.A.R.E. Program like some of the suburban stations, you know like going into the high schools and talking to the kids."

"Yeah, I know."

"I hope you don't mind Ray, but I elected you for this assignment. I really need someone I can depend on to work with the school administrations. We don't have any officers available to put in these schools and the brass doesn't seem to understand."

"So what do you want me to do Captain?"

"I need you to work with Mike Brunson, the principal at Woodward High School. They are having a lot of problems with teachers' cars being vandalized, drug dealing, and gambling on football games in the hallways. You know, the usual activities that gangs engage in.

"Well did you tell Mr. Brunson that I'm having problems with the same gangs, but its even worse on the streets? I have to deal with rapes, murders, robberies, etc., you know just the usual things kids do now a days."

"Ray, I hear you. One of the reasons I volunteered you is because Woodward is your Alma Mater and you have two daughters who attend school there. You also seem to understand how to work with gang members. I need a man who can get results. So how about it? Are you up for the challenge?" "Okay, okay, I'm sold on the idea. So what's the good news?"

"A detective position is coming open and I think you deserve it.

Not only do I believe you deserve the position but I believe you are ready for the next level. How's that baby boy?" Tom said, offering his friend a fresh cigar. "Care to have a good smoke with an old friend my brother?" Tom said, smiling at his friend.

"I sure would!" Ray said, happy to hear the news. Time flew as Tom and his friend smoked their cigars and jaw jacked for the better part of the morning. They talked about doing some fishing sometime in the next week, football this weekend and how good it would feel to be dressed in plain clothes as a detective. "Captain Safeway" the intercom on Tom's desk blurted out interrupting their moment. "Yes, Mrs. Whitehead," Tom answered Ray's wife playfully.

"When you and my husband get through having so much fun in there, Officer Tony Ward is waiting to see you."

"Thank you Hazel. Please send him in. I've got someone I want you to meet," Tom said to Ray as he stood up.

"Come on in Officer Ward," Tom said holding his office door open

"Ray this is Officer Tony Ward, fresh out of the academy. Officer Ward, this is Sgt. Ray Whitehead, head of rookie training in the department."

"Nice to meet you Sgt. Whitehead," said Tony, shaking Ray's hand.

"Likewise, Officer Ward."

"Have a seat gentlemen," Tom said. "Officer Ward received excellent grades at the academy Ray, so I requested him and five others to fill in some of the gaps. All I received was him and a promise that more officers were coming."

"Well one good officer is a great start for now."

"How soon do you think you can start training him Ray? There's some time and a half in it for you if you can start tonight."

"Sorry Tom. Tonight I promised my daughters I would meet them at the Woodward football game.

"Well take Officer Ward with you. He might enjoy the game and if not, he's sure to enjoy the fight afterwards." Captain Safeway said laughing.

"Yeah, he just might," Ray said as they all stood up.

"Good luck Officer Ward. You're being trained by the best."

"Yeah right. Come on Officer Ward. Let me tell my wife I'm working late and then I'll show you around until it's time to hit the streets."

Ray and Officer Ward kicked it around the station for a few hours reviewing the dos and don'ts of a uniformed officer, including the stuff not taught at the academy. Ray shared his personal opinions of the job, the people he worked with and his philosophy as to why kids in the streets act the way they do.

Ray continued as he and Ward entered the parking garage. "If these kids paid as much attention to their teachers as they pay attention to the rap stars like 2-PAC, some of these kids might graduate and make something of themselves. Most rap seems to encourage kids to shoot and kill everything in sight."

"Yeah, you've got a point Sergeant. These kids allow themselves to be misled these days, but it's more than just 2-PAC and his music. Its the illusion of street fame and power that's got these kids self destructing."

"I suppose you've got a point there too, but there's a lot of factors that go with that, and rap music is one of them." Ray continued to drive and talk as they exited the police garage and took a right onto Hamilton Avenue.

"Look," Ray said pointing to a few kids on the corner as they stopped at a red light. "What does it look like they're doing over there Officer Ward?"

"My guess is that they're probably selling drugs."

"You're damn right! Those kids don't look older than thirteen or fourteen, standing right there in front of us selling weed or crack! They act like they could care less that we're sitting here watching their transactions! Now that's outright disrespect Officer Ward! What does the academy teach you do in a case like this?" Officer Ward looked at Ray knowing that there was a better answer than what the police academy taught.

"You turn your lights and siren on like this and watch them scatter like cockroaches!" Ray said laughing as he watched some of the kids almost break their neck trying to get away. "We could get out and chase a few down, but not right now. We'll just sit here for a second and let them think we're coming after them." In less than a minute, all the dope dealers were gone. Satisfied that he had let them know who was really in control, Ray turned the lights and siren off and continued driving up Hamilton. "This is the Northside, an area known to be heavy in drugs and gang activity. There's a gang called the

'Ruff Riders' who operate on this side of town. By no means show any fear. Otherwise, they will never respect you or that badge you're wearing. When they don't want to give you respect, that's when you put your foot down and take it, just like I did back there. You've got to know how to think fast because your life and that of your partner may depend on it one day. If you let the criminal elements out here intimidate you, you may as well find another field of work to get into. Tonight, I just want to show you some of the major players you're sure to come in contact with, then we're going to check out that Woodward game." Ray continued to talk as he made his way through the Northside. "You'll never learn this job," and suddenly Ray had to hit the brakes to keep from ramming into a Cadillac sitting in the middle of the street. Music was blasting loud enough to make the trunk rattle. The driver was talking to some girls outside of the car. Ray sat there for a second or two waiting for the driver to wake up and realize that the police were behind him. After three seconds, it didn't take a rocket scientist to figure out that these people could care less who was behind them. That pissed Ray off royally. He saw one guy sitting in the back seat with two in the front. "You see what that loud music does to these kids' brains? Who in their right mind just challenges the police like that for no reason?"

"That's what rap music does to these kids nowadays! It gives them false courage!" Officer Ward said.

"Well it looks like you get to make your first arrest tonight," Ray said after calling for back up. "You ready?"

"Yeah, let's do this!"

"I'm going to hit the lights and when they take off, a cruiser should be up the street waiting to cut them off."

"What's the next move? Do you think they will get out and start running?" Officer Ward asked.

"I doubt they'll run because if they were dirty, they would have moved on when we pulled up." Ray hit the flashing lights and prepared for the chase, but the car didn't move. The driver turned the music down a notch or two but the rap continued to bang with plenty of bass. The situation totally pissed Ray off as he jumped quickly from the cruiser unsnapping the safety from his weapon. He rested his hand on the pistol grip as he pointed the floodlight into the punk's car. As Ray and Officer Ward started towards the Cadillac, Ray told him to take the passenger side. "If any one of them makes a sudden move, shoot his ass!" Ray instructed as they approached the car from the rear. "Let me see your hands driver!" Ray shouted.

By now, two more police cruisers had moved in. The music in the Cadillac continued to boom and entertain those on the sidewalk. The music blared:

> "*I don't wanna live no more,*
> *I keep hearing death knocking at my front door,*
> *Living everyday like a hustle*
> *Another drug to juggle*
> *Another day, another struggle.*"

By this time, Ray was beside the driver and shining his flashlight on the radio. "Turn off that damned radio!" Ray shouted into the car. The driver, obviously a teenager, didn't look to be intimidated by the presence of the police. He reached over, detached the faceplate from the radio and handed it through the window. The music continued to bang with enough bass to rattle the windows.

"Turn it off yourself!" the driver said laughing in Ray's face.

"You little sarcastic son of a gun!" Ray screamed. He started to yank open the door and then changed his mind. "Since they act as if they can't understand us, then we're going to act as if we don't see these damned door handles!" Ray said to Officer Ward snapping the safety back on his gun.

At that moment, each officer reached inside the car and grabbed a handful of something on somebody. They proceeded to snatch the teenagers out of the car through the windows bumping heads, knee-caps and funny bones along the way. No one could hear the teenagers screaming in pain because the music continued to blast from the car.

> "*It's too much trouble in the world,*
> *can anybody feel my pain?*
> *The world keeps changing on a nigga*
> *it's too much stress where I maintain.*"

As the officers wrestled the teenagers to the ground, the strong rap lyrics continued to pound away in the night.

"I don't wanna live no more,"
I keep hearing death knocking at my front door,"

Once the three suspects were cuffed and laying face down on the pavement, Ray searched frantically for the faceplate to turn off the offensive music.

"Living everyday like a hustle
Another drug to juggle
Another day, another struggle."

Click. And there came blessed silence. Ray felt a sigh of relief escape as the harsh and deafening sound of the stereo was silenced. As Ray's ears stopped ringing, he heard the laughter of the crowd that had gathered on the sidewalk. That pissed him off even more. "So everybody wants to be comedians tonight?" Ray yelled. He instructed the officers to grab a body, "Anybody!" he shouted.

Suddenly everyone started running as officers grabbed, tackled and roughed up some of the teens that were standing around smirking and giggling.

"Oh, its not so funny now huh? Cuff 'em and stuff 'em!" Ray shouted as he dusted himself off from the scuffle. Then, stepping up on the curb, Ray looked at the three suspects on the ground.

"Don't you hurt them you crooked ass cops!" someone shouted over the commotion.

Ray looked at the back of their jackets, 'Ruff Riders'. Ray just shook his head and motioned for all of the officers to come closer so he could talk with them over the noise that the crowd was making. He bent down and started checking the pockets of the suspects and began talking to the officers as if teaching class. After emptying the first suspect's pockets, Ray held in his hand a school ID card. "Gentlemen, what we have here is three, I guess wanna be Ruff Rider gang members. This Ruff Rider wanna be is just a kid who he thinks he's a man!" He reached over and thumped the suspect hard on his head. "He's fourteen years old, in the eighth grade, and wearing a jacket that prompts the use of drugs and gang violence! Can you believe that?" He reached over and again thumped the suspect on the head.

"Hey man, don't thump me like that no more!" the suspect cried out. SLAP — Ray cut him off with a smack that was probably heard around the corner. "Shut up, Mr. Man, when I'm talking! You wanna act like a man, I'm gonna treat you like a man!" Ray moved down the line to the next suspect who was only fifteen and a Woodward Ruff Rider as well. Ray thumped him three times just for being plain stupid. Next up was the driver. Ray leaned over him a little and said, "You see officers, I recognize this face. His name is Michael Roberts. Say hi Michael," Ray introduced Michael to his friend Thumper.

"Ouch! You ain't got nothin' on me!" Michael yelled.

"I busted Michael, a.k.a. "Street", and one of his friends with over a pound of marijuana and several bottles of ecstasy pills two years ago." Ray informed the officers. "Somebody tear that car up! We might get lucky! This is one of the problems we have on our streets gentlemen. The juvenile system gives them a year, maybe a year and a half, and then they're back on the street! Isn't that right Street?"

This time Street spoke up because he didn't want to be thumped again. "Yeah man, I did eighteen months for that little bit of shit, so you can back up off me," he said from his face down position on the ground.

"I'll back up off you all right! How old are you now, sixteen or maybe seventeen?" Ray asked while thumping him on the ear.

"Damn man! Cut that bullshit out!"

"Remember Street, you're old enough to get bound over to the grand jury now. If you have anything in that car, I'll make sure you get bound over to face big time and then bent over in the big house when you get there!"

"The car's clean Sergeant," Tony stated after he and two other officers completed the search.

Ray bent down and started talking to Street again. "Looks like you got lucky tonight Street. We didn't find any of your narcotics. I'm not surprised because I know how smart you drug dealers think you are. I didn't expect to find anything on you tonight but maybe later," Ray said while thumping him hard again on his ear. "Officer Ward!" Ray shouted over his shoulder. "Read me the name off the registration of that car." Ray continued to talk to the officers as they searched for the title and registration to the Cadillac. "Mr. Roberts here is a known drug dealer. He has served eighteen months for dealing and now he's are problem again. He's only seventeen according to his drivers' license and lives in the Winton Terrace projects. "You know what Street? You've got drug dealing written all over you and one day your luck is going to run out. That's when I'm going to put you and your Ruff Rider boys away for a long time. As far as you and your two other followers are concerned" Ray said, standing over them and pointing, "I'm gonna teach their asses a lesson or two about following behind a punk like you!" Ray stood up and started talking to all the officers. "All we have is a 211, a loud music ordinance. Personally, that's not worth the paperwork, so un-cuff them and let 'em go. We'll get our chance at these boys again." Ray slapped Street across his neck while an officer was standing him up to remove the cuffs.

"Man, you're gonna get enough of putting your hands on me!" Street said to Ray while rubbing his wrist where the cuffs pinched his skin.

"Oh yeah?" Ray stepped face to face with Street. "You got enough courage boy to try me?" Ray asked while thumping him on the forehead.

"Every dog gets his day," Street replied while staring into Ray's eyes.

"Look at you boy, that's your problem! You look high as a kite!"

Ray stepped back and looked deeply into the other two punks' eyes. "I'll be damned! All three of you look like you just jumped off a damned spaceship! What you been getting high on, boys? Some weed? Some dro? Oh yeah, maybe that ecstasy. Yeah that's it! Ecstasy, the superman drug. That's why y'all were acting like tough guys sitting in there! All three of you are probably zooming out of your brains off that ecstasy and marijuana right now as we speak. Stay right there!" Ray ordered as he walked over to the Caddy that Tony had moved to the curb. He proceeded to lock all the doors and made sure the windows were up and secure. "I can't confiscate the car because we didn't find any contraband even though I know you bought it with drug money. But what I will do for you tonight gentlemen, is keep you from getting into any more trouble," and he slammed the driver's door closed. "Oops, I think I just locked your keys in this pretty Cadillac. I hope you've got a spare. My bad fellas, it was a honest mistake!" Ray said smiling at the boys. "But if you don't have a spare, then use some of that drug money to catch a cab! All three of you look stoned out of your damned minds. Go home and sleep it off! Let's go officers. We've given enough of our attention to these three young men."

"Yeah, beat it," Street said as he continued to rub his wrist.

"Did somebody say something?" Ray asked as he was opening the door to the driver's side of the police cruiser. "My hearing is very good."

"Well hear this!" Street said stepping off the curb. Prince reached out and grabbed him before he got into it again with Officer White-head.

"No, no! Don't hold him back! Let him write a check that his ass can't cash!" Ray said pointing at Street. "You need to stop listening to that rap music boy. It's giving you false courage." Then suddenly Ray snapped his fingers as though he remembered something he forgot to say. "Since you relate to rap so well, I got a rap I wanna lay on you. Tell me if you like it." Then Ray began beating on top of the police car as if making a beat he could rap to.

They call me Sgt. Whitehead
from district four
I'm like the Lone Ranger
to all the poor
every time you slip or trip
when I come pass
I'm gonna slap these cuffs
on your drug dealing ass
So remember every time
you make a drug deal
I don't care if it's crack,
weed, or prescription pills
As soon as I catch you
with your pants down
I'm gonna place you butt naked
in a cell downtown.

"How did you like it? Was it me or what fellas?" Sgt. Whitehead said laughing at his little joke.

"That shit was whack, you fake ass rapper," Street said.

"I bet you can't do better," Ray said between chuckles as he got into the police cruiser. Making a U-turn, he stopped and yelled to Street,

"As you boys say, don't hate the playa, hate the game!" Ray drove off still laughing at his own joke.

"They look pretty upset," Tony said laughing.

"Who cares, they'll get over it," Ray said hanging a right onto Hamilton."

"You feel like seeing a good football game?"

"Sure who's playing?"

"The two best teams in the city - Woodward and Elder. Kick off is in thirty minutes. Let's ride."

CHAPTER 2

Prince, like many young African American men, grew up in a very crowded, intense, and poverty stricken situation. He was an only child, born and raised in a low-income housing project in Winton Terrace by a mother who was often missing for two or three days at a time. Two days after his seventeenth birthday, his aunt Tammy was sitting in the living room waiting for Prince to arrive home from school. Aunt Tammy was cool as a fan. She showed Prince maternal love, an emotion he was unfamiliar with. She was always concerned about Prince's welfare, knowing that life had tossed him the burden of looking out for himself and his mother who was a heroin addict. When you see someone you love start to crumble right before your eyes, age becomes nothing but a number and your will to survive instinctively takes over.

Young Prince was branded a man by circumstances before he even had a chance to enjoy his childhood. Since the age of fourteen, when Prince was just in the eighth grade at Woodward High, he looked after his mom, himself, and the household. They lived in a two-bedroom section 8 apartment in Winton Terrace, one of the lowest income housing projects in the city. Rent was just fifty bucks a month with section eight qualification. Prince had paid it faithfully every month for two years now. He delivered the rent to the office himself. No one ever asked questions because it was normal for Prince to run a money order up to the office for his mother every first of the month. When his mother was home, she was either passed out or turning a trick to support her habit. Food was always scarce because she never spent her food stamps on food. They were more valuable on the black market. If she wanted to eat, she ate what Prince brought in the house and that was usually cereal, milk, Snickers, Milky Ways, Pop Tarts, etc., all the things a fourteen year old liked to eat. Prince had lived that way for two years now. The only time he got a balanced meal was in the school cafeteria or at Aunt Tammy's house.

Aunt Tammy always asked Prince over for a meal when she got her welfare check. "Prince, baby you need a few dollars in your pocket."

"Nah, Aunt Tammy. I'm cool. It don't take much to get by over here."

Tammy always wondered how such a young kid could hold down a household all by himself and still go to school. For the life of her, she could never figure it out.

School was fun for Prince. That's where he made all his friends. He was the only ninth grader who hung out with the older crowd at Woodward High. He was also the only one in school who sold dollar marijuana sticks at lunchtime for those who liked to have a smoke break on the school's back stairwell. At lunch everyday, for over two years, Prince had sold weed to the potheads in school and pills to the pill heads. He did not discriminate; all money was good money and Prince had a regular clientele that looked for him at every lunch period. With every dollar he made, he added to his growing bankroll. He only dipped into his stash when it was time to pay the rent, buy food for the house or visit the local weed man in the 'hood to re-up. Prince had big dreams of being rich one day.

On the weekends, he would treat a few friends he went to school with and lived in the project, to a movie or Woodward football game. Prince didn't mind sharing and his generosity paid off in the long run. Those same friends would become his loyal protégés later in the game.

Now that he was seventeen and in the eleventh grade, he was feeling pretty good about himself and his accomplishments even though the situation with his mother hadn't changed much over the past couple of years. But today was a good day as he jumped off the bus and walked up the street toward home. He couldn't wait to get in the house to put the day's earnings in the pickle jar under his bed. Prince came in the door and saw his Aunt Tammy sitting in the living room and it nearly scared the daylights out of him! Holding his chest as if he was about to have a heart attack, he looked at his Aunt Tammy as if she was a ghost.

"Damn Aunt Tammy, you can't be scaring me like that!" Closing the door behind him, Prince headed towards the refrigerator for a glass of Kool-Aid.

"Prince baby, come in here for a minute so your Auntie can talk to you."

"Aunt Tammy, I hope this isn't one of your 'How to Be a Man' pep talks, because I'm fine, really. My mom's fine I guess – wherever she is. I haven't seen her in a few days. I'm doing well in school and I just passed to the eleventh grade."

"No honey, I'm not here to lecture you because you've shown me over the past few years, that you're more then capable of taking care of yourself. I came to ask you how you felt about moving in with us."

"I'm sorry Auntie, but that's a negative. You've already got too many mouths to feed as it is. Plus I'm cool right here. Why are you asking anyway?"

"Well, I got some bad news. They found your mother and she's dead, baby. They found her this morning in a hallway in the West-End with a needle sticking out of her arm. I'm sorry Prince, baby. I was always afraid this would happen."

Prince just looked at his Aunt and shook his head in disbelief. He really was not surprised at all. He had prepared himself for this moment a long time ago. He wasn't naïve, especially at this age, to the way of life his mother lived.

"Does this mean I have to move Aunt Tammy?"

"Not really sweetheart, not if you don't want to. I know you can take care of yourself. The only question is how long it will take for the welfare department to find out your mother's gone and cut the section eight off."

"Well, I'm willing to take my chances. I've been rolling this long by myself and I've got a few dollars saved up. I'll be alright."

"Okay baby." Tammy stood up and gave her nephew a big hug. "If you need me you know how to reach me."

"Would you do me a big favor though Aunt Tammy?"

"Sure baby, anything."

"Would you make all the funeral arrangements and cover for me when the school gets on my case? And if I pay for it, would you put a telephone in here in your name?"

"That's not a problem. As a matter of fact, that idea makes me feel much better about you staying here. Just let me know when you're ready."

Prince dipped into his pocket and pulled out a wad of singles. "How much do you think it'll cost to get a phone put in? Will fifty dollars get it done?" Prince asked as he counted out fifty singles. "If you need money for the funeral arrangements, I've got that too."

Tammy just couldn't hold back her tears as she gave Prince the biggest hug she could give. It touched her heart deeply to see such a young boy trying so hard to be a man.

"Prince, I don't want your money sweetheart. Use it to buy some food baby. I just wanna tell you I love you, nephew, with all my heart, and to please be careful with whatever you're doing."

Prince couldn't look his Aunt in the eye any longer for fear of becoming emotional. He knew he had to be strong. "Life tramples those who become weak," he thought to himself. "Aunt Tammy, when you get home, will you tell Fats and Street that I'm gonna need their help moving my mother's stuff outta here?"

"I sure will baby. As a matter of fact, those two little Negroes can stay down here for a while and keep you company if you like. It's a shame to say it, but they might learn more from you then they'll ever learn from their no good daddy." Fat's and Street were Aunt Tammy's two sons.

"Thanks Aunt Tammy." They hugged again before she left for home. Prince thought of his two cousins and shook his head as he closed the front door.

Prince sat down on the floor to let everything soak in. For the first time in his life, he felt fear; fear of the unknown and of actually being alone. Although his mother was hardly ever home, he knew that at some time or another, she would surface. His biggest fear was of being a failure. For the next couple of days Prince just laid around doing nothing. On the third day, he got a knock at the door. His first thought was to sit there and act like no one was home, hoping whoever it was, would go away.

"Open up little nigga, I know you're in there! Don't make us kick this damned door in!"

Prince recognized the voice of his cousin Street. He smiled and got up to answer the door but before he could get the door completely open, Fats and Street had him in a group bear hug.

"Hey baby boy, your family is here! You ain't got to deal with this shit all by yourself! That's what family is for!" Fats said. Fats was the rapper of the family, fourteen and in the eighth grade at Woodward. Street was seventeen and probably the craziest of them all. The boy just didn't care, but Prince loved him like a brother.

"Moms said you were over here by yourself, and you might want some company. So blam-blam, here we are! Let's bring on the good times!"

Prince shut the door and looked up at his cuz like he was fourteen karat crazy. "What good times fool?" Prince asked sitting down on the couch.

"Damn, look!" Street exclaimed while pointing to the pile of money on the floor.

"Who does that belong to?" Street asked.

Instantly Prince jumped on his money, having forgotten it was in plain view on the floor. "Don't even think about it nigga! This is my cheddar and I'm saving it!"

"Baby cuz! Saving it for what? Nigga while you saving it, you should be flipping it! Ain't that right little bro?" Street said.

"Big bro, you late! How you think Prince came up on all that paper?" Fats said. "This little nigga got Woodward sewed up on the reefer side."

"Damn Fats! Why you putting my business in the street like that?"

"Ah nigga, this is family! Street don't count."

"Hold up, fuck the chitter chatter! You mean you're making money like this at Woodward?" asked Street. "Ah shit little nigga! We got to talk!" Street said putting his arm around Prince.

"I know you of all people, ain't thinking about getting back on the block! Street have you forgotten that you just got home from doing an eighteen-month bit for weed and pills? Nigga, the next time you get caught, the man is sending you to the big house for some years!" Prince said.

Fats just sat back listening to the family debate, hoping his brother won because he was ready to get some money too, but he just never said anything to Prince.

"Listen little cuz, bump the bullshit! I ain't and never will be too scared to get some money! Plus, I got the perfect plan," Street said.

"And what's that, Street?" Fats chipped in.

"Oh, so you're siding with your brother huh?" Prince asked laughing. "Okay, Street let's hear it."

"It's simple. You and Fats keep doing what you do at Woodward and I'll work the block. You know that's what I do best," Street said. "Let me think on it for a few, but right now you two niggas are supposed to be helping me clean this mess up," Prince said.

Prince thought for a month about the conversation he had with his cousins and continued to sell his little joints and nickel bags to his regulars. Sometimes he would test the waters a little and see how fast a few twenty bags went. He was impressed with the quick flip, and that's what made Prince so dangerous. At seventeen he was smart and had a business head on his shoulders. Of course, Fats and Street by this time had moved in with Prince. Everyday for three months, Street worried the shit out of Prince. Fats was different and real cool about the situation, even though everyday in school Fats was with Prince while he took care of his business. Prince liked Fats' approach to things - real cool, calm and collected. He was just testing his cousins to see if they were really ready to get their feet wet and deal with the demands of the dope game. There was a lot out of life Prince once wanted for himself in the up and coming years. His biggest dream, like any other brother in the projects, was to see his mother out of the ghetto. "Well, that's one dream gone," Prince thought to himself.

"Hey Cuz," Fats said coming down the back stairwell, somewhat startling Prince at his sudden appearance.

"What's up Fats?" Prince asked from his seat on the bottom step.

"Lunch bell just rang baby. Let's go to the cafeteria and get a bite to eat."

"Wish I could Cuz, but I got to hang down here and get rid of this little bit of weed I got," Prince said.

"The last? Ah cuz don't say the last of the killer is about to be gone! That's not good!" Fats exclaimed.

"What you mean, that's not good? Ain't we got bills to pay?" Prince asked.

"Yeah, yeah, but today is my birthday and I was kind of hoping to get my smoke and drink on tonight."

"Damn Fats!" Prince said as he stood up to give his cuz a hug. "Man, I must have too much on my mind 'cause I completely forgot my bad Happy Birthday Baby Boy!"

"Thanks Cuz! You know this is the first time I get to enjoy my B-day with you, so I hunted you down to ask if it was okay to kind of throw a little party at the crib tonight after the big game."

"That sounds lovely!" Prince said.

"Well, I had to ask you first because after all, it is your pad we are crashing at."

"Listen Cuz, it's blood-in-blood-out with me when it comes to family. For your fifteenth birthday it's mandatory that we party. You only become fifteen once," Prince said giving Fats the soul shake. "As a matter of fact, let's do hit the cafeteria - my treat on your day!"

"Sounds like a plan baby boy, 'cause I'm starving like Marvin!"

On their way up the stairs, coming through the double doors on the third floor that led to the entrance of the school cafeteria, was Ms. O'Bannon. The infamous "hall monster from hell" as students often referred to her. Ms. O'Bannon was over fifty, very old fashioned and obsessed with trying to take a bite out of crime everyday she came to work. She had been working at Woodard for over ten years now as one of the school's hall monitors. She took the job when her husband, who was a police officer, was killed in the line of duty. Ms. O'Bannon's problem was she often became a little too determined to catch kids doing something wrong, which caused her to make a fool of herself on several occasions. When she was foolish, it completely irritated students and school officials alike. But Ms. O'Bannon was special, so a lot of things she did were either ignored or overlooked by the school principle, Mike Brunson. He simply allowed her to be Ms. O'Bannon. She was more of an annoyance then anything else. "Ah hah, caught you!" Ms. O'Bannon said blocking their progress.

Prince and Fats looked at Ms. O'Bannon as if she had lost her mind. "Caught us doing what Ms. O'Bannon? Going to lunch?" Fats asked as they snickered at Ms. O'Bannon.

"Caught you running up the steps! Now I done told you two boys before about running in the halls! Next time, it's after school detention for both of you!"

"Yeah right, Ms. O'Bannon. We promise not to run anymore. Now can we please go get something to eat?" Prince asked.

She continued, "I've got my eye on you two boys. I know you've been smoking down there in that basement." She sniffed a couple of times as though she smelled something.

"Damn Ms. O'Bannon, go find something to do!" Fats muttered under his breath as she moved aside.

When Fats opened the cafeteria doors both he and Prince cussed, as the cafeteria was already crowded. "Thanks to Ms. O'Bannon, we didn't beat the rush," Fats said to Prince.

"I see that! Fuck it, somebody's got a table where we can sit. Let's roll over this way. I see some homeboys from the block."

"Hey Fats, over here!" somebody yelled. Fats looked around and spotted Sticky sitting at a table with all the fellas.

"Listen Prince, I'm gonna slide over here and let the homeboys know about the party tonight after the big game."

"I got cha cuz, I'll be over there shortly after I kick it with my cats over here."

"Beat Elder -Woodward Riders - No 1" was on banners all over the cafeteria as everybody talked excitedly about the football game tonight.

"Woodward Riders!" Fats yelled as all the homeboys stood hugging and slapping five to Fats. This was the V.I.P. clique as they called themselves. There was Jeff Wright, a.k.a.'Blaze', who was the city's top ranked quarterback. He was credited with winning two state championships for the Woodward Riders, Charles Carter, a.k.a.'Hit Man', who was the number two receiver on the team, and last but not least, there was Jason McNickles, a.k.a.'Sticky Fingers', and ranked first in the state in receiving yards. Together, the three were the heart and soul of the school's success as a football program. With two state championships under their belts and in hot pursuit of another, they were the real deal on the football field. Tonight they had a big game against another school that was also undefeated and considered Woodward's biggest test in a long time.

The school's bookie Hustleman, sat quietly at the table counting his slips.

"Hey Fats. Where's Prince going?" J.Blaze asked as they all sat down.

"He had a couple of cats to holler at. Bump that! Listen up, I got lovely news." Fats said.

"What?" everybody asked at the same time.

Fats jumped up from the table and jacked on his slacks. "Today's a player's birthday! I'm now legal at fifteen!"

Everybody at the table stood up, screaming and hollering "Birthday Boy" and playfully punched on Fats.

"And the party tonight is on me, at my cuz's crib after the game!"

By this time, the whole cafeteria was paying attention.

"What's the address?" somebody yelled.

"Winton Terrance, 5969. Be there!" Fats said.

"This nigga ain't bullshitting," Sticky said.

"Ah shit, it's on," J.Blaze said. "Oh, I'm throwing the rock for five hundred yards tonight and running in two touchdowns on these boys."

"Yeah nigga," Sticky Fingers replied. "You better share half that five hundred you planning on throwing for me. I got a twenty yard per catch average to keep up to stay number one in the state," Sticky said, bragging. Plus I got a new end zone dance I need to practice on, so it's mandatory that I catch at least two touchdowns tonight!"

"Yeah, I hear you niggaz plotting and planning over there," Hitman said as he added his two cents. "Just don't forget I'm the fastest and the number two receiver in the state, next to my protégé over there," pointing at Sticky Fingers. "So make sure that rock is shared equally tonight on that football field because I need mines too!"

"Man listen, everybody's gonna get their share of the glory so don't start trippin'. Just come with your game face on and it'll be like business as usual. Now, what about the party?" Sticky asked. Who's the D.J.? You know, I got all the equipment."

"That's a good question," Fats said. "Me and Prince didn't discuss that part.

"Well I'm locked in. I'll D.J. the party," Sticky volunteered.

"Hey, Prince, come here!" Fats yelled as he waved his arm.

Prince looked up from the conversation he was having and put a finger up to say in a minute.

"All three of y'all come on," Fats yelled. "We got plenty of room over here. Plus we got plenty of shit to talk about."

Prince looked at his two homeboys, Dino and P. Funk. "That's my cuz Fats screaming over there. Come on, let's go see what he's talking about."

When they all got through introducing themselves and giving each other dap, Prince asked Fats if he was going to eat.

"Hell yeah, I'm going to eat! That's one of the reasons I called you over here and the next reason is Sticky wants to know if he can D.J. the party tonight."

"Yeah Prince, you know I got skills and I got this bomb Kenwood system I just got with my five-finger discount." Sticky said.

Prince just looked at Sticky and laughed. "I bet over half this school thinks your nickname came from catching all those footballs but we know the real reason why you're called Sticky Fingers!" Everybody who really knew Sticky laughed because they knew he was a thief before he became a football star.

"Come on Fats, lets get something to eat before the chow hall closes," said Prince.

"We'll catch you cats at the party tonight," Fats said as he and Prince started towards the chow line.

"You know what Fats?" Prince began to ask but he stopped in midsentence watching as four of the finest girls at Woodward walked by and started to exit the cafeteria.

"Hi Fats," one of girls said.

"Oooooh wheee!" was all Prince could say.

"Hey China Doll - what's up baby?" Fats asked.

"I'll see you in math class, or are you coming?' she stopped and asked.

"I'll be there. Listen, this is my cuz Prince and he's throwing a birthday party for me tonight."

"Hi Prince," China said

"Hey, Ms. Lady. Excuse me, not to be rude, but I think I see a super star!" Prince stated as he stepped away and headed toward the other three ladies.

"Which one of your girls is my cuz digging on?" Fats asked, as he and China watched Prince walk right up to one of the finest girls in the school.

"That's Danielle," China said. "She's a senior."

"Excuse me Miss, but can I ask your name?" Prince asked speaking to the hottest girl he had ever seen.

"Danielle," she answered.

"Danielle, um that's pretty," Prince said. "Well Danielle, I'm Prince and I just wanted to know if you ladies would like to come to my cousin's birthday party tonight after the game?"

"I don't know. Maybe. Let me see what the girls have in mind for tonight."

Suddenly Ms. O'Bannon flew through the door, screaming with the assistance of her bullhorn, "Lunchtime is over! Return to class!" Prince was pissed at Ms. O'Bannon's timing. She just killed the moment for him.

"What's wrong cuz?" Fats said over all the loud commotion.

"Ms. O'Bannon just chased Danielle off before I could catch her number or give her directions to the party."

"Don't worry! I told China Doll, so if she's down she'll be there."

"Man I'm salty! We didn't get a chance to eat a damn thing," Fats yelled.

"Let me call Street and tell him about the party and see if he can bring a brother a Happy Meal."

"Tell him to bring two," Prince said. I'll be downstairs in the front."

"Nigga, you just trying to catch up with that girl."

"Man just make that call and get us some grub!"

Fats dialed Street's cell. It rang until his voice mail came on. "Shit!" Fats said and hung up. He started downstairs, waiting until he caught up with Prince out front before he tried again.

Upstairs Cindy, China Doll, Gina and Danielle were having a discussion about the party. "I think we should check it out," China said. "All the players are gonna be there."

"You mean all the thugs, don't you?" Cindy said closing her locker.

"Girl, you know you love them thug niggas for some reason."

"Fats ain't no thug for real," China said.

"I don't see how you can say that, when you know his cousin supplies the whole school with marijuana," Cindy said.

China, Gina, and Danielle laughed at how Cindy was carrying on. For reasons they didn't understand, she just didn't like that crew.

"Well Danielle, what you gonna do? After all it was you who received the personal invitation," asked China Doll. She and Danielle were best friends. Most of the time when you saw one, the other was not far away. They all waited for Danielle's answer.

"Why don't we just go to the game and decide from there," Danielle said taking the safe route out of the situation.

The sixth period bell rang, and everyone decided to meet out front after classes to catch the bus home together.

By the time the last bell of the day rang, the front of Woodward was already crowded. Fats still hadn't caught up with Street, but he left another message to get up to the school with some food for him and Prince. When school let out, that's when everybody just kind of hung out to watch all the fly honeys come out and jump in all the show boating rides that cruised by. While Fats kicked it with everybody, going from one small group to another, Prince was busy selling the last little bit of weed he had.

"You sold all the killer didn't you?" Fats asked Prince as he walked up counting his money.

"Don't worry I got your back for the party tonight." When Prince looked up after counting his bankroll, he noticed three guys across the street in the parking lot looking his way but turning their heads when he noticed.

"Hey Fats," Prince nudged his cousin. "Why are those niggas over there looking so hard in our direction?"

"You peeped that too, huh?"

"They aint from Woodward, that's for sure."

"Say my brothers," Stickyfingers and Hustleman said as they walked up.

"Who are those niggas Sticky?" Prince asked, as the three guys turned to walk away.

"I don't know, I've never seen them before, but we can always find out."

"Naw, they haven't violated or nothing, they were just staring too hard," Prince said.

"Listen, we've got a meeting in the locker room in fifteen minutes," Sticky said. "I just wanted to run down to see when you want me to bring my equipment over and set up."

"Here take the key. Now you can decide when." Prince said.

"Alright," Sticky said taking the key. Suddenly his eyes got big and he started screaming and pointing at a Cadillac pulling into the school lot.

"I'll be damned, that nigga wasn't lying!" Sticky said as his mouth hung open.

"Who wasn't lying?" Fats asked as they all stared at the beautiful white Cadillac sitting pretty on twenty-inch rims.

"That is phat!" Prince exclaimed. "But who is it?"

"Ah man, ya don't know?" Sticky asked.

The music was banging loud from the stereo system in the Cadillac.

"Who ever it is, they're coming with a banging system that's for sure."

"They're rolling hard with that 2-PAC bumping," Hustleman said.

As the Cadillac moved slowly through the parking lot, everybody in front of the school stopped what they were doing. Heads began bobbing to the music and several of the students started dancing. When the car stopped rolling, the driver door swung open and Street got out.

"How you like me now?" Street yelled as he got out looking brand new in some fresh gear.

"This nigga is fooling!" Sticky and Hustleman hollered. "I got to have one of those one day," Sticky said.

Street walked up to his brothers. Fats and Prince were totally speechless and Hustleman's mouth hung open in disbelief.

"Nigga, what you done went out and did?" Fats asked as he walked around the car admiring it.

"Go ahead and tell them!" Sticky hollered.

"Yeah cuz, go ahead and tell us because I'm almost dying to know," Prince said.

"Little cuz, I got tired of being broke, so I handled my business," Street said.

"So what you do big bro?" Fats asked as he looked inside the Cadillac. "Nigga I robbed a bank," Street answered.

"He's a gangsta, that's all I got to say," Sticky said.

"Naw that nigga is a Ruff Rider! That's what he is!" came Hustleman. Prince just looked at Street, and started clapping his hands. "Naw, that nigga is a damn fool! I've got to give you a standing ovation because you've got balls the size of coconuts!"

"I agree with Prince," Fats said. "But for real though, you should have let somebody know what you were up too. That shit could've easily gone against you my brother."

"Man bump all that righteous shit! I'm in it to win it and as far as I'm concerned, anything goes in the game of survival," Street said. "When you two niggas are ready to start getting some real money like we talked about, let me know! Until then, I'm down for whatever!"

"I'm down wit you bro, don't get me wrong," Fats said. "Ain't nothing wrong with having heart; that's what true soldiers are made of. But, you've got to be smart about your hustle, man!"

"Yes sir, that's a fact!" said Prince flashing his large bankroll. "You've got to be smart about your hustle and today I was smart enough to get paid in full but I didn't have to rob a damn bank to do it!"

"Damn I hate to leave this interesting conversation, but fellas the coach said be there or ride the bench," Sticky said. "I don't think I wanna be like Sport Coat tonight, riding the sideline, so I got to get to this meeting."

"I feel ya baby boy," Prince said. "We'll get up with you later!"

Everybody, as always, gave each other love and the ole soul shake before parting company and made plans to meet later at the party.

"Let's go for a spin, we got some partying to do!" Street suggested.

"Oh yeah," Fats said. "We're throwing a party at the crib tonight! Since you're big money today big bro, you can hook us up on the drinks." Street had to laugh as he cruised out of the school parking lot onto Reading Road with Fats, Hustleman and Prince riding in the new caddie.

"Little Bro," Street yelled over the pumping music "tonight is your night Fats! It's whatever you want!"

"Well if it's like that," Fats said, turning around to slap five with Prince in the back seat "we might as well drink Incredible Hulks and Patron all night long!"

****

Danielle called China Doll to see if she had decided to attend the party tonight after the game, being that Gina and Cindy had decided not to go.

"What's up girl?" China asked. "Why are Gina and Cindy acting like they're too good to go to this party?"

"Girl I can't call it. I guess they got some type of complex about being around thug type niggas."

"I'll bet you it's because of their daddy," Danielle said.

"Well, if they allow their daddy to police their lives like he polices the streets, more power to them. But I personally ain't into square dudes - they're too boring," China Doll said.

"Yeah, plus they ain't got cheddar like them nigga's do!" Danielle just laughed at China Doll's statement. "Girl you keep money on your mind don't you?"

"Yup, sure do and I keep my mind on the money too."

"Well, girl it's starting to get late. I got to do my hair and nails before I get over there," Danielle stated.

"Well, hurry up girl! I'm not trying to be late for none of this action tonight!"

****

"Hey Prince!" Fats yelled over the music as Street rode through the city showing off his new ride.

"Is your cup empty yet?"

"Almost," Prince replied.

"My cup is empty!" Hustleman yelled as the alcohol began to take effect.

Fats passed the bottle to the backseat. "Look what I got," Fats said holding up a fat blunt of dro.

"Oh yeah! Hustleman said. "That will kick this buzz all the way up! Fire it up!"

"Here Prince, you do the pleasure little cuz," Fats said, handing Prince the blunt.

"Don't forget to puff-puff and then pass. And, don't burn my leather seats." Street yelled from the driver's seat.

****

"Girl hurry up in there!" China Doll yelled through the bathroom door to Danielle. "How fine you trying to get?"

"Baby girl, when you trying to look your best, it takes time and finesse," Danielle said stepping out the bathroom.

"Oh my, my, my!" China exclaimed. "You must be on a mission tonight because I ain't never seen you put it on like this before!"

"You like?" Danielle asked turning around showing off her almost see through silk body suit that hugged every curve God gave her.

"Your looking for somebody, and I think I know who that somebody is. But let me tell you now, girl, Prince ain't your type of dude."

"I like Prince and to be honest, his way of life is interesting but girl, I ain't got it twisted. I know exactly who I'm dealing with and I'm not looking for a husband," Danielle said.

"Oh well, to each his own," China said. "It ain't a husband I'm looking for either, just a nigga with Benjamins in his pockets. Now let's get moving girl, I'm ready to pop my thang!"

****

"Hey Street, change that CD man! I ain't feeling that shit," Prince said.

"Yeah, throw that PAC CD in there so we can get the blood flowing in this muthafucka," Hustleman said. "I'm feeling rather foxy back here in this back seat."

"All right my brothers," Street said as he put 2-PAC in the CD player. Pass that blunt up here!"

****

Daylight had turned to dusk, and the blocks were starting to get crowded as Street turned the music up louder. In the 'hood, the only thing that mattered was money, women, and pretty cars. If you wanted to be considered a player, you had to have all of the above to be recognized. Street leaned hard in his new Caddy as they rode up Hamilton Avenue blowing the horn at the homeboys on the block.

"Party at my crib tonight!" Fats yelled out the window. Prince and Hustleman relaxed, jamming to the hit tunes of 2-PAC. They were feeling the moment as the lyrics spoke on the only lifestyle they understood.

> *Let us Pray*
> *Heavenly Father,*
> *hear a nigga down here*
> *Before I go to sleep"*

"Turn that shit up!" Fats yelled as he started getting hyped and pumped up.

> *"I see mothers in black cryin'*
> *brothers in packs dying,*
> *Plus everybody's high*
> *too doped up to ask why,*
> *Watching our downfall*
> *witness the end,*
> *It's like we don't believe in God*
> *cause we living in sin,*
> *Maybe it's just the drugs*
> *visions of how the block was,*
> *When crack came*
> *it was strange how it rocked us,*
> *Tore us apart*

perhaps a modern day genocide,
It's when we ride on our own kind
is when I wonder why,
What is it we all fear
Maybe it's the reflection in the mirror,
We can't escape our fate
the end is getting nearer,
So who do you believe in?
I put my faith in God
blessed and still breathing,
even though it's hard,
that's who I believe in."

"That's the shit!" Hustleman said. "Pass me that Hen Dogg back here my nigga. My cups on 'E' again."

"Nigga who do you believe in?" Fats yelled as he passed the bottle of Hennessy and Hypnotic to the back.

"Nigga, I believe in me!" Hustleman exclaimed as the liquor started talking. "As long as I'm blessed and still breathing, I believe in me!"

"Nigga, pass the joint," Street hollered over the music. "Believe in that!"

Street slowly turned the corner at Chase Street. The four rode in silence for a moment as they listened to the booming lyrics, moving their heads to the music and looking at who was looking at them.

"There's no way to survive
in the city it's a shame,
Niggaz are dieing daily
from hollow point bullets to the brain,
Well I survive or I will die
is what I wonder,
Puffin on blunts
to keep from going under,"

"Hold up! Stop!" Prince yelled, making everybody jump out of their skins at the sudden outburst.

"What's wrong?" Street asked while hitting the brakes on the Cadillac.

"Back up and turn that down for a minute!" Prince instructed while sticking his head out of the window. He waved at two girls whose attention he was trying to catch.

"I'll be damned! Its Danielle and China Doll!" Fats said spotting the girls.

Street stopped the Caddy as his cuz began his rap.

"What's up Ms. Lady?" Prince asked.

"Hi Prince," Danielle said somewhat surprised to see him.

"Hi Prince. Hi Fats, Street, and who's that in the back?" China Doll asked, moving closer to the Cadillac.

"Hi Hustleman."

"Hi China Doll," Prince said still eying Danielle.

"What's up Doll Baby?" Fats asked, leaning out of the window.

"Listen, let me out and ya'll can kick it while I holla at Danielle," Prince said, getting out and closing the door.

"Well, turn that PAC back up since we kickin' it," China said. "And what's that y'all drinking?"

"Turn the music back up while I pass this liquor to China Doll," Hustleman said.

> "Getting lost in the madness
> blunted getting tipsy,
> Got my pistol out the window screaming
> Lord come and get me,
> Oh God, help me
> I think I'm losin' it,
> I got my 45 at the ready
> with an extra clip"...

"Hey Danielle, you want me to pour you a drink?" China asked her friend. "Yeah girl," Danielle said and turned her attention back to Prince as they continued to talk on the sidewalk. "Pour me a drink too," Prince said, watching China shake her behind back and forth to the beat of the music.

"Girl you feelin' it, ain't cha?" Danielle yelled at her friend as everyone seemed to be enjoying themselves. By now a crowd had gathered and everyone was jamming to the music playing through the system of the car. "Where's the rest of that killer?" Fats asked of anybody who was listening. By now, no one was feeling any pain.

"Here's the last blunt right here," Prince said.

"Let me fire that baby up. You nigga's already got your buzz working," China said as she grabbed the blunt from Prince's hand.

> *"Dear mama I know you worry*
> *cause I'm hardly home,*
> *Every other night in jail*
> *got you patient by the phone,*
> *Wanna shake it cause I can't take it*
> *got me livin in hell,*
> *Like I'm walkin with a secret*
> *that'll kill me if I tell,"*

"Here Street," China said passing him the blunt through the car window. As soon as Street took a big hit from the blunt, Prince peeped the police turning the corner.

"One time-one time," a voice yelled out.

"Put that weed down!" Prince yelled.

Street tried to talk, but the weed smoke sent him into a coughing fit. Fats panicked and started eating the blunt he snatched from his brother's hand. Hustleman was in his own zone in the back seat. No one had the presence of mind to turn down the stereo, so it kept blaring 2-PAC.

Prince watched Fats, hoping he could finish eating the blunt. He began to step away from the Cadillac with Danielle by his side. He was grateful that China Doll had the presence of mind to move out with the liquor bottles. A loud music ticket would beat getting a dope ticket any day.

Sgt. Whitehead sat and waited in his cruiser behind the Cadillac. Everyone watched and held their breath as Sgt. Whitehead and the other officer walked up to the car. By now, Street had stopped coughing. From the sidewalk Prince could tell that Street was high as hell. "Ahhh shit," Prince said to Danielle. Sgt. Whitehead looked pissed as he shined the flashlight on Street.

"Turn that damn music down right now!" Sgt. Whitehead shouted into the car. Street looked up at Sgt. Whitehead and for some reason, thought he looked funny. He started laughing.

"Here Mr. Policeman," Street giggled. Still laughing, he handed Sgt. Whitehead the faceplate to the car stereo.

"Turn it off yourself."

Everyone who heard Street burst out laughing. For a split second, Prince thought Sgt. Whitehead was going to snatch the door open and yank Street from the car. The crowd continued to snicker. The music was still blaring, so Prince couldn't hear what Sgt. Whitehead said to the officer on Fats' side of the car. Prince knew Sgt. Whitehead had a temper from the way he cracked heads on the block. More officers were reporting to the scene as backup. They began searching, grabbing, clawing, and pulling at Street, Fats, and Hustleman trying to snatch them through the car windows.

> *"I gotta live my life like a thug nigga*
> *Until the day I die*
> *Don't judge me*
> *Until you know why"*

Prince was standing there getting more and more upset as he watched the ugly scene unfold before his eyes.

"Come on baby," Danielle said as she pulled on Prince's arm. "Let's go sit in my car until the police leave."

"That sounds like a good idea! Where's your car?" Prince asked

"Come on, it's over here," Danielle said pointing to a burgundy Ford Contour. She began digging in her purse for the keys. They got into the car and sat there in silence for a moment watching as Sgt. Whitehead slapped and thumped the boys on their heads. "And they wonder why we act the way we do out here in these streets," Prince said finally, breaking the silence. "Look, there's no need for all that."

"Well, let's just hope they don't arrest them," Danielle said. "That wouldn't be a nice birthday for Fats."

"Yeah, I guess you're right. So are you coming to the party if there is a party?"

"I was thinking about it. I'm still undecided," Danielle said.

Prince leaned back in the seat and got comfortable before he asked the next question. "What if I told you I was looking forward to seeing you tonight, would it make a difference?"

"That's the problem. I haven't decided if it would be wise for me to get involved with you and be part of all of this," she said pointing at the confusion outside the car.

Prince hunched his shoulders, as if not really having an explanation for what was going on. "I'm not really a judgmental type of person Prince, but baby the life style you're mixed up in just doesn't have a bright enough future for me."

"Danielle, what I do ain't for everybody, but for the moment it beats doing nothing. I'm all I've got and everyday I wake up I got to keep that in mind."

"But," Danielle began, "does life have to be so hard? Aren't there other choices Prince that might make your life a little less dangerous? I mean, don't get me wrong, I understand your circumstances, but I'm just having a hard time understanding the choices."

"That's because you're looking at the whole picture upside down," Prince said. "This shit I do isn't by choice, it's by force. I didn't ask to be here but now that I am, I'm gonna survive the best way I know how. Now if you'll excuse me, I need to see about my brothers."

As Prince got out of the car, Sgt. Whitehead was still preaching to Street, Fats, and Hustleman as the other officers uncuffed them. "Damn why don't this house nigga go harass somebody else?" Prince thought. "The black officers always think they're picking up points by beating down their own kind." Prince stepped closer to hear Sgt. Whitehead's closing statements.

"That nigga is a clown," Prince said after the cruiser disappeared.

"Full of his own bullshit. Damn!" Street said looking into the car.

"How am I going to get my keys out of the car?"

"Don't panic," Danielle said. "I've already called a lock smith and charged it on my credit card. He said he'd be here in about an hour."

"I guess I owe you for that," Prince said to Danielle.

"No you really don't," Danielle said. "I did it out the kindness of my heart. Do you know anything about that?"

"Oh, yeah. I know a lot about it," Prince said with a smile.

"Well, we'll talk about it later at the party," Danielle said. "Right now I've got to go get China so we can get to the game."

"The Game! Ah shit!" Hustleman yelled. "I can't wait an hour on this chump! Man you niggas know how much money I'll miss if I don't get to that game before it starts and collect our bets! I can't afford it! I need that money! Will somebody help a brother out? I got five dollars for gas money," Hustleman said directing it at Danielle.

"If you don't mind Danielle, can my boy ride with you and China to the game?" Prince asked.

"Sure Baby, it's cool," Danielle said. In the meantime, Prince, Street, and Fats sat and waited on the locksmith.

CHAPTER 3

On the way to the game, Hustleman practically begged Danielle.

"Baby please hurry up! Can't you drive just a little bit faster? I've got to be there before kick-off or we can't make no money on this game."

"Hustleman, I'm already speeding! What you want me to do run red lights too? It can't be that serious!"

"You just don't know! What time is it, China Doll?" Hustleman asked. "Is it past 7:30 yet?"

"It's 7:20 Hustleman and we're almost there. So would you please sit back there and take a chill pill? The game doesn't start for another ten minutes."

Hustleman pulled his cell phone out of his pocket and scrolled his phone book until he found J. Blaze's cell number. Hustleman pushed send and prayed like hell Blaze had taken his phone with him to the football field. He usually did and put it inside his shoes on the bench. The phone rang once, twice, and then three times before his voice mail came on. "Shit!" Hustleman said closing his phone. By the time he looked over the front seat to see how close they were, his cell started ringing.

"Turn that music down a minute! It's Blaze. My nigga, please tell me you ain't kicked off yet." Hustleman said into the phone.

"Naw man we're still stretching on the field but you've only got about ten minutes. Where the hell are you at and why you cutting time so close?

"My nigga, your not going to believe what we've just been through!" Hustleman began telling Blaze about Sgt. Whitehead and how he performed with the thumping, slapping, and shit talking that the gang went through.

"I thought you were going to say he pulled you over for that bank robbery Street did. I got to tell Hitman and Sticky about this bullshit!" Blaze said. "Listen man, if we're gonna get this money, you better hurry up! Everybody is looking for you to place their bets and the whole stadium is jam packed!"

"For shizzle my nizzle, I'll be there in a second! How much time do I got?"

"Ah shit, the refs are blowing the whistle right now. Hurry up nigga! I got to go. Holla at me when you get here." Blaze said.

"Damn," Hustleman said under his breath "that damned White-head!"

By the time they made it through traffic and arrived at the stadium the game was just beginning. Running like the cops were after him, he dashed and dipped between the crowds of people until he reached the entrance that led to the field. Luckily, the Woodward players were on the sideline closest to him. He ran to get a closer look at the scoreboard. Hustleman was hoping the score was still zero when he noticed Elder lining up to kick off. When Hustleman looked at the board his heart sank. The score was seven to nothing in favor of the visiting team. "How in the hell did Elder get a touchdown so fast? Shit, that's not good," he thought.

"Excuse me sir," Hustleman said to an older gentleman, "how did Elder get a touchdown so fast?"

"They ran the kick off back ninety yards," the man replied. "It looks like Woodward has their hands full tonight!"

"Damn!" Hustleman said under his breath. "You ain't ever lied!"

"It's still early though," the gentleman continued. "Maybe we'll return our kick off for a touchdown too and even the score."

Hustleman watched the Elder team line up to kick off from the thirty-yard line. He looked at the gentleman who decided to stand and watch the kick off too.

"I'll see ya later partner. I've got a few friends to find," as Hustleman parted company. He walked around to the Woodward end zone. He didn't look behind him so he didn't see Sgt. Whitehead enter the stadium. He and his trainee Officer Ward were no more than fifty feet behind him.

"Hustleman, Hustleman, over here nigga!" Blaze yelled over the cheerleaders.

Hustleman looked around until he put the voice calling his name with a face that looked familiar. "Right here man," Stickyfingers and Hitman both yelled as they stood with their helmets in the air.

"Hey," Hustleman said.

"My bad I was caught up in the game."

"What we gonna do, get this money or what?" Blaze asked.

"I saw those seven points on the board and thought we were dead in the water," said Hustleman.

The announcer on the stadium intercom was saying:

"Woodward receives the ball on the five yard line; he runs it to the twenty before being gang tackled by Elder, but there's a flag on the play. Off sides on the kicking team! Elder has to kick over but farther back this time."

"Hey look! There's Sgt. Whitehead standing at our end zone!" said Blaze.

"Ah shit," Hustleman said ducking a little bit farther down in his coat.

"Listen Hustleman, I think I got a pretty good idea that'll fix Sgt. Whitehead," Blaze said. "Let us take care of Whitehead and you get up there in the stands and get those bets. Let 'em have the seven points. It ain't going to help. You know how we do. It's business as usual. We could spot these boys two more touchdowns and still blow 'em out, so just get up there and start collecting money my nizzle."

"Elder lines up to kick the ball off again, the kicker approaches the ball - it's a trick! It's an onside kick that appears to have caught the Woodward Riders off guard! Lets see what team fell on the ball. Great call by the Elder coach! It looks like Elder has recovered the ball at their forty yard line with a fresh set of downs!" the announcer said excitedly."

Things were quiet on the Woodward sideline as the team contemplated the impending disaster.

"I'll be damned!" Blaze muttered.

"Looks like a dog fight," said Hitman.

"Go get that money!" Blaze told Hustleman. "Hurry up and then give me the thumbs up sign when it's cool to turn the heat up on these chumps because they done pissed me off with that slick shit!"

While Hustleman went into the stands to begin collecting money, Blaze, Hitman, and Stickyfingers walked the sidelines discussing their game plan.

"What's your 'pretty good idea' for Sgt. Whitehead?" Sticky asked

Blaze as the three found a seat on the bench. "I'm really interested in hearing this one."

****

Coach Andrews was a good coach and everybody loved him, but when he got pissed like he was now at Woodward's special teams for getting tricked, he wasn't shy about voicing his opinion. If you were standing too close, you got an ear full of some serious profanity. The coach was cussing his head off but his three star players weren't paying much attention because they had other problems to worry about.

"Now what's the 'pretty good idea'?" Sticky asked again.

"I'll tell you when the time is right," Blaze said turning around looking in the stands for Hustleman. "Right now we need to be focusing on this money because I'm broke. So, we gotta hold back for a second until Hustleman gets all four pockets full of cash. Then we'll turn up the heat and blow these ol' boys out. We'll each have a pocket after the game." Blaze explained as he watched Hustleman go to work in the stands.

"Well he'd better stuff my pocket!" Sticky said. And he better stuff it fast because we're playing for all the marbles tonight and I don't feel like spotting these white boys no more points!"

"My nizzle, just be cool and stop stressing about these white boys! Can't nobody in this city beat us! There's two halves to this game and we're still in the first, so be cool and just relax!" Blaze said as he got up from the bench and walked towards the rest of the team. He glanced down the field to see if Sgt. Whitehead was still standing at Woodward's end zone.

"Elder gets another first down! It looks like they are marching straight down the field on the Woodward Riders! They're already within field goal range at Woodward's 20 yard line!"

Blaze watched the Elder Wildcats celebrate on their sideline. He continued to watch them until Coach Andrews interrupted his thoughts.

"You ready son?" Coach Andrews asked as he placed a hand on his star quarterback's shoulder pads. "As you can see this team came to play tonight!"

"I got us coach, don't even sweat it." J. Blaze said confidently. "I'm not worried about these cats at all! They better be worried about me because me and my amigos came to play!"

"Speaking of your amigos, where are those other two?" coach asked as he looked around for his two receivers, Sticky and Hitman. "I hope they know there's a lot of college scouts in the stands tonight here just to see you three play ball. So if you want those scholarships they're handing out and possible pro careers you're always talking about, you better get your heads in this game!" the coach told Blaze.

"Here we are coach!" Sticky and Hitman said putting on their helmets.

"It's third down and ten for the Elder Wildcats on the Rider's twenty yard line. Elder's quarterback, Chad Clemons, the city's second rated QB next to J. Blaze of Woodward, looks over the defense of the Woodward Riders and goes under center to call the play.

"Sixteen-forty-eight!" called Chad as he stepped back into shotgun formation. "Twenty-nine, sixty-two!" Chad motioned for his receiver on the right to fade to the corner of the end zone. "Hut, Hut GO!"

"Elder's Quarterback Chad steps back into the shotgun and just beats the play clock! It's a fade to the end zone! Oh a Woodward player at the last minute breaks it up! Elder will have to attempt a twenty-five yard field goal. The kick is up and it's good! Elder 10, Woodward 0! That Woodward offense better get busy ladies and gentlemen, or they might get upset here at home tonight! This Elder team is hungry for an upset!"

Sticky strapped on his helmet and then looked at his quarterback, J. Blaze and then at Hitman.

"What about you my nizzle, are you ready or what?"

"I was born ready," Hitman answered, strapping on his helmet.

"The question is," J. Blaze said putting on his helmet, "is Hustleman ready?"

"Damn I forgot about him!" Sticky said. "That nigga better hurry up and place them bets! What more do they want? We've already spotted them ten damned points for their money!"

"Hitman! Run over there real quick and tell Hustleman I asked what's the hold up?" Blaze instructed.

"Look out, here comes Coach Andrews!" Sticky announced.

"Listen guys. Hey hold up Hitman! Hitman!" the coach yelled as he watched his starting receiver run off while he was trying to give some last minute instructions before the offense took the field.

"It's okay coach," Blaze and Sticky said wrapping their arms around the coach. "His mom just wants to wish him luck."

"We got business to take care of! We need instant offense and I've got the first three plays right here! We need seven points on this possession and here's the plays I want you to run." The coach looked up and noticed that neither of his players was paying him any attention.

"Um hello guys, are you listening to me or am I talking to myself?" Coach Andrews demanded as Blaze and Sticky were busily looking around for Hitman.

"Yeah coach we got cha baby, don't worry," Blaze said. "These three plays, touchdown all in this possession. We got it baby-don't even worry," Blaze reassured the coach and turned his attention back to the stadium stands.

"Yeah Blaze! Something like that!" coach said suspiciously while eyeing Blaze and Sticky. "Listen you two wise guys! We're down ten points against a good team! Remember this is for the number one title and your careers in football! So I suggest you two find Hitman and get out there and do your thing!" the coach barked as he walked away rather irritated.

"All right coach," Sticky yelled. "Don't worry we got this!"

"Man we better not lose this game messing around with Hustleman."

"Just be cool Sticky," Blaze said, cutting him off.

"Okay, Mr. N.W.A.P.," Sticky said as he turned to watch the kick off.

"Hitman! Damn, what took you so long?" Blaze asked as Hitman ran back for his helmet.

"Alright you two! Let's go! We got the ball on the twenty yard line," Sticky said.

"Offense! Let's go!" Coach Andrew yelled. "We need points and we need 'em now!"

"*Coming on the field is Ohio's leading passer, Jeff "J. Blaze" Wright,*

Woodward's first 1,000 yard rushing quarterback."

"What did Hustleman say?" Blaze asked as they all three ran on to the field to join the huddle.

"That nigga is racking in so much cash he's got Danielle and China Doll helping him hold some of it! He said he needs just a little more time and he'll be ready," Hitman explained as they got to the middle of the field.

"More time! Shit we're already down ten damn points!" Blaze said counting to make sure he had enough players on the field.

"He said that's what got them betting heavy up there! Everyone took the ten points with Elder," Hitman whispered.

"So what we gonna do?" Sticky asked in disgust, not liking the idea of bullshitting in the first place.

"We'll give Hustleman a little more time to get that money. Now huddle up!" Blaze ordered. He looked around at his teammates in the huddle before deciding on what play he wanted to run first. "All right everybody, let's do this! We're gonna open the game up with a half back sweep to the right on two. Ready? Break!"

"Woodward starts their first serious offense on their own twenty. Blaze brings his offense to the line with Jason "Stickyfingers" McNickels out to the far right and Charles "Hitman" Carter out to the far left, with two running backs in the backfield. J. Blaze steps under center and watches the movement of the defense."

"Red, fourteen, blue, forty-nine, Hut one Hut two, Go!" Blaze grabbed the snap and pitched to his running back that only gained two or three yards before being gang tackled by the Elder defense.
"My what a surprise! Woodward starts off running the ball! I didn't expect that being down ten points when their bread and butter have been passing all year!"

"Come on, huddle up!" Blaze yelled. "Good run - good run!"

"What the hell was that?" Coach Andrews asked his assistant coach.

"That wasn't one of the plays I gave Blaze!"

"It's now second and seven for the Woodward Riders".

"What's the next play Mr. N.W.A.P.?" Sticky asked coming to the huddle a little pissed at the results of the shitty play Blaze had called. Blaze knelt down in the huddle and looked at all the plays written down on his wristband before deciding on what to call next. "Double reverse boys! Left to right on one, everybody block a man!" he called. Even though Blaze called Sticky's number to run the reverse, Sticky still wasn't happy because he knew it was too early to be calling a damn reverse but that's what his boy called and that's what they ran.

"Down- Set- Gray forty seven-Blue twenty-two, Hut one Hut two, go!" Blaze rolled left towards Hitman and pitched the ball. Hitman caught it in stride and handed it off to Sticky coming around the other end. Bam-Pow-Bang was all that was heard as two Elder defenders dumped Sticky so hard on his head. The crowd ooh'ed and ahh'ed at the punishing hit. Sticky jumped up a little wobbly, but he made it back to the huddle to give Blaze a piece of his mind for setting him up to get his head almost taken off. "Thanks a lot my nizzle for almost getting me killed! If you want me to finish this game, I suggest you not call any more plays like that!" Sticky complained as he snapped his chinstrap.

"My bad dogg," Blaze said helping Sticky put his shoulder pads back into his jersey.

The coach screamed for a time-out. "Hey you three get over here!"

"Come on Mr. N.W.A.P," Sticky said to Blaze as the three walked to the sidelines.

"What the hell are you doing Blaze! Those aren't the plays I sent in!"

"My bad coach, I was trying something new hoping to confuse them a little bit," J. Blaze explained to the coach with a straight face. Nobody knew that they were really point shaving.

"Well what you just tried made us lose three yards!" Coach Andrews screamed at Blaze. "And, you almost got one of your own players killed in the process! It's third down and we need twelve yards! Throw the damn ball!"

"This series of downs just doesn't look like the Woodward Rider's who have been throwing the ball all year!

Blaze turned to Hitman as they were heading back to the huddle.

"How long did Hustleman say he was going to need? 'Cause I can't hold back much longer."

"He said he would give us a thumbs up sign when he had all the bets in," Hitman said.

"All right," J. Blaze said, "everyone in the huddle! We need thirteen yards. Hitman and Sticky go fifteen yards and give me a buttonhook. I want both backs to split left and right just in case we go on a two count." As they broke from the huddle, Blaze pulled at Sticky's jersey.

"What does N.W.A.P. mean?"

"It means Nigga With A Plan," Sticky explained calmly as he trotted to his position. "And your plan doesn't seem to be working out in our favor." J. Blaze looked at Stickyfingers who was at the far right of the formation. Then he looked out far left at Hitman before bending down under the center to snap the ball. "Black-Red-Blue-Green," barked Blaze. Stepping back into the shotgun, he looked at Sticky and gave him the finger. "Hut-one Go! Blaze took the ball and purposefully scrambled, throwing the ball away. Forth down and the punting team came on.

"Blaze come here son," the coach said. "What's the problem? Is your arm hurting you son?"

"Naw coach, just a little nervous, I'll be all right," and he sat down on the bench next to Sticky and Hitman.

"Woodward looks a little flat on their first set of downs. Let's see if Elder can capitalize on their mistakes. If so, the morning sports page will have a new team in the number one spot and that will surprise a lot of people come tomorrow."

The three amigos sat in silence until Blaze told Hitman to go check on Hustleman.

"So this is the plan? Get the money, but lose our number one ranking and future scholarships? Man, have you gone crazy?" Sticky asked Blaze. "I mean for real, dogg have you lost your damn mind?

Because just in case you've forgotten, there's college scouts at all our games now that we're seniors and for this little bit of money you could cost us our dreams of playing together at the next level!"

"Man I'm only giving Hustleman three more downs and then we roll. I just need this money bad, my nigga and I know you can use a few extra chips in your pockets too." Blaze told his partner in crime.

"We've been getting money and winning championships for three years now and I haven't failed us yet so have faith Sticky! Don't start panicking on me now!"

"Hey," Hitman said after returning from talking to Hustleman.

"Hustleman said some niggas from Withrow just bet five hundred on Elder after seeing those last three downs."

"Say what?" J. Blaze and Sticky asked at the same time.

"You heard me! Three niggas who play football for Withrow just took the ten points with Elder for five hundred dollars!"

"Damn!" Blaze exclaimed. "We got that kinda cash waiting on this game?" He turned around from his seat on the bench to glance up in the stands at Hustleman. Hustleman nodded his head at Blaze and gave him the thumbs up.

"Oh, it's show time for real now!" Blaze said. "Hustleman just gave me the signal and now it's time to give these boys a show they'll never forget! Man I need that money!" He suddenly became all business.

"Lets get out there and do what we came here to do!"

"I'm ready whenever you two nigga's get ready," Sticky said. "I don't need that money that damned bad but if you do my nigga, then come on and let's go get it! Because as far as I'm concerned, we shouldn't have been bullshittin' in the first place!" And he walked away with an attitude.

"What's wrong with him?" Hitman asked Blaze.

"He's just trippin', that's all," Blaze explained. "You two just catch the damned ball when I put it up there and we'll win this game, cover the points, and keep our number one ranking. I got this under control," Blaze said as he began tightening the laces on his shoes. Hitman and Sticky jogged in place trying to stay loose.

"After scoring a quick ten points, Elder's offense seems to have lost a little of their steam. Instead of the high powered offensive game this match up between these two number one teams was billed to be, it looks like we're gonna get a defensive chess match tonight! Elder has to punt the ball for the third time with one minute forty-seconds left in the first quarter. Woodward fans are starting to get a little restless. J. Blaze and his two amigos better be

ready to turn it up another notch when their offense hits the field."

"Hey Dad!" came a familiar voice breaking Ray's concentration on the game.

"Well, hello ladies!" Ray said getting plenty of hugs and kisses from his two lovely daughters.

"What you doing standing way down here?" Gina asked.

"Well, I thought I was getting the best seat in the house by standing here at Woodward's end zone thinking their offense was gonna do plenty of scoring. So far, none of that scoring has happened. Basically, Officer Ward here and I have just been standing here kicking it."

"Hi Officer Ward," Gina said. "Since my daddy hasn't introduced us, I'm Gina and this is my sister Cindy."

"Hello ladies and please call me Tony. It's my pleasure to make your acquaintance," as he shook each of their hands.

"Oh cut it out," Ray said laughing. "I was gonna introduce you two, but you didn't give me a chance! Tony, they seem to think that I play Mr. Overprotective."

"You do," Cindy said.

"And it's another first down for Woodward at the fifty yard line!"

"Looks like the Woodward Riders might be on the move," Ray said watching Woodward's offense break the huddle.

"Where are they?" Tony asked pulling his eyes away from Gina's graceful figure.

"They're at mid-field," Ray answered.

"Who are the Pretenders and who are the Contenders in this game? Woodward looks like they're on the move sitting on the fifty-yard line. Woodward's Q.B. J. Blaze is starting to look more confident and comfortable as this game progresses, with triple receivers on the right and Stickyfingers lined up in one-on-one coverage on the left. J. Blaze steps under center, snaps the ball, drops back, throws over the middle toward the end zone. Jason McNickels high steps it into the end zone for Woodward's first score of the game with a leaping, spectacular catch! Sticky is doing his sticky dance! The Woodward crowd comes alive as the stadium rocks. The extra point, snap, hold and the kick. It's good! Elder 10, Woodward 7.

"Wow!" Ray said to Tony. "That was a pretty catch wasn't it?"

"It sure was!" agreed Tony.

"See, I told you if we stood right here at Woodward's end zone, we would have the best seats in the house! It was so close it almost felt like we were right on the field with them," Ray said.

"Yeah I think your daughters missed out because they were walking away when Woodward scored," Tony said.

"Woodward lines up to kick the ball off. Elder takes the touchback, so the ball starts on their twenty yard line. I think that touchdown stunned Elder a little bit because once again their offense can't produce. This is adding to Woodward's momentum! If Elder doesn't watch out and start playing on both sides of the ball, they could easily get steam rolled by this Woodward offense. It's the post-season showdown as the Woodward offense takes the field with excellent field position from the Elder thirty-yard line after a punt and speedy return by Hitman Carter. Watch out! It's the league's come back kids! J. Blaze steps under center - hut one, hut two, hut and hands the ball off to his running back. He scoots through the middle of the line for a gain of six yards! It looks like Woodward is starting to click on all cylinders! J. Blaze takes the snap and drops straight back, slinging a tight spiral to Hitman their speedy receiver on a five yard out pattern. He catches the ball at the thirty, twenty, ten and he's knocked out of bounds just short of the end zone at the one yard line of Elder! They smell a come back by the come back kids!

The coach sent in a play with the full back. Blaze called the play in the huddle. "Halfback fake on the two count."

"Woodward steps to the line of scrimmage with a full house in the back field. Elder thinks a run from the one yard line for a touchdown, but J. Blaze has something else in mind. Blaze fakes the hand off, keeping the ball on first and goal and takes it to the house himself for the go ahead touchdown! With the extra point good, Woodward takes the lead 14 to 10 with five minutes left before half-time!"

"Damn!" Ray said slapping high fives with Tony. "That was sweet how he fooled everybody and just tiptoed into the end zone! Man I think Woodward is gonna win it all again this year!"

"They might," Tony said. "They sure look good."

Blaze ran to the sideline after scoring the touchdown with his adrenaline flowing off the Richter scale. The team was going wild and waving Woodward towels over their heads at the fans in the stands. Hustleman was in the stands doing the cabbage patch dance, kind of rotating hips in a full circular motion. Danielle, China Doll and Kenya were standing and clapping with the rest of the fans. However, the three dudes who bet five hundred dollars were not happy at all. Woodward's team morale was high for the first time. Sticky was going off, "You know we're the Shiznit!" he was yelling.

"Yeah Nigga, Yeah Nigga, Yeah Nigga, Ruff Rider, Ruff Riders, Ruff Riders!" the football team was screaming until the whole stadium was screaming 'Ruff Riders' with them.

"You da Man!" Sticky exclaimed, slapping Blaze on top of his helmet several times. "This is Mr. N.W.A.P!" Sticky yelled at the top of his lungs.

J. Blaze grabbed Sticky and gave him a big bear hug because he loved Sticky like a brother. Then he pulled Sticky's facemask up to his and said, "I told you nigga, never doubt your boy cause I got your back for life!"

"This Woodward team is pretty exciting! I'm looking forward to seeing these boys in the playoffs and hopefully, the state championship. Elder must realize that they're now in the lion's den. They've got five minutes before half time to answer the bell and silence this Woodward crowd that's in a complete frenzy. I tell you, I think this Elder team is stunned! Let's see what they do with this kick off. Woodward's special team just completely manhandled Elder's return man!"

The Elder coach gave some last minute instructions to his quarterback before sending him on the field. "Don't worry about the crowd son. Just move the ball down the field and put points on the board before half-time."

"Sure Coach," and the Elder quarterback ran to the huddle.

After two running plays that netted a total of three yards, Elder found themselves in a third and long situation. Walking up to the line of scrimmage, Elder's Q.B. Chad Clemons changed the play when the Woodward Riders showed a blitzing formation. "Red 32, Blue 14, hut one, hut two," and Elder's quarterback dropped back and threw the long ball to his favorite receiver. It looked like a possible completion until a Woodward defender showed up at the last minute to break up the play.

"Forth and long. Elder must punt the ball with just two minutes left before half time.

"You think Woodward can score before the half Tony?" Ray asked as they both watched Elder line up to punt the ball.

"I don't know Sergeant," Tony said as he watched a few pretty ladies walk by. "I guess it depends on whether or not they get a good return."

"I guess you've got a point there," Ray said.

"Look at those boys! They're fired up and having big fun! It's times like this that I feel blessed to be able to work with some of these kids through the D.A.R.E program," Ray said to Tony.

"I guess it does have its rewards," Tony said, as he watched the Woodward offense take the field.

"Here they come!" Tony said pointing to the Woodward players trotting onto the field.

"Well, they don't have much time. They might have enough time to get a field goal," Ray said.

Woodward came out of the huddle in a four wide receiver spread, with triple receivers to the left. J. Blaze pointed to his two top receivers, nodded his head at Hitman, and then checked over the defense with a focused, hard look. Then he pointed to Stickyfingers and tapped his helmet twice.

"That's a new look from the Woodward quarterback. It looks like the three amigos have their own personal signals! Let's see if it helps them out."

"Ready-Set-Down and Go!" Blaze hiked the ball on a quick count catching Elder's defense off guard as they were still switching their defense to match up with Woodward's passing formation. Seeing a soft one on one coverage on Sticky's side, Blaze immediately zipped the ball to him as he stepped a yard from the line of scrimmage. Sticky put a move so sweet on the Elder defender after the catch, that the fan's oohed and aahed as Sticky used his speed to streak down the sideline before being knocked out of bounds at the Elder twenty yard line.

"Oh my goodness! What a move by #81, Jason McNickels. He just completely shook the shoes off of Elder's corner back, Tim Little!"

"Wow!" Ray exclaimed. "Now that was one of the best moves I've seen this year!"

"You ain't never lied," stated Tony. "That was pretty nasty wasn't it?" As both officers were completely engrossed in the offensive clinic the Woodward Riders were holding, Mike Brunson the school's principle was crossing the track heading straight towards them.

J. Blaze looked up at the clock then stuck his head back in the huddle to talk to his teammates. "We've got forty three seconds to score so everybody listen up. Option right on two, everybody block a man."

Blaze broke the huddle looking beyond the defense toward the end zone. He saw Mr. Brunson engaged in conversation with Sgt. Whitehead. Stepping under center, Blaze began to call the next play. "Blue fourteen, Red twenty nine."

"Well Woodward looks like they're about to run the ball with forty three seconds left and the ball on the twenty."

"Good evening gentlemen. I see you're enjoying the game," Mr. Brunson said to the two officers as he walked up behind them. Sticking his hand out as he introduced himself. "Hi, I'm Mike Brunson, principle of Woodward High."

Ray looked down at the principle, who was fairly short at five feet.

"My pleasure Mr. Brunson," Ray said as he shook the principle's hand. I'm Sergeant Ray Whitehead and this is Officer Tony Ward," Ray said as they shook hands.

Ray's attention was torn between watching Woodward line up to run the next play and Mike. Brunson.

"So, you're Sgt. Ray Whitehead of District Four," Brunson continued. "I've been in touch with Captain Safeway from your district requesting your department's assistance here at the school, but I haven't received a response yet.

"Yeah, we've been pretty busy lately," Ray said. "But the Captain did mention to me that the school has been inquiring about some help here at Woodward."

"Yes we have Sergeant Whitehead. We've got problems here at Woodward that's way beyond my staff's ability to deal with. I was hoping in the near future to get you to bring your D.A.R.E. Program here to talk to these kids."

"Well, Mr. Brunson that sounds like a possibility," Ray said. "Why don't you call this number Monday morning," as he handed the principle one of his D.A.R.E. business cards, "and hopefully we can get your school on the schedule."

Mr. Brunson took the card from Sgt. Whitehead and stuck it in his shirt pocket. Before the principle could say what else was on his mind, Ray had turned to watch Woodward's offense run the next play.

J. Blaze takes the snap and rolls right. He fakes the option pitch to his running back as his blocker in front of him has opened up a hole! Blaze shakes left, then he shakes right. He's got one man to beat for the touchdown. He's at the ten yard line, the five, four, three, two and he's gonna score! Oh no! He slips and falls down at the one-yard line just short of the end zone! My oh my what a run! He's gonna be a force to reckoned with when he plays college ball next year. Every major division one school wants him! But rumor has it he's leaning towards Ohio State hoping to take his two amigos with him. Ohio State has mentioned possible starting positions. Wouldn't that be special for these three kids to be able to continue their winning chemistry together at the next level?"

"Damn, he's a hell of an athlete!" Ray said as he watched Blaze shake and bake his way down to the one yard line and then slip and fall.

"It looked like a invisible hand just came out of the turf to trip up Woodward's quarterback at the one yard as he lost his balance just inches shy of the goal line."

Sticky was jumping up and down as he watched his partner Blaze cut in and out of traffic heading straight for the end zone. "Go Blaze, Go!" Sticky and Hitman yelled as they ran toward the end zone to celebrate. So when Blaze fell at the one-yard line all by himself, Sticky and Hitman were the first ones there.

"Damn clumsy ass nigga!" Sticky said helping Blaze up.

"Call time out Hitman," Blaze instructed as he stood up looking at the clock. The whistle blew.

"Time out, Woodward," the ref said, pointing to the Woodward sideline.

Blaze, Sticky and Hitman ran to the sideline to talk to the coach.

"What happened Blaze? You all right?" the coach questioned.

"Yeah, I'm all right. I just slipped that's all. Give me some water," Blaze said somewhat out of breath.

"Listen," Coach Andrews said to his three star players. "We've only got twenty one seconds on the clock with no time outs."

Blaze cut the coach off. "Don't worry coach, we're going in." Blaze took one more sip from the water bottle then offered it to Sticky and Hitman who both declined. He looked into the stands for Hustleman's face among all the screaming students. He found him and stuck his thumb up and then turned it down. Blaze took his hand and motioned across his throat, "Off with his head!" Hustleman nodded his understanding. It was revenge time. Blaze threw the water bottle down on the ground, put his helmet on and told Sticky and Hitman to come on.

"Sergeant Whitehead," the principle continued.

Ray was applauding the Woodward cheerleaders' performance.

"Yes, Mr. Brunson," Ray answered completely annoyed that the principle was still trying to talk about high school security.

"I just left my office after talking with the parents of a sixteen year old student, who says she was raped by two of our football players."

Ray and Tony stopped with their attention now completely focused on the principle. "Did she say which players allegedly committed this rape?" Ray asked.

"She won't say. But another source, who wouldn't leave their name, called the school this afternoon and said she witnessed Jeff "Blaze" Wright and Charles " Hitman" Carter having sex with some girl in an unoccupied classroom in the back of the school this afternoon."

"I'll be damned," Ray said turning his head towards the field of play as Blaze walked on the field.

"Sticky remember, we only got two shots at this plan," Blaze said as they walked on to the field. "So make sure you line Sgt. Whitehead up in my sight. Hitman, you come around and pop Sticky's man out the way so he can't touch the ball."

"Alright," Hitman said excitedly about Blaze's plan.

Sgt. Whitehead watched the quarterback more closely now.

"Damn, is this nigga staring at me?" Blaze thought, as he glanced in Whitehead's direction. "Ain't this a beeyotch!" he thought to himself. Blaze was really pumped about the play he was about to call as he continued to bring the team to the line of scrimmage. He looked left at Hitman and then right at Sticky before he bent down under center and began to call the play that he hoped he could make happen. "Green 42, Red 19, Grey 21, hut one, hut two, Go!" He stepped back as Stickyfingers cut across the back of the end zone. Blaze fired a hard bullet right at Stickyfingers' head just as Hitman hit the defender hard and knocking him down to the ground. Sticky ducked just in time to watch the ball sail right past his head to hitting Sgt. Whitehead square in the middle on his face. The blow knocked him to the ground instantly. Officer Ward and principle Brunson tried to catch the sergeant but he fell hard. Blood started gushing out of Sgt. Whitehead's nose.

"Huddle up, Huddle up!" Blaze shouted trying to get the play started before the last few seconds ticked off and the opportunity to score a touchdown would be lost.

"My goodness! Is he all right?" Principal Brunson asked while looking at the bloody mess on Sgt. Whitehead's face. "Call an ambulance! He doesn't look so good."

Ray mumbled something.

"What'd you say Sergeant?" Officer Ward asked kneeling down to hand Ray a handkerchief to wipe the blood from his face.

"I'll be fine," Ray whispered, "I'm just a little dazed. Just let me lay here."

"Hut one, Hut two. Touchdown on a quarterback sneak by J. Blaze." Blaze went over by the fallen sergeant at the back of the end zone and spiked the ball with authority.

"What the hell was that?" Coach Andrews asked another member of his staff.

"I can't call it coach," as they started for the locker room for half time. Blaze, Hitman and Sticky ran off the field while holding up one finger at the screaming crowd.

"Ruff Riders, Ruff Riders! That's my nizzle!" Hustleman yelled as he, Danielle, China Doll and China's home girl Kenya clapped and cheered with the rest of the Woodward fans. The score was Woodward 24 Elder 10.

"Hey y'all!" Look at Mr.Tuff Cop holding his face," Hustleman said pointing to the area where Sgt. Whitehead was being attended.

"Who's that helping him off the ground?" Danielle asked.

"Girl, that's our little itty bitty principle, Mr. Brunson," China Doll said laughing.

"When Blaze threw that ball and hit Sgt. Whitehead, he fell on top of Mr. Brunson! I was watching the whole thing!" China said.
After everybody had a good laugh at Sgt. Whitehead's unfortunate accident, Kenya elbowed China and said, "Ooh girl! I didn't tell you about the bullshit Monica got started today!"

"Aw shit," Hustleman complained. "I think it's time to hit the concession stand cause Kenya's getting ready to start gossiping."

"Ah nigga" don't be hating because I didn't give you none yesterday night. You need to be trying to listen to what I got to say because it's about your boy anyway," Kenya said pointing her finger at Hustleman.

"Wait a minute," China Doll said laughing and holding up her hand. "Before you go there Kenya, tell us a little more about yesterday. Me and Danielle want some of that gossip first."

"Oh yaw on that," Hustleman said joining in on the laughter.

"Girl it really ain't nothing," Kenya said giggling. "The nigga just popped over to my house late last night drunk as hell trying to get a bootie call and my momma ran his ass off." Kenya said as China Doll and Danielle started laughing.

"That's all right," Hustleman said. "I know you put your momma on me. Its cool how you played me."

Kenya laughed and then gave Hustleman a big hug because it was all in fun and games. They all really had a lot of love for each other.

"Don't worry baby. I'm gonna give you some one day, maybe." Kenya said, "But what I wanna tell you is this afternoon, Monica came to class walking all funny like she had been riding a horse or something, so I was joking with her like we always do. Now everybody knows how Monica has the hots for Blaze."

"Man, Blaze don't want that ho," Hustleman said, "so she really needs to get over it.

"Well, Blaze may not have wanted her but he sure wanted a piece of that ass," Kenya said as she dropped her bomb, "because she skipped 5th period with Blaze and gave him some in an empty classroom."

"Oh yeah?" Hustleman asked. "That's interesting."

"So I was joking with Monica because she was having problems sitting at her desk. I told her about running up on these niggas that's wearing a size 12 or better, you might get more then you bargain for."

"That's right girl," China Doll yelled as she high fived Kenya. "Them nigga's do be swanging mighty low don't they?"

"Dig this though," Kenya said as she continued, "that's only half of it. She fell for the banana in the tail pipe trick. She wanted Blaze so bad that she told me she did Blaze and Hitman one after another."

"You bullshitting!" China and Hustleman said at the same time.

Danielle just sat and listened because she didn't know Kenya that well.

"No bullshit! So I asked her how did that happen and guess what she said? Blaze told her if she really wanted him, she would give Hitman some too."

"She fell for that?" China Doll said shaking her head.

"She is rather special, isn't she? So I told her she needed to go home and soak in the tub," Kenya said. "She looked like she was about to pass out from the pain. I kind of felt sorry for her because not only did she allow herself to get played but she picked not one but two niggas with a size 12 to give her virginity too."

"Oh my God girl!" China exclaimed. "Monica was a virgin?

"You thought she was fucking, but for real she's been faking all this time. She's been telling me for the longest time that she wanted Blaze to be her first."

"I'll be damned!" Hustleman said as he watched the Woodward team come back on the field.

"That ain't all," Kenya said. "Guess what this dumb ho did? Instead of just taking her ass to the bus stop and catching the bus home, she goes to the principle's office and tells the secretary, Mrs. Brown she's sick.

Mrs. Brown calls Monica's mother China Doll said.

Yup, girl that's what happen," Kenya said. "When Monica's mom came, she noticed Monica was walking funny. She thought something wasn't right so she made Monica pull her pants down in the car and seen that her panties were covered with blood. Her mom hit the roof and took Monica back into the office yelling for Mr. Brunson."

Hustleman saw it coming, and almost too scared he asked, "What did Monica tell them?"

"You know what she said. That girl's terrified of her mother. She said she was raped by two guys she didn't see. At least that's what she called and told me from the hospital."

"The hospital!" Hustleman said. "You mean to tell me she's going through with this bullshit? Boy oh boy, my niggaz ain't going to like this news!"

"Yup," Kenya said. "It's deep and it's her fault. Her mom made Mr. Brunson call an ambulance to take her to get checked out and then called the police. So I'll be willing to bet that's why Mr. Brunson was talking to Sgt. Whitehead."

"You're probably right," Hustleman said deep in thought.

"Damn, now that's fucked up!" China and Danielle both said.

Everybody looked towards the direction of Sgt. Whitehead, but he had already left.

"I think I need to make a phone call, but my cell phone is in your car Danielle," Hustleman said.

Woodward was beginning to run the score up on Elder at this point. They had already scored 3 touchdowns and a field goal while they were talking in the stands.

"China, you ready to go to the party?" Danielle asked.

"I've gotta walk to the car so Hustleman can get his cell phone. The game is a blowout so we may as well go get our drink on."

"What party yaw going to?" Kenya asked. "I wanna get my drink on too."

"Girl, you didn't know Fats was having a birthday party tonight after the game?"

"No I didn't," Kenya said putting her hands on her hips as she stared at Hustleman.

"Don't stare at me girl! I would've told you but remember your momma ran me off before I could," Hustleman said laughing.

"Well you can roll with us," Danielle said.

"Now what about all this money in my purse Hustleman? When you want that?"

"You can give it to me at the car. I've got to count it up anyway.

From the looks of the score, Elder won't be coming back. It's already the 4th quarter."

"Well let's ride then!" China Doll said as everybody started down the steps of the stadium.

Not one of them noticed the three guys in Withrow jackets following them out of the stadium. Five hundred dollars was a lot of money to be taken for, and by the third quarter, those three brothers, who just happened to be gang members from Withrow High, realized Hustleman had hustled them.

"Open the car, Danielle and get in. We'll make the money transaction inside."

Once Hustleman had gotten all the money from Danielle, he counted it and stuffed the money in all the pockets of his jeans.

"Are you going to be okay carrying all that cash Hustleman?" Danielle and China asked. "If you want, we'll wait on you."

"I'll be all right," Hustleman said. "I'm just going to go back inside and wait on my niggas to come out the locker room. We'll meet you at the party. Oh yeah, where's my phone?"

"Here it is," China said handing Hustleman the phone.

Hustleman disappeared into the darkness. While Danielle was pulling out her parking space, she couldn't stop thinking about what Kenya said about a man having a size 12. She hoped Prince wasn't that big down there because she hadn't told him that she was still a virgin. Leaving the school's back parking lot, Danielle turned right, heading towards Winton Terrace driving slowly as she prepared to make another right heading south on Reading Road.

Suddenly, several gunshots could be heard off to the right somewhere in the darkness on the school's side lawn. Danielle's first reaction was to hit the brakes. China Doll yelled out, "Don't stop bitch! Those was real gunshots!"

Three guys in Withrow jackets ran across Reading Road to a parked navy blue Cutlass in the shopping mall parking lot across from the school. "Look! It's them niggaz from Withrow! Everybody start praying right now! Pray hard that them niggaz didn't just shoot Hustleman for that little money he had!" Kenya said.

Danielle instantly became nervous and confused. She started to make a U-turn in the middle of the street. Oncoming traffic came and began blowing their horns.

"Hold up girl before you get us killed! Fuck turning around!" China Doll yelled. "Drive this motherfucka over the sidewalk and through the grass!"

China and Kenya remained calm because they were from the 'hood and the sound of gunshots was a norm for them. But Danielle was a different breed. She was from the suburbs where gunshots were hardly ever heard. When they saw the fallen body, Danielle slammed on the brakes. All three of them jumped from the car at the same time. They didn't know it was Hustleman until they reached the downed figure. Suddenly, Danielle's car began to roll slowly down Woodward's side lawn. "Danielle!" Kenya screamed. "You didn't put the car in park!" She started running and managed to catch up with the car and stop it.

China started talking to Hustleman who was bleeding all over the place. "Get his phone," China said to Danielle. Danielle pulled Hustleman's bloody fingers from around the phone. She could hear somebody yelling from the phone.

"Help is on the way Hustleman! Hang in there my nigga! Hold on baby boy! Talk to me!" Danielle listened for a second then she softly said, "Hello?" somewhat scared to say anything else. Suddenly the voice became a little familiar to her as the voice shouted, "WHO THE FUCK IS THIS?" Danielle still didn't identify herself until the voice asked, "IS MY NIGGA ALIVE? Who ever this is, tell me, is my nigga still breathing?" Suddenly she recognized Prince's voice.

"Yes Prince," Danielle said. "He's still breathing."

"Danielle, is that you baby"? Prince asked.

"Yeah baby it's me," Danielle said and started crying.

"Baby did you see who did it?" Prince asked.

"Yeah baby we saw them," Danielle said.

"Alright listen to me baby! Get out of there right now before the police arrive. Come straight to me, you hear me baby?"

"Yeah, I hear you baby," sobbed Danielle.

"Then move right now and bring that phone!" and Prince hung up.

Danielle looked up through her tears and told China and Kenya what Prince said.

"Well, we better get moving," China said as she grabbed Danielle's hand.

"Kenya you drive."

CHAPTER 4

Ray and Hazel Whitehead were high school sweethearts. They married at a young age when Hazel discovered that she was pregnant with their first child. Ray was in his third year in the armed forces when he found out that he was going to be a father. He knew it was a blessing. Ray and Hazel named their daughter Gina, daddy's little princess. They decided to marry and build their future together. Now eighteen years later, with another daughter and an excellent career as a police officer, Sergeant Ray Whitehead was on top of his game. But this particular Sunday morning, Ray was feeling a little violated. That's about the best way you could describe how he felt about his painful face. When Hazel awakened and turned to her husband, she took one look at her husband's face. Frantic, she shook him out of a deep sleep to go look in the mirror.

"Honey, wake up! Baby wake up!" said Hazel with sincere concern in her voice as she shook her husband harder.

"Huh, what's the problem?" Ray mumbled with his eyes still closed. "Baby, it's your face! Wake up!" and she shoved him hard again. "Okay, okay, I'm awake," he said putting his hand on his head. He felt a headache coming on.

"Baby look," she said holding a mirror up to Ray's face. "Can you see?" Hazel asked.

"Hold on baby, I can't open my eyes," said Ray.

"I know and I want you to see why. Come with me Ray," and she grabbed his hand and led him to the bathroom. She turned on some water and told Ray to rinse his face. When he splashed his face a few times and his eyes opened enough for him to see, Ray looked into the mirror and almost fainted.

"My face, it's my face that hurts, oh my God!" he said, in a shocked tone. "I can't walk around or go to work looking this way! No one will believe a football did all this." Overnight, Ray's eyes had swollen nearly shut and were almost the size of golf balls.

"He sure got you good didn't he? You need some ice. I'll be right back." Hazel went into the kitchen for ice. Gina was eating a bowl of cereal and when she saw her mom getting the ice, she knew it was for her dad. "How's Dad?" she asked. "He'll be fine. He looks a little like a raccoon about the face, but once the swelling goes down, he'll be just fine," said Hazel as she wrapped ice cubes in a kitchen towel.

"I guess he should consider himself pretty lucky that football didn't break his nose," said Gina.

"Yeah, he's pretty lucky, but you couldn't convince him of that this morning from the way he looks," replied Hazel.

Gina giggled at the thought of her father looking like a raccoon.

"What you laughing at?" asked Ray as he walked into the kitchen wearing a pair of sunglasses. Gina and Hazel couldn't help but laugh at how he looked.

"I'm glad you ladies find my pain amusing," Ray said grumpily as they followed him into the living room.

"Where's the newspaper?" asked Ray. "My eyes may be black, and blue, and swollen, but they still work. So, can anyone tell me where's my Sunday paper?"

"Cindy's got it upstairs Dad. She's looking for a part-time job," replied Gina.

"Well, I've got a job so I don't need the classified section. Cindy!" Ray called up the stairs.

"Yeah Dad?" came a yell back.

"Can your Dad get his newspaper this morning?" he asked loudly from the bottom of the stairs. Footsteps could be heard as Cindy rounded the corner of the stairwell coming down the steps.

"Oh my Dad, you look awful!" Cindy said with wide eyes as she looked down at her father. Even in sunglasses Dad you can't hide those black eyes!"

"Thanks for your input on the matter, although I didn't ask. Now hand over that paper young lady."

"Sure, it's all there minus the want ads," Cindy said as she gave him the paper.

"You mean to tell me you don't have any jokes this morning about my new look? Your sister and mother have already said I resemble a raccoon," Ray said as he took off his sunglasses.

"Dad, seriously you look terrible and I'm pretty sure you feel just as bad, but I'm kind of upset and emotional right now. After you read the Metro section of the paper you're going to be upset too!" Crying,

Cindy ran up the stairs.

Ray turned in a state of confusion as he looked in the direction of his wife and daughter, who hunched their shoulders indicating they didn't have an answer to Cindy's outburst. "What's wrong with her?" Ray asked as he took a seat on the coach and laid the paper out on the coffee table.

"I'm not sure what's bothering her," said Hazel.

"I know what's bothering her," said Gina as she opened the refrigerator, taking out the orange juice and pouring herself a glass.

"Oh yeah?" Ray asked. "Well, what's her problem then since you and your sister want to keep your parents in the dark about what's going on in this house?"

Gina thought for a minute about the young life laying in the hospital bed, in critical condition fighting for his every breath. She nearly started to cry but she maintained her composure as she told her parents about Hustleman getting shot three times last night in the school parking lot.

"Say what?" Ray exclaimed. "I was at that game last night and I didn't hear any gun shots."

"It didn't happen Daddy until you left at half-time after you got hit with that ball."

"Yeah, but there were other officers at the game for security after I left!"

"They were all inside the stadium watching the game when the shots were fired. It wasn't until late in the 4th quarter when it happened. By the time the officers ran across the football field to the parking lot, Hustleman was laying there bleeding."

"Hold up, just wait a minute!" Ray said. "Honey, where's my glasses? I need to read this because too much is going on at that school."

"Look in the bedroom baby. I think I saw your glasses on the dresser," Hazel yelled from the kitchen to her husband who had already disappeared.

"I found them," she heard him say. Ray walked back into the living room and sat down on the couch in front of the paper. He thumbed through the paper until he found the Metro section. It didn't take long to find the headlines he was looking for.

"Shooting at Woodward/Elder game! Teen shot three times. In critical condition at University Hospital. The Millvale teen was shot in the upper torso while in the parking lot of Woodward High School sometime around 9:30 p.m. Witnesses reported hearing the gunfire from the stadium. It was reported that three suspects were seen running from the scene of the crime. One witness, who asked to remain anonymous, stated, "We heard three shots and then everyone ducked for cover"

Ray stopped reading. He had read enough. He took off his reading glasses and set them on top of the paper. Then he leaned back on the couch thinking to himself, "Why do these young black males keep shooting and killing each other? It's almost everyday the department has to pick up the pieces of another young life."

Gina saw the pain on her father's face as she got up to comfort him. "You can't save the world Dad," Gina said giving Ray a hug. "Unfortunately, this is the reality we live in now."

Ray was a tough cop because he had to be. But that didn't mean he didn't care about the many young lives he saw self-destruct everyday as a police officer.

"Hustleman is everybody's friend Dad," Gina said. "Every year he is voted class clown, because he loves to make people laugh."

"Cindy and Hustleman have the same home room teacher. That's why she's so emotional this morning. They are good friends."

Ray rubbed his hand over his bald head a few times. His mind was already racing about how to handle the investigation. The one good thing about this situation Ray thought was at least he had a potential witness living right under his roof. He got up from the couch and looked at his wife and daughter.

"Cindy," he yelled from the bottom of the stairs. "Get down here!"

"I'm coming, just a second," Cindy replied. "I just got out of the shower."

"Now Ray, remember she is your daughter," Hazel said. "So don't be interrogating her like she's some thug off the street. I'm going to stay right here and referee this whole conversation," she said placing her hands on her hips.

"What's all the commotion about?" Cindy asked taking a seat on the bottom step tying her sneakers.

"Your dad would like to talk to you honey about your friend who got shot last night, but if you don't want to talk about it sweetheart you don't have too."

"You mean Daddy wants to be Sgt. Whitehead and question his daughter this morning. Is that what this is all about?" said Cindy with a slight smile on her face.

"Basically, in a nutshell," Gina said from across the room to her baby sister.

"Wait a minute you two," Ray said taking the floor and cutting off his wife and daughter. "If anything, the two of you are treating this more like an interrogation than I am. I just want to ask my baby girl a few questions about the shooting, and what she might know. She may have information that could help the department in catching the suspects who shot this friend of hers. So if you two don't mind, can I talk to Cindy without any interference?"

"Now Cindy, while your mother starts some breakfast, will you give me a little insight on what's going on at this high school?" Ray asked while sitting back down.

"Well Dad, all I know is that Hustleman was supposed to have gotten robbed before he was shot."

"So, this could've been a robbery gone bad huh?" Ray asked.

"Yeah, that's what the word is around school."

"Gina said you were friends with this Hustleman guy. Have you ever seen him with large sums of cash? You know, enough to make someone want to rob him?"

"Not really Dad. Every game night he and his boys place some bets on the game, but heck, they've been doing that ever since Woodward started winning all their football games."

"And who are his friends?" Ray asked. "Do they carry large sums of cash too?"

"From what Kenya told me last night over the phone, you stopped Hustleman and a few of his boys last night before the game." Ray thought about it and then it hit him. "You mean the Cadillac I stopped that smelled like a marijuana factory? That car was being driven by Michael Roberts, a.k.a. Street, a known convicted drug dealer! These people are your friends?" Ray asked raising his voice.

"No Dad, I didn't say they were all my friends. I'm just cool with Hustleman, who to the best of my knowledge, isn't a drug dealer."

"I sincerely hope not young lady, because I know that crowd and it's only a matter of time before I catch Street with his pants down. "So," Ray continued. "This could've been drug related if Street was around?"

"But that's the thing Dad. Nobody was with Hustleman except a few girls from the school." "I thought you said he was with his boys." "His boys were playing in the football game. J. Blaze, Hitman, and Stickyfingers are his boys. I don't know this Street guy."

"You're confusing me now. If he was in that Cadillac with Street but at the game without him, that means he went to the game with somebody else because I locked their car keys in the car."

"Danielle and China Doll brought him to the game after you and your officers left." Cindy replied.

Ray rubbed his bald head again like he always did when he was trying to think. "Something's not making sense," Ray said mostly to himself. "So what else did this Kenya girl tell you?" asked Ray. "And who is this Kenya anyway?"

"We call Kenya 'Ms. Bell', short for telephone bell because she calls everybody with the latest gossip.

"That's interesting," Ray said with a little chuckle. "Maybe I need to be talking to Kenya. So did she say if your friend Hustleman had a large amount of cash on him? What's really a trip about this whole thing is I personally checked this Hustleman's pockets myself, just thirty minutes before he arrived at the game. If it's true what you say Cindy, that your girlfriends brought Hustleman to the game after I left them on Chase Street, then where did the money come from? At that time, he had no money, just his school ID. So were did the extra cash come from?"

"Oh yeah Dad. I didn't tell you but Kenya said Hustleman had four pockets full of money and right before he got shot, Danielle gave him more money out of her purse in the car. She said he cleaned up on mass bets he made on the game."

"Okay, I see now," Ray said, snapping his fingers. "Hustleman likes to bet large sums of money on high school games, right?" he said looking around the room at his family. "Are we paying attention in this room or am I talking to myself?" Ray looked at his family. "Can I get some feedback here?"

"What you need Daddy is a little support," Gina said playfully. Everyone laughed for a minute, having some family fun. But, everyone knew Ray was making valid points.

"If Hustleman didn't have money before the game but had his

pockets full by the time the game ended, that means he was collecting bets with the intention of not paying up if he lost or," Ray said putting a finger up to stress a point, "he collected all that money because he knew he wouldn't lose."

Cindy looked at her Dad to say something but changed her mind. Gina had a puzzled look and was silently asking, "Okay Dad, now where are you going with this."

"I see you ladies are still lost in the sauce" Ray said jokingly, somewhat proud of himself for unraveling the puzzle. "The moral of this story is, Cindy said these guys were friends. Hustleman showed up a little late. Remember when I introduced you girls to Officer Ward and we were talking about how sluggish Woodward's offense looked at the very beginning of the game? I'll bet you that was when the players on the field were giving their friend time to collect the bets. The stakes were higher because Elder lucked up and got an early kick off returned for a touchdown. Now Mr. Hustleman has to give up those points in order to collect the bets. Who wouldn't take seven points with a team that was undefeated? Now do you follow me?" Ray asked. "That's why he had so much money. They probably took every sucker up in the stands on such a loser bet!"

"That makes sense," Hazel said as she finished making breakfast. "How did you come to that conclusion Dad?" asked Cindy, getting up to wash her hands.

"How did I figure that out my dear?" asked Ray feeling as if he was the new Sherlock Holmes of the twentieth century. "I felt in my heart that the quarterback for Woodward hit me in the face with that ball on purpose. I watched the whole play. It didn't make sense at the time and I couldn't figure out a reason until you told me this morning that they were friends. If Hustleman were late, then the quarterback wouldn't have known about me pulling his friends over because Woodward's offense was on the field before Hustleman got to the game. That means he used a cell phone, or sent word somehow to tell his friends that he would be late and why. That was a good enough reason for his friends to stall on offense while their friend used that time to collect the bets. If I'm not mistaken, Woodward's first three possessions were three and out."

"Yeah Daddy, you got a point," said Cindy from the bathroom as she washed and dried her hands.

"Yes sirree," Ray said. "That game didn't start until Hustleman gave the signal. That's when Woodward started scoring as if Elder wasn't on the field. Remember how Blaze just mysteriously slipped and fell on the one-yard line and then on the next play rolled out and hit me in the face? After that, I was through. I didn't know what the hell was going on! I guess they scored and then laughed at their little get back on me. It's cool because I'm gonna get the last laugh."

"I think I'm gonna call Kenya tonight and see what other juicy gossip she's got for a sister," Cindy said walking towards the living room. "Food's ready!" Hazel announced. "Would you two detectives like to bring your discussion to the kitchen?"

"Yeah, bring it back in here, I wanna hear some more," said Gina.

"You're a day late and a dolla short, 'cause the discussion is already over! We've got a game plan!" Ray said as he started towards the table. "Don't forget now, everyone's invited to the Safeways for some soul food Sunday and brandy tonight, so don't disappear," Ray stated as he prepared to dig into the hot grits and butter that his wife had just put before him.

"Good," said Cindy. "I don't have to do dishes tonight being that it was my turn! Ha, Ha, Ha."

"Ohh, Cindy that's cold," Gina said. "What about Aunt Deborah? You didn't say a thing about seeing her."

"Aunt Deborah's cool," said Cindy between bites of bacon and eggs. "That's my girl, but tonight she looks better doing the dishes than I do."

They all laughed at that one, but they also knew Aunt Deborah was special. She was always there for the Whitehead family. Ray sat and ate his breakfast in silence while the girls talked. Ray was wondering to himself how he was going to prove that the Woodward Riders point shaving was the reason behind the shooting. It's probably going to be a felony, Aggravated Attempted Murder.

CHAPTER 5

Beep---Beep---Beep, was the only sound that filled the hospital room of Marvin Lawson, aka Hustleman, as he laid unconscious and fighting for his life. One of the three slugs had embedded itself only inches from his heart. All three bullets had been successfully removed. But he had lost a large amount of blood while waiting on the ambulance and five hours of surgery. At first, the doctors had Hustleman listed in critical condition, giving him only a fifty fifty chance of seeing the next day. But by Sunday morning, his status had been upgraded to stable as his vital signs continued to improve. Up until this morning, only immediate family was allowed to visit Hustleman.

Prince explained to the doctor that Hustleman lived in a foster home. "We're the only kin he's got," Prince said extending his arms towards the Ruff Rider members who had been camped out on the waiting room floor since Friday night.

The doctor looked everyone over before giving his reply.

"Marvin's condition is improving, but he's still fighting for his life. It's obvious that you kids care a great deal for him and right now that's exactly what he needs. Some support will benefit him greatly if he is going to pull through this. So, I'm going to allow you gentleman to visit him for a few minutes but only under one condition."

"Anything Doc, you got my word on that," Prince said.

"His heart is still weak and if you upset him in any way, his heart could stop. No noise, no emotions, no loud talking. He needs to rest," the doctor instructed.

"You got it Doc," Prince said through clenched teeth as he tried to hide the anger and pain he felt for his friend. He loved Hustleman like a brother.

"Someone needs to contact his foster parents or whoever his legal guardian is, because by law, the hospital can only release a minor to his parents or police. You kids don't look like either one to me," the doctor said. He looked at Marvin's chart and then back up at Prince. Marvin's in room 711 and for now I'm only granting a few minutes of visiting privileges, so go visit your friend."

"Thanks Doc," said everyone while shaking the doctor's hand. They filed out of the waiting room toward Hustleman's room. The hospital staff stopped what they were doing as Prince, J. Blaze, Sticky, Fats, Street, Dino, P. Funk, and Hitman turned the corner, walking past the nurse's station towards room 711. Prince pushed the door open slowly, and being as quiet as one person could possibly be, put a finger to his lips telling everyone to be quiet as they tiptoed into the room.

Everyone quietly found a seat and just stared at Hustleman, who was still unconscious. Concerned expressions covered everyone's faces, and every pair of eyes observed Hustleman's severe condition. They surveyed the tubes in his nose, IV's in his arms and the bloody bandage around his chest covering his bullet wounds. The emotions were thick.

Prince was the first to break the silence as he leaned up from the chair he was sitting in and lightly touched Hustleman on his leg. "Hang in there my nigga. Your family is right here," he whispered softly. Then Prince took his hand away, leaned back in his chair and closed his eyes thinking.

J. Blaze stood up and put a hand on Prince's shoulder, "I need to take a walk for a minute, and I'll be back."

"All right my nigga," Prince said understanding how emotional everyone was.

Half the crew had fallen asleep. Prince was too busy thinking to sleep. He sat quietly for several minutes. J. Blaze had returned and quietly entered with the Sunday paper. He made sure the door closed behind him as he walked around the room nudging those who were asleep. After he had quietly gotten everyone's attention, Blaze opened the paper to the Metro section and quietly began reading the article about the shooting.

"Police Investigate Woodward Shooting" read the caption.

"I just picked this up downstairs so everybody listen up," Blaze said, as he began to softly read, *"Cincinnati Police are investigating the shooting of a Woodward student, who was gunned down Friday night at the Woodward/Elder football game. The victim is identified by police as Marvin Lawson, (no address available), was shot three times in an apparent robbery. Witnesses say they heard the shots and saw three young black males wearing Withrow jackets running from the scene of the crime."* J. Blaze stopped reading as he allowed this information to sink in with the rest of his brothers.

"They ain't lying, because I saw the three niggas in the stands at the game. They bet five hundred on Elder with ten points," J. Blaze said.

"You think those nigga's caught on and realized you was point shaving?" asked Prince.

"Maybe afterwards, but so the fuck what? That don't give them the right to shoot my nigga up!" Sticky said quietly.

"I'm wit Sticky on that one!" J Blaze said. "We gave them ten points with Elder who was undefeated just like us. That was a heads up bet and those nigga's lost!"

"Well, whatever the reason. It's all irrelevant now because they drew first blood and as far as I'm concerned, we got to answer the bell," Street said.

Everyone shook their heads in agreement as they looked towards Prince to voice his opinion. Prince stood up quietly and walked over to the big glass window in the room. He looked deep in thought then turned and asked everyone in the room. "Is everyone prepared to put their life on the line for this cause? I love that nigga right there lying in that bed. When he bleeds, I bleed. Now ask yourself that question before you get in this shit too deep."

"My nigga, I'm down for whatever! My heart don't pump Kool-Aid," Dino said.

"What about everybody else?" Prince asked. "Can you stand the pressure? Because this is a whole new ball game if we go after these cats." Everyone seemed to agree, but Prince didn't get the sense that everyone was speaking from the heart. "I guess time will tell," thinking to himself as he turned back to the window.

For the first time, Street spoke up to voice his opinion. As he began to speak, his voice was shook with emotion. He was taking Hustl-man's condition hard. That wasn't good because not only was Street the oldest of the crew, he also was the most dangerous. "All I wanna know is," Street began to ask, "if those niggaz was down with the Warriors? If they are, you niggaz better not be bullshitting 'cause we gonna have to go to war with that gang. And that's gonna leave a lot of dead brotha's in the streets!"

"Damn, I didn't think about those niggaz being in with the Warriors! Them niggaz do have a pretty large gang at Withrow," Prince said. "Man, listen! I don't give a fuck how many gang members the

Warrior's got! If they shot my nigga up, I'm shooting their ass up. It's no mystery where my loyalty is at!" J. Blaze said in a loud whisper and waving his arms around the room. "I'm loyal with my life on the line for this crew!"

"Is that how everybody feels?" Prince asked quietly as he looked around the room. "Well, it looks like the stakes have just gotten higher but before we make a move, we need to find out if the Warriors are claiming responsibility for the shooting."

"And how we gonna find that out?" Sticky asked.

"Don't we play Withrow this Friday at their house?" Prince asked Sticky.

"Yeah," Sticky said.

"Then we'll find out then when we play them on their field," Prince said.

"We're gonna go to war on their turf? Hitman asked.

"I didn't say that! What I said was we will find out Friday if any of them robbed and shot Hustleman," Prince said.

"I don't care how we get down; just count me in," Street said with pure anger and malice in his voice.

"We're gonna need," Prince started to say as the door to the room opened.

In walked China Doll, Kenya, and Danielle. Expressions of shock were written on their faces as they looked down at Hustleman.

"Ssshhh," Prince said with his fingers to his lips. "The doctor said to make sure we don't disturb him." Prince walked up to China Doll and Kenya and gave them a hug. "He's going to be alright. We talked to the doctor and he said all the boy needs is some rest."

Danielle walked over to Prince and gave him a hug. "How you holding up baby?" Prince held her in his arms for a minute and then said. "I'll be alright after I get some fresh air. Somebody give me a cigarette!" Prince demanded.

"For what? You don't even smoke," Danielle said.

"Well, do you have a joint?" When she shook her head no, Prince said, "I didn't think so. I need something to calm my nerves."

"Here little cuz, I feel ya cause this shit got me stressing too," Street said handing Prince a pack of Newports and a lighter.

"Relax baby, 'cause everything is gonna be alright. As a matter of fact, all you niggaz relax," Prince said, "and start thinking about if you really want to get off into this gangster shit. Look at the bright side. Hustleman is still here with us and that's a lot to be thankful for.   Street, keep the order up in here while I go downstairs to clear my head."

"I got you baby," Street said from the chair he was slouched in trying to maintain his composure. Everyone was on edge by now and tension filled the room.

When Prince walked to the door and pulled it open, the noise from the nurses doing their everyday duties filled the room. He turned and looked at every face in the room. He stated, "This shit ain't over, it's just begun." He softly closed the door and he headed toward the elevator. After Prince left, a very uncomfortable silence filled the room. Everyone seemed to be at a loss for words. Danielle, who was standing next to Kenya, saw that she looked as if she was struggling to keep it together. She gave her friend a hug. "You okay girl?" Danielle whispered. Suddenly a tear appeared. "I don't know Danielle. I can't stop thinking about Hustleman's body laying on the ground covered in all that blood," Kenya said between sobs. China reached over and gave her friend a big hug and a few Kleenex for her tears.

Street sat motionless in his chair, staring at Kenya as China and Danielle tried to comfort her. The pain was palpable and it cut deeply through every heart in the room. He tried to keep his anger in check but it was beginning to boil over as he heard Kenya speak of his friend laying there helplessly in his own blood clinging to life. A look of danger consumed his facial expression as the vision of death began to flicker and dance within his eyes. Through clinched teeth, he spoke quietly but with malice, of the evil that was bloodthirsty for revenge and confrontation. "Get that Bitch out of here now with all that crying shit!" he said sounding like a completely different person.

Everyone heard the anger and Kenya snapped, "Fuck you!" she said through her sobs and tears. "He's my friend too."

Like a cat with the speed of lighting, Street was across the room with his hand around Kenya's neck squeezing with the strength of insanity that temporarily consumed his emotions. He had Kenya dangling like a rag doll in the air. The color of her face started to change as she pulled at his death grip. Fats, J. Blaze, and Dino were the first to restrain Street, as China and Danielle calmly tried to talk to him. "Fuck who Bitch?" Street asked through clenched teeth as he stared at her shocked expression. Slowly, he relaxed his grip and the color in her face began to return to normal. Once Danielle was sure Kenya was out of danger and Hustleman wasn't affected by all the commotion, she called Street a 'loose cannon' and stormed from the room.

In the mean time, preoccupied with his own thoughts, Prince sat quietly smoking his cigarette. He was confused as to how and why the circumstances in life had brought him to this point. How could it be that just simply trying to make ends meet could have brought him to this point? Seeing a good friend almost killed over a high school football game was a tough reality to face. Then, to contemplate murder as a fair exchange only made the burden that much heavier. Prince leaned back on the bench and let his mind wander for a moment thinking of all the consequences he would face and thought, "My oh my, how things have changed from selling nickel and dime bags and betting on football games." He chuckled somewhat at the thought and sat up to watch an ambulance pull around the corner. "Now its heroin, crack cocaine and decision time. What decision will I make?" Prince asked himself.

"Um, excuse me?" The sudden intrusion startled Prince from his thoughts.

"I didn't mean to scare you," Danielle said.

"Oh, its cool," Prince said sliding over a little. "Have a seat. I was just out here chilling and kind of gathering my thoughts."

"So, what decision will you make?" Danielle asked as she looked straight into "those eyes" that she personally called them whenever she was around Prince.

"What decisions will I make?" Prince repeated somewhat confused. "What are you talking about? I don't understand." Prince said hunching his shoulders a little.

"I heard you asking yourself that question when I walked up, and I'm curious to hear your answer."

"Oh, so you were eaves dropping on a brotha?" Prince asked laughing.

"Oh my how I love that smile!" Danielle thought to herself.

"So now you're waiting on an answer." Prince leaned back and asked, "What difference does it make?" He was toying with Danielle a bit.

"Don't play Prince! I think you know what difference it makes to me. We've been cool all through high school. I've watched you grow from a 7th grader selling joints in school to what you do today and I know what that is," Danielle said, with a look that said 'don't lie to me'. "Now one of your closest friends is laying up there fighting for his life and a room full of loose cannons that's ready to do whatever you say. So I'm coming to the source, who by the way I just happen to care about, to get my question answered."

"Damn D, slow down baby! It sounds like you're close to tears. What's up wit dat?" Prince asked somewhat tenderly.

"I'm sorry Prince," Danielle said quietly as she looked away. "I have never told you but I have tried to show you every time I was around that I care about you a great deal. Now that I see you going through some serious changes, I couldn't hold it in any longer."

"I see, um well," Prince started, fumbling with his words, "I don't quite know what I'm gonna do," he finally said.

Danielle looked up at Prince and leaning over, gave him a small kiss on his cheek. "Just be careful and remember this ain't the movies baby. This is real life," she said.

"Yeah, tell me about it," Prince said

"Oh yeah!" Danielle said grabbing Prince by the arm. "I almost forgot! You got to go get your cousin Street. He's trippin.'"

"What did he do?" Prince asked as he heard somebody screaming his name. "Girl hold that shit down! I'm right here! Come here Kenya!" Prince said as he stood up trying to figure out what was going on. Kenya ran straight into Prince's arms crying and sobbing. Prince held her for a minute. "Calm down girl! Hey, hey, calm down and tell me what happened!" Prince said as he grabbed Kenya by the shoulders and sat her down next to Danielle. Then Prince saw the red fingerprints on her neck and instantly his eyes turned to fire as his whole demeanor changed. "Who in the hell did this shit? I wanna know right now!"

It didn't take long for Kenya to answer 'Street' between sniffles.

"Here he comes!" Danielle said pointing to Street who was marching toward them. Everyone else was trailing along behind him.

"I see him," Prince said through clenched teeth as he stood in the middle of the sidewalk.

"Calm down I'm telling you Street!" J. Blaze said.

"Nigga, you can't tell me nothing!" Street yelled back as they came closer to Prince.

"But I can tell you nigga," Prince said to Street. "Now what the fuck is on your mind cuz?" Prince asked stepping toward Street. "Why is her neck like that nigga, huh?" Prince yelled. "You beating on woman now?" Street turned around and walked across the street to the parking garage. Prince looked around at everybody else. "Will somebody tell me what his problem is?"

Fats and Sticky spoke up first. "He's just taking Hustleman's situation kind of hard and when Kenya started crying upstairs, he told her to shut up and she said fuck you or something like that and he snapped," Fats explained holding his hands up as if asking 'what can I do?'

"Man, Who's all driving?" Prince said as he ran his hands through his short curly hair.

"Me, Dino, Sticky, and of course Street"

The sound of glass breaking interrupted the conversation as everyone looked toward the parking garage. A car alarm began to shriek

"What the hell is that nigga doing?" asked Prince.

"He just stuck his fist through that window," Blaze said shaking his head. "He's taking this pretty hard."

"Man, go get that nigga out of here Fats," Prince said to his cousin as everybody started to cross the street. "Tell that nigga I said to get his mind right or I'm through with him."

"I got you cuz," Fats said pissed off at his hotheaded brother.

"Sticky come here for a minute!" Prince yelled. "Take Kenya with you and tell everybody to go to the spot, I'll be there in a few."

"Come on Kenya," Sticky said helping her up off the bench. "How are you gonna get around?" Sticky asked Prince.

"I'm gonna be rolling with Danielle. I've got a few runs to make so I'm depending on you to have shit in order by the time I get back. Also take China Doll back to the apartment with you."

"All right my brotha, I'll handle this until you get there," Sticky said as he started across the street. Kenya and China Doll strolled across the street behind him. They all avoided going anywhere near the loud noise of the car alarm. The police would be arriving soon to investigate the commotion.

Danielle stood up from her seat on the bench only to be pulled back down by Prince. "Act normal as if we don't even hear that alarm. I wanna wait and make sure everybody gets out of that garage without being pulled over by the police. I know somebody seen Street acting a damn fool." Prince said. "So why don't you tell me exactly what went down upstairs while we wait. It's obvious that you're a little upset by whatever you saw," Prince said to Danielle.

"Street was wrong for choking Kenya the way he did. He's a loose cannon that's in dire need of some anger management if you ask me," Danielle said.

"I agree with you," Prince said in a nonchalant way as he watched an expression of surprise come over Danielle's face. "What's that look about? You seem a little surprised by my answer."

"Well, I am! I expected you to come to your cousin's defense and try to give me every reason to justify his actions."

"Under no circumstances will I ever attempt to justify any man's reason for putting his hands on a woman. Just because he's my blood don't make him an exception. But we all make mistakes, and it's not my place to pass judgment on those whose only crime is their lack of understanding."

"A lack of understanding? Now you've lost me. What does a lack of understanding have to do with your cousin almost chocking a girl until she couldn't breathe? You've got to explain that to me because now I think I'm suffering from a lack of understanding."

Prince had baited Danielle with that one and she took it, hook, line, and sinker. "I'll tell you in the car," Prince said observing the police talking to the owner of the car. "Right now we need to get out of here."

They both stood up and started walking towards Danielle's car. Prince looked around to make sure there were no eyes following them. Danielle unlocked the car and they both got in and drove off.

"Turn left at the corner. I need to go over the river to Newport, Kentucky and get some liquor for the party tonight," Prince said.

They rode in silence for a while. Prince was preoccupied with his own thoughts. Danielle reached for the knob to turn the car stereo on when Prince finally spoke. "Before you turn that on, let me explain something to you about my perspective about Street," Prince began. "True enough Street was wrong in the manner he handled himself by disrespecting Kenya, but I also know his actions came from the love and frustration of seeing somebody he cares about clinging to life. Hustleman is close to all of us because we have been like family since

I can remember. Street just doesn't know how to control his emotions and anger when they surface. He usually lets his temper get the best of him. Kenya knows this. Everyone in the family knows this because we all grew up together. Kenya should have seen that coming. Hustleman was very lucky compared to the others we've lost along the way, but that's life in the ghetto everyday baby. Personally, I'm just thankful that this incident didn't result in me having to attend another one of my friends' funerals."

Danielle looked over at Prince with a look of admiration. Although she knew they came from two different walks of life, she felt his pain, and for the first time, took notice of his strength.

"Personally, I'm tired of struggling," Prince said. "I've been on my own since my mother passed away two years ago. Since then, me and my brothers, which I call my family, have been doing everything in our power to keep a roof over our heads. In your eyes, we may not have a lot to be thankful for and what we do to earn our daily bread may be against the grain. If I had a mother and father who owned a beautiful home like you do, in a quiet neighborhood, and who has obviously benefited from the balanced nourishment of love from two parents, I probably would be better off too. But that's not my reality. It's yours, so I've got to do the best I can with what I've got to work with."

Danielle sat back and let what Prince had said sink in before she cleared her throat and responded. "So what you're saying is because of your hardships in life, what you do should be considered acceptable even though it's illegal and puts you in harm's way?" Danielle asked.

"What is it I do Danielle?" Prince said somewhat irritated.

"Sell drugs and fix a few football games."

" Would you rather see me standing on the intersection of I-75 holding a sign begging for handouts?" asked Prince sarcastically.

"You got any better ideas? That's why I don't like trying to explain myself to people who don't understand the reason behind my actions. You'll never be able to understand until you've personally been confronted with all the elements of my struggles."

"Let's drop this conversation for the moment Prince, because I don't want to fight or argue with you over this matter simply because we have different opinions. I just wanted to express to you that I feel that you're not giving yourself a chance at life."

"Chance at life? You must believe in fairytales! The only chances any young black man may have in life can be counted on one hand! Slinging crack, rap, or sports are the only chances any black man may have in this life! Any other decent paying job that requires an education is controlled and dominated by white corporate America. If you're not highly educated and willing to kiss a lot of ass, a black man doesn't stand a snow ball's chance in hell in today's work field!"

"Hum, that's an interesting analogy."

"Ha-Ha-Ha, you've got jokes girl! That's more then just an analogy," Prince said shaking his head. "Danielle that's reality baby, my reality, so don't get it twisted! Remember we live in Cincinnati, where opportunities for black men are far and few in between. Just be thankful that you were fortunate enough to have been blessed with a balanced upbringing. My pop was never in my life."

"Why is that?" asked Danielle.

"Because he was a dope addict who stayed around long enough to get my mother hooked on his poison, then like a coward, he ran when the responsibility of parenting surfaced."

"What was his name, Prince?" Danielle asked.

"The same as mine - Prince Hernandez. My pop was Puerto Rican. All I can remember about him was he was a career criminal who had almost every aspect of crime covered."

"So that's why they call you Prince! I always thought it was your nickname. Well Prince Jr., what liquor store are you trying to get to sir?" Danielle asked jokingly.

"Any store over here will do baby; it's all cheap."

Once they found a liquor store, Prince bought a few bottles of top shelf Remy Martin and a box of blunts to roll the weed.

"Where to now?" Danielle asked after Prince returned to the car.

"To my crib. It's time to party a little bit and discuss a few things with the family. Who's that you're listening to?" Prince asked enjoying the mellow tunes flowing from the car's stereo system.

"Oh, that's Dave Hollister's "Real Talk CD". He's a lot more mellow than what you're used to."

"Oh yeah, and what makes you come to that conclusion?" Prince asked as he leaned back in the car seat enjoying Dave's smooth groove.

"Well, being that you and your crew seem to listen to nothing but 2-PAC and other hard-core rap, I didn't think that Dave would be your style of music," Danielle replied.

"Well, Ms. Lady, for your information, I'm down with any sound that I can relate to. Rap just happens to be my first preference with 2-PAC as my favorite artist because he raps about my reality."

"Well, this guy sings about my reality!" Danielle said reaching over and turning up the volume.

Prince was bumping his head to the rhythm, "I'm feeling that! That's a pretty hip tune! We might have to slow dance off that cut one day." Danielle smiled, "I thought you might like it. Isn't it strange how music can help people relate to one another even in times when communication doesn't work?"

"Yup and that's a fact," Prince said. "Music has been a way of communication in our culture since the days of slavery. Song and dance has always been sort of a metaphor in helping black folks cope with adversities in life. But, I'm sure you knew that though didn't you girl?" Prince asked with a smile.

"I guess" Danielle said.

"Don't you listen to your music according to what mood you're in?" Prince asked.

"Yes I do," Danielle replied.

"Well, so does everybody else. Music can be used to enhance emotions, no matter what mood you're in. There's a song in everybody's life that relates to their personal experiences that they might be going through and that's why my boys and me listen to 2-PAC. He raps about our lifestyle," Prince said.

"You've got a point, but there's only one problem," Danielle said.

"What's that?"

"Your emotions always seem to result in violence and that's what I want to get you away from," Danielle said.

"That's my way of life. The ghetto is all I know and to survive in the 'hood, there's a code of rules and ethics a man must live or die by. Unfortunately, sometimes violence is the only thing people in the street understand, especially when the lines of communication fail. I know that's not what you wanted to hear, but sometimes the truth hurts." Prince stated.

While Danielle thought about what Prince said, she knew in her heart she would never be able to change Prince's perception of himself or the way he viewed his lifestyle. The music that was opening her heart to this wonderful guy she thought she was falling for, was now making her sad. She knew not only was it wrong to want to change a man to love him but in Prince's case it seemed practically impossible.

"You know what? I think I'm tired of this CD," Danielle said and reached over to turn off the music.

Prince started laughing. "Nah" he teased her. "I thought you liked that CD," Prince said.

"I'm not feeling Dave right now, plus we're almost at your house and I wanted to tell you something before I dropped you off," Danielle said.

"OK, I'm listening," Prince said as she pulled up in front of his apartment.

"Do you think, for the right woman under the right circumstances one day, you could change?"

"That's a hard question baby, because it depends on the situation. If you're wondering that one day, I might consider changing my lifestyle for a chance to be with you, that's a possibility."

His answer lit Danielle's face up more than she wanted Prince to see. "That's all I wanted to know," Danielle said.

Prince opened the car door and got out with bags in hand. "Call me tonight if you get a chance." he said.

"Alright baby. You be safe okay?" Danielle said with a smile.

Prince leaned inside the car and gave her a kiss on the cheek.

"I'm always safe girl," Prince said closing the door.

Danielle pulled off and blew her horn, leaving Prince standing there. Prince had heard through the grape vine that her mom and pop were both doctors and they were living phat some where in a big pretty house, but that didn't phase Prince. "This is my home," he thought to himself, looking up the walk to the apartment he and his crew shared.

"Hey, Prince is here!" somebody said from the open door to the kitchen.

"Hey my nigga!" Blaze greeted. "We thought you got lost."

"Nah man," Prince said. "I was just spending a little time with Danielle."

"Oh yeah my brotha, I feel ya," Blaze said smiling as he slapped hands with Prince. They laughed walking up the sidewalk toward the Winton Terrace apartments they now called the 'Club House'.

When Blaze pulled the screen door open with Prince on his heels, everybody was sitting around in the living room watching a movie on the big screen, smoking blunts, just chillin' and relaxing.

"Turn some lights on in this spot so a nigga can see," Prince said closing the door behind him.

"What's up cuz?" came a deep voice from the darkest corner of the living room.

"What you got in them there bags baby boy?" the voice came again." Prince recognized the voice of his cuz Street and motioned for him to follow. The rest of y'all niggaz just hang tight and don't get too damn high smoking that shit because we got some serious shit to talk about."

"Alright my nigga, we got cha," Sticky replied from his seat on the couch.

Prince turned and threw his arm around Street's shoulder as they walked into the kitchen chit chatting. "So did you straighten your hand with Kenya for that bullshit that happened at the hospital?" Prince asked as he set the bags of liquor down on the kitchen table.

"Yeah man," Street said in a quiet voice. "I owe you an apology too cuz, for losing my cool. My bad," Street said. They slapped dap and all was forgiven.

"We need to decide what we're gonna do about Hustleman," Prince said as he sat down at the kitchen table.

"You know how I want to handle the situation," Street said leaning up against the wall. "A fair exchange sounds appropriate to me."

"That's how I feel too," Prince said running his fingers through his short Afro. "An eye for an eye," Prince said to himself. "Well," Prince said, "If we do this, that means we're pretty much committed to seeing this shit to the end, which as you know, means some bloodshed. Are we ready for that?" Prince asked.

Street looked at Prince. "All we know is the ghetto and killing is what we've been living around our whole life. So if you're wondering if I'm afraid of the rules of the game, nah cuz. I'm down for whatever. I'm tired of starvin' out here in these streets."

Prince leaned back in his chair and looked at the ceiling for a second, then let out a loud sigh of frustration from thinking too much. "Yeah cuz, I'm tired of starving out here too."

Street walked over and put his hand on his cousin's shoulder. "I'll get the gang together and send China Doll and Kenya home."

"Nah man, I need to talk to the girls too. Kenya told me some shit about a rape at school. Blaze and Hitman's names were both mentioned and that concerns me.

Street stopped briefly to look back at Prince before stepping out the kitchen. "Oh yeah?"

"Yeah man. Sounds like some more shit we got to deal with," Prince said.

"Whatever, we'll deal with it," Street said throwing up his hands. He went to get everybody for the meeting in the kitchen.

Chapter 6

Tom had just sat down in his den and turned on the TV to catch the N.F.L pre-game show when the doorbell started ringing.

"Would you get that honey?" Debra yelled from the kitchen. She was cooking some soul food dishes for the first time in her life.

The doorbell continued to ring, "Tom," Debra yelled.

"Here I come honey," Tom said still glued to the TV set trying to hear what they were saying about the Bengals.

Suddenly Debra appeared in the door. "Never mind, I'll get it myself!" starting toward the door.

Tom wanted to get up and get the door but they were talking about the Cincinnati Bengals' chances of beating the undefeated Kansas City Chiefs. As a matter of fact, everybody in the city was talking about the Bengals and their miraculous turn around from twelve straight losing seasons.

"If the Bengals win today," the commentator was saying, "it'll place the Bengals in a position to be in the play-offs for the first time in over 12 years! It's a great job this new head coach has done for this team! He has gotten this team believing in themselves again! The Kansas City Chiefs come into Paul Brown Stadium as just the 10th NFL team to open the season with a 9-0 record or better."

"Wow! I didn't know that," Tom said to himself while glued to the television.

"But I did," Ray said entering the den."

"And only one of those 9-0 teams, the 1972 Miami Dolphins, remained undefeated."

"Hey Ray!" Tom said getting up from his chair to give his best friend a hug. After they embraced, Tom stepped back to get a better look at his friend's face and just shook his head at the sight of his swollen black eyes.

"So you think the Woodward quarterback did that intentionally, huh?" Tom said as he turned and walked toward the well stocked bar in the room.

"I'm pretty sure Tom, but it's cool," Ray said.

"By the time I get through with those kids, this face will haunt them in their dreams."

"Well have a seat and get comfortable. Let's have a drink and watch a little football while we discuss how to handle the situation. I'm having a martini, and you?"

"Brandy on the rocks," Ray said.

"My oh my, a brandy this early?" Tom asked.

"Yeah, that's how I'm feeling right now, I've got so much on my mind," Ray said.

"That's not good! Is there anything I can help with?" Tom asked.

"Not really. I've just been racking my brain all night over this alleged rape that the school principle told me about," Ray said.

"What's troubling you about it Ray?" Tom asked as he handed Ray his brandy and took a seat in the other recliner.

"If this young lady was actually raped, why report it to the school principle? Why wasn't it reported to the department?" Ray questioned.

"It makes me wonder if a rape actually took place or if it was consensual and then later called a rape. You know how these kids play games."

"Well, Ray, you're a 16 year veteran on the police force and this isn't the first time you've had to piece together a case that requires you to separate facts from fiction to get results. Don't start assuming what is the truth. Maybe you need to go up to the school and see for yourself."

"I've been thinking about that," Ray began, "But..."
Knock-Knock-Knock

"Am I interrupting anything?" Cindy asked as she stepped into the room.

"Hi Uncle Tom!" Cindy said giving Tom a hug. "I'm sorry, I just wanted to know the score of the game. But I see you guys weren't really watching it."

"Well, I guess we weren't" Tom said kind of looking over at Ray.

"It looks like half time," Cindy said. "Oh look, the Bengals are winning, 17-3!" she said happily.

"Hum, that's interesting. Bengals beating K.C. Who would've thought?" Ray said.

"Don't get too excited, it's only half time. You know how the Bengals can blow a lead." Tom said.

"You've got a point there." Ray laughed.

"Well, I'll let you two finish talking. I just wanted to know what the score was. Aunt Debra and Mom are still getting the food together, so we've still got a while before dinner is served," Cindy said walking toward the door.

"Cindy how's school? You're not having any problems or anything are you?" Tom questioned.

"Of course not!" she responded. "I'm not scared of any of those gang bangers. I just took dad's course in self-defense to sharpen my Tae Kwon Do skills but I do feel sorry for some of the other students who aren't as fortunate. The bangers pretty much run the school."

"That's a shame because there's really not a lot we can do without offending somebody in this city. People think these kids are angles because they're in school and that really pisses me off to no end." Tom said.

"Let me see what I can do tomorrow," Ray said. "It may not be as serious as we think. We might be able to remove a few kids and shake the tree a little bit."

"Dad, it's more serious then that!" Cindy said.

"If you remove the problem from that school then you'll probably have to shut the whole school down because there's Ruff Rider gang members all through Woodward. You'll see when you come up there tomorrow. For every problem there is a solution and I'm sure Ray will find it," Tom said. "Now, how come I haven't received a hug from my other baby girl?" Tom asked. "Gina!"

"Yeah, Uncle Tom," came Gina's soft voice from the kitchen. Gina was the quiet one, a mama's girl, as everyone liked to call her.

"She's probably still playing that electric chess set. I'll get her," Cindy said.

"You don't have to get me girl!" Gina said as she moved past her sister to give Tom a hug. "I'm sorry Uncle Tom. I didn't mean to be rude. I just thought you and Dad had some important things to discuss and I didn't want to disturb you."

"How you young folks say it? Don't make me salty at you," Tom said with a smile as he gave Gina a hug. "So, I hear you've decided to stay at home and work at the bank rather than go to Ohio State next semester." Tom said.

Gina was silent for a minute, before she said. "Yeah, I'm not ready to leave home yet."

"Leave home? Dang girl, Ohio State is only up the highway!" Cindy blurted out. "Keep it real Gina! You just didn't want to be away from Momma."

"Cindy, mind your own business!" Gina snapped back. "Uncle Tom wasn't talking to you!

"Shoot, I can't wait to graduate this year!" Cindy said as she stood in the doorway.

"You can stay in boring Cincinnati if you want, but I'm getting outta here on the first thing smoking!" Cindy stated emphatically as she disappeared into the other room.

Tom and Ray just laughed.

"That's why we're different," Gina shot back.

"Whatever you do is fine with me Gina," Ray said to his eldest daughter. "It's whatever you like baby girl."

"Thanks Dad," Gina said. "I just want a break from the books for awhile."

"Well hell, I didn't go to college until four years after I graduated! I was a confused youngster when I came out of high school. So you take your time sweetheart. You'll get there," Tom said.

"You boys need anything from the kitchen while I'm heading that way?" Gina asked.

"Nah baby girl. Just let us know when supper's ready," Ray said.

"Sure will Dad," and Gina went back into the kitchen and started arguing with Cindy.

"Those gals are as different as night and day," Tom said.

"Yeah, you got that right, but it's cool," Ray said. "I'm just kind of concerned about Cindy and how the kids at school might treat her once I start making my presence felt at the school."

"I wouldn't worry about that. Cindy can handle herself," Tom said. "What we do need to be concerned about is putting a team of officers together to help you question some of those students about the shooting."

"I'm already shorthanded on the task force as it is and I need every available officer I got on the streets. People are getting robbed and shot every day!" Ray said seriously.

"That brings to mind something I wanted to talk to you about,"

Tom said getting up from his chair. He closed the door to the den. "Would you like another drink?" Tom asked as he walked to the bar.

"I guess one more won't hurt," Ray said. "I've got a feeling I just might need it since you had to close the door to say what's on your mind."

Tom fixed them both a drink, and then picked up a folder of papers that was sitting on the bar and handed them to Ray along with his drink.

"What's this?" Ray asked taking a sip from his drink looking up at Tom.

"That's the employee file of two officers the Chief informed me on Friday that he was transferring from district five to our Violent Crime Squad."

"Under my command of course," Ray replied opening the folder.

"Replacing you Ray will never be an option. You've earned your stripes in the streets and no one will ever question that," Tom stated.

"So what's the concern?" Ray asked.

"Well, everyone knows with your experience and excellent job duty performances, not to mention leadership qualities, that you are a shoo-in to get that detective position."

When Tom said that, Ray's stomach knotted up.

"I smell a rat Ray, but I can't prove it because the smell is coming from higher ranking officials. But, on Friday, the chief sent me two officers that he decided to transfer in to help our body count on the streets."

"Oh yeah, well we need more than two but I guess we gotta take what we can get," Ray said taking a sip from his brandy.

"The chief also informed me that he already had Jim Spencer's resume out for the detective position I recommended you for. He was waiting on your resume so he could decide who was best qualified for the position."

"Hold up!" Ray said. "First of all he should have already had my resume. I gave it to you Tom two weeks ago and I'm not even going to insult you by asking if you turned it in because I'll bet my life on it that you did!"

"Yeah," Tom said. "I asked the chief about that and his response was and I quote, 'I'm sorry Tom, but I never received it,' and I just kind of said uh huh, I see chief. I'll fax you another one."

"Let me get this straight. The chief transfers two officers into the district, with what sounds like a promise, for a detective position. I've spent the last sixteen years of my life on this force busting my balls to earn a detective's shield. That's a crock of bullshit, Tom," Ray said calmly taking another sip from his drink.

"I pretty much went over Spencer's personnel file almost all day yesterday trying to get a read on this guy. He is a sixteen-year veteran, no strikes against him and was second in command in District 5's, Violent Crime Squad. On paper, he looks squeaky clean and a tough competitor for the detective position. Should he somehow get it, not too many people would look twice."

"Can they really do that Tom?" Ray asked in disbelief.

"I see now that the department will go to any length to keep minorities at a lower level." Tom went on to say, "I called a resource I know in that department who told me 'off-the-record' that rumor has it Spencer is banging the chief's daughter and could be his future son in law".

"Well, I'll appeal it if he does give it to him," Ray said. "I can do that, can't I?"

Tom gave Ray a funny look as if to say, 'I wouldn't trust that one either'. "My resource went on to tell me that last year Spencer was disciplined behind closed doors by the chief for making a racial slur toward another officer. Then just last month, he was supposedly observed by a lieutenant on the Violent Crime Squad, stealing cash from a drug bust. Something's not right here and we both know it. I believe what's in the dark will eventually come to light but it might be in our best interests to sit back, relax, and not go over the top. Let this thing come to us because it's gonna come, and when it does, some heads are gonna roll!" Tom said tapping the folders.

"That makes sense," Ray said.

"So just play with me because I got your back. Do your homework on these two jokers; you've got their files. I'm putting them on your beat so you can keep an eye on them."

"I like that idea," Ray said smiling as he opened their personnel jackets and began reading about each officer.

"*Officer Jim Spencer, a Western Hills High School graduate has been a Cincinnati police officer since October 1986. Before joining the force, he worked as a resident assistant at Talbert House, a halfway house. His last performance report called him a 'dependable officer who makes sound choices."*

"Sound choices, huh, I bet," Ray said to Tom.

"Keep reading," Tom said. "I want to see what jumps out at you."

"O.K.," Ray said continuing.

"Officer Robert Adams. A Maderia High School graduate, this 31-year old has been a Cincinnati police officer for five years. His latest performance report calls him an 'outstanding beat officer with a working knowledge of his beat and its residents."

"Hum," Ray said to himself. "Comparing what I've read about the two, my assessment would be," Ray said slowly, "that Spencer would be the leader and Adams the student."

"That's good," Tom said. "Very good because that was my thought as well, so in dealing with these two always keep in mind that Adams appears to be the weakest link," Tom said.

Tom Safeway did not make Captain with his fat looks. Twenty-five years of dealing with every crime imaginable got him in the Captain's chair. Ray admired his friend for his intelligence and wisdom.

"Dinner's ready," the girls announced from the kitchen.

"Good, 'cause I'm hungry," Tom said getting up stretching his entire six foot frame. He rubbed his big belly that actually fit his frame and said he was hungry enough to eat a horse.

"Let's go get some of that soul food you been telling me about," Tom said slapping Ray on the back. That was the first of many times that officers Spencer and Adams would be the topic of conversation between the two friends.

"Guess what?" Ray asked as they set their empty glasses on the bar and started towards the dining room.

"What's that partner?" Tom asked resting a hand on Ray's shoulder.

"We didn't catch the final on the Bengals game!"

"Yes we did, you just wasn't paying attention! The Bengals won 24-19 on a late kick off returned for a go ahead touchdown by that young talented rookie Tab Perry they drafted from UCLA and now we're tied for first place with the Ravens."

"Watch the news tonight and catch the highlights," Tom said patting Ray on the back as they entered the dining room to a warm welcome from the girls.

"Welcome to the first annual Safeway/Whitehead Soul Food Sunday!" the girls announced as Ray and Tom observed the neatly prepared dining room table.

"Boy, you sure can tell this is a special occasion!" Tom said as he checked out the nice soft texture of the napkins that rested on top of each plate. "We haven't used this china in years," Tom said.

"That's because we didn't have a reason to until now," Tom's wife Debra said from the kitchen as she was unsuccessfully trying to open a bottle of wine for dinner.

"Here, let me help you with that Deb," Ray offered as he entered the kitchen.

"Thank you Ray, since my husband didn't notice."

"Okay, Tom," Hazel said as she walked up to the table, "let me give you a grand tour of the table, so you'll be familiar with each dish on the menu."

"All right then, because I'm starving." Tom said.
Cindy and Gina stood by giggling, because they knew he wasn't ready for the menu.

"Right here," Hazel began, "is cranberry sauce and over here is mashed potatoes, macaroni and cheese, and black eyed peas."

"Black eyed peas huh? Okay," Tom said nodding his head, "I'm hip to that food group. What about these three pots?" Tom asked pointing.

Cindy and Gina thought the question was really funny. Tom turned to them and asked what they were laughing about.

"Never mind them," Hazel said grabbing Tom by the arm. "In this pot, there's what we call collard greens and in this pot we have," and the room suddenly went quiet as all eye's were on Tom, "chitterlings."

"Chitterlings," Tom repeated as he stared at the pot. "Aren't chitterlings hog intestines?"

The question rocked everybody on their heels with laughter except Tom. He was serious.

Hazel patted Tom lightly on his arm. "Yes honey," and in a playful voice she said, "chitterlings are hog intestines, but they've been scraped and fried. It's a popular dish from the south that is often prepared for holidays."

Tom looked around the room, and then he looked over at Cindy and Gina's smiling faces. "Oh I see the two of you are getting a real big kick outta this."

"Now remember Tom, you said you would try whatever we prepared, so be nice," Debra said to her husband.

Ray finally popped the cork on the wine and started towards the table. "Wait until you check out the main course," Ray said laughing as he sat the wine down.

"Whatever it is, it's got to sound better then pig intestines," Tom said looking at the pot with suspicious eyes.

"For the main course," Hazel said lifting the lid, "we're having pig feet."

Tom's chin hit the table as his mouth gaped open. "You've got to be kidding me!" Tom exclaimed. "Pig feet?" His facial expression brought the house down in laughter.

"What's wrong buddy?" Ray asked. "Wasn't it you who said you would try anything once?"

"Yeah, well I didn't mean that literally," Tom said as he picked up a fork and moved the feet around in the pot.

"Stop that!" Hazel said grabbing the fork. "No playing in the food! Now everyone sit down so we can say grace. And you two stop acting so silly!" Hazel said to her two daughters.

"Okay mom," they both said still giggling.

"Well don't expect me to 'pig out,'" Tom suddenly blurted. Everyone started laughing all over again.

"And this was Ray's idea right?" Tom asked, looking across the table at Ray. "I owe you! And don't think I'm not going to get you back," he said with a wink of his eye.

Everyone sat around the table hand in hand, to bless the food.

"Who's going to say grace?" Hazel asked looking at her husband.

"I think Tom should honor us with grace," Ray said as he looked over to Tom.

"Oh, you just don't quit huh," Tom said smiling. Ray winked back at Tom, "You can do it." Tom sat for a moment to gather his thoughts. Gina and Cindy were still shaking with suppressed laughter. "Okay, I can do this. Is everybody ready?" Tom asked as he looked around the table.

Dear Lord,
Please bless this soul food were about to eat

Especially the chitterlings and pig feet

Somebody giggled but Tom went on...

> *In the name of Jesus,*
> *for his blessing we pray*
> *please don't let these pig feet*
> *get up and walk away*
> *Thank you,*
> *Amen.*

Hazel and Debra shook their heads, but Ray and the girls had to laugh as Tom's moment of culture shock. Everyone sat down and prepared to eat, but Tom just kind of watched.

Tom continued to watch his friends and wife and suddenly asked Cindy if she knew a Ms. O'Bannon at the high school.

"Yeah, who doesn't know Ms. O'Bannon?" Cindy said sarcastically. Gina let out a low whistle, "Ms. O'Bannon is off the hook!"

"Yeah, she's another hall monitor from hell. Don't none of the students like her," Cindy said.

By this time Ray had filled his plate and was chowing down on some of the pig feet.

"So what's up with Ms. O'Bannon?" Ray asked Tom in between bites.

"Oh, she's having a parents meeting at the school tomorrow at 6:00 p.m. So I told the principal when he called, that you would love to be Ms. O'Bannon's keynote speaker at the meeting. I hope you don't mind," Tom said smiling at Ray.

Ray's mouth froze. For a second, you could almost see what he was chewing. "That's cold blooded Tom!"

"I feel for you Dad," Gina said as everyone laughed at Ray's misfortune.

"Ms. O'Bannon's parent meetings can get pretty ugly sometimes. Over a hundred parents have attended the last few meetings to complain about something," Cindy said.

"I think it's their bonding time," Gina said.

"I'm sorry Ray, I must have forgotten to tell you!" Tom said with a smile. "You better prepare a speech because you're just the man they want to talk to."

Tom reached for the pig feet and held the pot up as he shoveled a foot onto his plate. Tom looked down at the foot and then looked up at Ray. "See, I told you I'd get you back. God don't like ugly," and Tom burst into laughter almost knocking his pig foot onto his lap.

CHAPTER 7

Like a child without a care in the world, Danielle slept peacefully on Monday morning as pelts of raindrops beat at her bedroom window. Curled in a tight little ball and sound asleep, she dreamed and dreamed until her dream became her reality. Restlessly, she shifted positions holding her pillow tightly as if in search of some security or comfort as she spoke to the object of her desire that was visibly clear to her subconscious mind.

"Oh Prince, I've wanted you for so long," played through her subconscious mind as she lay bundled up in her yellow canopy bed. The thought continued but with more emotion and intensity, "Oh baby, I've been wanting you for so long please don't stop," and then her small young body began quivering and shaking as if she had been sleeping out in the cold. Then her eyes opened and for a second, she was disoriented. She lay quietly, letting her eyes focus and realized it was just a dream. She pulled the covers tightly around her neck and listened to the raindrops fall on the roof. Remembering the vague dream, she felt between her legs for the wetness that was always there when she thought or dreamed of Prince. The alarm clock started buzzing it's wakeup call, slightly startling her. Okay she thought, time to get ready for school.

Wide-awake now, she looked for her robe as the early morning October chill in her room made her shiver a little. Her parents were away on a business trip, so she had the entire house to herself. She missed her mom because she was always up with breakfast prepared. It was one of the few quiet times of the day when Danielle had her mom all to herself. But this morning she had to fend for herself. "I guess I'll shower and get dressed," she thought "and if time permits, I'll eat a bowl of Captain Crunch cereal." She had to be at school before the tardy bell ringed. No one ever wanted to be placed on the tardy list because that meant an hour with Ms. O'Bannon in detention after school. So Danielle hurried, or at least attempted to, but the soothing beads of hot water beating on her back were relaxing and she began to daydream. Danielle thought Prince was so fine with his curly hair and beautiful brown eyes. He was always a gentleman when they were together but she knew his life style would be an issue if they were ever to get serious about their friendship.

When Danielle's parents bought their big house in the suburbs, she refused to attend any more private prep schools protesting that it would be in her best interests to attend a public school. She wanted the diversity a public school would offer. Danielle knew that she had led a sheltered life and she wanted a more rounded perspective of how to relate to people of various walks of life. She wanted to become a social worker and help people who were less fortunate. Her mother thought it was a wonderful idea so she supported her daughter's decision, but her Dad disagreed. He wanted Danielle to follow them into the medical field. But Danielle was adamant in her decision to attend the local public high school.

Suddenly the phone in Danielle's room began to ring bringing her back to reality. "Shit! I'm going to be late! That's all I need is detention with Ms. O'Bannon!" she thought as she dried herself. She checked the caller I.D. and the phone rang again. She put the phone on speaker.

"Yeah girl, I know!" Danielle said recognizing Kenya's number.

"What are you doing girl? We're going to be late!" Kenya's voice filled the room as Danielle ran around the bed and into her walk-in closet.

"I'm sorry Kenya- my bad girl. I'm on my way out the door right now!" Danielle said.

"Girl you better hurry up, or you, me and China Doll will be kicking it with Ms. O'Bannon today after school."

****

Sgt. Whitehead didn't look too bad by Monday morning but he was still a bit puffy around his eyes. Feeling rested and refreshed, he and his new partner pulled into the parking garage of District Four. Ray had picked Tony up at his house because his car was acting up.

"Oh yeah, thanks Sarge for giving me a lift this morning," Tony said as they entered the building from the garage.

"Man don't mention it," Ray said "I understand how it is on rookie pay!" slapping Tony playfully on the back. "Listen, meet me back here in fifteen minutes. We've got to be at Woodward High School by

8:30.

Tony headed towards the cafeteria in search of some hot coffee while Sgt. Ray Whitehead headed upstairs to see the Captain and meet the infamous Jim Spencer and his partner. He was not looking forward to the meeting either one of them but unfortunately he had no choice in the matter.

"Hi Ray," the captain's pretty receptionist spoke as Ray strolled by.

"What's up Fancy?" Ray asked. "Where's the Captain?' Ray said as he pointed towards Captain Safeway's empty office.

"Oh, he's showing the two new officers around," Fancy replied.

"Well tell him I stopped by. Let him know I'm on my way to Woodward and I'll be back sometime this afternoon." Ray turned around and headed back to the garage to meet his partner thinking about Fancy and all the rumors going around the station about her. 'Fancy Pancy' was what they nicked named Officer Yvette Storey. It was either 'Fancy Pancy' or 'Home Wrecker' because she was all that and a bag of Doritos. Her fellow officers decided on 'Fancy Pancy' because her walk was all they could remember when someone asked her if she wanted some fries to go with that shake. Ray laughed at his thoughts. "Yeah girl you're lucky I'm a married man!" Ray whispered to himself. Tony was leaning on another cruiser enjoying a donut and a cup of coffee when he asked Ray "Did you see them?"

Ray stopped somewhat startled as Tony interrupted his thoughts.

"See who?" Ray said as he reached in his pockets for his keys.

"The captain and those two officers you were telling me about," Tony answered.

"You saw Spencer and Adams with the captain?" Ray asked.

"Captain Safeway brought them through the cafeteria while I was getting my coffee," Tony said buckling his seatbelt.

"What did they look like to you?" Ray said pulling into traffic.

"Like cops!" Tony said laughing.

"Oh it's like that," Ray said laughing as they pulled out into traffic heading down Reading Road towards Woodward.

****

Honk- Honk- Honk sounded the car horn outside. Two heads peaked around the curtains in the front room. Honk- Honk- Honk-came Danielle's horn again

"Ain't that a beeyotch?" Kenya said, looking around for her umbrella. "She's going to rush us after she made us late. The hell with the umbrella!" Kenya told China Doll as they both ran out dodging raindrops. It was raining harder now, so the girls pulled their coats over their heads and ran towards Danielle's car trying not to get their hair wet.

Danielle was smiling when Kenya and China Doll finally got in and shut the door. Kenya looked over at Danielle and started to say "Hi" until she noticed Danielle smiling.

"What's so funny crazy ho?" Kenya asked. Everybody started laughing and slapping each other Hi Fives. They were the best of friends and when they referred to each other as bitches and 'hos', it was all in good nature because that's how the sistas from down the way kicked it. Beeyotch this and Beeyotch that, you know how they do. So they carried on, "Ho I know you was up all night thinking about that nigga!" Kenya said smiling as she talked about Danielle's crush on Prince. "That's why your jive ass couldn't get outta that bed this morning!" Kenya said snapping her fingers with the quick side-to-side two snaps.

Danielle just drove and smiled, not about to try and out talk Kenya because everybody knew that was a mistake. "So you really diggin' Prince like that?" China Doll asked from her relaxed position in the back seat. "I thought you knew," Kenya said.

"I mean it ain't like I'm stuck on him," Danielle said in her own defense. "I just think he's interesting and fine."

"Come on girl, keep it real!" Kenya yelled. "Tell China how you're thinking about letting Prince bust that cherry!"

"Damn Beeyotch!" Danielle exclaimed. "Why don't you tell all my business?" "Oh my bad" Kenya said laughing. "Girl you know we all girls and we got your best interest at heart!"

"I ain't trippin!" Danielle said. "Yeah I dig the nigga and I'll probably give him some if he acts right!"

"Baby if that's what you feel, go for it!" China Doll said. "Prince is an all right brotha. I can't hate on him but as a friend, I will tell you to be careful because he's a street nigga and his loyalty is to his way of life. It may keep him from being faithful to just one woman."

"Tell it like it is girl!" Kenya said pointing towards a bus stop across the street. "See that bus stop? Last night, me and my sister caught

that bitch Monica who screamed rape on Blaze and Hitman, sitting on the bench waiting on the bus." "Oh yeah?" asked Danielle.
"You're bull shitting girl", China Doll stated sitting up in her seat smiling."
     "No bullshit, for real!" Kenya said."Look at how swollen my knuckles are!" and Kenya stuck out her left hand out for inspection. "We beat that lying ass bitch down for a whole half hour and then we left her there bleeding!"
     "Damn girl!" China said holding Kenya's hand looking and feeling the swollen knuckles. "I bet you that 'ho' won't tell now!" and everybody started laughing, and they laughed all the way to school.

****

Woodward was a large school and in the usual design, there was a half circle visitor parking lot in front. Ray pulled into the circle and immediately noticed that parking was limited. He was running late so he found a space in the fire lane and parked.
     "Hey girls come on! Let's get to class!" Ms. O'Bannon said clapping her hands. "That means you two over there! First period bell has rung ladies and gentleman!" Ms. O'Bannon shouted at the scattering students when she noticed Ray's police cruiser parking in the fire lane. She stood there with her little hands on her hips as Ray and Tony exited the police cruiser. "Um excuse me!" she said in a very nasty tone.
     "You can't park there, it's a fire lane! You're in the way of our school buses. You two are police officers, correct? You know better!" Then she turned and disappeared through the front doors of the school.
     Ray and Tony were more than a little surprised and stood there for a second looking at the little lady with the big mouth. "I should ignore her little sarcastic ass!" Ray said turning back to the car.
     Tony just chuckled a little and shook his head.
     Ray was a little upset though as he kept saying, "that little something, something, something, should be glad to see the police at this something, something, something school! I guess I'll park in the back where the students park! I see now that this morning isn't starting off so good!" Ray told Officer Ward as they headed toward the back of the school.
     "Being that my car wouldn't start this morning, I think I might have to agree with you on that."

"My goodness!" Ray exclaimed. He slowed the cruiser and stopped to admire a '67 Ford Mustang. Ray wanted to get a closer look and he walked around the car. By the time he reached the front of the car again, Tony was standing there shaking his head.

"You see what I see?" Tony asked.

"Yeah!" Ray said, pointing at the tinted windows and shiny new spinning rims that cost about ten thousand dollars.

"Dope boy car!" they both said at the same time.

At the other end of the parking lot, Danielle was looking for a parking space when Kenya pointed out the police. Suddenly Danielle's cell phone began to ring and she handed it to Kenya, "Here, answer this while I park." Kenya flipped the phone up and saw that it was Prince.

"Hey Baby, what's up?" Prince asked.

"I'm sorry but this ain't your baby!" Kenya said laughing. "But hi anyway".

"Where's Danielle? And stop playing so much on other people's damn phone, girl!"

"She's right here, parking. Hold on."

"Yeah baby?" Danielle answered.

"Listen girl, your first period teacher didn't show up, so your class has got a study hall in the auditorium."

"Is that where you at?"

"Yeah baby, we're on the stage behind the curtains getting tatted up."

"You know I don't like those ugly tattoos. Did you eat breakfast like I asked you to start doing?"

"Naw baby I didn't have time. I was visiting Hustleman at the hospital." "Well I'm going to go get you something to eat, and by the way the police are out back looking at cars."

"Shit, as long as it ain't Whitehead I don't care!" Prince said.

"I can't tell who it is. Is there anything in particular you want to eat?" "Nope, whatever is cool with you."

"Okay baby. I'll see you in a minute," Danielle said and hung up.

"Guess what ya'll?" Danielle said happily to Kenya and China Doll. "We've got study hall this morning!"

"Oh yeah!" Kenya said. "Shit girl lets go get some breakfast then!"

"Ms. Patton must not be over that cold she got," China said of their English teacher. Danielle started the car up and pulled out slowly,

"Where are we eating?"

"It doesn't make a difference to me," Kenya said. "How 'bout the Waffle House girl because that can of ass whippin' I opened up on Monica's ass has made me hungry as hell. I was too pumped up last night to eat."

China Doll looked back at the cops as they parked and got out. "Damn, I wonder if Sgt. Whitehead is here to investigate Monica's bullshit?"

"Sgt. Whitehead! Where?" Danielle said stopping the car in its track as China pointed out the back window.

"I'll be damned! It sure is!" Danielle picked up her phone and quickly called Prince.

"Yeah girl?" Prince said

"It's Sgt. Whitehead baby and he's coming in the back door!"

"Oh shit! That's where the fellas are at!" Prince said. "Good looking out! I'll call you back after I warn them niggas!"

"I can't believe some of the cars these dope dealers drive!" Ray said, as he made sure the cruiser's doors were locked. "I've been working all my life and I still can't afford a ride like that."

"I feel you," Tony said as he put on his police hat. "That's why that life style is so tempting to these kids."

"What door we going in?" Ray asked.

"I think that one," Tony said, pointing to the one that looked like it was cracked.

The door was cracked and it was cracked for a reason. It was cracked so Low Down, one of the newest members of the Ruff Riders, could keep a look out. But he was slipping and it cost him. "Man, let me hit that blunt!" Low Down said taking his eyes off the door. "I bet ten more dollars you don't sixty-eight on your next three rolls."

"Bet nigga! Put your money down!" Fats said to Low Down from his knees as he began to roll the dice. "Anybody else want some of this action?" Fats asked as he rolled the dice. The dice bounced off the wall just as Low Down took a big puff off the blunt. His phone started to ring.

"You smell that?" Ray asked.

"Yeah I smell it."

"Come on!" Ray whispered as he stepped quickly but lightly towards the cracked door. Just as he heard somebody say, "Don't touch my money!" he yanked the door open. "Everybody freeze!"

The surprise made Low Down start choking on the weed smoke as he was bending over picking up his money. "It's Whitehead!" someone yelled.

"Hold up Low down!" as Ray grabbed him by his jacket and pushed him against the wall. "Grab him!" Ray said pushing Low Down towards Tony. Then Ray took off towards the other teenagers. "Come here!" Ray commanded as he ran through the hallway door. He chased the teens up the stairs. By the time Ray made it to the top of the steps he was out of breath but still moving. He opened the doors at the top of the stairs but all he could see was a sea of students coming and going. "Shit!" Ray said to himself as he looked through the crowd of students.

"You looking for someone Sergeant?" Ms. O'Bannon asked standing in the front of the school's trophy case.

Somewhat winded, Ray asked her if she had seen a young man running down the hall.

"He ran in there," Ms. O'Bannon said motioning toward two doors that read 'Auditorium'. "But you won't catch him in there!" and Ms. O'Bannon walked away chasing students to class.

Ray bent over to catch his breath, resting his hands on his knees.

"You okay?" Tony asked, as he walked up dragging Low Down along in handcuffs.

"That son of gun was quick!" Ray said between breaths. "I thought I had him, but these damn floors are too slippery," Ray said.

Low Down smirked at Ray, "Better luck next time Mr. Policeman."

"Shut up punk! You weren't so lucky and it's gonna be my pleasure to boot your ass back to juvenile detention! Yep, that's where you are going today Mr. Smartass! Did you shake him down?" Ray asked Tony grabbing Low Down and bumping his head against the wall.

"Yeah I shook him down. He threw his blunt down on the ground. Besides that, he was clean."

Ray kicked Lowdown's legs apart, making him spread eagle on the wall. "Who was your buddy that ran?" Ray asked as he started patting Lowdown's pockets.

"I don't have any buddies and this is brutality, I know my rights!" Lowdown said with his face mashed against the wall.

"You don't know jack shit!" Ray informed him. He pulled him away from the wall and handed him over to Tony. "Here watch him while I look in the auditorium for this other guy." He stepped over toward the auditorium doors and pulled one open to peak inside. His eyes almost popped out of his head at what he saw. There were kids dancing to loud music, paper airplanes flying back forth, and a corner that looked like lovers' lane as girls were sitting on guys' laps. "Tony! Come and look at this!" Ray yelled. He opened the door wide enough so everybody could look in.

"That's our study hall. Not a pretty sight huh? Hi, I'm Coach Andrews head football coach. I couldn't help but notice the commotion, being that you shot right by my office like the building was on fire." Ray let the auditorium door close. "Did you happen to get a glimpse of the guy I was chasing? I saw him making a drug transaction."

Coach Andrews laughed a little, "Welcome to Woodward High. No, I didn't get a look at the young man you were chasing, but there's only one group in this school who handles those types of transactions. Come on to the office. Mr. Bronson is expecting you and I'm sure he can help answer your questions."

Ray looked a little pissed as he walked toward the office; mean mugging any student who dared to establish eye contact with him. Coach Andrews worked his way through the sea of students until he reached the principle's office. He held the door for Sgt. Whitehead and Officer Ward to enter with Low Down in tow.

Ray stepped in and turned around grabbing Low Down by the front of his shirt. He shoved him in a seat in a far corner of the room. "Watch him Tony and don't take off those cuffs. I don't care how much he complains!"

"Hi, I'm Ms. Brown," a lady said getting up from her desk. "Mr. Bronson will be right with you. He's in a meeting with a parent."

"Thank you," Ray said removing his hat. "You wouldn't happen to have a name for this gentleman right here would you?" pointing to Low Down.

"Oh yes," Ms. Brown said. "That's Leonard Milton, one of our 9th graders."

"Say what, a 9th grader!" Ray said surprised. "You've got to be kidding me!"

"No Sergeant. Leonard is one of many 8th, 9th, and 10th graders who are active gang members at this school."

"Well, why don't you kick them out if you know they're gang members?"

"Because, it's against the law to deprive any one of them an education. I'll tell the principle you're here," and Ms. Brown disappeared.

Suddenly the hallway door opened and the loud noise of the students filled the room as Ms. O'Bannon entered the office. "It's about time you got caught!" pointing her little boney finger in Low Down's face.

"You know this guy?" Ray asked.

"Yep- sure do. I caught him once before smoking pot in the back hallway, but I couldn't catch him."

"Well I caught him," Ray started to say when the principle appeared. "Sgt. Whitehead, a pleasure to see you and thanks for coming! This way please. I've got someone in my office that would like to meet you. Coach Andrews you too please." Ms. O'Bannon tried to pull up the rear but the principle put his hands up holding her back. "I'm sorry Ms. O'Bannon, but if you'll excuse us, this meeting is rather personal. See if the officer guarding Leonard needs any help," and he closed the door in Ms. O'Bannon's face.

Principle Bronson turned and looked at Mrs. Johnson and then over to Sgt. Whitehead and Coach Andrews. "Gentleman, this is the mother of Monica Johnson. She alleges that her daughter was raped last Friday by two of our football players.

"Do we have names?" Coach Andrews asked looking straight at Mrs. Johnson.

Before Mrs. Johnson could reply, the principle interrupted, "That's the problem. The accused players' names came from an anonymous caller who spoke to my secretary, Ms. Brown."

"Hold up!" Ray said. "All I want to know is did the rape actually take place?"

"Yes, I would say so," Principle Bronson said.

"And why do you think so?" Ray asked.

"Because she told me and her mother on Friday, right here in my office, that she was having sex in one of the rooms in the back of the school," the principle said. "Her appearance, at that time, was disheveled and she was very upset."

"So why didn't you contact the police at that time?"

"Because she was too scared to give me their names. So I left the decision to her mother," the principle replied.

"Then why didn't you contact the police?" Ray asked Mrs. John-son.

****

"I wouldn't have said it if I didn't mean it," Prince replied.

"Yeah, I hear you," Danielle said. "But we'll talk about it later." She noticed that the second period study hall was starting to file into the auditorium.

"Here comes the noise," Danielle said.

"What noise? You mean the music?" Prince asked.

"Naw, all the 2Pac and Snoop Dogg wanna bees!" Kenya said. Everybody laughed at Kenya's little joke. "For real, half these niggaz can't rap and you niggaz know it!" Kenya said, taking center stage as always.

Stickyfingers hated it whenever he heard somebody talking out the side of their neck, and even worse when that somebody was always Kenya. "Bitch shut the fuck up! You're always talking goofy. You're just mad because every time these niggas battle, you lose your money 'cause you always bet on the nigga that you think is the cutest!" Everybody started laughing at Kenya because Sticky was telling the truth!

Kenya always bet on the best looking rapper, and the best looking one was usually the worst one.

Second period study hall filled the auditorium with music, chatter, laughter, and of course, Kenya's favorite the battle of all the rappers. All the rappers in the school liked to battle before lunch period, so they could hustle lunch money. So the battling began and the bets were made. The crowd was the judge.

****

The meeting in the principle's office was still in progress, and Ms. O'Bannon was still posted outside waiting for the meeting to end. She was on a mission as she waited to tell Sgt. Whitehead that she wanted him present at this week's open house meeting for concerned parents and she wasn't about to be turned away. So while she was standing there patting her feet, a tapping noise caught her attention. She heard it again and peaked around the corner at Officer Ward who was look-ing at a magazine.

Tony looked up at Ms. O'Bannon, "Yes, what is it?"

Ms. O'Bannon suspiciously shifted her eyes from Officer Ward to Lowdown.

Fats and P. Funk were tapping on the glass door trying to get Lowdown's attention. "Damn!" Fats said. "Is the nigga knocked out or something?"

"Tap on the window again but harder." P. Funk said. Tap- Tap-Tap. Lowdown heard it this time, but so did Ms. O'Bannon. "I knew I heard something!" she said as she stuck her head around the corner to peak again.

"Oh shit!" Fats said jumping back. "Ms. O'Bannon just stuck her head out!"

P. Funk jumped himself, but not sure as to why. "Oh shit! Did she see you?"

"I don't know, but I got Lowdown's attention! I'm going on with it before she makes her move. You better be ready to run…" Fats peaked until he could see Lowdown, then he lifted his hand and pointed his finger at Lowdown and wiggled his thumb. Then Fats mouthed the words through the window so only Lowdown could see. "WHERE'S THE GUN?"

Ms. O'Bannon saw the hand making the motion and she yelled, "Watch out, HE'S GOT A GUN!" Ms. O'Bannon scared the living day lights out of Officer Ward, who almost panicked when he heard the word gun.

Lowdown finally understood what Fats was asking, so he yelled over the commotion, "I lost it shooting craps," meaning he had left the pistol in the hallway where they were shooting dice.

Fats said, "I got it! Now let's go 'cause here comes Ms. O'Bannon!" and they took off running down the hallway.

Ms. O'Bannon was up and out the door after them but she was too slow.

Tony was standing there in complete disbelief and shaking his head when Ray, the principle, and Coach Andrews showed up to investigate all the commotion.

"Did I hear somebody say GUN?" Ray shouted as he looked around the office.

"You sure did! That woman is crazy!" Tony said.

"I'm assuming its Ms. O'Bannon that you're referring to?" the principle asked already knowing the answer.

"Listen, I think its a very good idea for us to address the parents at your open house this Thursday, but right now we better get this guy locked away," pointing to Lowdown. "If somebody owns up to the incident involving Monica, contact me at the station. Coach I'm going to grant your wish and let you first talk to your players before I bring them into the station for questioning."

"Thank you Sergeant," Coach Andrews said shaking Ray's hand with respect. "These kids need more people like you to show them some love, because they obviously are not getting it at home."

"Half these kids don't have a home," Ray said kicking Lowdown's foot. "Get him moving, so we can go lock him up," Ray said to Tony. Both Ray and Officer Ward grabbed a handful of Lowdown's bubble coat as they pulled him up from his seat on the bench as they escorted him out of the office into the student traffic that was moving back and forth through the school hallway. Ray looked around for the best route to take, being that their cruiser was parked in the back of the school.

P. Funk watched them from his posted position in the lobby behind one of the big round pillars.

Ray started towards two doors that appeared to lead downstairs. He stopped and felt the pair of eyes that were watching. "Something wrong, Sarge?" Officer Ward asked holding onto Lowdown's jacket a little tighter.

"Hold on to him while I go back to the office," Ray said. Like a puff of smoke, he disappeared.

P. Funk was just about to break and run, until he saw Sergeant Whitehead stop, look around and then run back into the office. "What the hell is he doing now?" P. Funk thought as he waited to see Sgt. Whitehead's next move. Then he went and told the gang that Lowdown was on the move.

Fats found the 38 snub nose behind the heater. He put it in his coat and made his way through the school hallways making sure Ms. O'Bannon wasn't around. He made his way safely back to the auditorium after checking to make sure he wasn't being followed, then he opened the door and ducked into the side entrance of the auditorium.

Prince looked up and motioned for Fats to meet him in the back room on the stage. "You have any problems?" Prince asked Fats as soon as they were alone.

"Naw playa, everything cool," Fats said reaching in his pocket.

"Did you find the gun?" Prince asked.

"Yeah, here it is." Fats pulled out the pearl handled snub nose 38 and handed it to his cousin.

"Good Job Dogg! That nigga Lowdown owes you for this one!" and they both started laughing. Where's P. Funk?" Prince asked as he reached in his pocket and pulled out a plastic bag of some good killa.

"I told him to chill and watch out for Whitehead, so we'll know when he's gone," Fats said.

"Yeah, we don't need that simple ass nigga in our mix. He's a damned fool! Find somewhere to hide that piece while I roll this blunt."

"Who's that battle rapping out there? They sound kind of nice with their flow," Fats said to Prince.

Prince lit the blunt and took a couple of tokes. "Here hit this, it'll calm your nerves."

Fats grabbed the blunt just as Hitman and J. Blaze walked into the room. "Fats you got competition jocking for your spot kid!" Blaze said teasing.

"What's up?" Hitman asked. "And let me hit that too while ya back here taking a break."

"Who the hell you nigga's screaming about? Can't nobody beat my flow!" Fats said as he took a big hit off the blunt before he passed it to Hitman.

"Who ya talking about?" Little T-Baby Prince asked from his seat in the corner. T-Baby was a fourteen-year-old sophomore who could rap with the best of them.

"They say he can rap, but he don't never want to battle my cuz, so as far as I'm concerned he gets no recognition," Prince said standing up and putting his arms around his cousin's shoulders.

"Yo listen! Where's this nigga at?" Fats yelled feeling good.

"Naw man chill out!" J.Blaze said laughing and playfully grabbing Fats as to hold him back. "Let's finish this blunt."

"You niggaz gonna keep pumping me up and I'm gonna have to show that young boy who I am!" Fats said. "I did hear a little of his flow and it didn't sound too bad but he can't out rap me!"

"Here Fats," Hitman said. "Just hit this killa nigga because you're starting to talk too much!" Everybody just laughed. When Ray stormed back into the office, he startled principle Bronson, who was standing there talking to Ms. Johnson about Monica.

"Listen up everybody!" Ray said looking at principle Bronson. "Come with me! It's time to start confronting the problem that plagues this school!" Coach Andrews walked up and stood next to the principle and Ms. Johnson, looking as puzzled as everyone else.

"Don't look at me like I'm 14 karat crazy! Come on! We're gonna deal with this shit right now!" and he stormed out the office.

"Deal with what shit right now?" asked Principle Bronson turning to Coach Andrews. Somewhat scared, he felt that the school board didn't pay him enough to take on gang members. "I'm not sure about this," he started to say when Coach Andrews grabbed him by the arm.

"Come on Mike and stop acting like a coward," Coach Andrews said. The auditorium was jammed packed with students screaming and hollering as usual. I got my money on T-Baby half the kids were yelling, I got my money on Fats was what all the Ruff Riders were screaming. "Put your money were your mouth is 'cause we can fade any bet you wanna make!" Prince said.

"Yo-Yo-Yo fuck all the talking! Does your boy want to battle or what?" Fats yelled as he jumped off the stage.

"Ah shit, they about to battle for real'" somebody said as students moved closer to the front. Prince pulled out a stack of money and dropped five hundred dollar bills on the stage. "Can you niggaz fade that?" Prince asked

"Man you ain't said nothing!" and T-Baby flipped a roll of bills to Prince. "What nigga, you thought I was broke?" T-baby laughed.

"Don't let this smooth face fool you baby!"

"Yeah, Yeah, Yeah! That's what I'm talking about!" Fats said getting pumped up. "Okay," Prince said, as he held his hands up for silence.

"Here's the rules. Anything goes. The crowd judges by the flow and you got to rap at least 5 verses. Everybody cool with that? Now get your bets on and let the games begin."

"Come on Fats! Put it down baby!" somebody yelled from the back. "Fats I got money on you! Do the damn thang!" The crowd circled the two, with everyone trying to get closer so they could hear the rhymes they spit.

Stickyfingers stood next to the boom box, waiting for the coin toss.

Prince flipped a quarter. "Call it in the air!"

"Heads!" Fats yelled.

The coin hit the floor at T-Baby's feet. "Head's up!"

"Yeah!" Fats yelled. "Now get ready nigga to feel my flow!" Fats stepped towards T- Baby and said, "I'm the best at this shit!"

"You ready Fats?" Sticky asked. As soon as he pushed play and the music filled the room Sgt. Whitehead made his grand entrance, opening up both auditorium doors like a gangbuster with Lowdown leading the way.

"What is this nigga trying to prove?" Fats asked Prince who was still standing on the stage.

"Come on!" Ray said to the principle and Ms. Johnson who were pulling up the rear. "You can't let these punks see you acting scared!" Ray whispered to them. "Just follow my lead." The closer Ray got to the front, the louder the music got. "Turn that music down so I can talk!" Ray yelled to no one in particular.

Sticky looked over at Prince, who shook his head 'no'.

Ray now stood in the middle of the crowd with a fist full of Lowdown's jacket in his grasp. "I'm not playing with you young punks! I will call enough cops up here to arrest every last one of you!" Ray shouted as he turned in a slow circle pointing his finger and checking out faces. "Man, you're out of your jurisdiction! You can't arrest any body up in here!" Dino declared from his seat on the stage.

Ray let Lowdown go and walked towards the radio. He pulled his handcuffs out and dangled them in Sticky's face. "Either turn that radio off, or put these on," Ray said in a very calm but deadly tone.

Sticky reached over and pushed the pause button.

"Now, that's better! I can hear myself talk because I got something to say." "Dig man! Why you sweatin' us so hard Dogg?" T Baby asked. "We got to deal with you on the block, and now in school too? Damn nigga, don't you got nothing better to do?" Prince added.

"Damn boy! You got a lot of mouth don't you?" Ray said looking up on the stage. "Who are you? The spokesmen for this group of wanna bee's?" Ray asked. He wanted confrontation to see who was in the group and taking charge. He tried to push buttons that would get responses. "Not all are gang members," he thought surveying the crowd. But he noticed all the navy blue bandannas that indicated gang membership.

"Dig man! Go on and speak your piece so my boy you got over here in handcuffs can beat your stupid charge and get back to his family!"

"Who are you, since you like to talk so much?" Ray asked stepping through the crowd.

"That's none of your business! Just think of me as your worst nightmare!" Prince said. "Yo listen everybody! This man can't do nothin' to us as long as were on school property. Turn the music back on and ignore this nigga!" Prince said as he walked away. He said something else, but Sticky had hit the pause button and the sound of the strong bass beats drowned out the last part of Prince statement.

But Ray was certain that Prince had said something about his daughter Cindy and it sent him into a mad frenzy. "Do what to my daughter?" Ray shouted pulling out his nightstick and leaping onto the stage. The Ruff Riders started to make their move before Ray got to Prince. Coach Andrews saved the day by grabbing Ray in a bear hug in midair. "Come on Sergeant Whitehead," the coach whispered in Ray's ear as Ray shouted and kicked trying to get loose. "You don't wanna do that."

"You better listen to the coach chump!" Prince said from the stage,

"You don't wanna do that. It's against the law and you can't break the law!" Prince shouted as the coach pulled Ray towards the side exit. That's when everybody started laughing. The entire auditorium of students erupted into loud taunting laughter and it infuriated Ray.

"If you so as much as look at my daughter wrong you young punk, I'll hunt you down and beat you until your own Mama don't recognize you!" Ray screamed at Prince as Coach Andrews continued to hold Sergeant Whitehead for dear life.

"We gotta get him outta here!" Officer Ward yelled at Coach Andrews while holding Lowdown and pulling him toward the side exit. "I ain't playing with you!" Ray continued to scream. "I ain't playing with none of you young punks! I'm gonna break this bullshit up and put all your asses in jail!"

Coach Andrews finally managed to get Ray to the exit door. Ray grabbed a trash can and threw it cross the stage at Prince, "Remember punk gangsters don't live that long! I'm gonna be your worst nightmare from here on out! Remember that!" and with one more push, Coach Andrews and Officer Ward were able to get Ray out into the hallway that led to the back exit of the school.

CHAPTER 8

When Patrick O'Donnell took the job as Cincinnati's Police Chief, he could not have imagined his tenure would see riots that ripped the city apart or the indictments against his officers for taking bribes. But this week he was celebrating his tenth anniversary as Chief, which is twice as long as the average term for major cities.

Unlike most Chiefs of Police, who serve at the pleasure of the Mayor or City Council, O'Donnell had retained job protection under the Civil Service, meaning he couldn't be fired that easily. He had been called a racist and accused of cover-ups by a long line of critics who had repeatedly called for his resignation. But no one had ever been able to provide proof to support any of the accusations. So this stubborn German-American home grown Northside cop had remained at the helm of the police force.

The crisis had started from the day he walked into his plush downtown office. Twelve days into the job, two officers were shot and killed. Then, Jeffrey Wilson, a 30-year-old black man, was stopped for expired license plates and beaten to death. This prompted an investigation by Internal Affairs into the department's use of force. That had been ten years ago, and since then the Chief and the police department had been under scrutiny for one reason or another.

"All-in-all, it's been a rough ride," the Chief had said. "But there's just no foolproof way to fight the kind of crime that's on the streets these days," he had been quoted as saying. "So I do the best I can but unfortunately you can't please everybody."

The Chief's cockiness had never set well with most of the officers, but no one ever did more than just whisper their disapproval of how he handled things. It was well known that when you whispered your opinion, you had better make sure that whisper didn't get caught up in the wind.

Unfortunately, the Chief's future son-in-law Jim Spencer didn't get the same respect as the Chief did. Officers talked about Jim Spencer like a dog around the precinct, not because he was the Chief's soon to be son-in-law, but because of recent rumors about him being on the take. No one really knew what Officer Jim Spencer's bag was, but the rumors persisted. In the Chief's eyes, officer Spencer could do no wrong. "We love to hate what we don't understand," was the Chief's defense.

That's why Ray Whitehead watched with pure hate and disgust as Spencer and his partner Adams walked towards him as he waited outside Tom's office. He had no use for the cocky cop. Individual arrogance, as far as Ray was concerned, didn't mix with community relations and he believed good community relations were key to fighting crime. Ray disliked Jim Spencer for what he stood for because he didn't respect or understand what purpose he served the department or the uniform he wore. Ray believed that cops like Spencer hid behind the big blue wall of steel that signifies the code of silence for all the wrong reasons and Ray didn't respect him at all.

Ray stood leaning against the wall talking to Fancy, Captain Safeway's secretary, while waiting for the captain to finish his phone conversation. Feeling the tension in the air mounting as the two officers approached, Ray began to feel somewhat uncomfortable. Just as he decided to go do something else, Tom ended his phone call. Ray looked through the glass window of the office waiting for permission to enter. Just as he was about to go in, Spencer and Adams walked up to the door, tapped on the window and just walked right in. "That was a mistake," Ray thought to himself. Nobody just walked into the Captain's office without a personal invitation, so it was no surprise to see them ushered out and the door slammed shut. "Don't ever walk into my office again without an invitation!" Tom screamed at the two puzzled officers. The door slammed with such force that the glass rattled. Ray turned his back to the two cops trying to hide his amusement at their embarrassment.

Spencer looked at his partner who seemed to be a little red in the face from the sudden outburst. "Damn!" Spencer said as he watched the Captain walk around his desk, sit down, and not once glance in their direction.

"What an ass hole!" Adams muttered under his breath, turning to have a seat in a nearby chair.

"Hate me now, love me later," Spencer said as he turned and noticed Ray across the hall. He looked down at Adams who had also noticed the black Sergeant. "That must be the nigger Whitehead we've heard so much about," Spencer said under his breath.

Ray realized that the two officers were talking about him and turned to glare in their direction. His hard look caused Fancy to ask Ray what was wrong. "Why you looking like that?" Yvette asked.

Suddenly, the Captain got up and walked over to open his office door. "You two, let's talk!" Tom said pointing at Spencer and Adams. Ray was still thinking to himself in disbelief, "I know that white boy didn't just call me a nigger! Naw, he didn't let that come off his lips!"

"Let's go Ray," Tom said breaking his thoughts. "You're a part of this meeting too."

Ray stepped towards the office following Spencer and Adams, still wondering about what he thought Spencer said.

"Close the door Ray. Everybody have a seat," Tom said as he sat behind his desk. Ray closed the door and took a seat in the corner forcing Spencer and Adams to sit in the two hot seats directly in front of Tom's desk.

Tom waited until they both were seated before he looked up. "You two need to learn the number one rule in this department, and that is no one, under any circumstances, invites themselves into my office without me offering an invitation."

"But..." Adams started to say.

"There are no buts Officer! Now do we understand each other?"

"Yes sir," came the reply from both Adams and Spencer.

"Now that that's understood gentlemen, let us get properly acquainted with each other, since we will now be working together. Have either one of you met Sergeant Ray Whitehead?" Tom asked pointing to Ray.

"We haven't personally met," Spencer said looking back at Ray, "but I believe our paths have crossed."

"Well Sergeant Whitehead is the team leader of command for this department's new trainee program and drug task force."

"Oh yeah, I was the team leader in command at District 5 Drug Task Force," Spencer said. Tom shook his head in acknowledgment. "Yes, Officer Spencer. I read that in your file and I'm sure an officer with your street knowledge could be of use to this department."

Ray looked up at Tom for the first time wondering where he was going with that statement of praise. But Tom continued as he stared down at some papers on his desk.

"It also says in your file that in May of 2000, that you were counseled for using a racial slur while role playing in a training class and in November 2002, a suspect asphyxiated while being subdued by you and Officer Adams here."

"Well my future father-in-law conducted the investigation that cleared both cases," Spencer responded.

"I understand this. If I may continue, I just got off the phone with the Chief and his instructions were for me to place you two," Tom said pointing at Spencer and Adams, "where needed until your resume for Detective in the Narcotic's Division is reviewed. Which means, I have the pleasure of placing you and your partner on our street task force under the command of Sergeant Whitehead. Do you have a problem with that?" Tom asked leaning back in his chair.

"No sir," Spencer and Adams replied.

"Okay then," Tom said slapping the top of his desk as he stood up and began walking to the door. "You gentlemen can wait outside for further instructions from Sergeant Whitehead, because this meeting is adjourned."

Ray wanted to laugh but didn't. Spencer arose from his chair with an obvious attitude and walked out into the hallway. Adams, who was the follower of the two, got up and followed Spencer without saying a word. Standing side by side, the two looked like Mutt and Jeff with Adams being much shorter at 5' 7" and Spencer standing at a towering 6' 6".

Tom closed the door behind them and returned to his seat behind his desk. He looked over at Ray and said, "I know something isn't right with those two, I can feel it. But I can't worry about it and I don't want you to start worrying about it either Ray. We've got too many other problems out there in the streets to worry about. Whatever those two and the Chief have in common, if it's not right, it will come to light. Until then, we've got to continue doing what we do best, fighting crime in the streets."

"That sounds fair to me, but you are giving me the authority to use those two where ever I see fit, right?" Ray asked.

"That's right, but watch yourself. Now tell me, what happened at the school yesterday. That's what I'm concerned about," Tom said with sincere interest.

Ray proceeded to tell Tom how bad the conditions were at Woodward High and how the Ruff Riders basically had all but one person at the school scared to confront them. Ray told Tom how he went back to the principal's office yesterday and convinced everyone to follow him to the auditorium. He explained how he had staged the confrontation to obtain help from the group to identify who were gang members. He also wanted to know who were the leaders and who were followers. Ray convinced the Principal that before he could start removing the bad apples, he first had to find them. The scene in the auditorium was just an act to get everyone close enough to get a good look at all the gang members. Today, they would come down to the station and go through all the mug shots of known juveniles involved in gang activities.

"Who's this Ms. O'Bannon lady?" Tom asked with a smile. He listened to Ray's description of the old lady who was known as the hall monitor from hell. "She sounds interesting, I'd like to meet her. You say she's coming in to the station this morning?"

"That's wonderful," Tom said smiling at the thought of a little old lady not scared of taking on a dangerous clique such as the Ruff Riders.

"Supposedly everyone in administration at Woodward will be here this morning, so we can look over mug shots and discuss strategy." Ray said.

Tom thought it was an excellent idea. "Good thinking Ray. So what time are you expecting them?"

"Oh, about 9:30 this morning."

"Good, Good, Good," Tom said while puffing on his cigar. "Take them across the hall to my conference room so you'll have some privacy."

"Sure, that sounds like a good place to meet," Ray said standing up, "plenty of light and plenty of room."

"Well, the room is yours for as long as you need it." Tom said shaking Ray's hand.

"Look at them!" Adams said from his chair in the hallway. "They're shaking hands like old friends Spence."

"Yeah, I see," Spencer said standing to adjust his police belt.

"You might come in second for that Detective position," Adams said as he leaned back and smiled at Spence. "Two friends and a stranger."

"Man, fuck you Rob." Spence said to his partner. "My father-in-law is the Chief! Remember that fuckhead!" Spence said angrily. "That position is mine and when it is, I don't wanna see your sorry ass around begging for favors!"

"Ah Jim, be cool! You know I was just joking with ya partner!" Adams said.

"Yeah right!" Spencer said walking toward a nearby water fountain. He almost knocked over a man that was shorter than his partner Adams.

"Excuse me," the short man said.

"No pardon me sir," Officer Spencer said stepping aside to allow the little man to pass.

"Um," the little man stopped and said, "excuse me one more time, but could you point me in the direction of a Sergeant Ray Whitehead?" Mike Brunson asked Spencer.

"Sure, second door on the left," Spencer said pointing towards Tom's office.

"Thank you." Mr. Brunson said as he stepped back around the corner. "Come on," the principal said to Coach Andrews and his secretary Ms. Brown who were waiting to see if Ms. O'Bannon and Ms. Johnson had arrived.

"Did you see them?" Brunson asked.

"Not yet," Ms. Brown said.

"Well come on. Let's go tell Sergeant Whitehead the news," Mike said.

Officer Spencer bumped into the principal again just as the group turned the corner.

"OOPS! Pardon me again. I know you're pretty tall," Mike said. "But I'm not so short that you can't see me!"

"Sorry!" Spencer said unapologetically.

"Come on, his office is this way," the principal said to his group.

"Well Ray," Tom said opening the door for his friend. "When they get here call me."

"I sure will," Ray said, stepping out just as Mike Brunson was approaching.

"Coach, there's Sergeant Whitehead," Mike said approaching Ray and shaking hands.

"Hey Coach, Ms. Brown," Ray said shaking hands with everyone. "Where's Ms. O'Bannon?" he asked somewhat disappointed.

"Oh, she's coming," Ms. Brown said. "She and Ms. Johnson have a little surprise for you."

"Oh yeah, I'm sorry," Ray said stepping aside to introduce the Captain. "This is my Captain, Tom Safeway. He's given us his full cooperation on anything we need to restore order at your school."

"My pleasure Captain Safeway," Coach Andrews said shaking his hand. "We need all the help we can get."

"Who's that?" Tom asked noticing the strange trio walking in their direction.

Ray turned to look while still talking to the Coach. "Yeah, who's that?" He saw two ladies in scarves and dark shades turning the corner and leading a child with a Halloween mask on her face of Cinderella. Ray looked in bewilderment for a second before realizing it was Ms. O'Bannon. He nudged Tom in the side. "That's Ms. O'Bannon Captain. I told you she was special!" Ray ushered everyone into the conference room to review photographs of the suspected gang members. Prince was also assembling his troops at the school auditorium.

"Gang members only." he instructed the Ruff Riders standing security at every entrance. "Only gang members get in this morning," he said from his position on the stage as he watched the seats begin to fill. "That looks like everybody," Fats said to Prince as he looked around.

"All right come on, we got to get this started before we get any interruptions," Prince said. He stepped to the edge of the stage and motioned for everyone to hold the noise down. From the looks of things the Ruff Riders had about 40 to 50 members present and that was enough to get the word passed around. "Everybody in this room knows what tomorrow is, but for those who don't, tomorrow night we play at Withrow."

At the mention of Withrow's name, angry insults began to swirl through the auditorium. "We owe those niggaz!" somebody shouted. "Hold up!" Prince said. "I ain't finished yet. Yeah, we owe them niggas ten fold, but a rumble at the game could cost the football team. So, tomorrow's not the time." Prince looked around at all the members to see if he had gotten his point across. Some were shaking their head in agreement, some were fixing the belt on their sagging jeans and some were busy adjusting their bandannas on their heads. "Them niggaz are gonna pay for what they did to Hustleman and that's a fact," Prince continued. But it's got to be the right time and place. So tomorrow, I don't want nobody packing guns in the stands. Leave your gun in the car. The police know we got beef with these cats, so they'll be all over the place and I don't wanna see anybody going to jail. Those niggaz ain't going to make a move at the game and we're not either."

"You sure about that?" one member asked.

"No, I'm not sure about that Tiny, but that's my call. Now does anybody have a problem with that? Tomorrow night we go in peace and represent. After the season is over, we settle our beef on the street. We meet here at the school at 7 pm in the back parking lot."

"Yo! J.Blaze!" one member yelled.

J.Blaze looked up from his conversation with Sticky. "Yeah, what's up my nigga?'

"Good luck dog, I hope we blow them niggaz out."

"For Shizzle my Nizzle, that's a given my brotha!" Blaze said slapping five with Sticky. "Where's Hitman?" Prince asked looking around. "I think he's hanging out with Street on the block." Stickyfingers replied. "For anybody that wants to go, I'm going over to the hospital to visit Hustleman this afternoon. Anybody is welcome to come along," Prince said. "Oh yeah, and everybody put on their colors tomorrow, because I want these cats to know how strong we are."

****

It took some time before everyone was present at the police station. Ms. O'Bannon was telling Ray and Captain Safeway how she convinced Monica to come to the station and face her fears. "Myself and a few other parents from our group talked to Monica for three hours," Ms O'Bannon was telling Ray and the Captain.

Tom was just looking at Ms. O'Bannon in amazement as she was talking, really enjoying the little woman's 'go get 'em' attitude. "Ms. O'Bannon, I must say it has really been a pleasure making your acquaintance this morning," Captain Safeway said trying to make an exit. Ms. O'Bannon continued to relate her story. "So I told the girls that if it made Monica feel better hiding her face when she's outside, then we all will wear a disguise."

Once everyone got settled in, Ray began his presentation. "Now if we can get started, I'd like to show everyone some photos I've prepared." He stepped towards a stack of four photo albums that sat in the middle of the big table giving one to the secretary, Ms. Brown.

"Even though you work in the office and don't see many of the gang members, I want you to pay close attention to the names because you handle the daily detention sheets at the school. If there is a name that you recognize as having been in detention, I want you to tell me. Coach Andrews I want you to look through your book and see if you recognize any players on your team. We already know you've got three starters in there, the quarterback and two receivers, so I'm willing to bet you've got more you don't know about."

"Probably so," the coach said opening the book. He was not very happy about what was happening to his 14-0 football team. Ray felt his pain and patted the coach on his back.

"We're not going to lock them up Coach, so don't worry," Ray said. "We're just going to round 'em up and try to talk some sense into them before they completely self destruct."

"They've already self destructed," Ms. O'Bannon said.

"Come on now Ms. O'Bannon, work with me here! Not all these kids are bad! We might be able to save a few. Here," Ray said pushing the third book her way. "You and your brother James go through this book since the both of you deal with these kids up close."

Ms. O'Bannon had told her brother about the meeting with Sergeant Whitehead, being that he was an activist who had formed an organization called Citizens On Patrol. He had lost his oldest son to a drug overdose two years ago. He had been a one-man task force since that day chasing drug dealers off corners and shutting down crack houses with nothing but a bullhorn and pure determination.

Ray picked up the last book and walked over to Monica. "Its important that you look at these pictures very closely. I want the guys who violated you, but I can't do it without your help, understand?"

"As long as I don't have to go back to that school." Monica said.

"Don't worry sweetheart. They won't jump on you again," Ray promised. He touched her shoulder and then bent down and gave her a hug. "I'm gonna make sure of that."

"I want everyone to review each photo and name carefully. I'm gonna step across the hall and speak with my Captain. Take your time."

"How's it going?" Tom asked as Ray shut the door behind him.

"Okay, I guess," Ray said kind of thinking for a second.

"What's on your mind?" Tom asked.

"I'm gonna need a couple of extra officers to put at the school until I get order restored. I don't have a couple officers to spare." Ray said.

"You have Spencer and Adams. They worked with the gang unit at District 5," Tom said.

"Yeah, that's it, a perfect fit. That will be a great first assignment for those two. Where are they?" Ray asked looking out the office window.

"I sent them down stairs. I didn't need them hanging in front of my office watching what I was doing."

"Well then, that solves my problem. I should take them to the meeting with me at the school tonight," Ray said.

"What meeting is that?" Tom asked.

"Ms. O'Bannon and her brother James use the school auditorium to meet with the parents about school and neighborhood problems every month, and tonight is their monthly meeting. I've been invited to speak to the parents."

"Well every little bit helps. You've got my full support."

"Thanks Tom. I think I'll surprise Adams and Spencer with the news at roll call in the morning," Ray said with a smile. "It's gonna be my pleasure to throw those two into the fire and see what they're made of."

"Just be careful and play it by the book."

"I always play it by the book, you know that," Ray said winking at Tom as he left the office.

"You might want to give your newfound friends a lunch break," Tom said looking at his watch.

"Is it that late?" Ray asked checking his watch. "Damn, time flies when you're not paying attention. They should be finished by now, I'll talk to you later."

"Yeah, good luck," Tom said as Ray shut the door to his office.

When Ray walked back into the conference room, everyone was putting on their coats preparing to leave. "All finished?" Ray asked.

"Just in time for lunch. I'll be looking forward to seeing you tonight Sergeant," James said shaking Ray's hand.

"It's gonna be my pleasure." Ray said. "What about you Ms. O'Bannon" You gonna be there as well?"

"I wouldn't miss it for the world! I think tonight's meeting might be one of the better ones." she said.

"Monica are you all right? Did your recognize anyone?" Ray asked.

"She's still unsure Sergeant Whitehead," Ms. Johnson spoke for her daughter. "Give her a day or two. I think she saw a few faces that scared her a little. She's still not convinced she's safe and to be truthful Sergeant Whitehead, I'm not either. So I told her to think it over before putting herself in harm's way."

"I understand," was all Ray could say. That must of been how everybody felt, because once they left Ray saw that not one single photo was on the table. He stood there wondering why and at the same time, knowing the answer. "Yeah it's time to convince these people that we're all on the same team. Tonight's meeting could be the perfect start." He grabbed the photo albums off the table and headed downstairs to see if his wife wanted some lunch.

****

Word passed like wildfire throughout the school during the afternoon. Everybody was to be at the Withrow and Woodward game but no guns. Many of the Ruff Riders didn't agree with being on another gang's turf and not packing, but Prince had said no weapons and his word was law. The gang was chilling in back of the school when school let out. Street's caddie drove up with it stereo jamming to 2-Pac.

"I feel like partying tonight!" Prince said. "Yaw niggaz wanna go up to Brandy's and have a few drinks?"

"I thought we was going to check on Hustleman?" Fats asked.

"We are after we hit a few clubs. You down or what?" Prince said leaning on the front of the car talking to Danielle. "What about you baby girl?" Prince asked her. "You feel like hanging out tonight?"

"It's a school night." Danielle reminded him.

"Ah girl, cut it out! You know your parents are out of town," Prince said. "So what you worrying about?

"I've got exams next week and I need to study, but maybe I'll chill for a little while. I can't do an all nighter." Danielle said.

"Don't worry girl." Sticky said. "We'll have you tucked in before midnight.

"Listen, call your girls Kenya and China and tell them were rolling tonight about 9:30, okay?" Prince said giving her a kiss on the cheek.

"All right baby," Danielle said jumping off the hood of the car. "So you getting ready to head over to the hospital now?"

"Yeah baby girl, it's about time we blow this spot. I'll get up with you later. We'll meet you at the club."

Prince, Fats, Street, J.Blaze and Stickyfingers all got in Street's Cadillac and rolled past Danielle. "I'll holla," Prince said out the window.

"Damn! I like this Cadillac!" Stickyfingers exclaimed from the back seat. "This is a sho-nuff Ho catcher here, but I ain't about to rob no bank like your crazy ass Street did to own one of these."

"Sometimes my brother, you gotta do what you gotta do to get what you want in this world." Street said from the driver's seat. "But nigga you got it made with your skills on the football field, so I don't know why you're sweating this small shit any way!"

"Yeah I hear ya, but there's still gotta be an easier way for a playa to get a Cadillac," Sticky said laughing.

"There is man if we can keep your silly ass out of trouble! Its called the N.F.L.," Prince said.

"Yeah, that sounds good," J. Blaze cut in, "but a brotha ain't trying to wait another four years to get it."

"Nigga, college ain't a guarantee for your black ass anyway!" Sticky said to Blaze. "Not if that Monica chick comes back to town with them rape charges."

"That bitch better not show up with that bullshit! What she better do is take that ass wiping Kenya gave her as a warning for her ass 'cause I only gave her what she asked for," J. Blaze said.

Prince just shook his head. "I still can't believe you and Hitman boned that girl like that."

"For rizzle my nizzle! The girl wanted it and then got mad after Hitman hit it!" Blaze said.

"You better hope the coach don't find out or both you niggaz will be riding the bench tomorrow and everyday after that," Sticky said.

"Naw, I doubt if the coach would even believe her because he knows how these chicks be sweating the star Q.B." J.Blaze said.

"Yeah right, Mr. Superstar. You just better be crossing your damn fingers 'cause I got a feeling we ain't heard the last of Monica Johnson," Sticky said.

And he was right. But unfortunately she hadn't found the courage to tell yet, but that could change in time.

"Yo! Hold down the chatter. I can't think up here for you niggaz screaming and yelling back and fourth!" Prince said shutting everyone up in the car. "Dig Street! Cruise through the 'hood so I can see if business is jumping."

"Business was good last night for them rocks, I know that." Street said. "I don't know what the weed did, but those dope fiends fell in love with that batch of crack I cooked up."

"Well, if that's the case, then we'll keep selling both. You feel me?" replied Prince

"We need to get some of that YA YO too," Street said.

"I told you it takes money to purchase heroin and we haven't been in the game long enough to be handling that type of cash. Now make a right turn on North Bend so I can check on these niggaz!" Prince shot back. All Street was concerned about was expanding and getting money. That's why he was the only Ruff Rider who just simply said bump school all together and started hustling full time.

"Since we can't talk, can we at least get some music?" Fats asked from the backseat.

"Yo, park behind that red car," Prince said getting ready to jump out. "Listen, I ain't going to be nothing but a minute and then we'll go check Hustleman at the hospital."

****

After taking a two-hour lunch with his wife, Ray settled down in the cafeteria to jot down a few notes on what he wanted to discuss at tonight's meeting. There was so much to discuss. Everyday, there was a new wrinkle. Lost in his thoughts and trying to remember everything he wanted to put before the parents, he spent the remainder of the afternoon in the cafeteria. Ray hadn't seen Spencer and Adams since this morning. They did a great disappearing act. He looked at the clock on the cafeteria wall; he had ten minutes before it was time to pick Hazel up out front. As he gathered his notes, he wondered if Tony was feeling better. He had called in sick. Ray thought highly of his trainee, "Now there's a good cop."

****

Prince walked down the street counting the stash he picked up from the house joint. "Three grand, not bad!" he thought as he rolled the bills and slipped a rubber band around them. He reached the car and flipped a baggie of weed to Fats in the back seat. "Here's your weed! Now smoke and relax while I figure out some shit."

"Good looking," Fats said with a smile, getting all happy. He loved that weed. "Just what the doctor ordered," he said sticking his nose in the baggie.

"Yo, get us to the hospital. I gotta check on my little brotha." Prince told Street. "The weed did pretty well last night, but you're right, the YA YO would make us rich." Prince told his cousin.

"Now you talking," Street said turning the big Caddie into traffic. "Yeah now you talking."

"Let them windows down while these niggaz smoke, and put something worth listening to on that radio." Prince said.

Street turned the beats up and the lyrics of Pac flowed through the speakers as well as his thoughts.

> *Time to question our lifestyles, look at how we living.*
> *Smoking weed like it ain't no thang,*
> *just kids faced with demon's,*
> *addicted to hearing victims screaming.*
> *Guess we were evil since birth,*
> *product of cursed semen's.*
> *Cause even our birthdays is cursed days.*
> *Born a thug in the first place,*
> *in the worst way.*
> *I'd love to see the block in peace.*
> *With no dealers or crooked cops to make our mothers weep.*
> *There are too many murders,*
> *too many funerals too many tears.*
> *Just seen another brother buried that I knew for years.*
> *Passed by his family, but what could I say*
> *besides keep yo' head up and pray for better days.*

They rode and smoke until the sun went down, jamming and kicking it around, but yet bonding like family at the same time. In the ghetto that's how the family structure worked, it's never about flesh and blood. That does not classify you as family in these times, it's loyalty and unity that determines who is family.

"Park in the garage. We can go through the hospital entrance on the back side and take the back elevator upstairs," Prince said turning the music down.

****

"Come on honey!" Ray shouted upstairs to Hazel. "Its almost seven o'clock. I'll be outside warming the car up," Ray said picking up the speech from the end table. He looked the speech over one last time.

"You still looking over that speech?" Hazel asked handing her coat to Ray. He helped his wife into her coat and then held the front door.

"Shall we?" he said.

"I suppose we should," Hazel said playfully as the two exited the house and walked down the driveway already ten minutes late.

Ms. O'Bannon was busy ushering parents, community activists and invited media people to the seats she had arranged for tonight's meeting. Microphones and tables were neatly placed on the auditorium stage so the guest speakers could talk and respond to questions that were directed from the audience. Ms. O'Bannon's brother James was busy handing out pamphlets about his 'Citizens On Patrol' organization, containing dates, times and locations of the next rally or demonstration. James specialty was shutting down crack houses wherever he found one and running dope dealers off city blocks with his bullhorn and picket signs. As a retired Captain of the armed forces, James feared very little and his determination was relentless when it came to fighting drug dealers. This was his daily mission, considering that his oldest son Troy had died from a 'Hot Shot' placed in a syringe by a dope dealer who thought had been screwed out of some money. The case was never solved and no suspects ever found, so James had dedicated his retirement years to fighting and exposing dope dealers all over the city. Maryann O'Bannon had just about everyone accounted for, so she thought. "Where's Sergeant Whitehead?" she asked her brother as she stood at the entrance to the auditorium.

"Haven't seen him," James answered placing his pamphlets down on a table by the door.

"Well we need to get started," Maryann said as they both walked down the center aisle. She stopped at the microphone in the middle of the aisle waiting until her brother reached his seat on the stage with

Coach Andrews and the principal Mr. Brunson.

"Where's Sergeant Whitehead?" Brunson asked James in a whisper as he sat down. "We can't start this meeting without him."

"Too late, my sister has started," James said.

"Can I have everyone's attention please? Hi, I'm Maryann O'Bannon and welcome to our third community meeting for concerned parents. Tonight on our panel, we have Mr. Mike Brunson, principal of Woodward High, Coach Larry Andrews, who's built the most successful football program in the history of the school, and retired Captain James Miller from the United States Army, who spends his free time organizing demonstrations for the COP program. He's always looking for new members, so if you're interested please get with him after the meeting."

Everyone in the auditorium applauded. Once everyone stopped clapping Maryann continued, but not until she turned and looked back at the auditorium door hoping to see Sergeant Whitehead making an entrance. "Unfortunately," Maryann continued, "our key note speaker Sergeant Ray Whitehead from District Four, hasn't arrived yet, but we're going to go on with the meeting as planned. I think everyone is familiar with how this works. If you have a question, feel free to step up to this microphone and address anyone on the panel about any issue of your concern."

Ray was having the same problem he had the last time he visited Woodward. There was no parking available in the front, so like last time, he went around to the back parking lot.

"My goodness!" Hazel said, "Look at all the cars! I didn't realize this event was going to be so big. How do we get in?" she asked.

"I guess this door. It's where I went in last time. I hope it's open," Ray said. Once they got into the quiet hallways of the school Ray could hear someone talking on a P.A. system. "I think they've started already. "Come on," Ray said speeding up their walk. The first parent, eager to ask the panel a question, was stepping up to the mike for the question of the night. "Hi everyone. I'm Yolanda Thompson and my question is..."

A banging from the door stopped Yolanda's question and sent Maryann flying to the door cursing the interruption. Ray felt a lump in his throat as he walked hand in hand with Hazel into a half filled auditorium with every pair of eyes watching in silence. Maryann showed

Ray to the stage side steps and then took Hazel with her to a seat next to hers. It was quiet; everyone could hear Ray's heels knocking on the wooden floor of the stage as he made his way to his seat with the other panel members. He pulled the chair out and then apologized for being late. "I'm really sorry I was late," he said sitting down. "I'm Sergeant Whitehead from District 4 Police Station and head of our Violent Crime Task Force in the department. I'm now investigating all criminal and gang activity at this school." The crowd applauded.

Maryann got up and walked to the mike. "Thank you Sergeant Whitehead for your attendance," and then she grabbed Yolanda and introduced her to Ray. "Sergeant Whitehead, this is Yolanda Thompson and she has a question she would like to ask the panel. If everyone is ready, I'm giving her the mike. Ms. Thompson, would you repeat your question?"

"Yes, my question is for Coach Andrews. In light of your football program being so successful, winning the state championship the last two years and being undefeated this year, please tell us your position on these rumors of rape. I have heard that two of your star players may be involved. Will you suspend them from tomorrow's game at Withrow knowing it could cost the team an undefeated season?"

Coach Andrews cleared his throat, and silently cursed his luck at being the first one on the hot seat. He pulled his mike closer to address the question. "I think that there are a lot of allegations, but to date there hasn't been anything proven and no charges have been brought."

"Hi my name is Judy Myers and my question is for Sergeant Whitehead. These kids believe they're being wrongly punished, picked on and discriminated against by your police department and because of that, they are rebellious, swearing never to be knocked down quote unquote by anyone in the system ever again. That seems to drive them more then anything else. What do you think?"

"Um, that's a good question," Ray said pulling the microphone closer. "For some reason, the police department is always labeled the bad guy, no matter how we handle any situation. We do have some problems just like any organization, but everyday we give our lives to the cause of serving others. Some of the kids we are talking about are responsible for 75 murders to date. Ninety percent of the homicides we've had were drug related. Discipline begins in the home and without it; many kids become drug dealers and my problem to deal with. No child, man or woman has the right to play judge, jury and executioner in this world. It is my mission as a law enforcement officer to find a solution that'll keep our streets safe."

"Hi, I'm Sue Wilson from the Cincinnati Enquirer and my question is for Sergeant Whitehead as well. You say and I agree, that no one has the right to play judge, jury and executioner. So my question is don't you think some of these kids are rather young for the choices they make? Do you think they're being influenced or brainwashed by the violent rap lyrics in today's music?"

The crowd applauded at the reporter's question. Ray rocked back in his chair making sure to choose his words carefully. He didn't want to offend anyone, but he intended to tell it like it was from his point of view. "Yes and no," Ray said. "Yes, I think the violent content of some of these rap songs at times consumes these kids, and I do mean consume. Many rap songs seem to glamorize crime. The problem is that these kids want to be successful, but they want to be successful on their own terms. With crime being glamorized, many are willing to take by any means necessary shortcuts to obtain their vision of success. Many believe that crime is their only road to fame and riches. The street lifestyle seems to look like a savior to some who don't have direction or mentors to help provide direction in their lives. On the other hand, rap music isn't the only factor leading kids astray. But lack of parenting allows violent rap to fill the void far as I'm concerned. When a child has no one to provide loving discipline, they will look elsewhere." The applause was thunderous. The next question was directed to Principal Brunson. "Mr. Brunson I'm a concerned parent and I would like to know what the school is doing to get through to these kids?"

Principal Brunson scooted his chair to the table until his chest touched. "If I stop these kids in the hallway and inquire about their personal problems or behavior patterns their excuse is, "Hey that's the environment I come from and I don't care what you think." If you try to get these kids to conform to the rules and regulations, that's when you're going to see the most resistance. They have never had any structure at home. They don't want mentors these days. They prefer their own way of doing things rather than listening to outsiders, whom they feel for the most part, can't relate to their trials and tribulations in life.

I think teachers can be tremendous role models. But there has to be more role models in these teenagers' lives from their home to really have a chance to stem the tide of negative pressure they face outside in the real world. And, that has to start from their family structure first. Then a teacher has a foundation from which to build a successful young adult." Again, the applause was thunderous. The principle had made a valid point.

"Excuse me," Ray said into his microphone. "Before the next question is asked, I would like to elaborate a little more on what Principal Brunson just said. What we need to be concerned about is why buckets of blood from our youth keep running in the streets? We can sit here and blame the lyrics of rap songs but that's something we can't change. We as parents and educators should be asking ourselves why this music is so hypnotic to our children. In 1992, the Supreme Court upheld the First Amendment, the right of free speech, for any rapper to rap about whatever he or she wants. So singling rappers out as a source of our problem is not an answer. Worrying about City Council and what laws can be made or changed isn't the answer either. Why worry about voting to change the history of our city, when we can't even change the history of our children's behavior? If there was a law that needed to be passed that'll have any effect on the problems we face today, it should be nobody could have kids until somebody with some sense and parenting skills gives them permission and that's just the bottom line. I'm telling you, people are failing as parents and it's just that simple." Ray looked out over the crowd of parents, and then looked over at his wife.

"You go boy!" she mouthed as she stood up and started the standing ovation. She felt blessed to have such a wonderful and caring husband who helped her raise two beautiful girls. She knew that both of their daughters would achieve greatness.

CHAPTER 9

Sleep hadn't come easy for Sergeant Whitehead last night. For some reason his mind continued to play visions of some of the most horrific cases of abuse and child endangerment he had seen over his many years as a police officer. The replay seemed to have been triggered by the tales of disrespect some of the parents told about their encounters with their children. It was absolutely shocking to hear one mother tell how she came home from work one evening to find her daughter laying unconscious on the bathroom floor in a pool of her own blood after sticking a coat hanger up inside herself trying to abort a baby she didn't want. To hear that woman's testimony was enough to bring tears to any man's eyes. It made Ray think even more about other incidents in the past when officers had found newborn babies in dumpsters, left for dead.

All too often parents repeated again and again at the meeting last night, *I don't know what's wrong with my child.* Ray knew better. He knew exactly what the problem was. Your child is either on drugs or there are no rules and regulations that govern your home. You have allowed your child to be exposed to the vast amount of mind controlling substances that are on the streets, schools, and clubs these days. You forgot to watch your child. It amazed him to see how naive most of these parents were to not see it coming. It's just mind boggling Ray thought as he got out of bed, making sure he didn't disturb his wife as he made his way through the early morning darkness of their house towards the kitchen to put on a pot of coffee. Once he got the coffeepot started, he went to see if the morning paper was in the front yard. He turned the alarm system off and tiptoed through the grass to pick up the paper. The fresh October morning breeze felt good and peaceful, so Ray stood and enjoyed the moment before returning inside to check on his coffee.

"What are you doing up so early Dad?" Cindy asked scaring the wits out of her father.

"Girl!" Ray exclaimed jumping at the sound of her voice. "Don't play like that!" as he shut the front door. "What are you doing up?"

"I heard the alarm being turned off, so I looked out my window and saw you in the front yard," she said walking towards the kitchen.

"Yeah, I didn't sleep all that good last night. I went to that community meeting last night at the school. By the way, how is everything at school lately? You haven't had any problems have you?" Ray asked as he took a seat on the couch.

"No Daddy, I'm fine. No problems at school. Would you like me to bring you a cup of coffee if it's ready?"

"Yes please, thank you." Ray removed the paper from the plastic cover.

"So how did the meeting go?" Cindy asked bringing two cups of coffee into the living room and giving one to her dad.

"It was wonderful and I'm glad I went. I met so many interesting people and heard many interesting stories. Um, this coffee tastes good." Ray said taking another sip.

"I heard the media was there," Cindy continued kicking her feet up on the coffee table.

"The newspaper wrote an article on the meeting and that's what I'm looking for now. I'm curious to see if the 'Enquirer' gave us some good press this time. It seems as though they blame the police for all their problems," Ray said checking out the front page.

"You must not be going to work this morning," Cindy said sipping her own coffee.

"Why you say that?" Ray asked looking up from the paper.

"Because you don't look like you have any intentions of getting up off that couch anytime soon," Cindy said standing up with her cup in hand.

"While you're up would you get me a refill?"

"How can I say no?" Cindy said picking up his cup.

Ray turned to the Metro section still looking for the article. He looked until another article caught his attention. Ray read the brief article, then stopped and read it again as if not believing what he read the first time, and then he just looked up at Cindy as she sat his coffee down.

"What's wrong with you?" she said. "They must have given the meeting some bad press from the way you look. Let me see the paper."

"Hold up," Rays said putting his hand up. "Bump my article, listen to this. Two 8-year-old boys and an 11 year-old schoolmate were arrested yesterday, after they were accused of burying a loaded handgun in a playground sandbox. They were apparently plotting to shoot and stab a third-grade girl during recess, authorities said Thursday. Sheriff Ray Thornton said the boys intended to harm the girl because she had teased two of them."

"Oh my! Where did that happen?" Cindy asked.

Ray looked back at the article. "It happened at a school some where in Montana. Isn't that a shame?" Ray said shaking his head.

"That is sad," Cindy said.

"It just amazes me how kids so young can become so angry and deadly. That's why I'm going to go ahead and put Citizen's On Patrol out on the street to help the department to try and deter some of this crime."

"Who is Mr. O'Neal? Is he any kin to the hall monitor Ms. O'Bannon? They act like they are related." Cindy asked reaching for the paper.

"From my understanding, he's her older brother who's retired from the army for the past four years," Ray said in between sips of coffee.

"Oh yeah, I remember him. He's a retired Captain. Wow, Dad you should see all the medals he's got pinned to his uniform! Captain James O'Neal is his name if I'm not mistaken."

"Yup that's him. He's a pretty impressive person and seems to be pretty dedicated to helping the department get some of these drugs off the street." Ray said.

"Did he tell you that he had a son that went to Woodward?"

"He mentioned it at the meeting last night, but that was about it. I did ask his name but he didn't elaborate, so I left it alone."

"I really don't know much about their business. All I know is what Mark has told me over the summer. Mark O'Neal is his name and he's cool, I like him." Cindy said.

"Like him! Hold up baby girl, let's talk."

"Not like that Dad," Cindy said shaking her head. "Although he did tell me that when we were sophomores he had a crush on me. But that was two years ago, we're both seniors now. He told me that he and his Dad had a bunch of differences between them because he likes to smoke pot."

"Say what? Captain O'Neal's son is a weed head? Now this is getting interesting. Tell me more."

Cindy stopped looking at the newspaper and looked over at her dad laughing.

"I gotta get ready for school and I'm not about to sit here with you gossiping about the O'Neal's business. Remember," Cindy said standing up pointing her finger at her dad, "you promised Mom no more police work in this house."

Ray leaned over quickly and placed his finger to his lips. "Shush, girl before your mother hears you! You trying to get me in the doghouse? Now tell me more. You might have something valuable I can use."

"Cut it out dad, you're begging now. If I tell you this time will you promise no more questions?" Cindy whispered.

"I promise, I promise," Ray said pulling Cindy's arm. Now sit down and fill your Dad in before your mama wakes up."

"Okay, Okay," Cindy said sitting back down. "One day Mark was showing me how to create a few programs on our computer in the computer lab, and I asked him how he manages to make the honor roll every semester when he's high on pot all the time. He told me weed makes him happy."

"Happy, yeah O.K., go on."

"He said every since his older brother got killed, living around his pops had been depressing and stressful because they don't really communicate. Captain O'Neal kicked his older brother out the house, after he found two used syringes in the bathroom trashcan. Mark watched the confrontation and stood by as his father made Troy pack his clothes and leave. That was the last time Mark saw his brother alive. Two weeks later they found him dead with a needle in his arm."

"Oh yeah?"

"That happened two years ago, so Mark said he started smoking pot real heavy because it makes him happy."

"You mean it helps him cope with the depression of losing his brother."

"Possibly, but because of his desire to smoke weed, his aunt, Ms. O'Bannon doesn't approve but lets him be. His father, Captain O'Neal is just happy Mark decided that life was worth living. Mark cut his wrist and tried to end his life when his brother was found dead. Mark says he's only close to his Uncle Ben who's also in the army. They communicate through e-mail a lot. Mark loves hearing about the exciting missions his uncle e-mails him about. He lets me read a few and they do sound pretty exciting. Now if you're through holding me hostage Dad, can a sista get ready for school?"

"Hey, good looking out baby girl. Yeah, you go on and get ready." That was interesting he thought while relaxing on the couch.

"And guess what?" Cindy said before going up the stairs. "Even though he smokes dope and listens to country music staying on the honor roll has earned him a four-year ride at Duke University. He says he wants to study computer science. I think I need some of what he's been smoking," Cindy said laughing and running up stairs.

Ray couldn't get the words out fast enough, he was gonna say something to the effect of beating the tar out of her if she did, but Cindy was gone.

It took Ray the better part of thirty minutes or so to do three things, get a shower, get dressed and head to work. That's how anxious he was to get to the station to meet with James O'Neal and discuss their plans of working with Citizens On Patrol at roll call. Tom is gonna love this plan, he thought as he backed out of his driveway. He saw a wonderful opportunity to get the community involved. Ray was so ecstatic, that he almost didn't see the parked car behind him as he sped off.

"Morning," Tom cheerfully addressed several officers he passed in the halls heading to his office.

"Good morning," James O'Neal said from his seat next to Ray's desk. "Beautiful day," James said standing up and walking towards the Tom to shake hands.

"It certainly looks like we're in for some sunshine today," Tom said shaking James' hand.

"You must be waiting on Sergeant Whitehead."

"Yes I am," James said.

"Well come on in and chat for a while. Ray should be here shortly. I was just about to sit and enjoy my morning coffee and paper, before I start my day," Tom said.

"I've already had that opportunity and on my way to a second cup," James said.

"I understand you're a retired Captain. Rumor has it that you are an activist against drugs. I must admit I admire your determination, Mr. O'Neal. I'm glad to see someone in the community step up and support the police force. I also had an opportunity to read some of the article in today's paper about the success of last night's meeting."

"Yeah! I've got a lot of fed up parents involved in my organization and more joining every day," said James.

"I sure wish I knew your secrets in recruiting some of these parents, because I've been trying for years to get the community involved. But they act as if they don't trust us. Maybe now they'll get a chance to see what fighting crime is like and what we go through everyday."

"Well Captain Safeway sometimes it takes one of your own to bring the truth to the fight, so…"

A knock on the Captain's window interrupted James. Ray opened the door and stuck his head in. "I hate to interrupt you two gentlemen, but I've got over thirty officers waiting on roll call. If you don't mind, I would like you to introduce James to the boys in blue this morning."

"Oh sure, sure by all means," Tom said getting out his chair to shake James' hand again. "When you get through Ray, stop by and fill me in. And by the way, lovely PR work in this morning's paper."

"Oh, you saw it!"

"You mean you haven't," Tom said walking around his desk.

"No, I was looking at the paper some what upside down this morning. Read this." Ray said pointing to the small article. "It'll give you a whole new perspective on the criminal element we're dealing with."

Ray and James disappeared in the direction of the Officer's Conference Room where morning roll call took place. Meanwhile, Tom shut the door to his office and sat back down to read the article Ray had brought to his attention. "Two eight year olds and a eleven year old plot to kill school mate at recess." Tom read the article and it had the same impact on him as it did on Ray. What are these kids thinking? Tom was just thankful this time it was somebody else's problem to worry about and not his. God knows this department has enough to worry about as it is. "Jumping Jesus!" Tom said sitting back down at his desk. "How much more can I take?"

****

"All right Gentlemen quiet down," Ray said as he and James made their way through the sea of officers. "Before I begin," Ray said, "let me see a show of hands of those interested in some overtime for tonight's game at Withrow versus Woodward? For those who don't remember the last time these two teams played each other, a student was robbed and shot by three unknown assailants. We can't have incidents like that tonight and we can't stop the game from being played. So I'm beefing up security with more foot patrol and some horse patrol. Should matters get out of control, at least we'll be prepared and if need be, I will have the riot squad on stand by. So if you're interested in some overtime, place your name on the overtime list that's going around the room. Last night," Ray continued. "I had the honor of being part of a community meeting that was held at Woodward High School. Several parents, teachers, and community activists expressed a lot of concern about the criminal activity going on in that school. After conducting a small investigation, I discovered quite a bit of criminal activities that seem to be gang related and that concerns me. Most recently, a rape allegedly took place in a classroom by two Woodward football players." Ray looked up and shook his head. "Gentlemen, we can't have that, so I'm assigning two officers this morning to work at the school for security purposes. Those officers will work Monday through Friday from 8 to 4 until I say otherwise."

Most of the officers were smiling and whispering amongst themselves at the thought of which two unlucky candidates would be selected. After all, who wanted to work around a bunch of kids all day? Nobody wanted that job!

"Today I brought someone with me. His name is Captain James O'Neal who is retired from the army. He has now dedicated his time to working with the COPS (Citizens On Patrol)," Ray said motioning to James. "He has volunteered to help us fight crime on the streets. Give this gentleman a hand!" and Ray stepped back as James took the floor. The applause was loud from the officers who were familiar with the work the COPS were doing on the street.

"Thank you," James said recognizing many faces. "I see a lot of officers that know me and what the COPS program is about. I take what I do very seriously for those who don't know me. Albert Einstein once said, 'The world is too dangerous to live in, not because of the people who do evil but because of the people who sit and let it happen.' And that's why I'm here this morning. At some point in time, the community is going to have to stand up and get involved, because it is our kids who are dying. Some of us parents have come to realize that if you want a change, you must confront the beast. The officers applauded and James shook his head, his voice becoming a little louder. "I tell my people, we must take to the streets; you must call authorities to report any crime you see. I tell all the parents that it takes a whole village to raise today's child. These kids are not real killers; they're just young human beings that are easily influenced by a combination of things."

James paused for a minute, stuck his hands deep into his pockets and looked up at the room full of officers. He noticed he had everyone's undivided attention. "We're talking about kids as young as 9 and 10 years old. That's not a killer. That's a child with no direction. He's easily influenced because he's confused and probably feeling pressured by his peers. So, I can understand how the false lavish lifestyle of the streets has such a strong influence considering that most of these kids probably came from nothing. I can see how that tough violent nature of rap music could consume a kid as Sergeant Whitehead says because violence is how they mark their territory in today's drug culture. So where do you start if you really want to reach these kids?" He looked around the room, "It starts at home ladies and gentleman, and that's why I do what I do. Get the parents and community involved and then these kids will listen. They are not going to shoot their mother or their buddy's mother." Everybody got a good laugh out of that one, but also everyone knew James did have a point. "Thank you for your time," James said as he stepped back.

"Captain James O'Neal gentlemen," Ray said stepping forward. "Now let's keep rolling so we can wrap this up," Ray said as he put his glasses back on and looked down at some paper work. "The COPS will have police radios, so his people can report whatever crime they see. I want every officer who signed up to work overtime at tonight's game to be here at the station with full riot gear at 5pm. Game starts at 6 pm." Ray shuffled through some more papers. "OK, that looks like that's about it. Oh yeah, hold it." Ray said, as officers were getting ready to leave. "Adams, Spencer!" Ray shouted over the chatter. "Since the two of you are the two new guys on the block, you get the babysitting job at the school."

Laughter was all Spencer heard as his face turned red from embarrassment. "That prick!" he whispered to Adams as he looked up across the room at Ray.

"Is there a problem?" Ray asked staring back at Spencer from the front of the room. Spencer shook his head. "I gotcha," he said sticking his thumb up. "I guess I can baby-sit while I wait on my detective position." Before Ray could respond, Officer Ward had stepped up to ask Ray a question. "Hey Sergeant Whitehead, what's my assignment?" "Hey Tony, listen I'm gonna be spending some time getting Mr. O'Neal set up with radios and instructions. So I want you to head on up to Woodward and keep an eye on Spencer and Adams for me."

"All right," Tony said putting his hat on.

"Yeah, do that for me and I'll pick you up for the game tonight."

"Okay, I'll see ya later then," Tony said

"All right my man, be safe."

****

Officer Adams drove through traffic heading north on Reading Road and Spencer sat quietly in the passenger seat obviously fuming over having to spend his eight hours patrolling high school hallways.

"Yeah I would say that, but what can we do?" Adams said. He always looked to Spencer for every answer. After all, Spencer was the veteran.

"I tell you what. We aren't going up to that high school right now. To hell with that! Turn this damn cruiser around! Let's go check on our boy Pretty Tony at the pool hall, he might have some valuable information for us. Then we'll get some coffee and donuts and head up to the school. I'm not jumping through no hoops for that nigger. He's not the boss of me. I don't care if he does have more stripes than I do." Spencer was pissed off and he cursed and rambled on throughout the whole ride. Adams just drove and listened, just as he always did.

"Make a left on McMillan. Pretty Tony should be standing on the corner or inside the pool hall. Hell, them niggers don't have no jobs other then selling that poison, so he should be there."

All of the sudden there was loud music blaring from a Cadillac speeding past. "What in the hell? Catch up with that Cadillac!" Spencer yelled.

"Damn nigga, pass the blunt!" Sticky screamed over the music.

"Here nigga fire this up," J. Blaze said.

Sticky leaned back in his seat and blazed the blunt up, "This shit is sure nuff the P Funk!" "Turn right on McMillan," Prince said over the music to his cousin Street. Street bent the corner turning on red, puffing on his own blunt as he leaned on the driver's door bobbing his head and singing the lyrics.

Everybody run for cover, ahh shit
Thug life motherfucka duck quick
Thug life forever catch these two shots
Every nigga on my block drop two cops
Dear lord can ya hear me when I cry
When I die I hope I'm strapped, fucked up and high
With my hands on the trigger like a thug nigga
Trying to survive the life of a drug dealer

Out of the corner of his eye, J. Blaze caught the reflection of flashing lights in the glass window of the bank across the street. "One-time! Cut that shit down, hurry up, put that shit out!" Blaze barked to Sticky. He slapped Sticky's hand down when he tried to raise the blunt to his lips. "One-time, nigga, put that shit out! Open the sunroof!" Sticky said coughing a little because Blaze scared the shit out of him.

"Just be cool, and pull over right there." Prince said opening the sunroof.

"Pull up and block their path," Spencer instructed. He unsnapped the safety from his weapon and reached for the door handle at the same time. Adams didn't wait for the Cadillac to come to a complete halt before swerving the cruiser into its path.

"Ah motherfucka!" Street screamed slamming on his brakes to keep from hitting the cruiser. Then another black and white appeared on the scene.

Prince looked out the passenger window evaluating the situation.

"These chumps are about to start fooling. You niggaz be cool."

"Get out of the car!" Spencer yelled being the first to exit the car. He didn't see Sgt. Whitehead's cruiser.

Ray's police cruiser came to a stop blocking Adams from opening his driver door. "No, you get back in YOUR car," Ray said pointing his finger at Spencer. "Get to your post or be relieved of duty for insubordination! You make the call."

Spencer holstered his weapon and looked at Ray with daggers in his eyes.

"I've got a whole room of witnesses plus a Captain who heard me tell you what your assignment was this morning," Ray said. "Now either get in that car without saying a word or I'll be glad to do the paper work."

Spencer was no dummy. He knew when a plate of good ole crow was in order and he ate it with a smile, this time, as he walked back to his cruiser. Adams was much too glad to drive off.

Ray was pissed as he jumped back into his cruiser. "You kids find somewhere to be!" and he jumped back into his cruiser. "I should have burned their asses!" Ray said to James who was riding shotgun.

"You have that problem often?" James asked.

"Only from a few, who can't seem to see these stripes on my sleeve. They're blinded by the color of my skin. Unfortunately racism does live on in the Police Department." After everybody in the Caddy got over the shock of being pulled over and witnessing two white cops being checked by Ray Whitehead, the good weed they were smoking kicked in and the whole car busted out laughing. "Did you see that white cop's face when Whitehead told him to put his damn gun away and get his dumb ass back in the car?" Sticky said. He was the comedian of the family. Prince was holding his stomach, doubled over with laughter. J. Blaze had one hand in the air laughing and saying, "Hold up! Man that white boy was so mad his whole head and police cap turned red. I thought his head was going to pop!" Sticky yelled as everybody started cracking up again. Prince finally manage to speak, "Alright, alright, alright nigga! Damn cut that shit out! We gotta pick Hustleman up and we can't be sitting here laughing all damn morning. Stickyfingers, you can be one silly ass nigga!" Prince said. Street started the Caddy up and pulled into traffic heading towards Burnet Avenue to the hospital. "I'm starving." "Me too," Prince said. "We'll grab some lunch after we pick up Hustleman. We can't afford no more close calls like that this morning, so keep the volume on the low."

The hospital was only a few blocks away, and Hustleman was starting to get impatient waiting outside in the hospital courtyard. He could see the street from the bench he was sitting on resting his weak legs, with his cane in his hand. When Street's Caddy rolled up to the curb, and blew the horn, Hustleman looked but didn't move.

"What's wrong wit him?" Sticky asked.

"He can't walk that good, so come on," Prince said exiting the car.

"Damn you niggas took long enough!" Hustleman said when Prince and Stickyfingers were within earshot.

"Yeah man, we had a small problem. How you feeling?" Prince asked while helping Hustleman up.

"Oh aw-ooooohh shit!" Hustleman screamed through clenched teeth as Prince tried to help him take baby steps. "Sticky! Get his other side. Why you standing there daydreaming?" Prince yelled.

Chapter 10

Cindy was feeling pretty good as she was grooving to some Out-Kast in her Chevy Tahoe on her way home from school. "If roses really smelled like pooh pooh pooh..." is what she was singing as she pulled into their driveway. She didn't want to turn the truck off until her jam went off. "Caroline – I know you like to think your shit don't stank but lean a little bit closer cause roses really smell like pooh pooh poooooh"

Cindy was jamming and rocking back and forth snapping her fingers. "When roses really..." and that's when she saw the flashing police lights in her rearview mirror. She jumped and cursed her luck; because she knew her Dad would have a speech. She tried to outsmart him by jumping out of her truck to apologize, hoping Ray wouldn't carry on outside. But, better luck next time, because Ray was heated and Cindy peeped it as soon as the police cruiser door opened.

"Don't try to jump out now and apologize, because I have told you about that loud ass raggedy stereo." Ray said pointing at Cindy. "Keep it up girl! Just like I giveth that truck, I'll taketh it away."

"Okay Dad, my bad just chill." Cindy said running up and hugging Ray.

"No, don't try it." Ray said shrugging his shoulders to shake her hug off. "I heard that stereo all the way up the street. It goes to show you that I know that music is mesmerizing to you young kids. I slipped right up behind you without trying and you didn't even know it. One of these days you're gonna listen to your ole dad," Ray said lightly thumping Cindy on the head.

"Ouch," Cindy said playfully giving Ray a hug.

"That's how I be thumping them knuckleheads I catch doing the same thing. You just got off lightly"

"Ah come on Dad."

"What girl? I'm in a hurry." Ray said walking up the driveway.

"Can a sista borrow a couple of bucks to go kick it with tonight?"

"You know girl, you're good, real good!" Ray said pulling his wallet out.

"Oh yeah, guess what, guess what Dad?" Cindy suddenly said excited for the first time. "Today, we had the auditorium to ourselves."

"Girl, how much are you talking about?" Ray asked looking through the bills in his wallet. "Here take this twenty."

"Twenty? Come on Dad. Sweeten that just a little bit, please! You know I got to put gas in this big hog you got me." Cindy said with a smile.

"Man, you're good," Ray said snatching another twenty out of his wallet. "But, before you get this other twenty, you got to give me some information." Cindy put her hands on her hips. "Who do I have to rat on now?" Ray smiled dangling the twenty in front of Cindy. "It's an easy one, don't worry. I sent two cops to the school today and I want some juicy info on those two for this twenty I'm holding."

Cindy grabbed the twenty out of his hand. "You mean the two white cops?"

"Yeah! Yeah! Those two."

"What they do? You could've got that info for free dad!" Cindy said laughing. "Cause I was just trying to tell you. Those two white cops caught them smoking weed in the auditorium and started chasing gang members all over the school. They couldn't catch none of them, so they ran them all out the auditorium. That's how we got the auditorium all to ourselves today."

"Oh yeah?" Ray said smiling.

"But that's isn't all. After school, they caught a few of them and had them up against the wall going through their pockets. Mark and I watched the whole thing from the computer lab window."

"You know what?" Ray said turning to go in the house. "That was worth another twenty, but you can't get it."

"That's alright. I got you for two of them. I'm not greedy," Cindy said laughing. Ray grabbed the mail out of the mailbox while Cindy opened the front door and walked in.

"Where's Mom?" Cindy asked taking off her jacket and plopping down on the couch. "She went to pick Gina up from the bank." Ray said as he put the mail down and opened the garage door.

"I think Gina really likes that job at the bank." Cindy said.

"Well, why wouldn't she?" Ray said pulling boxes down off some shelves. "Banks pay good money."

"But it's too stressful." Cindy said flicking buttons on the cable T.V.

"Too many banks have been getting robbed in Cincinnati.

"You can't be scared to live your life Cindy. Plus banks are a lot safer than you think." "Yeah, I hear ya. What are you doing home anyway?" Cindy asked. Ray came out the garage carrying a big duffle bag and a small brown box. "I needed to grab some audio equipment and extra riot helmets." He opened the front door and picked up his gear. "Cindy?"

"Yeah Dad," Cindy said looking up from the television.

"I got to hurry so call Tom and tell him I'm on my way. If you go to the game tonight, be careful and watch your back."

"Sure Dad," Cindy said jumping up and closing the front door for her father. "I wouldn't miss that game for nothing in the world," Cindy said to herself as she looked for the phone to call Uncle Tom.

Ray rolled though rush hour traffic in deep thought like always. He was trying to think of how to stay two steps ahead of every problem that tested his police skills. "How do I prevent these gangs from clashing tonight? Man, this is a tough call," as he pulled up to Tom's house and blew the horn.

The front door instantly opened and Debra stepped out waving to Ray. "Tell Hazel to call me".

"Alright, I'll tell her." Ray yelled through the window.

Tom walked out the house and kissed his wife goodbye. "I'll be home late tonight honey," as he walked to the car and got in.

"Good morning," Ray said giving Tom the rock to hit. "How did you sleep?"

"Like a hunted buffalo with one eye open," Tom said rather seriously.

"Yeah, I feel you," Ray said as he drove toward the police station. "A lot is going on right now isn't it?"

"A little too much, and it's starting to aggravate me."

"What's the matter? Did something else come up that I'm not aware of?" Ray asked turning onto Interstate 71.

"No not really, I'm just concerned about the safety of all the parents that are going to be at this game tonight and secondly, a rumor I heard about Chief O'Donnell and his son in law Spencer."

" I knew it was something." Ray said.

"It's a lot deeper than you think. It seems that a few years ago, when the Chief was Captain, he saved Speencer's career after he was accused of shooting an unarmed suspect."

"Hmm," Ray said as he drove along looking for their exit on the highway. "How did he manage to get past an internal investigation? That doesn't sound right."

"Yeah tell me about it! My resources tell me that the first supervisor on the scene wrote in his report that he didn't see a gun on the suspect. Then he changed the report from not seeing the gun, to finding one behind some trashcans that had the suspect's fingerprints. Everybody seems to be pretty closed mouthed about the whole incident."

"Well all I know is something's not right and I'm not laying down when the time comes for my detective position," Ray said pulling off the exit. "I'm letting you know that right now Tom."

"I didn't expect you to Ray. If you don't mind telling me, where exactly are we going?"

"I thought I would show you the layout of Withrow's Stadium, before we went to the game. That way we'll have some idea at how to best position every officer we put out here tonight."

"That's good thinking."

"You know I was surprised to hear that Spencer and Adams did such a good job today, making their presence known at the school especially after I had to check them early this morning for riding around making traffic stops."

"I suggest you keep an eye on those two," Tom said looking out the window watching the students that stood around.

"I guess the stadium is around back," Ray said as he drove slowly looking at the students himself.

"This school looks like a college campus," Tom said.

"Yeah they've got quite a few tall building here," Ray said looking up through the front windshield of the cruiser. "Look, there's the stadium entrance." Ray drove through the gates. "That's good," he said to himself. "What's good?" Tom asked.

"Oh, I was just thinking that the gate only allows two cars at a time. That's good cause I was thinking of placing a few officers there to look out for cars carrying gang members," Ray said parking the cruiser.

"That sounds good. Maybe place some horse patrols at each end of the driveway."

"Yup, that's what I was thinking too. What about putting a couple surveillance teams on the roof tops?"

"That'll work too. As a matter of fact, I think that's where we should be. That way we'll have a view of everything that's going on."

"Well, I've seen enough," Ray said.

"Let's get to the station and put our plan into effect. It's getting late". Ray looked at his watch before pulling off.

****

Spencer placed a coin in the coffee machine at the precinct cafeteria and was waiting for the cup to fill when a couple of other officers walked in and started to tease him.

"So how was school today Spence?" one officer asked as they both laughed. Spencer joined in on the little joke. "School was fine boys. It was like taking candy from a baby," he said laughing while he reached down and grabbed his cup of coffee.

"Where's your sidekick?" the other officer asked.

"Who, Adams? He's around," Spencer said taking a sip from his coffee. Then Spencer walked out of the cafeteria bumping right into Tom spilling coffee everywhere. "Oh shit, I'm sorry Captain," Spencer said as he attempted to brush off Tom's suit jacket.

"Cut it out. I'm fine."

Ray couldn't help but laugh. "Come on Tom. Officer Spencer if you're on overtime, then we'll be meeting in the conference room in ten minutes. Thank you," Ray said over his shoulder as he and Tom turned the corner. Adams saw what happened from down the hall. He didn't dare laugh but he wanted to as he walked up to his partner. "You and Sgt. Whitehead just love to bump into each other, don't you?"

"Who asked for your opinion? Come on so we aren't the last ones to roll call."

Ray and Tom were looking at a giant picture of Withrow's stadium as the room was filled with officers for tonight's task force. "If we place officers here, here and here, then the crowd control in these areas would be covered," Tom said pointing at the picture.

"And, if any immediate adjustments need to be made, we can make them from our position up here," Ray said pointing to the rooftop.

"Yeah right," Tom said shaking his head up and down.

"Okay then, I think it might work." Ray said clapping his hands and patting his friend on the back.

"We better hope it works or your ass is in more hot water," Tom said. "Well while you brief everyone on what's going on, I'm going to get the surveillance equipment ready."

"Alright then Tom," Ray said. He turned to face the room and started roll call. "Okay gentleman. Let's make this as quick as possible because it's already getting late. I'm going to call out a few names. If you hear your name, come up here. Lieutenant Mike Wilson, Sergeant Phil Thomas, Officer Paul Bentley and Stan Jefferson. You men will be second in command during tonight's operation. You will only answer to me or Captain Safeway via radio transmission from this rooftop," Ray instructed as he turned and pointed to the photo. "There will also be another radio team on this rooftop over here. Security, at times, may feel like they're in a chess match tonight, because I will be moving people all over the place. When I see a problem, I won't hesitate to shift a unit in that direction. We can't afford a blood bath at a high school football game and it's as simple as that. I want fifty men in full riot gear on standby and I want officers to move in packs of five while patrolling the grounds. There's going be a lot of kids and parents present. Lieutenant Wilson," Ray said looking to his right. "I want your unit to cover the front gates. Watch for weapons. Are there any questions so far?" Ray asked the room.

One officer raised his hand.

"Let's hear it," Ray said pointing at the officer.

"Do we have to wear our vests tonight?" the officer asked.

"Look everybody. I understand your bulletproof vests get uncomfortable, so look at your vest tonight as if it were a condom. At first, it may be a little uncomfortable, then you get used to it. In the end, it'll save your life. So, yes everybody in vests tonight. Now anymore questions. We need to be sharp tonight men or asses will be on the line. We've got forty five minutes to get radios, tear gas, shields, batons and whatever gear you need and then report to the garage."

****

Danielle and Prince had decided to kill some time at the mall. Prince had settled down from being so upset over having eight hundred dollars stolen by Spencer.

"Crooked ass cops!" he kept yelling until Danielle was able to calm him down and put him into the car. Now they were sitting in the food court of the mall enjoying some ice cream from Baskin Robbins.

"So you think we'll make a good team huh?" Prince asked.

"That depends on what you're ready for. But I do feel as if we have some chemistry."

"I don't know if my life is ready for a girlfriend right now, but I dig you too. I thought you were about to go away to college?"

"I am," Danielle replied.

"So why you trying to get a relationship going when you know you're leaving?"

"You really want the truth? I think I'm afraid you won't be around when I come back."

Prince looked up from his ice cream.

"Where am I going?"

"You know how your lifestyle goes. Don't play."

"Damn girl, quit burning bread on a nigga. This shit is already scary enough as it is."

"Well you know, I didn't mean it like that."

"I know girl," Prince said playfully. "I also know me, and we need to be getting out of here, 'cause people are waiting on us."

"Everybody's not at the school yet." Danielle said looking at her watch. "Come on girl and stop being lazy!"

"I'm not being lazy! My legs are tired from walking around this mall," Danielle said slowly getting up. Prince walked up behind her and put his arm around her to help her up. "You want me to carry you?" Prince joked with her. "No silly, but you can drive," she said handing him the keys.

****

Mark was still at school in the computer lab. His intentions were to wait until after school, when it was much quieter, and he had enough peace of mind to sit down and e-mail his Uncle Ben. He was in deep thought wondering what type of mission his uncle was on this time and what country he was in when suddenly his thoughts were interrupted by a loud roar of motorcycles pulling in out back. Mark jumped up and ran to the window to investigate. Several cars and students were starting to arrive and get a little rowdy. He never went to any of the football games, but Cindy had told him how wild they got sometimes. So he watched with interest for a little while until he sat back down to finish e-mailing his uncle.

"Dear Uncle Ben", he typed. "I've been waiting on your e-mail. It sounds like you're all right. I'm praying for your safety and speedy return home from the war. I'll be graduating soon and I hope you make it. I haven't decided on a college yet. Maybe when you get home, you can help me. Your mom is fine. She's still called the hall monitor from hell :) at the school. Right now she's helping my Dad with his activist work. They've formed a group called "Citizens on Patrol" and they're helping the police run gang members off the street corners. I met a new friend. Her name is Cindy. I'll introduce you two if you get back in time to catch my graduation. She's real cool and doesn't make fun of me. Well, I gotta go. You be safe.

Your nephew, Mark."

He sent the e-mail and shut the computer down. Then he jumped up to take another peek out of the window to see what was going on. The roar of more motorcycles came around the corner of the building. Mark looked on with excitement as he watched the pretty bikes ride past. "Wow! Look at that Kawasaki," Mark said to himself. "That baby is bad. I wish I could be a gang member."

The bus transporting the Woodward team pulled up. The team started filing out the door to a screaming and yelling crowd of students and cheerleaders. More Ruff Riders were pulling up with sparkling brand new bikes of all kinds. Every set of Riders from every neighborhood had been told to meet up for tonight's game and they were showing up, ready for whatever.

J. Blaze was standing on the side of the bus talking to one of the cheerleaders, when he heard a car with a loud stereo pull around the corner. "Hold up baby. I hear my nigga coming around the corner!"

"Hey Blaze!" Sticky and Hitman yelled as they trotted up to him. "Where's everybody at?" Sticky asked.

"I thought I just heard Street pull in. Let's walk around here," Blaze said moving around the bus.

"There he is!" Sticky said pointing at Street.

Street hit the horn when he saw his crew. "Here I come!" Street yelled out the window. "Listen girl, I'll get up with you after the game. I gotta holla at my boys," Street told the little honey he was talking to.

"Alright Street. You ain't playing are you?" she asked.

Street reached over and popped the red sex bracelet she had on her wrist. "Now do you believe me?" he asked.

She lit up like a Christmas tree and clapped her hands. "I'll be ready baby," and she walked away popping that thang.

Street leaned back inside the Cadillac and pulled up slowly to where J. Blaze and the crew were standing.

"What's up kid?" Blaze said giving Street some dap.

"Where's everybody at?" Sticky said. "It looks like everybody else from all the other sets are here but ours, judging from all the bikes."

"I just passed Prince on Reading Road," Street said getting out of the car. "So he should be here shortly. Yo Hitman," Street yelled spotting his boy and Lowdown kicking it with some new cat. "Who's he?" Street asked pointing.

"Oh this is my homey Hicks from around the way," Lowdown said as they walked up.

"Yeah? How come I haven't seen him before?" Street asked.

Sticky and J. Blaze spoke up at the same time. "Lighten up Street. He's with Lowdown, so he's cool."

Hitman looked up and saw Prince approaching. He was thankful to see him because Prince was the only one who could calm Street down when he got started. "Look," Hitman said breaking the tension. "There's Prince right there."

****

"Alright everybody. Listen up," Ray shouted. "In about forty five minutes, this stadium is going to be full of people that are depending on us to keep them safe and I intend on doing just that. All officers in plain clothes, I want you to blend in and keep your eyes and ears open. Wilson, you take your crew right now and secure the entrance. Remember if anyone looks suspicious, pull them aside immediately and search thoroughly."

"Gotcha Sarge. Come on boys," Wilson said to his crew as they moved out.

Ray looked around for a second then called Bentley. "Bentley, I want your crew to secure the grounds and I'll move you around for crowd control."

"Sure Sergeant Whitehead."

"Make sure each officer has two pairs of cuffs and a full canister of mace," Ray said. "Now Thomas, I want your team to stay in the shadows, since you've got the riot squad. Just make sure, if there's a need, you've got rubber bullets, tear gas or whatever ready to go. I just pray to God, we don't need any of this stuff." When everyone was in position, Ray turned and looked to Tom and Tony. "I guess we better get up on that roof and get ourselves into position."

Ray made a radio check after they set up the cameras and video equipment that offered the best view of the field. "Here Tom," Ray said handing him binoculars. "Look through these and tell me if I adjusted them right."

Tom grabbed the binoculars and kneeled down on one knee looking around the stadium. "They're fine, I think I might hold onto these."

"Good, okay now Tony how's your end?"

"I've got this baby on ready," Tony said tapping his camera.

"Radio check," Ray said into his radio.

"Team one in position, sir. Team two in position, sir. Team three in position, sir," came the responses.

"Okay keep your eyes open," Ray said.

The stadium was beginning to fill and as expected, parents sporting their schools' colors were filling the seats on both sides. The announcer was testing the PA system for tonight's play by play. Sports broadcasters from every station would be in attendance to cover this blockbuster of a game.

****

"Everybody on the bus!" Coach Andrews yelled looking toward his three star players.

"Okay Coach. Alright y'all it's show time!" Blaze said to his crew as they all hugged and passed around dap.

"Yeah, that's right! It's show time!" Sticky yelled.

"You brothers be safe on that field and remember we got your back," Prince said as he waved his arms around indicating everybody. "We're all family and we're going to represent like family tonight. Now get out of here. Let's do this shit." Prince turned and snapped his fingers and the bikes behind him roared to life as every Ruff Rider prepared to leave. "Remember, no guns. There's gonna be cops everywhere."

"Bullshit! I got my shit in the trunk." Street said.

"And that's where it better stay. Now let's get outta here," Prince said. "Hustleman, you ride with us in the caddy. We gotta keep an eye on you." "Alright," Hustleman said limping with his cane over to the car. "Hey Yo, T-Baby." Prince turned and said to one of the Riders on his bike.

"Yeah my nigga," T-Baby said riding up along the side of the caddy.

"Put Kenya and China Doll on a bike and Danielle you ride with me." China Doll and Kenya instantly ran and jumped on the back of the first bike they reached. "You don't have to tell us twice," Kenya said as she wiggled her behind on the seat.

"LET'S RIDE!"

****

The Woodward bus was noisy. The team was getting pumped. The bad blood between the schools had everyone fired up. J. Blaze and Stickyfingers were leading the charge.

"Who we be!"

"Ruff Riders!" everybody screamed.

"Who we be!" they yelled again.

"Ruff Riders!" everybody screamed.

"That's what I'm talking about!" J. Blaze said as he stood up. "Listen up everybody! I got something I wanna say to the Coach."

Coach Andrews turned around in his seat to watch J. Blaze walking up the aisle with a jacket in his hand.

"Coach, you're like family and you've always been there for each one of us at one time or another when we've had problems. So tonight we want to give you this Woodward jacket, because you're a Rider too in our book!" Everybody started clapping as Blaze and Coach Andrews gave each other a hug.

"Thanks everybody," the Coach said and put the jacket on. It was a school jacket, but it was a Woodward Rider's personalized jacket, that only Riders wore.

The bus took the next exit and Stickyfingers looked out the window as Withrow's lighted stadium came into view. "We're here!" he announced

"Damn look! It looks like the whole police force is here too," Hitman said as the bus passed police cars and vans parked on the street. Suddenly a loud roar of motorcycles made everybody look out the windows. They could hear Kenya and China Doll screaming as they flew past. "Street, stay behind the bus. I want them niggas to go through first and park their bikes before we get there. I wanna lay back here and slowly pull through, so we can get a good look at some of these Warriors' faces through these tinted windows," Prince said.

"Yeah, I want to get a real good look at them niggaz too." Hustleman said from the back seat. The bus pulled into the driveway with Street just behind.

"Damn! Look at all these cops!" Fats said. "I don't feel so bad now about not bringing my pistol with all these cops around. I know them niggaz ain't got one neither."

"You recognize anybody yet, Hustleman?" Prince asked as they cruised by plenty of niggaz with red bandanas wrapped around their heads. Some had Warrior jackets on and some just had t-shirts on.

"Naw, I don't see no familiar faces yet." They cruised by car after car of niggaz hanging out. "Wait! Him, that nigga right there talking! He was one of them!"

"What you want me to do? I got my heater under the seat." Street said ready to stop.

"Come on nigga! What we gonna do? Shoot the nigga right here in front of the police? Just find a parking space close by," Prince said.

****

In the meantime Ray was on the roof waiting and watching, when the Withrow team burst out of the building running into the stadium.

> *"The home team is entering the stadium bringing with them the number one defense in the city. Yes sir, its the number one ranked defense versus Woodward's number one ranked offense. It looks like we may be in for a treat tonight ladies and gentleman."*

"My goodness people are still coming in and I don't see much room left in the stands on either side for people to sit," Tom said looking through his binoculars.

"Yeah, I'm peeping that too," Ray said swinging his zoom camera from left to right trying to find a face to take a picture of.

"Ooh," Tony said

"What's wrong?" Ray said looking over at Tony wondering if he saw something. "The Woodward Riders just took the field."

"That's what you were talking about?" Ray said peeping back through his camera. "We're not here to watch the game, Tony!"

"Wait a minute, hold up," Ray said. "I think I've found a familiar face."

"Where? Who?" Tom said pointing his binoculars in the direction Ray had his camera pointed.

"It's the one I had words with at the school. I think he is the leader of the Riders at Woodward." Ray said taking pictures.

"Well, show me who on earth you are talking about," Tom said as he continued looking.

"He's in the fourth row from the top, blue bandana on sitting between two girls."

"You mean the one talking on the cell phone right now?"

"Yeah, yeah that's him," Ray said as he continued to take pictures.

****

The Woodward team began to warm up on the sidelines, but Blaze, Sticky and Hitman sat on the team bench talking to Prince on Blaze's cell phone.

"Yeah man! Hustleman spotted one of the niggaz already."

"One down, two to go," Prince said

"That's good, that's real good," Blaze said looking around, himself.

"Well y'all niggaz take care of your business and do them niggaz on that football field," Prince said.

"All right my brother," and Blaze flipped his phone shut and placed it in his shoe. "Hustleman done already spotted one of them niggaz."

"Oh yeah, so what's up?" Sticky asked.

"Ain't nothing up. We just want to know what they look like. They'll get theirs later," Blaze said.

"Alright guys, the coin toss," Coach Andrews said looking at his players and interrupting their conversation. "Or did you three forget that we have a football game tonight?"

"Oh, oh yeah, our bad Coach," Sticky said strapping on his helmet.

"Well we can't start the game without the captain to make the coin toss," the Coach screamed as the three of them trotted to the middle of the field. "Okay, everybody get ready," Ray whispered into the radio. "Here we go."

"Woodward has won the coin toss and they've elected to receive. Well, it looks like we get to see that high-powered offense of Woodward's first in tonight's match up."

Prince stood in his seat and looked around the stands, and then he sat back down and looked over at Hustleman. "Where's Street?"

Everybody looked around at each other, and Fats said, "I bet that nigga is up to no good."

Prince jumped up. "Come on we gotta go find that nigga, before he does something stupid. You girls stay here just in case he comes back."

"Look something's up," Ray shouted as he watched Prince and about five of his boys move out.

"Unit A! Unit A!" Ray shouted into the radio.

"This is Unit A," Spencer said.

"Spencer, there's five thugs moving your way wearing Riders jackets and bandanas. Keep your eye on them."

"I see 'em," Spencer radioed back. "The boys from Woodward. Yeah, that's them."

"Don't let them out of your sight," Ray shouted into the radio.

The game started with Woodward at the twenty-yard line. There was plenty of trash talking as Woodward broke the huddle and J.Blaze surveyed the field.

"This is Woodward's first possession and Woodward's quarterback breaks the huddle looking all business."

"Where did they go? Tom do you see them?" Ray asked.

"Not yet," Tom said peering through his binoculars.

"Are you getting this on video or are you still watching the game?" Ray asked Tony.

"Red 48, green 32," J.Blaze pointed at Sticky to go in motion. "Black 14 hut one Go!"

"J. Blaze sweeps to his right, stops and plants his feet and let's a bullet go down the field. Hitman catches the ball in stride at the fifty-yard line before he's tackled immediately. What a throw and catch by this Woodward team! Looks like they came to play!"

"Come on! Huddle up!" J. Blaze yelled.

"Good catch Hitman!" Sticky said slapping Hitman on his helmet.

"Alright everybody," J Blaze said as he kneeled down in the huddle, "this is where we show these boys. Double Reverse on two, ready Break!"

"J.Blaze brings his team to the line of scrimmage, he looks over the defense and calls the play. 69 Twist, 69 Twist, Blue56, hut one- hut two,Go!"

Street had found a dark corner to hide in behind the Warriors' bleachers. He laid and waited until he heard the loud sounds of the crowd cheering. He crept in a crouched position, until he was under the bleachers and pointing his 9mm at the backs of the three Warriors he felt were responsible and pulled the trigger. POW! POW! POW! Spencer had him in his sight, a direct shot at Street's back. He aimed and fired. POW! After firing three rounds from his 9mm, Street had dropped to the ground and into the weeds as Officer Spencer's shot bit a chunk of wood from the bleacher seat he had vacated just seconds before.

Gunfire suddenly erupted from the top of the bleachers from Warrior gang members returning fire. Spencer ducked back for cover, tripping and falling on his back. Street squeezed through the bleachers and disappeared, leaving the gun with no prints, behind.

At the sound of gun fire, all hell broke loose and both gangs went at each other simultaneously. Police began firing canisters of tear gas into the sea of people fighting in the middle of the football field. Everything was completely foggy and police were running around chasing gang members and beating them down on the spot. Street saw everything and cut around the edge of the chaos and ran into Sergeant Whitehead helping two ladies to safety. He stopped dead in his tracks, not because of Sergeant Whitehead, but because he saw two Warriors coming from behind with pistols drawn.

Tom was just coming to assist, when he noticed Ray helping Hazel and Gina to the school building. He ran as fast as he could screaming, "This way! This way!" Just as the words left his mouth, three shots rang out. Ray and Hazel shook with the impact and tumbled hard to the ground, dragging Gina down with them. Initially, Tom didn't see Ray and Hazel fall, not until he had fired several rounds from his snub nose .38 at the two gang members from Withrow who were shooting in his direction. Once Tom realized that Ray and Hazel had been hit he kneeled on the ground crying, not believing the fate of his closest friends. That's when the hard rain started to fall. Tom closed his friends' eyes and stood up watching the blood mix with rainwater. He knew now that it was time for a change. There was just too much killing going on.

CHAPTER 11

Ray had stopped taking pictures as he noticed the dark clouds moving in. "Just great guys! I think we're about to get rained on," Ray said to Tom and Tony.

"Might be for the best. I've sure got a funny feeling these gangs are going to go at it before this game is over," Tom said.

The Woodward Riders need five yards to keep this drive alive. The crowd is starting to get into the game J. Blaze steps up to the line, calls the play; awaits the snap, drops back. It's a quarterback draw up the middle and he's got it.

Sticky ran over and picked J. Blaze up. "Good run nigga, good run!" J.Blaze pulled Sticky closer. "I know who else shot Hustleman." J. Blaze said as they walked back to the huddle.

"Who?" Sticky asked.

"I'll tell you. Hold up and let's call this next play."

"Huddle up! Huddle up!" J. Blaze yelled to his team. "Alright everybody! We're in striking distance of the end zone. Let's go for it." Blaze looked over at Sticky.

"Just get open nigga, cause I'm coming at you."

That was an excellent call and run by Woodward's quarterback J. Blaze. I wonder what he's got up his sleeve now as he looks over the defense. "Red forty-two! Blue Green Hut!" J. Blaze takes a three-step drop.

Sticky made a double move and then shot past the defender. Blaze saw the separation and let a tight spiral fly in Sticky's direction. Sticky leaped to get it and out of nowhere, a Withrow defender hit him so hard that he lost his breath when he hit the ground.

"Oh shit!" Sticky moaned from the ground. Blaze and Hitman ran over to pick him up. "Wait a minute. Call time out and let me lay here for a second. I can't breathe."

"Come on nigga," Blaze said holding out his hand. "You just got the wind knocked out of you."

"That nigga hit me hard," Sticky said walking slowly to the sideline.

"He probably was trying to kill you too," Blaze said.

"One of their lineman told me on the field that their two cornerbacks are the ones who shot Hustleman."

"Now why would he tell you that?" Hitman asked.

"I don't know, and I really don't care, but I'm glad he did." Blaze said putting on his helmet.

"Time out!" the referee shouted

"Come on! We got some business to take care of," Blaze said.

After that big time hit Stickyfingers just took, let's see if J.Blaze calls his number again.

J. Blaze brought his team to the line of scrimmage. He looked left at Hitman and pulled on his jersey, and then he turned right and tapped his helmet in Stickyfingers' direction. "Team down! Ready! Set!" All of a sudden shots rang out. J. Blaze ducked. "Down, gunshots!" he screamed.

More shots were fired and all hell broke loose. People were running and screaming across the field.

"Nigga get up! We got to get outta here!" Sticky yelled as he and Hitman grabbed J. Blaze. They all took off running.

Ray snatched up the radios, "Unit A, what's your location?"

"Jumping Jesus!" Tom yelled looking in the direction of the shots.

"Shots fired! Far end of the stadium in the Warriors' bleachers." Ray shouted into the radio. "Keep that camera rolling, Tony!" Ray said as he snapped pictures.

The football players were fighting and you could see helmets flying back and forth. Students were fighting in all the chaos and Coach Andrews was doing his best to pull his players out of the madness.

Three more shots were fired. "The shots came from the top of the bleachers. We'd better get down there!" Tom yelled.

"Give me those binoculars! My wife and daughter are in those bleachers!" Ray looked for Hazel and Gina, but there was too much confusion. "Come on," Ray said as he took off for the stairwell leading down.

Ray hit the steps two at a time when he busted through the door leading out back. People were running and falling all over the place. Cindy heard the gunshots as she was waiting in line to park outside the stadium. When she saw a lot of students start to run her way, she frantically looked for her cell phone. She was concerned about her mother and sister in the stadium. She dialed Gina's number and got a busy signal. She tried again and it started to ring. When Gina answered, all Cindy could hear was screams and chaos in the background.

"Hello! Hello! Gina!" Cindy screamed.

"Cindy? Is that you?" Gina asked.

"Is that Cindy?" Hazel yelled as she was fighting the crowd trying to get down the stadium stairs. "Tell her to stay away from here! It's a madhouse!" Hazel screamed.

"Gina! Where's Daddy? Find Daddy!" Cindy kept screaming.

"We're trying! But they're fighting and shooting everywhere!" Gina screamed into the phone.

"Ray! Ray!" Hazel started yelling when she saw her husband coming towards them.

"There's Daddy! We're fine now." Gina said to Cindy.

"Don't hang up, until you get out of there. I'm stuck outside in the parking lot."

"Hazel! Gina! This way! Follow me!" Ray yelled. Suddenly a crash of thunder hit. Ray pushed his wife and daughter back toward the way he came. He saw Tom waving his arms motioning for them to follow. At that moment, a heavy rain began to fall and Hazel slipped on the wet pavement. Ray bent down to pick her up and out of the corner of his eye, he spotted Street running like a mad man in his direction. As if in slow motion, he saw two Warriors chasing Street. Ray saw them take aim at Street and heard more gunfire.

Gina lay buried under her parents' dead bodies. Tom kneeled on the ground crying as he tried to free Gina. The last volley of shots had everyone bobbing and weaving through the sea of running people.

Cindy's head was spinning, as she jumped out of her truck and started running against the flow of the crowd. "I know they didn't shoot my family! I just know it!" Cindy kept repeating to herself as she ran in the direction of the stadium.

****

"Oh shit!" Prince yelled ducking every time he heard a shot. "We got to get everybody outta here!" he said to Dino, Fats and Hustleman.

"Look, there's Prince running this way! Yo! Yo! Over here!" Sticky said.

"Listen up! We got to find Street and get the hell outta here! These niggaz got guns!" Prince said. "Come on, let's go! Jump on the back of somebody's bike and beat it!" Prince yelled. He looked at Fats. "You go find Street and I'll go get the Caddy. Meet me right back here."

"Alright," Fats said and he was gone. Prince turned to run and knocked Cindy over. She looked up and rolled her eyes recognizing Prince. Without saying a word, she got back up and took off towards the flashing lights on the other side of the football field.

"Fats," Street whispered to his cousin as he walked past the spot where he was hiding.

Fats stopped and looked over at a dark hole.

"Yeah Bro," Street said.

"Nigga, get your ass outta there and come on! Hurry up!" Fats said pulling at his brother's shirt.

****

Tom panicked for a moment thinking Gina had been shot because she wasn't moving, but she was breathing.

"An ambulance is on the way sir," Tony said.

"Spencer! Find me a blanket and some fresh water! Tom yelled looking around. He held Gina's shivering body, trying to keep her from shaking so bad. The rain had stopped and Tom was thankful to see two ambulances coming in the back entrance. "It's gonna be all right baby," Tom whispered to Gina as he held her in his arms. Gina was in total shock and didn't hear a word he said. The blank look on her face made it obvious.

The paramedics were strapping Gina to the bed. "She's in shock Captain," the paramedic said. "She needs a doctor."

"Hey! Hey! Hey!" Cindy screamed running toward the ambulance.

"Hurry up! That's her sister running this way." Tom said.

When Cindy made it to the ambulance, she ran right past the covered bodies of her dead parents. She wanted to know who was in the ambulance. "Gina! Gina!" Cindy screamed.

"Hold her back Officer Spencer!" Tom shouted.

"I'm trying," Spencer said.

"Help him Adams!" Tom shouted. Cindy was kicking, scratching and screaming. "Now you got to calm down Cindy. I've got something to tell you." Tom kept telling her.

"What! What! What! Cindy said screaming and crying. "What do you have to tell me?"

Tom looked at her and just said it. "Your parents have been murdered."

Her whole body went limp in Spencer's arms as she blacked out completely. "Hold her up! Call another ambulance!" Tom yelled leaping forward. Tom looked at Cindy wishing he could just faint like that and let somebody else be in his shoes. "Officer Ward," Tom yelled over his shoulder.

"Yeah Captain."

"Go up on that roof and take every piece of equipment to the station. Give the film and video to the lab and tell them I said I want photos delivered to my home in 24 hours."

"Yes sir," and Tony took off running.

CHAPTER 12

Word had traveled fast throughout the 'hood about Street shooting four of the top players in the Warriors outfit. "Man, did you hear what Street did last night? That young nigga shot up six niggas at the game last night!" someone said to another as they chilled on the corner. "Oh yeah," the other brother replied. Then later on that same brother told another. "Man did you hear what that crazy ass Street did?"

"Nah, man, what did he do?" the brother asked with genuine interest as they shared a pint of Wild Irish Rose on the corner.

"Ah, man, Jimmy told me the young nigga just pulled out two 9mm's and started shooting up all them Warriors."

"For real, man? You bullshitting, right?"

"Man, I swear," the brother said literally jumping up and down. "They said the nigga emptied both clips. Kilt about ten niggaz and split."

"Damn, that young nigga is a fool."

"Yeah man, he got heart." That was the ghetto morning report and by the end of the day as the story got passed along, Street became a legend overnight in the 'hood.

Come the next morning, the streets were busy with hustlers out on the block peddling their products. Hustleman leaned against one of the project buildings smoking a Newport and watching the morning's activities. Everybody but Prince was in the clubhouse crashed out, exhausted from all the drama and confusion from the night before. Hustleman checked his watch and then flicked his cigarette butt to the curb. He grabbed his cane and started limping toward the apartment when he looked up the street and noticed a bunch of cars pull in and park. He stopped to get a better look and saw a bunch of white people start to crowd the sidewalk in front of another apartment. More cars kept coming and more white folks joined the others. "What are all these white folks doing down in the 'hood?" Hustleman thought to himself as he limped towards a parked car to have a seat. Suddenly, a man jumped on a bullhorn and woke the whole neighborhood up. "You must stop selling drugs to the children," James O'Neal said into the bullhorn.

"What the hell?" Hustleman said to no one in particular as he stood up to get a better look. "This cat is tripping."

"The police are coming to confiscate any illegal drugs found on the premises. You will all go to jail," he yelled again through the bullhorn. Suddenly the apartment's front door burst open and out came Lowdown and his crony, Hicks. They ran across the front lawn right past all the white protesters who were screaming and cheering at the sight of the two half scared drug dealers.

"That's right run! The police are coming!" James yelled into his bullhorn. Lowdown and Hicks came flying down the street towards Hustleman so fast he couldn't help but laugh at those two niggaz.

"Yo, that white man is crazy!" Lowdown said bending over trying to catch his breath.

"What happened?" Hustleman asked laughing.

"Man, all I know is we were sitting there chopping up some dope and all these cars starting pulling up. Next thing we know ol' boy hit us with the bullhorn, talking about the police was coming. Shit man, I had to bail outta there!"

"We should run they ass up outta here," Hustleman said looking up the street.

"Yup, we sure should, 'cause they're making the block hot!" Hicks said.

"Lowdown, go inside and wake them niggaz up," Hustleman said.

****

Danielle lay quietly next to Prince listening to the birds chirp outside her window. She rolled over into his arms, laying her head on his chest. Prince arm went automatically around the soft body lying next to him. He then opened his eyes and focused on Danielle's soft body.

"Good morning," she whispered.

"Hey baby," Prince said in his own deep whisper.

"What would you like for breakfast?" she asked.

"I'm thinking about some more of you," he said caressing her body.

"Oh no, you've got to give me a chance to recuperate after last night's performance." Prince smiled at the thought. "Okay then, I'll take bacon and eggs," he said playfully pushing her off his chest.

"I'm gonna go jump in the shower and then cook breakfast," she said crawling out of bed.

"I'll take a shower while you're doing your thing in the kitchen." Prince laid back thinking about this really fly crib of Danielle's parents. "Boy oh boy," he thought, "I was sure sleeping on this chick. This girl got the life, the type of house only brothers like me dreams of living in!" He wanted to check out more of the house, so he found his underwear and slipped them on. As he sat on the end of the bed he thought for the first time about what happened last night. "Four cats dead! Street has gone and lost his damn mind. Damn that shit was crazy!" he said quietly to himself. "Shit's about to get hot and we got to lay low!" he thought to himself when his cell phone rang.

"Yeah, what's up?"

"Yo, it's me Fats," came the voice on the other end.

"Yeah, Fats what's going on?" Prince said lying back on the bed.

"Dig cuz, like I know you told us to lay low but we got some problems over here."

Prince sat up. "What kind of problems Fats?"

"That James O'Neal was over here with his bullhorn and a bunch of white people early this morning. We threw rocks, bottles, bricks and anything we could get our hands on at their asses and they ran off. Now the police are sweating us."

"Damn, I can't leave you niggaz alone for five minutes! Listen, get everybody in the house. Where's Street?"

"He's up stairs, you want me to go get him?"

"Nah, just go tell him I said to get out here and pick me up. I'm at Danielle's." Prince said.

Danielle stood in the doorway wrapped in a towel, looking very sexy. "What's wrong?" she asked. Prince flipped the phone on the bed and laid his head back down.

"Those niggaz, with that damn bullshit is what's wrong," he said looking up at the ceiling.

Danielle went over and sat on the bed. "Can I say something?"

"Sure, speak your mind."

"Has it dawned on you yet, that your cousin shot four people last night and you're hiding him from the law which can also get you involved?" she asked looking into his eyes.

"Yeah, I know but that's how the game goes on the street. You do me and I'll do you. That's a fair exchange on the streets and that's the law we live by."

"I understand all of that, just like I understand your commitment to your way of life. But I don't understand why you're willing to go to jail for something you didn't have anything to do with."

"Because real niggaz don't sell out on their friends and I'm a real nigga."

"You would choose your friends over us?"

"No, but I'm not turning my back on my people."

"Well that's a little too serious for me to be a part of. I'm on my way to college Prince."

"Well, don't let me hold you back. You've got your life to live and I've got mine.

"So it's like that?"

"How else can it be, Danielle?" he said getting up from the bed. "Look at all of this! It's your reality not mine."

"It could be yours too, if you want it to be."

"No baby, I can get mine on my own," he said while buttoning his shirt.

"Where're you going?"

"I've got business I need to take care of."

Danielle got up and walked into the other room without saying another word. Prince made a few more phone calls, before he slipped on his shoes to wait for Street.

Street, Stickyfingers, and J. Blaze rode in silence while driving toward Danielle's place. Street was the first to break the silence. "That chump O'Neal is starting to get on my last nerve."

"Man, it looks like everybody has been getting on your last nerve lately," Sticky said laughingly. J. Blaze laughed along with Sticky.

"Damn nigga, you got jokes this morning don't you?" Street said.

"Alright, chill out, before you start arguing," Blaze said from the back seat. "Turn left at the corner, Her house is on the right."

"They sure got some fly cribs up here," said Sticky looking around.

"Which house is it?" Street asked, slowing down.

"Right there, right there!" Blaze yelled, pointing. Street cut a sharp turn and whipped the Caddy into the driveway of a big brick house with a beautiful redwood door and blew the horn.

The door opened and slammed hard behind Prince. He turned and looked at the door and called Danielle a simple something under his breath as he ran over and jumped in the front seat after Sticky got into the back seat with Blaze.

"What's up with you niggaz this morning? Why can't you lay low like I asked you to? Come on drive! Get me away from this house!"

"Having girl problems, I see," said Street laughing.

"Ha, Ha, Ha, my ass! It was probably your ass who started the shit with the police this morning!" Prince said accusingly.

"Nah, it wasn't him this time," Blaze said from the back seat. "That would be Lowdown and his boy Hicks."

"Say what?" Prince asked turning around in his seat to face Blaze. "I just let that nigga in the gang yesterday and he's causing problems already. That nigga is starting to make me wonder about him.

"He's been making me wonder all along," said Street.

"Wait a minute! You ain't got no room to talk! It's your silly ass' fault we're hot as fire crackers right now!" Prince said looking again back at Street.

"Man, don't be trying to hate on me because I was down for taking revenge for my brother! I'm down for the brotherhood and I would've done the same thing for any other nigga in this car if a nigga tried to take you out!" Street said.

"Well since you started the job, you realize we've got to finish it, and soon, but tell the truth nigga, you were on something last night weren't you?" Prince asked.

"Yeah, I ain't going to lie. I had a hit of that ecstasy and when Hustleman pointed that nigga out, and the more I thought about it, the madder I got. So I came back, got my nine from under the seat and carried out my mission."

"Yeah, nigga you sure carried out your mission that's for sure! You scared the shit out of Blaze! He was suppose to be hiking the damn ball. When I looked over, the nigga looked like he was trying to crawl between the lineman's legs," Sticky said.

"Fuck you," Blaze said as everyone started laughing.

"Blaze was ducking," Street said still laughing.

"Yeah, man! Me and Hitman had to go pick his scary ass up," Sticky said.

"All right nigga, don't make me play the dozens," Blaze said getting serious.

"Okay, okay, my nigga I was just jugging with cha," laughed Sticky.

"Believe it or not I didn't think I was gonna make it out of there. 'Cause after I bust on them niggaz, I looked back and saw Officer Spencer beaming down on me, so I dropped to the ground just as the shots went off," Street said.

"Damn Spencer again. Well at least we don't have to worry about Whitehead any more," said Prince.

"That's what I was getting to. When Spencer fired, he tripped and fell. That was my chance to make a move, so I squeezed through the bleacher seats and got up to start running. That's when two Warriors spotted me, so I started up the track ducking in and out of the crowd 'cause I knew they were trying to get a good shot at me. Then it started raining and it was perfect because that tear gas on the field was burning my lungs. As soon as I made my break, I looked up and saw Sgt. Whitehead step onto the track right in front of me and that's when those niggaz started shooting. I didn't stop to see who got hit and I'm glad, because a plain-clothes cop immediately dropped those two chumps that were chasing me. When I saw that, I disappeared into the crowd," Street said.

"That must have been when you ran into us," Prince said. "Damn boy, you got balls the size of coconuts!" and they all laughed.

When they finally reached Club House, everything seemed pretty quiet. "Don't look like we had problems over here," Prince said.

"Look up the street at all the glass and rocks," said Sticky.

"Uh, yeah I see now," Prince said as he walked up the sidewalk. Hustleman opened the door to the apartment when he heard everyone arrive. Prince walked in looking around. "How you feeling my nigga?" he asked Hustleman.

"A little sore, but I'm making progress. I'll be off this cane in no time."

"Where's everybody?" Prince asked as they walked into the kitchen and took a seat at the table.

"Went to get some fast food somewhere. Those niggaz got hungry after all the drinking last night," replied Hustleman.

"Well, since it's just us, I guess I'll let you know what I've got planned. I called a meeting for tonight with all the top Riders of the organization. Now that we're at war with these niggaz, we need to pool all our resources together," stated Prince.

"You thinking about bringing all the Ruff Riders together as one?"

asked Street.

"Yup, that's exactly what I'm thinking. I believe it'll work if these niggaz don't get greedy," Prince replied.

"I'm wit it. Shit, that's how the Warriors got strong, by pulling together their whole organization," said Sticky.

"Well, I'm gonna see how these niggaz talking tonight," Prince said while walking to the fridge for a cold drink. Lowdown and Hicks had walked over to White Castle's for something to eat. Between the both of them they had managed to come up with a dollar and some change, just enough to get them two little burgers apiece. "Man, I'm still hungry. Those little bitty ass burgers didn't do shit for me," said Hicks.

"Well nigga, you should've had more than forty cents in your pockets. Then you could've gotten more. Now come on," demanded Lowdown.

"Let's snatch a purse," Hicks said as they started walking up Hamilton Avenue.

"You can snatch a purse if you want to. But shit is already hot as it is and I don't feel like running from the cops today."

"Yeah, you're right. We've already been chased by that O'Neal guy once today."

"Come on. Let's go over to the United Dairy and see who's hanging out." Prince sat in the living room watching television when the phone rang. "Yeah, who is it?" Prince asked snatching up the phone.

"Yo, baby boy, it's T-Baby. What time are we meeting tonight?"

"Hey, my brother, I'm sorry. What's up? How about eight o'clock right here?

"Sounds like gravy baby boy, I'll be there."

Prince hung up the phone and clapped his hands with excitement.

"It's on for tonight!"

Lowdown and Hicks were standing on the corner when Ray-Ray the neighborhood stickup kid started coming their way. "Look, here comes Ray-Ray. I'll bet you he's got a lick set up. Ray-Ray keeps a hustle. "What's up Ray-Ray?" Lowdown shouted, slappin' him five.

"What's up fellas? What you niggaz up to?"

"Out here on the grind. What you got cooking for the paper chase?" asked Lowdown.

"Nothing at the moment. I just came out the house." Ray-Ray answered.

"Well, we're trying to get some money together. Our pockets are like on 'E' man and I'm starving right about now," said Hicks.

"Look," Lowdown said pointing at Mr. O'Neal who was walking up the street with his sister Maryann O'Bannon.

"Damn, don't Ms. O'Bannon's ever take a day off? We see her in school all week chasing us through the halls and now she's out here chasing us off the block with her brother!" said Hicks.

"I got an idea. Ray-Ray you got a burner on you?" asked Lowdown.

"I keeps my pistol on me playa," said Ray-Ray patting his shirt where it was tucked away in his pants.

"Since O'Neal wants to sweat us all the time, lets rob his ass," said Lowdown. They thought it through as James and Maryann walked into the Juke Box Tavern right on the next corner.

"Well, what you think?" Lowdown asked the other two.

"Well, alright, I usually work alone but this once I'll roll with you niggaz," said Ray-Ray hesitantly.

****

Eight o'clock rolled around pretty quickly. Different niggaz from other sets of the Ruff Riders started coming through.

"Fix you a drink," Prince said as they strolled in. "There's food in the kitchen. When a few more of the gang gets here we'll get started." Prince told everybody.

****

Hicks did what Ray-Ray and Lowdown told him to do, and now he was back giving his report. "I walked in like you told me and asked to use their restroom. I looked around and counted five people in the bar including the bartender."

"Are you sure?" asked Ray-Ray.

"Yeah, I'm sure," replied Hicks.

Ray-Ray looked at Lowdown. "Well what you wanna do?"

"Let's do this shit! I ain't scared," said Lowdown reaching in his pocket for his ski mask.

****

"Alright, now that everyone is here," said Prince taking the center of the floor. "Let's talk about the business at hand. After last night whether you like it or not, if you're a Ruff Rider you're at war with the Warriors. Now, we can do one of two things. We can let this shit drag on and keep doing drive bys on each other or we can take advantage of the niggaz right now since we've got them hurt and finish them off." He paused a moment to let his words sink in before he continued. "All we have to do is wait for the perfect opportunity to knock two more of their leaders off and they'll be through."

"What two niggaz?" one of the homeboys asked.

"The only two niggaz left in charge; the same two that put three slugs in my nigga here," Prince said pointing toward Hustleman. "Once we knock those two cats off, the Riders could control half the city. And, that will mean more money in our pockets."

****

Once they all got ready, Ray-Ray eased his thirty-eight snub nose out of his pants and yanked open the door to the Juke Box. "Everybody freeze!" he yelled. "You and you! Don't move and nobody gets hurt!" waving his gun at several of the customers.

Lowdown went straight for the cash register and Hicks was supposed to help watch the customers with Ray-Ray. But he took his eyes off James O'Neal while reaching for a twenty-dollar bill that laid on the bar. James waited for the right moment to pull his weapon. He watched until Hicks reached for the money on the bar. James fired and everybody jumped at the sound. Ray-Ray fell to the floor bleeding from the chest and Hicks and Lowdown took off running. Before they reached the corner they ran right into the arms of two officers headed in their direction after hearing the shots.

****

"O.K. Prince, how do we hit these cats?" someone asked.

"I've got the perfect plan. They're having a Halloween party next weekend at their clubhouse. What better opportunity than to be in disguise to go commit a murder. I believe that'll be the time to strike." Everyone agreed with Prince. Killing these cats at a Halloween party sounded real clever.

CHAPTER 13

For two days now, Captain Safeway and his wife Debra had been camped out on the seventh floor of the Psychiatric Ward of the Cincinnati University Hospital. They patiently waited for a diagnosis of Gina's condition. After she fainted at her parents murder scene, she didn't responded in any way to the paramedics attempt to bring her back to consciousness in the school's back parking lot. As a medical procedure, although there were no physical injuries, both Gina and her sister Cindy, had been rushed to emergency for tests and observation.

Captain Safeway was at the front desk of the nurses' station requesting information or an update on the conditions of Gina and Cindy, who were both on the same floor right next to each other in rooms 107 and 108. He had been there almost forty-eight hours with little sleep and no peace of mind. He was worried about the well being of two girls who were like daughters to him and he was hurt emotionally over the loss of two people he loved. He felt as if he had lost part of his family. At this moment, he was agitated, mainly because for the last several hours, they had been denied visitation with Gina or Cindy per doctor's orders. Tom's wife Debra, had tried to comfort and settle her husband, but she knew she couldn't reason with him when he was in this frame of mind. Being the wife of a captain, she learned her lesson a long time ago about getting in the way of Tom's feelings regarding his job.

By now Tom was at the nurse's station demanding an explanation as to why he couldn't see Gina or Cindy. He was getting even more frustrated as the nurse attempted to explain that only the biological parents were allowed to visit at this time.

"The attending physician has restricted all other family members and visitors. I'm sorry Captain Safeway. I know how you must feel," she said.

Tom almost blew his stack and yelled at the nurse, "F--- your hospital policy! I'm the only family they got!" but instead he just stood there and stared the nurse. A tear rolled down his face, "Miss, I am the only family they have, I need you to understand this. Their biological parents, who also were very dear friends of mine, were, murdered Friday night at a football game. Forgive me if I seem a little unconcerned with your policy at this minute, but I am not going to sit here another day and let you and your hospital treat me as if I'm a nobody to these girls." At this point, Tom's voice broke off as the tears he had been fighting back for two days began rolling down his face. He dropped his head to hide his shame as his wife came over to comfort her husband and finish handling the situation.

"Hi, my name is Debra Safeway and we understand your position in this matter, Ms. Johnson." Debra read her nametag on the nurse's hospital whites. "If you don't mind, we would really appreciate your cooperation. If you would page or notify the attending physician of our concerns in this matter, he or she can give us some answers to our questions. Would that be okay, Ms. Johnson?"

"I'm sorry Mrs. Safeway. I'm only following instructions and I really do understand." Looking down at the charts before her, Ms. Johnson stated that the attending physician for both girls was Doctor David Schmidt, chief of Psychiatric Medicine. "He's scheduled to be here in the hospital in approximately thirty minutes. I will leave a message on his voice mail informing him of your request to speak with him personally. Would that be okay Mrs. Safeway?"

"Yes that would be just fine and would you please tell him that we'll be waiting right over there." pointing to the vending machines. "I think I need to get my husband a cup of coffee."

It wasn't long before a tall, slender, gray haired gentleman in a white lab coat walked up to Tom and Debra and introduced himself as Dr. David Schmidt, Gina and Cindy's physician. Addressing Tom, Dr. Schmidt stated, "I understand that you both are the closest to kin these two young ladies have."

"Yes we are, and I would like to know why for two whole days I've been denied the right to visit the girls," Tom challenged.

Dr. Schmidt excused himself for a moment as he started checking doors for an empty room to speak in private with the Safeways. Upon finding one he motioned for them to follow. "I want both of you to understand that we are first, doing the best we can to help these two young ladies weather a very sad traumatic experience. Both of these girls' diagnoses are similar but yet not the same. If you would allow me to explain, I'll tell you why. Gina's condition is more severe than her sister's. When Gina arrived at emergency two days ago, she regained consciousness in the emergency room and became so hysterical and violent that I was forced to sedate her for her own safety. After two hours of observation, she appeared to be sleeping calmly. I assessed her for any signs of irritability or distressing recollections of her traumatic experience. Upon seeing none, I wrote an order to have her admitted and placed in room 107 on this floor. This morning around 2 A.M., her sedative wore off and she made a suicide attempt by cutting both her wrists."

The color left Tom's face upon hearing the shocking news. Dr. Schmidt paused to see if the captain was all right before continuing with Gina's medical condition. "She lost a considerable amount of blood, but fortunately she didn't cut a main artery in either wrist. This is why I have restricted her visiting privileges. I have her on the highest level of suicide watch."

Tom and Debra were speechless, really not knowing what questions to ask the doctor. The obvious was to ask if she were going to be all right, would sound pretty stupid.

"Tomorrow, I intend to run a few tests on Gina to see how she responds. At that time I'll have more information regarding her condition and will be in a better position to explain what we are dealing with. But right now, I think it is in Gina's best interest to get plenty of rest."

"Well, what about Cindy? Is she under suicide watch Doc?" asked Tom.

Dr. Schmidt considered the question for a moment then replied, "Yes, I'm afraid so, considering the age of the child and the nature of the situation. Its best to be safe and assume at this point that she to is experiencing trauma even though it isn't as visible. The situation is appears to be effecting them differently."

"So what you're saying is that the traumatic experience was more severe in Gina's case than in Cindy's. Am I correct?" asked Tom.

"Exactly. The severity could be as a result of Gina having seen the bodies of her murdered parents, whereas Cindy didn't. In my opinion, although it's still too early to tell, I think both girls are suffering from a case of Acute Stress Disorder. This happens when a person has been exposed to a traumatic event in which the following has occurred; one, the person experienced, witnessed or was confronted with an event that involved an actual death or serious injury. Two, the person's response involved intense fear, helplessness, or horror. In both their cases, I'm sure you would agree these two young ladies were exposed and affected by their traumatic experience. Now, here's the catch. The prevalence of Acute Stress Disorder in those exposed to a serious traumatic experience depends on the severity and persistence of the trauma and to the degree of exposure, which is probably why Gina seems to have been more deeply affected than her sister. Symptoms of Acute Stress Disorder are usually experienced during or immediately following the trauma. The symptoms last for at least two days and either resolves within four weeks after the conclusion of the traumatic event. If the symptoms persist beyond four weeks, the diagnoses of Post Traumatic Stress Disorder may be applied. So, as I explained before, we are just in the beginning stages of our evaluations of Gina and Cindy. Therefore, it is too early to give you complete assessment of their conditions. There are so many different stages they may go over the next few days. I can say one thing though, I am very concerned in Gina's case, as she has already displayed a lack of willingness to live and see this through. That could mean that mentally and emotionally she feels defeated and wants to disassociate herself with any thoughts, feelings, people or conversations that might arouse recollections of the trauma she experienced. This is why, until I gain a little more knowledge of what she is going through, I think it is best that she not be allowed any visitors to remind her at this time."

"I see what you're saying now Dr. Schmidt, and it makes perfectly good sense to me. But in the meantime, what can we do to help the progress of their condition?" asked Tom.

"Well, first I've got to find out exactly what their condition consists of, then I've got to determine where their weaknesses and strengths are so we can focus on some sort of rehabilitation. My guess would be to collect items from home that they might be familiar with and that may provide some happy thoughts or feelings from past experiences. Things such as photos, a doll, jewelry, anything that you feel will bring back the happier times in their lives. I am grasping at straws at this point because I'm not really sure just yet. Let us just take this one-step at a time and hope for the best. Dealing with the conscious and subconscious mind has always been unpredictable and that is exactly what we're dealing with Captain Safeway. What would probably be best for you two right now is to go on home and get some rest. I'll contact you in a few days or if there are any changes, sooner.

"Thanks Dr. Schmidt," and Tom stood up to shake the doctor's hand.

"And I also thank you," replied Debra as she shook the doctors hand.

"You two get some rest and I'll be in touch," the doctor said as he left the room to complete his rounds.

CHAPTER 14

Debra Safeway woke up at her usual seven o'clock in the morning and was surprised to see her husband still in bed sleeping like a baby. "Honey wake up," she said, as she nudged her husband. She got a couple of groans before Tom mumbled that he wasn't going to work until he checked on Gina and Cindy. "Well in that case," Debra said, "I guess I'd better get breakfast so we can get our day started."

While Debra prepared breakfast, Tom crawled out of bed slowly. Sleep hadn't come easily last night. He was up until well after 3 A.M., counting sheep as his mind continued to twist and turn. The investigation had determined that Ray and Hazel had been caught in the middle of a gun battle that had nothing to do with them. "That was obvious," Tom thought, especially since he had killed two Warriors and Tony had identified the Rider gang member as Michael Roberts, also known as Street, as the one who got away. Tony had mentioned that he remembered him from some sort of confrontation he and Ray had with him and his gang. Tom knew in his heart that these young kids were somehow tied to other unsolved murders that had suddenly been turning up everywhere in the city. He knew he had to come up with a game plan because his gut feeling was that whoever was responsible or involved with these crimes was most likely the one he needed to take down.

After breakfast, Debra and Tom put what few things they could find for Gina and Cindy in the car as they prepared to go to the hospital. After going through some of Ray's and Hazel's belongings, Debra found a diary that belonged to Hazel and she decided to give it to Gina.

Debra held onto the diary herself, as she wanted to give it to Gina personally. Tom drove to the hospital in silence thinking to himself. Debra let her husband have his time, as she knew he had a lot on his mind.

Tom followed with bags in hand as Debra made her way through the hospital until she reached Gina and Cindy's floor. She stopped at the nurse's station and started to ask for Dr. Schmidt when the nurse told them that he was expecting them in Gina's room.

"Thank you," replied Debra as she and Tom started towards Gina's room. Pushing the door open to enter, Debra and Tom noticed Dr. Schmidt writing on a clipboard full of medical papers.

"Hi there," said Dr. Schmidt.

"How's she doing?" Debra asked as she and Tom stepped around the curtain to see Gina.

"She's still slipping in and out of depression. She seems to be pretty content with staring out of the window while holding her pillow as you see her doing right now."

Debra and Tom really were not prepared for Gina's blank stare. They were quiet and really didn't know what to say. Dr. Schmidt signaled them to follow him out into the hall. Tom set the bag down on a chair as he and his wife left the room behind Dr. Schmidt.

"Well, Gina's progress over the past few days hasn't been that favorable, but as I explained, the time frame for her condition is unpredictable. She hasn't quite exceeded the time table of her present diagnosis of Acute Stress Disorder, which means the more serious diagnosis of Post Traumatic Stress Disorder is not be in order for treatment in Gina's case. She obviously has the symptoms of Post Traumatic Stress Disorder as she avoids any thoughts, feelings or conversation associated with her parents' deaths. She's feeling a sense of detachment from reality and estrangement from others. She hasn't spoken a word since her arrival and her difficulty falling or staying asleep has been my primary concern. If she doesn't allow her mind to rest, I'm afraid she will continue to sink further and further into depression. Rest will help her to break the cycle of disturbing thoughts that continue to cause her sub-conscious mind to relive the traumatic experiences. In order for Gina to begin recovery she has to find healthier images, thoughts, and perceptions of her inner being in order to re-cycle her negative attachments to her trauma to positive perceptions that may provide hope and the willingness to live on, despite her losses. Is this making any sense to you?" Dr. Schmidt asked Tom and Debra.

"So what you're saying, Dr. Schmidt is that for Gina to fully recover from her trauma and depression, she has to start maintaining more positive thoughts. At least she must try to find a way to vent and release the anger she's feeling in a positive way. That will help her to view her surroundings objectively. Her reality will come back into focus and her life once again takes on substance," Debra said. "Basically yes Mrs. Safeway," Dr. Schmidt said. "Until she can find this relief valve within her present frame of mind, she will continue to experience intense psychological distress and pressure as she has more flash backs and recollections of the past that continue to replay in her mind. Until she learns how to combat this problem, I am afraid Gina will never be able to get past the pain and distraught feelings she's harboring over her parent's deaths. This does happen occasionally depending upon the nature of the situation, but not often. How soon a person recovers from depends on their own individual strength and the will to fight through the feelings of hopelessness. When the love for self surfaces with a renewed understanding as to why they should move on beyond their burdens of despair, they can continue to enjoy the full cycle of life. This is what Gina must accomplish. She must find a way to detach herself from the loss in order to realize the positive. What would probably be best in Gina's case right now is a lot of love and support. Familiar objects may cause her to respond positively. That's the beginning," Dr. Schmidt said.

"Well, I did bring some items from the house that belonged to Ray and Hazel, I don't know, maybe they'll help, maybe they won't, but it's worth a try," Debra said.

"As you know, you have to be very careful not to give her anything that may cause a relapse in her progress. I've taken her off suicide watch."

"The things we brought are in Gina's room," Debra said.

"I'll go get them," Captain Safeway said.

Upon returning with the bag, Tom set it on a chair in the hallway next to Dr. Schmidt. He sorted through the bag pulling out books, clothing and personal hygiene items, but bypassing all the photos of family and friends.

"Why not the photos?" Debra asked

"Well, in Gina's condition it wouldn't be a good idea to give her pictures of her parents portraying happier times. Her mind and emotions are still trying to adapt to the mental perceptions that are still vivid in her mind after seeing her parents' violent deaths."

"That makes sense," Capt. Safeway said.

"But the books are good, they will allow Gina to exercise her thoughts in other aspects, while providing her imagination with something else, other than her own problems to concentrate on."

"What about her mother's diary we found? Would that be okay to give her?" Debra asked.

"Sure, as long as there isn't a lot of pain and past misery inside. That's my main concern. Now on the other hand, Cindy, I think, can handle the photos and memories of her parents because she has displayed extraordinary signs of will power in dealing with the effects of her depression. So after your visit with Gina, I'm sure Cindy will appreciate some good company. She's been asking for you anyway, Captain Safeway."

"Oh yeah?"

"Yes she has, and now if you'll excuse me I've got a few more patients to see before lunch."

"Thank you, Dr. Schmidt. Tom, you go ahead and see what Cindy wants and I'll be in here with Gina," Debra said. With that, Debra turned to enter Gina's room only to find her fast asleep. She tiptoed around the bed until she was standing over Gina. Gina opened her eyes as she felt Debra's presence. Debra smiled, bent down and kissed her on the forehead and whispered, "I love you". Only Gina's eyes responded as she stared up into Debra's face and blinked twice. It took all of Debra's strength to fight back the tears that threatened to roll down her cheeks. The only thing Debra could think to do was reach for Gina's mother's diary and shows it to her.

"Look what I found," Debra said. She took one of Gina's hands and held it as she told her all about the diary and how she had found it. She went on to tell Gina about the beautiful and wonderful poetry that her mother had written. Debra pulled up a chair next to the bed and asked if it was okay to read one of her mother's poems to her. She searched through the diary until she came across the poem she was looking for. When she read the poem last night, she became so emotional she had to put the diary down. It had made her reflect on her own past experiences regarding loss. Debra thought that this might be the appropriate time to share this with someone. Someone who needed all the inspiration they could get. So she looked into Gina's eyes and started to read.

When you need a few words of inspiration
to help ease the pain.

Or a little love in the form of a hug
when you're trying to maintain.
Maybe you're possibly wondering
how to carry on.
How to face tomorrow
with the strength to move on.
How do you learn to live
without a loved one that's gone.
The answer is in Jesus
and the comfort of his arms.
Prayer can heal the pain
that still runs deep.
The Lord can provide strength
to those who are weak
His glory will shine a light
on the memories you cherish and keep
Of the ones you loved and lost
who are now resting in peace
Don't lose faith
as you try to place hope in each day
The Lord won't let you down
He'll provide a way
Sometimes things do happen
that we don't understand
But we still carry on
the best way we can.

When she finished, she looked into Gina's eyes and saw tears roll-ing down her cheeks, and to her surprise, she realized that she had been crying as well. Debra stood up and placed two books in Gina's hands. In the right hand she placed her mother's diary and in the left she placed the Bible. Gina took both books and clutched them in her arms as if they were the only two possessions she owned in this whole wide world.

CHAPTER 15

Although Cindy was aware of her surroundings and somewhat coherent this morning, she reached for the bandage on her head that covered the gash she got when she fainted after seeing the horrible sight of her parents' bloody bodies. She was still very distraught and angry. Losing her father was devastating and she felt her heart breaking into many pieces. Everything her father encouraged her to do or become in life seemed irrelevant. She lay back in her hospital bed staring at the TV when a light knock sounded at the door.

"Come in," Cindy said softly.

"Hi there," Captain Safeway said. "How are you feeling?"

Cindy looked at her Uncle Tom with a blank expression. "I'm fine I suppose. I've had enough nightmares to last me two life times."

Tom pulled up a chair and kind of slouched down in it, showing his exhaustion from the recent chaos of the past few days.

"You look pretty beat," Cindy said.

"I am. I'm completely exhausted."

Cindy knew Tom's words were sincere and from the heart. She knew how close he and her farther had been. "Have you found a suspect yet?" she asked. She knew how hard it was to solve a crime that continued to get colder with each passing day.

"Well, yes and no," he said, sounding unsure. "We have what my personal gut feeling says is a suspect, but to be honest with you Cindy, I'm a long way from finding the proof I need."

Cindy propped herself up in the bed, to get a better look at her Uncle Tom before starting to speak. "Uncle Tom, you know what troubles me the most? My Dad was the most caring, loving and understanding person I knew. He did everything a man could do for his family. To lose him before I could actually show him how much I appreciated him, has shattered my heart in a thousand pieces. I've been laying in this bed trying to figure out how I'm going to cope with that for the rest of my life. And then, there's the fear of knowing that my parents' deaths could go unsolved forever, just like the other unsolved murders in this city."

"Ouch!" Tom said. "That hurt, but I understand your pain and frustrations Cindy and you know I do. Believe me, baby I'm doing the best I can."

"I'm sorry Uncle Tom, I know you are because I know how close you were to my parents, but on the other hand, I also know that there's somebody out there who knows who's responsible for my parents' murders."

"You're correct Cindy, and right now I've got over twenty officers and detectives out there in the streets turning everything upside down looking for leads in this case. It's just so hard to get people to cooperate with the police and overcome their fears of these thugs. At least enough to want to come forth with information."

"I figured that much Uncle Tom, but in the mean time, I suppose the police department expects the family members to have faith and comfort each other through the heartaches and grief. What about family members who want to get involved Uncle Tom? What do you tell them? Let the police do their job. Is that what you tell them?"

"I know that's not what you want to hear Cindy, but basically you've got to let the system work for you."

"Well Uncle Tom, I'm not so confident in the system right now. I've been in this hospital room for almost a week and so far your system of trained personnel hasn't produced any useful information in my parents' murders and I've got a problem with that."

"Well Cindy, I don't know what else to tell you except that we're trying,"

"Uncle Tom you don't have to tell me anything anymore because I understand. Do you know what else I understand? I understand that with each passing day, the trail to my parents' killers gets colder, and before long, another case will take precedence. Then, before you know it, finding my parents' killers won't be your department's number one priority. Isn't that how it goes?"

"Not exactly. It seems you're already convinced Cindy that the system is going to fail you."

"No, I'm not convinced that the system is going to fail me, but I am convinced that the system needs some assistance in handling this matter. Your department and personnel are having a problem producing results and I'm concerned."

"You have a right to be concerned, but there are certain procedures the law has to follow in handling cases such as this."

Cindy looked Tom straight in the eye and said with the utmost sincerity. "That's the problem Uncle Tom. Your department is more concerned about following procedures then about following leads that might turn up evidence pointing toward a suspect,"

"I have a suspect in mind Cindy and a witness in the county jail who could possibly finger your parents' killer."

"And who might that suspect be?" she asked.

"It's against department policy for me to disclose information in an ongoing investigation."

"So that's how it is Tom? After being a friend of this family all this time, all of a sudden you want to play Captain Tom Safeway and withhold the name of the person who could have possibly been involved with the murders my parents. I think you've worn your welcome out and I would appreciate it if you would leave my room."

"Cindy" Tom said helplessly as he stood up over her bed. "I know you're upset but..."

"But nothing! I'm more than upset and I'm laying here not believing what I'm hearing come out of your mouth. That's all right though because if you can't find my parents killers, I bet I can, and that's without your help or permission." Cindy said with determination.

"Cindy, what you need to do is get some rest like Dr. Schmidt advised."

"Captain Safeway, there's nothing left to talk about. My mind is made up and it's obvious we're on different teams. Please excuse yourself while I gather my thoughts. Thank you, and close the door behind you," Cindy said as she turned her head away.

Tom slowly stepped towards the door, his feelings somewhat hurt, but he totally understood. "His name is Street," Tom said reaching for the door handle.

"Who is Street?" she asked.

"Michael Roberts is his name and he's the person I think is responsible for your parents' murders," Tom said as he waved good-bye before stepping into the hallway and closing the door behind him.

Cindy lay there deep in thought, tossing the name Michael Roberts over and over in her head until she fell asleep. Completely exhausted from worry, her sleep became sound within seconds as she slipped into a state of unconsciousness. Still as the night, Cindy lay there as the wheels of her subconscious mind began to turn. As she slept, the big picture screen that played in her head suddenly produced a clear image of the man she thought was her parents' killer. She was so terrified of the image that stepped from the shadows, she could think of nothing to do but run, and run, and run. Suddenly she heard shots and her mother's and her sister's screams. When she stopped to look, she saw nothing but a trail of blood as her mother crawled toward her, bleeding from a hole in her head and reaching out with one hand. Cindy was frozen in fear as she screamed out to her mother over and over again. MAMA, MAMA I'LL HELP YOU! Her awful dream continued. Out of the darkness came a figure and a shot rang out. Cindy screamed at the top of her lungs when the figure that stood over her mother with a smoking gun started to raise it in her direction.

"Cindy, Cindy, Cindy!" came an unfamiliar voice that interrupted the episode playing out in her mind. "Cindy, Cindy, Cindy!" came the voice again. She felt herself being rocked back and forth. She opened her eyes and through her blurred vision, she saw her nurse standing over her bed looking into her face. The nurse was saying something but Cindy's mind couldn't comprehend the words.

"Can you hear me Cindy?" came the voice again.

"Yes," she mumbled in a groggy tone.

"She's awake now doctor," the nurse said.

"Can you hear me?" Dr. Schmidt asked Cindy as he leaned over her. "You've been having bad dreams and I've ordered some medication to help you sleep better."

Cindy fought extra hard to completely regain her consciousness. She shook her head from side to side trying to tell the doctor that she didn't need any more sleeping medication. Dr. Schmidt held Cindy's hand as the nurse injected a sedative into the IV. She finally found her voice and said "I'm O.K. Doc. I don't need any more sleeping medication."

"It will make you sleep better. Just relax and rest Cindy."

She leaned back on her pillow as she watched Dr. Schmidt and the nurse exit her room. Cindy began thinking to herself that she couldn't stay in the hospital and continue to have nightmares of different versions of how her parents were murdered while the man who was responsible continued to walk the streets. She knew she had to at least try. She summoned all of her strength and lifted her right arm slowly towards the IV in her left arm. The sedative was beginning to take effect. If she was to carry out her plans, she knew she had to remove the IV from her arm before the medication completely subdued her and she lost consciousness. Sleep was beginning to consume her. As she reached for the IV, her reflexes became slower and her eyelids became heavier. Her plan of escape was becoming something she couldn't quite remember. Determination and will power was now the source of her strength as she fumbled with the tape over the needle. Time was running out as unconsciousness continued its unrelenting hold. With one last effort, she pulled on the tape holding the IV in place before surrendering to the darkness. Her final thought was to awaken in enough time to make her escape before first shift arrived to check on her condition.

Sleep came easily for the first few hours but then as the medication started to fade, the nightmares began again. But this time, she refused to be afraid of the demons that chased and taunted her in her sleep. She dreamed of the image of her parents' killer and she began to kick and scratch at the wispy face and eyes. She swung wildly as the image continued to come closer. Knocking over the IV stand brought the night nurse running to investigate the commotion. Seeing Cindy shaking and twisting violently in her bed made the nurse run to her bedside. Calling Cindy's name softly, "Cindy, Cindy, can you hear me? Wake up, wake up."

"I'm awake," came Cindy's groggy voice.

"You were having another nightmare," the nurse murmured. "You have a visitor in the hall who wants to leave you some flowers. It's after visiting hours but I'll give you five minutes if you want to see him."

Cindy's eyes were still trying to focus but she heard what the nurse said. "She said him. Who would bring flowers at this time of night? Her eyes finally focused as she looked around and noticed all her bed linen was hanging off the side. She suddenly remembered her mission as she watched the nurse beginning to clean up the mess. "Well, do you want me to let him in?" the nurse asked as she picked up the IV stand.

Cindy nodded her head as she watched the nurse walk to the door and tell someone to come in. She waited with curiosity as she watched the door to see who had brought her flowers. Mark O'Neal walked in slowly and said Hi. Cindy was shocked to see Mark but also happy because she knew she couldn't stay in the hospital another night.

"Okay you two, you've got five minutes and I'll be back," the nurse said.

Mark walked over to Cindy's bed and handed her the flowers. "I'm really sorry to hear about your parents."

"Thank you, Mark. You're so sweet," Cindy said smelling the flowers.

"Yeah, I heard at school today what happened, so I came by to see how you were doing."

"Mark, you're my friend right?"

"Yeah I guess," Mark said somewhat caught off guard by her question.

"Well, as a friend," Cindy began but then she stopped in mid sentence. She suddenly turned her head away and softly began to cry.

"Hey! Please don't cry," as he bent over and gave a kiss on her cheek and offered her a tissue to wipe her tears. "You'll make it through this Cindy. You've always been a tough girl."

That's when the dam broke and Cindy began to cry and sob. From her heart to the bottom of her soul, she cried and cried.

Mark stood helplessly and watched as he let Cindy get it all out. He knew from the pain he had felt when he lost his brother to drugs that Cindy would have many more days like this when the need for a good cry would help a little bit. Not much, but every little bit helps.

"Mark I can't stay in this hospital!" Cindy suddenly burst out. "My parents' funerals are tomorrow and the doctor won't let me go."

He walked over to the window and looked down at the street below, and then he looked back at Cindy. "So what's your plan?"

"Did you drive?" Cindy asked.

"Nope! My dad dropped me off."

"Look in my purse and get the keys to my Tahoe truck," Cindy said.

Mark reached down and opened her purse. "Okay I got them."

Cindy leaned up on her elbows and whispered to Mark. "My truck is in the garage across the street on the second floor. I'll meet you outside as soon as I can."

Mark stuck the keys in his pocket and stepped to the door. "I'll be waiting." And he was gone.

Mark was high stepping down the hallway when he bumped right into the nurse heading in Cindy's direction. "Excuse me," Mark said over his shoulder as he turned the corner.

The nurse stopped and looked, then hurried her pace toward Cindy's room.

Cindy was lying back thinking about her next move when the nurse poked her head in to tell Cindy to relax while she mopped up the medication on the floor. The nurse told her that she had to get a replacement IV.

"Can I get up to use the restroom?" Cindy asked wanting to test the strength in her legs.

"Sure, but be careful. The floor is wet," cautioned the nurse as she disappeared to gather her supplies.

While Cindy was in the restroom, she hurriedly filled her face bowl with ice-cold water splashing her face several times in an attempt to clear her head. Grabbing a towel, she preceded to pat her face dry as she opened the bathroom door to walk back to her bed.

The nurse had finished mopping and now she gathered the wet linen off the floor that had fallen into the spilled medication. Cindy walked to the other side of her room, looking out of the window onto the dark streets surrounding the hospital. She contemplated her escape while the nurse continued to straighten things up. "I'll be back Cindy," came the voice of the nurse as she exited the room. Cindy's mind started thinking of how and when to make her move. Suddenly the door opened and the nurse came in wheeling a new IV bag that Cindy was sure contained more sleeping medication. "I'm going to get you some fresh linens, then I'll be back to tuck you in."

Cindy knew it was now or never, so she ran to the door to peak out to check on the nurse's whereabouts. She watched the nurse head toward the nurse's station to answer the phone. She hurriedly ran around her room gathering what belongings she had and threw them in a bag. Then peeking out to see what the nurse was doing, Cindy saw her chance as she watched the nurse disappear into the linen closet for fresh bedding. Once the door closed with the nurse inside the closet, Cindy dashed down the hallway, locking the nurse in the linen closet. She dashed back to her room and grabbed her bag. She slipped out of the room and into the elevator. Cindy had escaped and it would be a while before anyone saw her again.

CHAPTER 16

To say that the County Jail was a little chaotic this Monday morning would probably be somewhat of an understatement. It was packed with two rival gangs who wanted nothing more than the opportunity to see the others blood spilled at any cost. The animosity between the Warriors and Riders presented many problems for the guards working intake. Police car after police car dropped off gang members that had been caught participating in the rumble.

"Put the Warriors on the West Wing and the Riders on the East!" Big Country yelled as each gang member was processed. Big Country's real name was Bill Scott, an ex-army man who stood six feet six inches and weighed three hundred pounds. They called him Big Country because he was a tobacco chewing, country boy who pretty much gave everybody hell. When Big Country made Captain and was given control of second shift operations, he didn't take any shit. "If any of these jokers get out of line, beat 'em down!" he instructed the guards. "Get 'em processed and upstairs under lock and key."

By the time the night ended, the West Wing was full of Warrior gang members with the East full of Riders. The noise was deafening as everybody screamed up and down each floor at their homeboys.

"Under no circumstances will the East and West wings be open at the same time. We don't want a riot on our hands," said Big Country.

"Yes sir, Captain," one of the guards replied.

"Okay then, now quiet these jokers down. It's past their bedtimes. Officer Barnes!" Big Country yelled to one of the guards walking away. Officer Barnes turned around. "Yeah Captain?"

"What floor did you place O'Neal?" he asked.

"He's right around the corner in a cell under protective custody, just like you instructed," Officer Barnes replied.

"Keep an eye on him."

James heard his name mentioned and jumped off his bunk to place his head against the bars to hear better. He was already a nervous wreck. "Keep an eye on him," James thought to himself. "Why they want to keep an eye on me? Do they think something is gonna happen to me?" He sat down on his bunk to think. There was a possibility he would be indicted on first-degree murder charges for his heroic efforts in stopping an armed robbery. James hadn't lost faith in the justice system at this point, but sitting on the fourth floor in protective custody hadn't done much for his morale either. For the past two days he had received nothing but around the clock verbal abuse and threats from the other inmates who seem to believe he would be better off dead. "No wonder the streets of Cincinnati are so dangerous," James thought to himself. "If these are the types of animals roaming our streets at night, every citizen in their right mind should arm themselves for protection."

"I'm gonna kill you cracker!" someone shouted at him from down the hall.

"You'd better hope you don't make it to population!" another voice threatened.

James took a deep breath and recalled the reasons why he had organized Citizens on Patrol. He was experiencing first hand the behavior patterns of criminals that roamed the neighborhoods. James felt secure in his decision to get involved in helping to fight the criminals who controlled the streets.

****

"Open up cell nine!" came a voice of authority.

James jumped a little and became slightly nervous hearing the voice and suddenly seeing his cell door pop open. He franticly looked around his cell for anything that could be used to help defend himself against any would be attackers. He picked up a small steel stool that was at the foot of the bed and raised it over his head just as two giant correctional officers stepped in front of his cell door.

"Mr. O'Neal take it easy," the officer said between chuckles. He and the other officer began to laugh at the sight of James holding the stool over his head. "We're here to escort you to your grand jury hearing."

James let out a sigh of relief and the tension in his body relaxed. He put down the stool as he stepped past the officers and into the hall. At that moment, the entire cellblock began screaming and shouting insults.

"You bitch police wanna be, I'm going to kill your white ass as soon as I catch you!" an inmate yelled. "You're gonna be my bitch up State!"

came another voice. The insults kept coming as the two correctional officers hurriedly escorted James out of the cellblock.

"They've been screaming day and night like that at me for the past couple days. I didn't know how much more of that madness I could take."

"Well, Mr. O'Neal, I don't think you're gonna to have to worry about that anymore. "From the looks of the courtroom downstairs, it seems like everything is pretty much going in your favor," said one officer.

"Am I going to my hearing right now or is there some holding cell I have to wait in?"

"Usually, you would wait in the bull pen with the rest of the suspects going to court this morning and we would come and get you. But since you seem to be a target, you will be placed in protective custody. Then you'll be moved to the courtroom when it comes time for the grand jury to hear your case. As James approached the bullpen with the two officers at his side, he observed a six by fourteen cage that held the other suspects. They were quietly sitting but hand cuffed and shackled to a steel rod drilled into the wall. James tried not to stare but he couldn't help it. He stopped dead in his tracks to meet the stare of a young man. James knew he was one of the robbers and a cold shiver ran up his spine as the hatred in the young man's eyes penetrated and burned an image into James' mind. It was a look that James would never forget as long as he lived. One of the officers broke the silence.

"That's Leonard Milton staring at you and the guy over there in the corner with his chin on his chest is Byron Hicks. They are the other two suspects that attempted to rob you and your friends last week." Opening the door before them, the officer poked his head inside to announce James' arrival.

"Send him in," the sheriff said grabbing James by the arm and motioning toward a chair. "Mr. O'Neal, I'm the sheriff for the courtroom this morning. I'm going to escort you to your seat when Judge O'Cain calls your case number. Do you understand, Mr. O'Neal?"

"Yes, I do," replied James, who was now a little confused and scared. He could hear the Judge banging his gavel over and over again screaming in the room next door.

"Order in this court, order in this court. The next case on the docket is the State of Ohio vs. James O'Neal."

As the sheriff pulled James from the bailiff's holding room into full view of the courtroom, half the courtroom stood and gave a standing ovation. The courtroom was filled to capacity. The news media were franticly crawling over each other to get closer with their microphones, but the sheriff pushed his way through until they made it to the table where James' lawyer was sitting. By this time Judge O'Cain was again screaming for order in his court, and the sheriff was making people sit down and be quiet. After the courtroom was restored to order, Judge O'Cain proceeded with the hearing and business at hand.

"This court of Hamilton County versus James O'Neal is now in session. Mr. O'Neal you have been charged with aggravated murder, felonious assault and the use of a firearm in a state licensed liquor establishment. How do you plead?" James' lawyer whispered in his ear, and James pleaded no contest to the charges. The judge continued.

"Mr. O'Neal, do you fully understand the charges brought against you in this courtroom today by the Hamilton County Prosecutor's Office?"

"Yes, I do your Honor."

"Today a jury of your peers will carefully consider the facts surrounding your case and then decide whether or not you should be indicted on said charges. Before I ask the grand jury to hand over their findings in this case, I want to address everyone in this court room, especially you Mr. O'Neal. As I interpret the law, there is no self-defense law in the State of Ohio."

James sat quietly next to his lawyer as the Judge continued to speak. He was sweating profusely as he tried to get a little more comfortable in his handcuffs and shackles. He stared straight ahead, and hung on every word coming from the Judge's mouth.

"Ohio law prohibits carrying a gun into a liquor establishment. But it does allow for self-defense in which a defendant such as you admits to committing a crime but for a reason. Those reasons must include that the gun was kept ready at hand for defensive purposes by a prudent person with reasonable cause to fear a criminal attack. Mr. O'Neal, it is my belief that on October 8th under complete fear, you shot Ruben Anderson in self-defense as he and two other accomplices attempted to rob 'The Juke Box Tavern' of which you were a customer. The Grand Jury has finished deliberating your case. The foreman has forwarded their findings to me."

"Mr. O'Neal please stand up," Judge O'Cain instructed. "On this day of Oct. 8th, 2003, the Grand Jury finds no probable cause for reasons to indict you on the said charges."

The crowd erupted into loud applause as friends and supporters of James hugged and shook hands. He felt a huge sigh of relief as the sheriff removed the handcuffs and shackles.

Reporters began to fire questions. "How does it feel to be free of all charges Mr. O'Neal? "Are you going to continue to organize Citizens on Patrol?"

"Yes I am," James said with a smile.

Judge O'Cain banged his gavel several times to restore order. "Mr. O'Neal, do you realize that you're not quite out of the woods yet? The prosecutor's office can possibly try you on other charges, at a later date if they feel they have a case. Do you understand this Mr. O'Neal?"

"Yes I do your Honor."

"Being a member of Citizens on Patrol does not give you the authority to carry a weapon and use it to fight crime in our streets. We have law enforcement for that. In my opinion, you're not a vigilante as some proclaim you to be or some sort of folk hero. What you are is a very lucky man to have not gotten yourself hurt or killed, or possibly hurt an innocent bystander. If you had missed and hit another patron at that bar, a gunfight could have erupted and you would've had more than you could handle. The bottom line Mr. O'Neal is that you were wrong to carry a firearm into a bar and take the law into your own hands. Do you understand?"

"Yes your honor I do," replied James.

"Then this court is adjourned. Good luck to you Mr. O'Neal. We will take a fifteen minute recess before hearing the next case," and with that, Judge O'Cain banged his gavel as he got up to enter his chambers.

As everyone moved from the courtroom to the hallway, James was thankful that the press had turned their attention from him to the Chief Prosecutor handling the case. As they drilled him with a hundred questions, James slipped by with his lawyer and family in tow, only stopping briefly to shake hands here and there with friends. Hamilton County Chief Prosecutor, Jeff White, continued answering questions until he had had enough then he just simply said to every reporter within earshot, "People in this community are fed up. It is a community that has had it with violent crime and this individual," pointing towards James, "who took vigilante action. I can't tell you why or how the grand jury came to their conclusion of not indicting Mr. O'Neal and ignoring the charges brought forth by the Cincinnati Police. That's why grand jury proceedings are secret. But, I will say before I go, those that are truly guilty in this case will be prosecuted to the fullest extent of the law, and with that, ladies and gentlemen I must go. I have two other accomplices in this case that are scheduled for grand jury proceedings as we speak and I need to be there."

"Mr. White, Mr. White," reporters yelled.

"No more questions thank you," said the Chief Prosecutor as he made his way through the crowd. He made it into the courtroom just in time to hear the grand jury's findings of guilty on eight counts of aggravated robbery for the two remaining suspects. He thought an eight-count indictment was appropriate for the crime and danger they exposed themselves and others too. Jeff sat back down at the Prosecutor's table as the judge asked for bond recommendations. Jeff stood up and recommended to the court that Leonard Milton and Bryon Hicks be held each on a $250,000 cash bond each with no ten percent. He explained why the two were considered to be flight risks or allow them a chance to get back on the streets to commit more crimes. That drew an objection from their defense attorney, Jim Bunch, who had been appointed Public Defender in the case.

"At least allow a ten percent or property value to be accessible to the prosecutor's bond recommendation for the defendants," he argued.

"That's a negative Mr. Bunch. Your clients' actions are responsible not only for the death of one of the accomplices in this case, but also the cause of inducing panic and fear in eight citizens, who were exposed to this dramatic experience when your clients decided to rob the tavern at gun point. So at this point, I don't see a need for this court to have any sympathy for any request you may make on behalf of your clients. Objection denied. Bond is set at $250,000 cash with no ten percent. Sentencing will be scheduled four weeks from today. Mr. Bunch, please have your clients stand."

As both defendants rose on each side of their lawyer, the Judge addressed them directly. "Gentlemen, I suggest both of you prepare yourself for a very long stay within the Ohio penal system, because I have every intention of prosecuting you to the fullest extent of the law for the crimes you have committed. It's as simple as that. You made your bed and now you've got to lay in it. Court is now adjourned." Judge O'Cain hit his gavel once as he entered his chambers.

In the back of the courtroom listening closely, but not saying a word was a familiar face that only the two defendants didn't recognize.

"Hey Tom, how are you doing?"

"I'm fine I suppose," replied Captain Tom Safeway.

"What brings you downtown in the middle of all this madness?" Jim Bunch said as he was leaving the courtroom.

"Well, I really came down to talk to Jeff, because I've got a special interest in this case and I knew Jeff was the Chief Prosecutor in the vigilante shooting case. I see that you have been appointed Public Defender on this one."

"Yeah Tom. I pulled the short straw on this case, but it's really an easy one. It's open and shut. These two young men were caught with their pants down and as you heard, O'Cain intends to give them a spanking they'll probably remember for the rest of their lives. So, what makes the Captain of Cincinnati's finest so interested in two small time crooks like my clients?"

"It's a long story Jim. Do you have time for lunch?"

"This must be really good Tom! Lunch with an old friend who's treating of course, and some juicy gossip. I wouldn't miss it for the world. How does UNO'S sound over on Race Street?"

Tom chuckled at his friend's sense of humor, even though what was on his mind didn't have him in a laughing mood. He faked it anyway, because it wasn't his friend's fault that he had so much on his mind these days. Fortunately, UNO'S hadn't received their lunch crowd yet, so tables on the outside balcony were still available. Taking a corner table for privacy, Tom and Jim seated themselves with lunch menus in hand.

"So what's troubling you Tom? Whatever it is sure has you pretty uptight. You haven't laughed at one of my corny jokes yet and that's strange for you because you use to love them."

"Damn Jim, does it show that bad?" Tom asked.

"Yeah buddy, it's kind of written all over your face. So what's up partner?" Jim asked in a somewhat serious tone."

"Well Jim, I've got these three folders here that are very important pieces to a puzzle that could possible solve over half the crime in this city and possibly give me a suspect in the murders of the White-heads.

"I'm looking at the folders. I see two mug shots, one each of the clients I'm representing in the vigilante case, but what about this third folder with no mug shot and just this name 'Prince'. What's his involvement?"

"Prince is the key. He's the man I need to bring down before this city gets turned up side down. Prince is the leader of the Ruff Riders and your two clients have been fingered as active members of this organization."

"Okay, I follow you so far. So what is it that you need me to do?"

"For the right information, I'm willing to offer one of them a 'get out of jail free' card," Tom said.

"You do know that Jeff White is lead prosecutor on this case?" Jim asked.

"Yeah, I know. I saw him in the batter's box in the courtroom. I'll convince him to see things my way. I will show him the facts and tell him he can have all the publicity on the case," Jim laughed.

"Very tricky Tom. You know Jeff loves the limelight and any publicity that might make him look good at election time. But there's only one problem."

"What's that Jim?" Tom asked.

"It'll be hard getting the prosecution to give up a bird in hand for two in the bush. This case has already received a lot of publicity and the public is screaming for a conviction. It's an excellent idea Tom, but you're going to have to find a better way to execute it. I just don't think the prosecution is going to give you the room you need in sentence reduction to offer either one of my clients in exchange for information against someone who is a known killer. Think about it Tom, would you snitch on a killer knowing that you were about to do at least ten years no matter what? Judge O'Cain made it perfectly clear today what was to be expected at sentencing for my clients."

"Damn Jim, I guess you've got a valid point there." Tom said, as he became lost in thought searching for another solution.

"I do have an idea that might work without you having to compromise at all with either of my clients." Jim said.

"I'm listening," Tom said, as he took a sip from the glass of water the waiter placed in front of him.

"When I first received notice that I was representing Leonard Milton and Byron Hicks, I pulled both of their jackets to review their criminal history before I went down to the County to conduct pretrial interviews. Their juvenile records were not too extensive as I'm sure you've noticed, some trafficking, auto theft, and a burglary or two. You know, the usual things you'd expect from 16 and 17 year olds, but nothing serious that would give you any indication they would be capable of committing aggravated crimes of violence. I just didn't see that Tom, and I still don't see it even after meeting these two young men. But, I can see the influence of the Ruff Riders written all over my clients. You're probably right about how dangerous this Prince is."

"That's why I'm sitting here talking to you, compromising my professional integrity as a lawyer Tom, by betraying the confidentially between me and my clients regardless of who they are or what they've done. But I want to help you Tom, so I'm going to take one for the team this time."

Tom was speechless because he knew Jim was right, so he sat there quietly and let Jim continue talking.

"Tom, my clients have been friends for a long time. Every crime they've committed, they've committed together, but only one of them, Leonard Milton, ever did any juvenile time in lock up and his partner Byron, only did 90 days and then six months in drug rehab. Twice he stayed at the Welcome House for substance abuse. I thought that was strange, so I sent for his substance abuse evaluations from the Welcome House. At the age of 16, Byron Hicks was diagnosed as a heroin addict. If you are to get any information out of either one of my clients, Byron Hicks would be your weakest link."

Tom shot up to attention at this information. "Are you sure about this Jim?"

"I'm positive. When I interviewed Byron last week, he was having serious withdrawals. They were so bad I had to feed him a Snickers to ease the monkey on his back before I could talk to him. He said he felt like he was going to die today in court, if he didn't get medical help."

"Oh, yeah?" Tom asked as his mind started turning. "I think I need to be talking to Mr. Hicks. Thanks for lunch, Jim. I owe you one," said Tom as he got up to say his good bye to his old friend and ran out of UNO's.

****

News traveled fast throughout the county jail of James O'Neal's release. Inmates all over were screaming bloody murder at the decision of the court.

"That's bullshit!!" Lowdown was screaming over the range through his cell. "How they gonna let that cracker get away with murder?" Lowdown was pissed off.

"Yeah Lowdown. I hear you my nigga," another Ruff Rider yelled out of his cell.

"And then on top of that, they gonna try and charge me and my boy with the murder! That's bullshit!" Lowdown said to himself as he sat down on the edge of his bunk cursing. Then he thought he heard someone crying. Lowdown quieted down and put his ear to the cell wall next to him and he heard it again. "Byron." Lowdown whispered to his boy next door. "You all right partner?" Lowdown didn't get an answer, so he knocked on the wall. "Byron you all right?"

In the next cell, Byron was on his knees crying and praying for strength, because he knew he couldn't do life in the penitentiary. He poured his soul out to the Lord, the only help he knew to call on in times of trouble.

Dear Lord, hear me as I pray
As I'm caught in the middle.
Feel my need for a better day
As I survive in the ghetto
In the school of hard knocks
Where my lessons haven't been easy,
In my heart I want to stop
Living a life that hasn't been good to me

But I do what I have to do
Please forgive me for my sins,
For you know what I've been through
Because you've always been a friend

Life gets hard sometimes
As you know I'm not a saint
I've grown weak with this pain of mine

I wanna quit but I can't

So through these bad times
Please show me the way
Lead me out of my salvation
Into the light of day
Understand my circumstances
Help me change tomorrow
Show me the path towards prosperity
So I don't have to beg or borrow.

It's not everyday
I take the time to pray
But I'm in my time of need
I can't afford to see my life go astray
As I struggle to find the right way
In my hopes to succeed
So when I call it's for good reasons
Reasons I'm sure you know
Reasons that can weigh heavy on a man's heart
Who's been trying to escape the ghetto?
Life is too precious to fail
Too short to be in and out of jail
As I try to stay out of harm's way
But when you've got to survive what do you do
Is my question as I turn to you
Dear Lord, please hear me
As I pray

Then Byron opened his eyes, still shaking as the monkey on his back suddenly made him double over and roll on the cold concrete floor sweating profusely. "Ohh God, help me," Byron said softly as he wrapped himself in a tight bear hug. Lowdown listened and heard his boy's pain. "Byron," he whispered. "Talk to me."

The pain stopped momentarily as he lay there motionless, rubbing the needle tracks on his left arm. "I ain't gonna make it my nigga," Byron whispered to Lowdown.

"Just hold on. I'm gonna get you a fix. Somebody up in here has got some heroin."

Byron managed to find enough strength to climb back on his bunk and that's where he stayed for the rest of the day. At daybreak they found him with a bed sheet wrapped around his neck and hanging from a light fixture in the ceiling.

"What a shame. I guess pressure will make some pipes burst," said the guard that cut Byron down.

CHAPTER 17

"Oh yeah, Spencer and Adams. I need to see you two." Tom suddenly said as he was gathering his paperwork.

Spencer and Adams stopped and looked at the Captain.

"Yeah, you two. Follow me to my office." Tom said walking straight toward both officers.

Spencer and Adams looked at each other and then fell into step behind the Captain.

"Come on in," Tom said holding the door open. "Last man in, shut the door and have a seat." He stepped behind his desk and sat down facing Spencer, and waited for Adams to have a seat before he began. Spencer had pulled out his personalized nickel-plated pocketknife and started cleaning under his nails. "Put that away," Tom said referring to the pocketknife. "Get serious because I have a very important assignment for you two."

Spencer and Adams were all ears, thinking at first that they might be in trouble.

"I want the both of you to pick up the investigation on the Ruff Rider gang where Sergeant Whitehead left off. I chose the both of you, because you've already been dealing with some of the members at the high school. I'm sure they all have vacated the school by now after all the shootings. So, since you two are already familiar with these kids, I want you to hit the streets and locate this 'Prince' or 'Street'. Can you two handle that without screwing up?"

"Sure no problem. Glad to be back on the street fighting real crime again," replied Spencer.

"Also Ray's daughter Cindy, the one who fainted in your arms, left the hospital last night and I believe she might be thinking foolishly and going after these gang members herself, so be on the look out for her too."

"No problem Captain, you can count on us," Spencer said standing up and nudging his partner.

"I sure hope so," Tom said. "If you hear anything about anything, call me immediately!" Spencer and Adams were off to take a bite out of crime, while Tom decided he'd head downtown to the county to talk to Byron Hicks.

****

Cindy's eyes opened wide at the sound of someone closing a door. She looked around and thought, "This isn't my hospital room!" She panicked instantly until a familiar voice brought her back to her senses.

"Did I wake you? I'm sorry," Mark said looking down at Cindy lying across the hotel bed. "I was just making a pot of coffee," Mark said pointing to the counter where the coffee was brewing.

She rubbed the sleep out of her eyes before speaking. "It's okay Mark, but what time is it?"

"Oh, it's about 10:30."

"Oh my aching head," Cindy said as she rolled over.

"You better lay still," Mark said looking at Cindy. "You bumped your head pretty hard on that sidewalk."

"Yeah, you can tell from the bump on my forehead. Remind me the next time I escape from a hospital not to trip and fall down. I can't believe I made it all the way outside to fall and bump my head on the damn sidewalk."

"Well you did and lucky for you, I was there to pick your unconscious body up and put you in your truck."

"Yeah, thanks Mark I owe you one!"

"Don't mention it. How about a cup of coffee?" he asked walking toward the coffee pot.

"Sounds great," she said trying to sit up.

"Don't move, I'll bring it to you."

"What hotel are we at?"

"Extended Stay," Mark answered. "Oh yeah," as if remembering something he forgot. "I've got to run an errand later but I'll be back. You think you'll be alright by yourself?" Mark asked.

"Why can't I go? I thought we were in this together," Cindy said sipping her coffee.

"We are, but I'm not a fugitive from the law," Mark said laughing.

"HaHa, I see you got jokes this morning."

"I was just joking, but on a serious note, I found out where and what time your parents' funerals will be today. I need to ride by there and check things out."

"Oh did you Mark!" Cindy said excitedly and giving Mark a big hug.

"Well, I heard you say in the hospital that you wanted outta there in time for your parents' funerals. At first I thought you were just talking but I can see that you weren't."

Cindy sat up on the edge of the bed and put her feet on the floor. "My legs feel weak, but I have to get up."

Mark jumped up trying to help Cindy. "Just take it easy," he said helping Cindy take baby steps.

"I don't know how I'm going make it, but I will some how." "Well, you've only got a few hours before the funeral starts and you're not moving well. Why don't you lie back down and I'll go get us some grub. Then you can eat and build up your strength."

"Yeah, you're right," Cindy said hobbling back to the bed. "Just bring me a cheeseburger and fries."

Mark headed towards the door. "You don't mind if I use your truck?"

"Of course not! How else are you going get there silly?" Cindy asked playfully as she began to lay her head down.

"Yeah, you get some sleep. I'll be right back," Mark said.

****

Prince had Kenya and China Doll come over to the apartment and cook breakfast for the family. When breakfast was almost ready, Kenya walked into the living room to announce that it would be served in ten minutes. She caught an ear full from Prince for interrupting their meeting.

"Alright, alright! Didn't I tell you that this was an important meeting and not to disturb us?" Prince angrily waving Kenya out of the room. "Now, like I was saying, we need to take a vote on what we decide to do. All in favor of doing the Warriors tonight, raise your hand." He looked around the living room at each of his trusted friends and commandos. Street, Hitman, Fats, Stickyfingers, Dino, J. Blaze, and Hustleman were all in favor of finishing the last two Warriors off at their school Halloween party tonight.

"I got one question though," Street said.

"What's that?" Prince asked.

"If we're going to kill these cats, why not rob their stash too? I know they've got to be sitting on at least a few hundred thousand dollars with all that territory they got locked in. Everybody knows that."

"It's up to the gang. I don't care. I just want the ones who shot Hustleman and I want all their business."

"Well then we're in," Street said slapping high fives around the room.

"Hold it, not so fast," Prince said. "We've got one more thing to vote on. Do we or don't we knock that activist James O'Neal off for killing one of the family? We've got to do something about him because he's bad for business."

The room went silent. Everyone looked at everybody else. Then Sticky spoke up. "You know the rules, an eye for an eye."

"Fair Exchange!" J. Blaze and Fats said. "You know how we play it, besides he brought it on himself."

"Okay then, let's eat breakfast," Prince said.

****

James O'Neal pulled into his driveway wondering whom the Tahoe truck belonged to. He looked around but saw nothing out of the ordinary, so he parked and got out the car.

Mark was just coming out of the basement were he lived at his father's house, when he heard the car door slam. He peeked out of the curtains and watched his Dad eyeing Cindy's truck. He opened the door, picked up the bag of things he had and stepped out onto the porch.

"Hey, where you going? Slow down for a minute," James said to his son.

"Oh, I'm sorry Dad," Mark said stopping long enough to give his dad a hug. "I'm just in a hurry to pick a friend up and go work on a school project."

"Wait a minute son. Have you forgotten that the Whitehead's funeral is today? I wanted us all to go as a family to pay our respects."

"Yeah, I know Dad but I borrowed my girlfriend's truck and I'm supposed to pick her up from work in a few. I might have to meet you there Dad." Mark knew the word 'girlfriend' would throw his Dad off balance, because he always worried Mark about finding a girl to spend time with.

"Girlfriend?" James asked with sincere interest. "Who is she and when do I get to meet her?"

"Ah Dad," Mark said walking toward Cindy's truck. "It's not that serious."

"Oh yeah?" James said lifting his eyebrows. "It's serious enough for you to be sporting her truck!" James said laughing. "Well, if you don't make the funeral, I suggest you not miss your Aunt Maryann's birthday party tonight."

Mark opened the door to the truck and tossed the duffle bag of belongings he had packed into the back seat. "Do I really have to be around all those old folks Dad?" Mark asked as he sat his laptop computer down on the front seat.

"You most certainly do have to attend," James said. "Besides you'll enjoy it, because she's got a big surprise coming tonight."

"Oh yeah?" Mark said jumping in the driver's seat and starting the Tahoe.

"What surprise is that?" Mark asked looking out the window at his Dad.

"Your Uncle Ben is flying in tonight for his mother's birthday."

Mark almost fainted. "You're kidding right?"

"No I'm not. Ben will be in tonight at 10 P.M. I was going to ask you to go and pick him up. But since you're all tied up with your new girlfriend," James said poking fun at his son, "I guess picking Ben up is out the question."

"Oh no Dad! No, no, I can do that," Mark said and changing his tone a bit.

"You sure?" James asked toying with Mark a little

"So where is the party?" Mark asked.

"She wanted it at the 'Jukebox.'" James said.

"The Jukebox Tavern?" Mark asked in disgust. "Why there after you just shot and killed that robber in there."

"Son, because that's where our friends are. We're not about to start living in fear because of these gangs."

"Yeah right Dad," Mark said not really trying to hide his disappointment.

"Well Dad, I got to go. I'll see you tonight at the party."

"Okay Son," James said slapping his son on the arm. "You drive safe and feel free to bring your girlfriend."

He laughed as he backed out of the driveway, heading towards the hotel to tell Cindy the good news.   His Uncle Ben was coming to town, and he couldn't believe it. He couldn't wait to see him!

****

"Okay everybody," Prince said pushing himself away from the breakfast table. "You couldn't ask for a better breakfast than that. Good looking out ladies."

"Yeah, good looking," Street said. "Them steak and eggs was really righteous."

Kenya slapped China Doll five. "Them niggaz was hungry. We appreciate the compliment. Now how about a tip or something from you big time playas? Kenya asked. "You know a sister got mouths to feed."

Prince looked around the kitchen at everybody and then went in his pocket and pulled out a crisp hundred-dollar bill. "Here's a tip for your services my sister. Now can I have a cup of coffee while we sit here and begin putting these wheels into motion for tonight?" Prince asked.

"Sure my brother!" Kenya said happily as she picked up the money and placed it in her pocket. "With a tip like that, you can get more than some damn coffee this morning if you want it!" she said playfully.

"If we're going to roll up into these cats' Halloween party, we need some damn costumes!" Street said.

"I know!" Prince said. "That shouldn't be a problem."

"Why we got to hit them niggaz at the school? Don't you think it's going to be hot up in there with police after what happened at the football game?" Dino asked.

"Why can't we just go spray them niggaz when we catch them on the block?" Sticky asked.

"Listen," Prince said, "it was ya'll niggaz idea to rob and then kill these cats. My vote was to just get rid of these brothers, take over their territory and be done with it but you niggaz wanted to rob these chumps. In order to do that, we gotta hit em when they're away from their money spots and tonight we know these chumps will be at that party."

"Alright," Fats said holding his hand up to change the subject. "We need costumes. It's just that simple."

"You're right, we need costumes. That's why I thought the Halloween party would be the perfect place to hit these cats, because everybody else is gonna be wearing costumes just like us and that way can't nobody tell nothing if they don't know nothing."

****

When Captain Safeway pulled into the precinct's parking garage this morning, he knew to prepare himself for the chaos that awaited his arrival upstairs in the department. His job was getting anything but easier. He wished he could just retire and leave this mess for someone else to attend. "There was a time when police work was fulfilling in this city," he thought to himself. "But lately, it's been divided by personal opinions and politics. It's time to shake things up a bit and make some reforms in the department's policies if the police is ever going to be successful in taking back control from the gangsters who control our streets and nightlife in this city." To Tom, at this point, that sounded like wishful thinking as he exited the elevator to his floor at the department.

"Captain Safeway – Captain Safeway!" yelled his secretary.

"Yes. Officer Storey. What can I do for you?"

"Chief O'Donnell is on line one asking to speak with you."

"Transfer him to my office and please take messages on any other incoming calls." Tom knew the shit was about to hit the fan, so he went into his office, hung his hat and suit jacket up and sat down. He took a deep breath and pushed the speakerphone button.

"Chief O'Donnell. Captain Safeway here."

"Hey Tom! How ya doing?" came the voice of Chief O'Donnell.

"I suppose fine, under the circumstances." Tom replied.

"Well I guess you know why I'm calling, Tom. I'm sure you've seen the paper and how bad the press made us look. I know you're doing the best you can, but when we start losing officers and having deadly shootouts at high school football games, I get concerned Tom. What's going on down there?"

"Sir, it was a very unfortunate situation and I lost not only two officers, but two of my best friends. But you can believe I'm gonna tighten the noose around the necks of these gang members from here on out."

"Now, that's what I wanna hear Tom. You've got to get after these gangs if you want results," Chief O'Donnell said. "The press screwed us again."

"Yeah, chief. I saw the headlines – 'Robbers Hold Up Tavern', 'Police Volunteer Shoots and Kills Gunman'." Captain Safeway said as he glanced at the newspaper sitting on his desk.

"Explain to me Tom, exactly how are the citizens armed when they volunteer to help patrol our streets in these high crime neighborhoods?"

"Supposedly police radios and whistles, sir."

"Well please make me understand how one of these citizens had in their possession a semiautomatic pistol, Tom. And, please don't tell me that somebody under your command authorized them to carry it."

"No sir. This gentleman, James O'Neal, was informed like the rest of the volunteers, to never attempt to stop criminals themselves. He acted on his own."

"Then Tom, I suggest you get in touch with the press and arrange a conference so you can explain to the people of Cincinnati how we are not recruiting vigilantes to help police fight crime in our streets. You let everyone know that this individual acted upon his own recognizance when he decided to take the law into his own hands."

"Yes sir, chief." Tom said.

"Clean that department up quick Tom, because I'm guessing you'll be getting a visit from internal affairs on this one."

"You're probably right chief."

"Well good luck Tom. If you need anything, just call. Keep me informed. You did the right thing by sending my son-in-law out there in the streets to catch some of these gang members. With him on the job, you'll get results."

Tom was furious after taking that ass chewing from the chief and he wasn't about to take it lightly. Tom knew the chief was right and the department was completely out of form in every aspect of command and it was time to rattle a few cages and get some results. He summoned his secretary, Officer Storey. "Yvette, come in here please." Tom spoke into the intercom. Yes Captain, Fancy said as she entered the Captain's office and shut the door behind her.

"As you know I just got off the phone with Chief O'Donnell and he's not happy with this department and I can't say I blame him either.

I'm taking over roll call for the first shift until I find a suitable replacement now that Ray is gone and I expect every ranking officer from every section of this department to be in attendance as long as I'm in attendance. I need a memo typed up ASAP to that affect and posted throughout the department."

"Yes sir," she responded.

"Also notify Mike Thornton, the public relations spokesman for the department, and inform him of my changes and request him to be at roll call this morning as well. This department is in dire need of a face-lift. And before you go Yvette, please have the shift Captain authorize any overtime for second shift with my permission should roll call exceed its normal time because I've got a lot of ass chewing to do and it might take all day to do it.

Yvette giggled as she said "yes sir".

"Thank you," replied Tom. He sat back in his chair and looked at the clock, it was 8:15 A.M. He had forty-five minutes to gather his thoughts and prepare a summary on points of trouble areas in the department. He knew he couldn't leave any stones unturned and he didn't have any intentions of doing so. Adams and Spencer thought it was pretty amusing hearing that Captain Safeway was taking over roll call until further notice. "Here comes the whip gentlemen," Spencer was saying as he cracked jokes in the locker room. With Captain Safeway taking charge this morning, the tension in the air was pretty thick and no one this morning seemed to be interested in hearing Adams' and Spencer's wisecracks. Everyone was filing into roll call taking the first available seat. It had been a long while since any officer had been killed in the line of duty. There were no smiles around the room. If Adams and Spencer weren't serious before, they got serious quickly when they walked into the room and saw every ranking officer in the department staring with eyes of interrogation at every officer who walked thorough the door.

"Have a seat gentlemen." Captain Safeway spoke loudly and with authority. "Would somebody please shut the door as we have lots to discuss this morning?" I've been instructed by my commander this morning to find out why this department is not being as effective as it should be in fighting the crime that continues to escalate every single day on our streets. Is there anyone in this room who feels that the obligation of a law enforcement officer is too much for them to bear? If so, please speak up, because I can arrange other job duties that might suit you better rather than having you on the streets wasting our taxpayer's money on your salary. The crime statistics over the past few months show a lot of negligence that I refuse to tolerate any longer."

With each breath, Captain Safeway's voice rose. "I want some answers and I want some solutions this morning or a lot of people's careers will be in jeopardy after this meeting. This weekend alone, Cincinnati suffered its most deadly night of an already increasingly violent year. Four fatal shootings took place in one night and two of those were our own officers killed and we still don't have a suspect. In Evanston, a known trouble area for gang and drug activities, a 16-year old was shot in the head, in Westwood- five people were found gunned down in the streets as a result of a gun battle that's still under investigation. Officer Johnson, aren't you this department's gang coordinator?"

"Yes sir," came the reply.

"Then can you explain to me how Thomas Kinton, a known member of one of our area's gangs, was found lying in the street at 2:15 A.M., at 1429 Republic Street, with a bullet hole through his chest. You have yet to question a suspect. Or how Antonio Berry, 21, of Madisonville, was shot multiple times at a gas station at 10:30 P.M. on Friday night and you have no eyewitnesses to the shooting. That's pretty mind boggling Officer Johnson and I would like to hear your input on this matter."

"Well sir, I really can't give you an adequate explanation as to why we haven't solved or made more progress on these cases – except to say that with the increase in gang wars and activity in the streets here lately, we've become pretty swamped in our department." he replied.

"Well, that must be the reason why gang members feel they can expand their turf all the way down to the heart of the city to fight their wars on Fountain Square. Well Officer Johnson, guess what? Today must be your lucky day, because you don't have to worry about that case any longer. Your wounded suspect died at University Hospital this morning. So now that case belongs to homicide. Today gentlemen, we have 20 confirmed homicides this year already. That is a 35% increase in murders over this time last year. That statistic has put Cincinnati breaking a 15-year record high. It is my job to make sure that record never again comes close to getting broken. If I have to shake this department up a little to ensure that everyone is doing their job to the best of their ability, I will. This is not a job you become lax in. You must be assertive and aggressive day in and day out while performing your job duties. Yes, we're understaffed" he continued. "That's why I'm sending Homicide more detectives to help with their case load and I personally, along with a few handpicked officers, will be working with the gang coordinator, Officer Johnson, to see if we can stop the drug related deaths in this city. I have reason to believe that the majority of our problems come from one primary source. My sources tell me that the name on the streets is 'Prince' and his gang, the Ruff Riders. I'm sure everyone has heard of the Ruff Riders. It seems that they control a large percentage of the drug trafficking in this city. This means that this 'Prince' character and his gang are probably responsible for more than half of our unsolved drug related crimes. Up until now, we haven't been able to collect any data on this 'Prince' because of the strong hold he has on the black community. He's like the boogeyman of Cincinnati. He stays invisible and he's ruthless in how he goes about dealing with the people he does business with. I intend to put a stop to this and for those who might have forgotten." He stopped for a brief second as if he was trying to choose his next words carefully. "Sergeant Ray Whitehead and his wife, Hazel, were gunned down in cold blood because of these ongoing gang wars. They were good friends, so I'm committing myself to bringing this gang down." Tom's voice became strained with emotion as everyone listened. "Now why do the people in the street know more than we do? I'll tell you why. Its because we're busy fighting among ourselves and not focusing and operating like the law enforcement officers we were trained to be. In order for us to be the most effective, we have to keep and respect the lines of communication we have with the community. And, I seriously hope I don't have to explain why that's so important to anyone in this room. As an example, I'm going to give you gentlemen some food for thought. If our communication were effective, we wouldn't have any need for the citizens of this city helping us do our work. We wouldn't be dealing with this problem of defending this department's integrity and reputation. As you know, one of these volunteers on patrol decided to take police matters into his own hands. He shot and killed one of three masked robbers during a robbery attempt. I don't call that gentleman heroic. I call that stupidity. The grand jury has decided not to indict

Mr. James O'Neal on the charges of murder and carrying a fire arm in a liquor establishment." A stir went around the room as officers heard of the grand jury's decision.

Tom continued, "The grand jury declined to indict Mr. O'Neal, because the guy he shot was an armed robber during the commission of a crime. As you know, the law regarding self-defense and defense of others, states a person has the right to use force to defend him and others. That's what the jurors based their decision upon. No matter what our personal opinions of the matter may be, the case is closed and we need to support the decision. The same jury indicted both accomplices Leonard Milton and Brian Hicks with aggravated murder, five counts of aggravated robbery with gun specifications and four counts of robbery. If convicted, the men each face a sentence of up to 33 years to life imprisonment. They are being held under a quarter of a million dollars in bond each, so I doubt if we'll have to worry about them again gentlemen. And yes, for those who are wondering – there will be public outcry about this one because Mr. O'Neal is white and these were young black kids. Considering the racial tension in this city, there will probably be some groups using the race card and their opinion of racial indifferences of the justice system to question the grand jury's decision. Do not feed into this!" Tom instructed. "Our job is to uphold the law and serve and protect those who need our services. It is not our place to quarrel over the justice of Mr. O'Neal going free while the two would-be robbers go to trial. Mr. O'Neal is not a hero, he's just a guy with a gun that did something foolish and got very lucky. "Well gentlemen, that's all the information I've got for roll call this morning. If there aren't any questions, let's hit the streets. I want any leads or information on Prince and his organization brought to me personally. I do not want to hear about any more citizens patrolling the streets with firearms. Ray and Hazel's funeral is this afternoon at 3:00 pm. I expect everyone to be there in support of our fallen officer. Okay gentleman, that's roll call," Captain Safeway shouted. "I'll see you boys this afternoon at the funeral," Tom said to the officers as they left the room.

Tom stood there for a second longer before turning around to face the other officers of authority that sat quietly behind Tom. "Did I forget anything?" Tom asked to no one in particular.

"No Tom, you covered all the bases," said Lt. Tommy Evans of Investigation. "But we all need to sit down at the round table and discuss strategy and future plans for dealing with the Ruff Riders.

"Yeah, you're right Tommy. But first I want to follow up on a few leads. I think I'll personally handle the interrogation process of those two Ruff Riders members. Maybe we can get one or both, if we're lucky, to roll over on this Prince guy.

****

Mark felt like he had three hands as he stood outside Cindy's room fumbling with the hotel key trying to open the door and hold two large drinks in one hand and a bag of burgers and fries in the other. He knocked on the door and stood there with bags in hand, until Cindy finally opened the door. "I thought I heard someone at the door, but I thought I was dreaming," Cindy said.

"Yeah, I hate these credit card like hotel keys. They only work half the time. But anyway, here's lunch," Mark said putting the bags down on the table.

"Mmm - McDonalds," Cindy said looking into the bag.

"How does your head feel?" Mark asked.

"That nap did me wonders. I think I feel a little bit stronger," Cindy said as she stuck a hand full of fries into her mouth. It's amazing how McDonalds fries can taste so good at times."

"I got some good news," Mark said smiling as he took his glasses off to clean them.

"I sure could use some good news," Cindy said as she started on her Big Mac. "Come on spit it out."

"We gotta go pick my Uncle Ben tonight from the airport," Mark said happily. "He's flying in to surprise his mother for her birthday."

"Who? Ms. O'Bannon, the hall monitor from hell?"

Mark chuckled a little. "That would be her. She's having her birthday party at the Jukebox Tavern. Why I don't know, but my Dad said that's what she wanted. Uncle Ben's plane arrives at 10 P.M."

"Well, I'm happy for ole Ms. O'Bannon. She got to see another year come and go," Cindy said.

"I'm just glad Uncle Ben is coming," Mark said. "I haven't seen him in awhile and it's always exciting to hear him talk about different missions the Army has sent him on."

"So, I finally get to meet you uncle," Cindy said putting her trash in a nearby can. She walked over to the mirror over the sink and began pulling on the bandage around her head.

"Hey, what are you doing?" Mark asked watching Cindy pull at the bandages. "I can't walk around with this thing on my head. I'm checking to see if my stitches have dissolved yet," Cindy said examining her head closely.

Mark started chowing down on his Big Mac and fries while he watched Cindy play doctor on her head.

"I think this bandage is too much," and she started unraveling the dressing that covered her stitches. "See?" Cindy said turning around to show Mark her stitches. "They're almost dissolved. All I need is a couple of Band-Aids."

Mark looked at the red scar across her forehead and turned away.

"If you don't mind Cindy, I'm trying to finish my lunch over here."

"Oh, don't tell me you're one of those guys with a weak stomach," she laughed. "I'm gonna jump in the shower real quick now that I've got this bandage off and then I want to at least drive by the church and pay my respects to my mom and dad. Since I'm a fugitive from the law, and can't go in."

"Are you sure that's a good idea? You know how many cops will be crawling all over the place, don't you?"

"We're not getting out of the truck. We'll just park somewhere out of the way, while I have my moment of peace with my parents," Cindy explained.

"Okay," Mark said backing off the subject "I'll be right here on this bed napping whenever you get ready."

Cindy showered and Mark catnapped on the extra bed. When Cindy dressed and did the best make up job she could, she still looked a mess. "I need to do something with my hair," she thought as she looked in the mirror. "Oh well, no one's gonna see me anyway." Satisfied with her appearance Cindy turned around and walked over to the bed where Mark was snoring and nudged him on the leg.

Mark jumped up and his glasses flew across the bed landing on the floor. Cindy couldn't help but laugh. "Come on boy," she said laughing and picking up his glasses. "You need to get some quality rest tonight 'cause you were dead to the world."

"Yeah, I guess I was kinda out of it, wasn't I?" Mark said yawning and getting up.

"We've got to go. The funeral starts in fifteen minutes. Where are my keys? I'll drive."

"Are you sure?" Mark asked searching in his pockets for the keys. "I'm awake now."

"It's okay honey," Cindy said kissing Mark on the cheek and taking the keys. I can drive."

****

Captain Safeway and his wife Debra had parked in a reserved space in front of the First Born Church of the Living God where the funeral for Ray and Hazel was being held. He looked over at his wife, then out of the passenger window at the three rows of steps leading into the church. "This is going to be one of the hardest things I'll ever do in life," Tom said as he leaned back in the driver's seat gathering his thoughts.

Debra reached over and began stroking the back of her husband's neck. "I know honey," Debra said comforting him. "Are you going to be okay?"

Tom shook his shoulders as if trying to snap himself out of his funk.

"C'mon," Tom said. "I've got to do this like it or not."

"Well let's do it," Debra said opening her car door.

"Hold on honey. Let me get that door for you."

****

"What street did you say the First Born Church was on?" Cindy asked Mark as they cruised down Washington Street.

"Here it is," Mark said. "Make a right at the corner."

Cindy made the turn and the First Born Church of God was sitting on the hill with three giant rows of steps leading to its entrance. She slowed to a crawl noticing the police cars parked up and down the street. Then she started looking for familiar faces in the gathering of people in front of the church making their way in to pay respects to her Mom and Dad.

Mark sat in the passenger seat quietly watching Cindy and the people in front of the church as well. He could sense Cindy's pain as he sat there wondering why he had to watch the only friend he ever had start to shed so many tears. To break the uncomfortable silence of the moment, Mark reached over and turned the CD player on and smooth jazz filled the air.

Through Cindy's eyes, everything seemed to be passing in slow motion as she slowly cruised by the church. She didn't bother to try and hide her pain as the tears continued to flow as the reality of her parents' deaths started to sink in.

****

After Captain Safeway helped his wife out of the car, James O'Neal and Maryann O'Bannon walked up just as Cindy's Tahoe truck rolled by.

"Look Debra!" Tom yelled letting go of his wife's hand. "That's Cindy in that truck!" As he turned to run after the truck, he bumped into James O'Neal. Tom looked at James then back at the truck as it continued up the street. "What is your son doing helping Cindy hide-out?" Captain Safeway asked James.

James was just as shocked as the Captain to see Mark with Cindy, and he remembered the truck as the same one earlier at his house. "I honestly don't know!" James said somewhat puzzled. "But I assure you that I'll find out. All I know is they're friends from school."

Tom scratched his head and thought about the tears he had seen running down Cindy's face. "You can tell she's hurting," Tom said to his wife. They began to climb the church steps.

"Yeah honey she's hurting," Debra said.

"Why doesn't she stop running and come on into the service? That's what I don't understand," Tom said as they reached the top of the steps.

" If you want to catch up with Cindy, I'm having a party tonight and Mark is supposed to be there. Maybe he'll bring Cindy along." Ms. O'Bannon said. "Where's the party and what time does it start?" Captain Safeway asked.

"The Jukebox Tavern, so I assume they'll show around eleven."

"Service is about to start," Debra whispered from the door.

"Oh," and Tom moved to his wife's side as James and Ms. O'Bannon followed. They made their way to the front of the church where people were standing by the open caskets and paying their last respects. Tom noticed that Coach Andrews and Principal Mike Brunson were seated in the front row where family and friends were seated. Captain

Safeway nodded his head in their direction.

"Good Afternoon Ladies and Gentleman," the preacher began.

"Welcome to the First Born Church of God. I'm Reverend Sweetwater. The reverend looked out over the hundreds of mourners gathered to pay their last respects to Ray and Hazel Whitehead and he just shook his head at the thought of what he was about to say. There was a strange calm in the room as everyone waited for Reverend Sweetwater's few words of faith and deliverance as he stood at the podium looking from face to face.

"Cincinnati's heart is broken today." He spoke with sincerity as he gripped the sides of the podium. "The sun came up this morning and it's still shining. But somehow, the world looks different as we prepare to say our last goodbyes to Ray and Hazel Whitehead. Of course, their deaths are no more tragic than the deaths of many of our sons and daughters, husbands and wives who have been lost in the aftermath of the violence that plagues our streets and it's a shame that we have to continue meeting like this." He paused for a moment before continuing.

"When we lose sight of the direction our children's lives are taking, this is what happens. You see it; you feel it and now you know it," the Reverend said pointing to Ray and Hazel's caskets. "If we don't find a way to guide and help these children, we're going to have many more of these unfortunate funerals. I personally knew Ray and the Whitehead family. They were members of this greater family, the same congregation that has gathered here today to pay their respects. In this church of God, we share and divide our problems in the name of Jesus Christ because only through his help and our teamwork will we ever find a solution to help resolve the complicated issues that face each and every one of us dealing with today's youth.

"There's got to be something more to offer than hatred!" the reverend stated as he looked up and shook his head. "Everyday I try to give my best to the cause of serving others. Violence is the easy way to settle differences. Violence is a poisonous drug we are injecting into our own brothers and sisters. It is completely insane and inhuman. If we don't come together, we've got some difficult days ahead."

Captain Safeway sat quietly, clinging onto every word of reason the reverend expressed. He was totally touched by the man's willingness and commitment to change. His words reinforced Tom's desire to bring the gang violence to a stop. "The Reverend is correct," Tom thought. "All this gang violence and senseless killing was doing nothing but filling the system with orphans and our cemeteries with kids. Its most definitely time for a change and it was the police department's responsibility to make it happen. Tom felt for a minute that the Reverend was talking to him personally.

"We may as well stop living for tomorrow if we can't find a way to change today! The Lord knows we can do better in raising today's child. You can't place blame anywhere but at home when you know you sleep with one eye open and worried half to death about your child that you haven't seen in days because he or she has been hanging out on street corners until the wee hours of the morning! And don't tell me and I mean nobody in this Church of God can tell me," the reverend screamed at the top of his lungs, "that they didn't know their child owned an illegal weapon that he carried in and out of your house everyday. Or that they had large sums of cash in their pockets that came from dope sales and you did nothing to discipline the situation!" The Reverend held up his hands for emphasis. "Please don't tell me you didn't know what your child was into until it was to late. We have no one to blame but ourselves. You can't blame someone else when you know it's our kids that are out here killing each other by the dozens everyday just for sport. Parenting isn't that simple!" he shouted. "We must pay more attention to our kids and many of these problems will go away but until that happens, don't bother to put away the mourning clothes your wore for Ray and Hazel because somebody else will be murdered tonight, or tomorrow or the day after! It's terrible and until we find a way to convince our children to put down their guns, it will continue to be our reality!"

"Praise the Lord," somebody yelled. "Tell the truth Reverend!"

The entire congregation stood and applauded Reverend Sweetwater's words.

As he looked out over the faces in attendance, he pointed towards Heaven and shook his head from side to side. "Dear Lord, don't let this rap music be the reason! We must do something before it's too late!" he said. "But what do the youth think? That's the important question. What inspires them to want to be stick up kids instead of educated men and women with careers? What makes a child want to throw their life away for the love of money before he or she even gets a chance to live? I don't know so you tell me!

Y'all ain't never just dreamt and pictured
Just looked at the whole situation
Cause once you looked at it — you know
They don't give a fuck about us

If I choose to ride
Thuggin till the day I die
Nobody gives a fuck about us
But when I start to rise
And become a hero in their children's eyes
Now they give a fuck about us.

Some say niggaz is hardheaded cause we love to trip
Some say we're off the hook with this thuggin shit
I see you trying to hide like nobody can notice
But you're a nigga like me
a member of the hopeless
See you're black like me
So you snap like me
Everyday in the struggle
Is our young black seeds
Cops are as crooked as the niggaz they chasing
We can't find no role models
cause all our father figures are basing.

They don't give a fuck about us!

CHAPTER 18

Almost every police officer came by the church to pay respects to one of their fallen comrades. Before the funeral service ended, at least every officer, except two, were in attendance mourning the loss of a good cop.

Officers Spencer and Adams were preoccupied with their own agendas as they cruised the streets. "I'm telling you buddy," Spencer was saying, "if we catch up with this Prince, he'll pay our price for protection. It'll be the easiest money you ever made. I'm talking about a few thousand a piece every month."

Adams listened to his partner as he drove. "I don't know about that Spencer. What if it backfires and somebody in the department finds out? I need my job."

"Aw stop being a wuss, for God's sake!" Spencer said. "Just let me do all the talking and you'll see how this game works. I used to shake down all the dope dealers down on my last beat and never got caught. It's our word against theirs and who do you think they'll believe?"

Adams was listening and pretended to play along because he didn't want Spencer to think he was a punk.

"Hey look!" Spencer said sitting up in his seat. He pointed at a Ruff Rider crossing Vine Street who disappeared into an alley a block up the street. "Didn't the Captain say he wanted us to start squeezing these Riders every chance we got?" Spencer asked.

"Yep, those were the last words I heard come out of his mouth."

"Well then, what we waiting for partner?" Spencer said laughing. "Let's go have some fun!"

****

On the corner of Race and Vine, an old player named June Bug was shooting his game at a young tender cutie pie trying to get his mack on when Adams and Spencer turned the corner. June Bug yelled, "One Time!" as he warned those in the alley who were shooting craps. Sticky Fingers stuck his head out of the alley entrance to see where the police were and in the process, was almost run over by Adams as he turned the cruiser into the alley to give chase. Spencer flung the passenger door open banging Sticky Fingers in the kneecaps. Screaming in pain, Sticky fell on the sidewalk at the entrance to the alley. Spencer stepped out of the car and kicked him in the stomach, then proceeded to raise his foot for another nasty kick when he noticed a crowd gathering around.

"Hold up man! You ain't got to kick a brotha like that!" June Bug said.

"Yeah, you ain't got to kick a man like that!" came another voice in the crowd.

Spencer grabbed June Bug and slung him up against the wall. "Who in the fuck do you think you are to be interfering with police business?" Spencer said to June Bug as he roughly shook him down.

"I'm a player, chump! The police don't scare me!" was June Bug's response.

"Oh, you're a player. Hah, well why don't I just take your player ass downtown, so you can play on playa" Spencer said as he let June Bug off the wall.

June Bug backed up a couple of steps and shrugged back into his clothes before he responded to Spencer's statement. "I don't fear you crooked ass cops! Take me downtown and I'll be out within the hour!" June Bug said.

"Well that's what's going to happen playa if you don't mind your own business!" Spencer said. "Now get out of my face, before I bust you for possession of this crack cocaine in my pants pocket."

June Bug didn't bother to push any further because he knew Spencer held all the cards. So he turned and walked away knowing that the crooked ass cop would plant some dope on him in a heartbeat.

Sticky lay moaning on the ground holding his stomach when Spencer bent down to whisper something in his ear. "Today's your lucky day boy, because I'm not going to run your ass in. Instead I'm going to leave you with a message that better be delivered in 24 hours. Tell your boy Prince, he better be trying to get in touch with me or I'm gonna bust his ass down to size before daybreak. Do you hear me boy?" Spencer asked.

"Fuck you," replied Sticky through clenched teeth. "You crooked ass cops don't scare me. One day you're gonna get yours."

"Well until we do punk, I suggest you and your so called brothers

walk lightly because I'm gonna be around every corner you turn waiting on your ass. Every time I catch you, this is what you're gonna get!"
and Spencer applied another football kick to Sticky's rib cage sending
him rolling over broken glass and into puddles of urine.

By now Adams and Spencer had sped away as Sticky Fingers was
trying to get up off the ground. He knew he had to get moving. The
pain in his side was intense. Everyone who had gathered around noticed the difficulty he was having trying to stand. Two strong pairs
of hands picked him up from behind and held him steady as his legs
tested the weight of his body. He was somewhat wobbly, but finally
stood erect. Sticky removed the urine soaked hooded sweatshirt. A
sharp pain shot up his back and into his tailbone. He realized he had
fallen hard on the steel of the 9mm he kept hidden away in the waist
of his pants in the small of his back.

The crowd that had gathered was thinning out, leaving only a few
who were genuinely concerned about Sticky's welfare. A little boy
walked up and handed Sticky his cell phone, which he had found lying
on the ground. Sticky thanked him and pulled out a wad of bills and
handed the little boy a five. After placing his money back in his slide,
Sticky tested his legs as he started limping towards his truck parked
across the street. Even with the pain he was feeling, the anger of what
just transpired had him totally consumed with hatred. There wasn't
a doubt in his mind that one day, revenge would be his on these two
cops. He swore by that as he sat in his truck, trying to regain his focus
before calling Prince to tell him about what just went down.

****

Kenya was sitting in the living room with China Doll watching the
soaps on TV when the phone started ringing. "Damn girl, I hate it
when the phone rings and I'm watching my soap operas," China said.

"Answer the damn phone," Prince yelled from upstairs.

"Hurry up commercial! Damn!" Kenya said and snatched the
phone up.

"Hello!" she said in an irritated tone.

"Damn girl, it's like that?" Danielle said over the phone.

When Kenya heard Danielle's voice she said "Girl what's up? Why
you just now calling? I'm gonna wup that ass when I see you."

"Ha Ha Ha," Danielle started laughing. "I miss you too, my nigga"

"Who is that?" China Doll asked Kenya.

"Girl, you ain't going to believe me if I told you. It's our girl, D." Kenya said.

"Danielle!" China exclaimed. "Let me holla at her!"

Kenya put her hand up to push China away, "Hold up girl. I'm still kickin' it with her! You'll get your turn."

"Yaw niggaz stop fighting!" Danielle said into the phone.

"So how's the college life?" Kenya asked.

"I'm loving it! I'm taking exams right now."

"Well you go girl!"

"What's up with that no good nigga of mines?" Danielle said.

"Who? Prince?" Kenya asked as she lowered her voice.

"That's the one" Danielle said.

"Stressing over losing you and running shit all over the city. Girl, these niggaz done blew up since you've been gone." Kenya said.

"Oh yeah?"

"Yep, girl these niggaz driving new trucks, taking trips, splurging like they got money growing on trees."

Danielle just shook her head and said, "I wonder how long it's gonna be now?"

"You wonder how long what's gonna be now?" Kenya asked.

"How long before my baby daddy is gonna end up behind bars or found shot to death somewhere."

Kenya gasped when she realized what Danielle was saying. "Oh my God! Prince got you pregnant and he don't even know?"

"Say what," China Doll said snatching at the phone. "Girl, I know I didn't here what I thought I just heard!"

"Hey" Danielle said into the phone. "Hold that down. I don't want him to know just yet."

Kenya looked at China. "Bitch, be cool, before you let the damn cat out the bag."

"I'll be in the city in a few days to let Prince see his son." Danielle said.

"But first, I wanted to see if he was still in them streets."

"Well girl, he's still in them streets. That's a fact. But he's a daddy now, so that has to count for something."

"You would think," Danielle said, "but like you told me before I even started kicking it with Prince; it's hard to compete with the fast lane and the fast money.

"But you know what? You are the woman who's got his heart. So he'll listen to you before he'll listen to his boys, his family and even himself because love has the power to do that."

"Hold on girl," Kenya said, "somebody's beeping in on the other end. Hello?"

"Get Prince!" the voice on the other end barked.

"Who the hell is this?"

"BITCH. Don't play twenty questions with me. Just get my nigga."

"Fuck you! Who you calling a bitch?"

"Hey," Prince yelled from the top of the stairs. "I thought I told you to hold that bullshit down."

"Telephone!" Kenya yelled and then clicked over to Danielle. "Call right back girl."

"Who is it?" Prince asked turning the corner and snatching the phone.

"I'll see you girl when I get in town," and the line went dead.

Prince looked at the phone and then at Kenya. "Who the hell was that?" Prince asked as he put the phone down on the receiver. The second line immediately began to ring and he snatched it back up.

"That was Danielle," Kenya said sarcastically.

"What? You was talking to my girl ho and you ain't tell me?" Prince was pissed for real now. "Hello!" he shouted into the phone.

"Damn my brother, maybe I should call back later." Sticky said.

"What's up, Sticky? Naw man, it ain't like that," Prince said "I'm just having a shitty ass day."

"Well, I guess I'll tell you about what happened to me today when we meet, because it seems like you've already got enough to worry about right now."

"Naw, speak your mind my nigga. What's going down?"

"Well, I just had a run in with Spencer and Adams this afternoon. Shit got ugly and they left the usual message of urgency to meet you. But this time they left a 24-hour deadline." Sticky said.

"Oh yeah?" Prince asked. "Well, I guess it's time to deal with these two cops, 'cause they obviously aren't just going to go away. Let me think on this shit for a minute and I'll get back," Prince said and hung up the phone. He looked over at Kenya sitting on the couch and asked what Danielle said.

"She said you need to get your shit together." Then Kenya flipped him the finger.

"Oh, so that must be your way of saying you ain't telling me. Yeah, okay, and fuck you too!" Prince said. "You's a simple ass beeyotch, you know that?"

"But I'm a good one!" Kenya laughed and slapped high fives with China Doll. Prince looked at both of them like they were half crazy.

****

Back at the hotel, Cindy was getting restless and tired of being cooped up inside. "Let's do something," Cindy said as she plopped down on the bed.

"Do what?" Mark said as he watched videos on the hotel tube.

"I got an idea," Cindy said. "Let's head over to the Bump in Kentucky, I know they're partying over there. They've got all the video games, pinball machines, pool, bowling and they serve food."

"Sounds great," Mark said "but I'm hurting for cash and that sounds pretty expensive."

"Don't worry about cash. I got you." Cindy said "But we can chill there until it's time to pick up your Uncle Ben from the airport."

"What time you talking about?"

"Like right now, dummy. We've only got about three and a half hours before Ben's plane touches down."

"Well okay, if that's what you want to do. Then let's do it!" Mark said.

"Great!" Cindy said jumping up. "Ready to go."

"I'll drive," Mark said snatching the keys.

****

Prince and the gang sat around the kitchen table listening to Sticky tell what happened with him and Officer Spencer earlier that afternoon.

"Man listen," Sticky said "them chumps came out of nowhere as if they were following me or something."

"You think it's about to get hot?" J. Blaze asked Prince from across the kitchen table.

"Well since that nigga Hicks left a suicide note telling our business before he hanged himself down at the county. I'm not sure what the police know." Prince said.

"I bet them two crooked ass cops know what's going on." Street said.

"Yeah, that's what I'm thinking." Prince said.

"That's why they're looking for you so hard, so they can squeeze a nigga out of a few bucks." Dino said.

"Well it's worth it. Just this one time," Prince said, "because we need to know how much the police know about us. We already know they want Street for questioning."

"Yeah, but they got to catch me first!" Street said slapping five with his brother Fats.

"Well, let's get this meeting going. It's getting late," Hustleman said as he rolled a blunt for the gang.

"We're still waiting on T-Baby and his two boys with motorcycles to show up," Prince said.

" And where's Kenya and China Doll?" Sticky asked. "They need to have they asses in here too."

"They walked to the store." Prince said. "When they get back, we'll start."

****

Cindy was having too much fun at the Bump, having fits of laughter until her stomach hurt watching Mark do his impression of Fred Flintstone bowling. "You look just like twinkle toes," Cindy laughed as she scored Mark for another gutter ball.

"Hey, this was your idea," Mark said sitting down. "I never said I could bowl." Cindy took her position in the lane, took two steps and let her ball fly.   "Strike!" she said. Then she turned to Mark and said "but you never said you couldn't either."

Mark looked at his watch, "I tell you what. We've got time for one more game and I bet I beat you."

"Yeah right," Cindy said.

A light tap on the kitchen door made everybody jump and reach for their guns. "Who the hell is it!" Prince said getting up from his chair and walking toward the back door with gun in hand. He raised his gun and said, "Come in."

When the back door burst open, T-Baby fell through doubled over in laughter. "Ha Ha Ha. I had you niggaz," he said between fits of laughter.

After everybody relaxed, Prince said, "Nigga, that's a good way to get dat ass blown off."

T-Baby stood up and regained his composure. "Boy, oh boy you niggaz look tense up in here!"

"Probably because we're ready to handle our business, but can't cause we had to wait on your slow ass." Street said.

"Well nigga, I'm here and I brought two of my best boys with me." T-Baby said.

"Alright then," Prince said. "Let's get down to business."

Ben O'Bannon was taking a nap in his first class seat, all decked out in his Army uniform that displayed many medals. He was a twelve-year veteran that had served in two wars and successfully carried out several secret missions for the United States government. He was in the eyes of the Army, the best of the best. During his last mission, a suicide bomber detonated a bomb near his command post killing two of Ben's closest friends. After being evaluated by the Army psychiatrist, Ben was taken off active duty and advised to take a leave of absence to relax and unwind. Now he was on his way to visit his family and surprise his mother for her 59th birthday. So the Army granted Ben a month to go home and relax before his next mission.

The 'fasten your seatbelt' sign above Ben's head began to blink. "Ladies and Gentlemen, please fasten your seatbelts, turn off all electronic devices, bring your seats forward and place your tray tables in the locked position as we prepare for landing. The local time is 10:00 P.M. in Cincinnati. Thank you for flying Delta Airlines." Ben relaxed in his seat and waited for the plane to land.

Boy, oh boy," Cindy kept saying as they left the Bump. "That was fun wasn't it?" she teased. Mark just ignored her.

"Oh don't tell me you're mad," she said as they walked towards the truck in the parking lot.

"Naw, I ain't mad. You won fair and square."

"Okay then, that's what I want to hear. Be a good sport about it." Cindy said. "Now let's go get Ben. The airport is right down the highway."

"Alright everybody, we done went over these plans four times,"

Prince said as he stood up and stretched his legs. "Kenya!" Prince called and turned to look at her.

"Yeah Prince?"

"What's your part? Tell everybody in this kitchen, what your part is in tonight's plan."

Kenya jumped down from her seat on the countertop and walked over and started pouring herself a drink. "Me and China Doll will ride with T-Baby and his crew on the bikes to the Halloween party and finger the last two niggas who shot Hustleman," she said taking a sip from her glass.

"Right." Prince said. "Then you and China Doll head outside and get on the bikes. When you hear the gunshots, start up the bikes and wait for T-Baby and his boy to come running out. T-Baby, what's your job?"

"Go into the party after Kenya and China Doll and wait for them to ask a nigga for a light. Then me and my boy Threats do they asses and get out of there."

"I hope it goes that smooth" Prince said. "Now J. Blaze, you got the fair exchange on James O'Neal. Take Dino and Hitman with you on that job. Stay in phone contact with me and don't make a move until I give you the go."

"Alright" J. Blaze said.

"What happens on your end depends on how successful the rest of the plan goes."

"What about us?" Street said. "Ain't we still going to rob these chumps?"

"Yeah nigga, damn! Give me a chance to get to your overly anxious ass." Prince said. "Take Fats and Sticky with you Street and be quick about it."

"Don't worry we will," Street said smiling.

While the Ruff Riders got ready to crash the Halloween party, Cindy and Mark were on the highway not far from the airport where Ben awaited their arrival.

"Take this exit. No, not that exit!" Cindy yelled.

"You think I took the wrong exit, don't you?" Mark asked Cindy from the driver's seat.

"Yup." Cindy said and sat back.

"Well," Mark said. "I think I did too, so I'd better turn around."

Cindy just shook her head. Now she could see the down side of smoking to much pot!

"So where do you think we should turn around?" Mark asked.

"Just get off at the next exit Mark and then get back on."

When Kenya and China Doll came downstairs dressed in black cat suits and their faces painted white with cat women masks, the gang was stunned.

"Damn girls!" Prince said as they all stood in the living room. "You got the dead presidents thing going on in here and I like it."

"Well you said make yourself a custom, so no one would recognize us." Kenya said.

"The painted face game is cool." Sticky said.

"Well, is everybody ready?" Prince said.

"Hold on, let me pop one of these pills and then I'll be ready."

"Wait a minute!" Prince said. "Don't be popping them damn pills nigga, cause you know that shit makes you go crazy."

"I got this," Street said. "Let's go take care of business."

"Okay, now we're back on track. Turn into the baggage claim area." Cindy told Mark. "He should be hanging out somewhere around here."

"I hope he didn't think we weren't coming," Mark said, as he looked around for anyone in a military uniform.

"Well if he did," Cindy said, "it's your fault cause you got lost." Now let's park and get out and look for the man."

"Hey, Mark," a strong voice called out.

Mark and Cindy looked up at the same time as a tall, clean-shaven man with a crew cut was walking their way.

"Uncle Ben..." Mark started as if he was unsure.

Ben walked up and sat his duffle bag down and just towered over Mark.

"Hey nephew, put it here" and Ben stuck out his hand.

Mark wished he hadn't stuck his hand out there, because Uncle Ben liked to have pulled his arm off shaking his hand.

"So, who's this pretty little lady? Hold it." Ben said. "Let me guess, Cindy right?" Ben said flashing a smile.

"How did you know?" Cindy asked in awe of the medals on Ben's chest.

"I got Mark's e-mails about you. Sorry to hear about your folks.

Any progress on the case yet?" Ben asked opening the rear doors of the truck to toss his bag in.

"No." Cindy said. "No progress yet, but I'm not giving up."

Ben walked around the truck and Cindy raised her eyes to look at Ben's face. "How tall are you?"

Ben laughed, "I'm six-eight."

"My, you are tall."

"Well let's go. We've got a party to get you to. You look a little tired, Uncle Ben." Mark said as he looked up at his tall uncle.

"Yeah…a little. I'm just gonna jump back here and take a little nap, until we get there."

Kenya and China Doll strolled through the party from room to room looking for their men, but neither of the gang members was there. So they danced in their cat suits, blending in with the other students dressed in customs. Suddenly Kenya nudged China in the side. China thought she had seen one of the Warriors, but she was checking out the guy in a custom that had a table around his waist and a lampshade on his head. Kenya walked over and asked him what he was supposed to be and he replied, "I'm a one-night stand you interested?" Kenya started laughing, but then realized she shouldn't be talking to him.

Suddenly the two guys walked in dressed in all red. Kenya spotted them and so did China Doll. She gave the signal to T-Baby and Threats who were just walking in the door dressed as pirates. China made her move first towards the exit and Kenya was three steps behind her.

Screams erupted along with gunshots. Kenya and China both backed the bikes up and gunned the engines to get them warm. T-Baby and Threats fired more shots and then jumped on the back of the bikes. They took off like bats out of hell across the school front lawn and into the darkness that offered them all the cover they needed to make a clean get away.

"Boy, he sure is tired," Cindy said as she glanced in the rearview mirror.

Mark turned around in his seat to check Ben out as well. "Yeah, he must have had a long flight," Mark said looking at his uncle. Then Mark adjusted his glasses and looked a little harder at what appeared to be a pill bottle lying on the back seat floor. "Hum, what's this?"

Mark asked picking up the bottle and showing it to Cindy. "You taking medication?"

Cindy took her eyes off the road for a second to look at the bottle and then grabbed it. She started to flip the interior light on to see better, but didn't want to disturb Ben, so she tried to read the label in the dark. "It looks like it says Benjamin O'Bannon. This is your uncle's medication." Cindy said. "It must have fallen out of his pocket or something," Cindy said handing the bottle back to Mark keeping her eyes on the highway as she drove. Just as Mark was about to take the bottle, she snatched it back again. "Wait a minute," Cindy said looking closely at the label again. "Zyprexa. Take one per day." Cindy said quietly.

"Yeah, what's up?" Mark asked trying to see Cindy's expression through the darkness.

"Mark, I did a paper in health class last semester on this drug Zyprexa. It's an antipsychotic drug for people who hallucinate! How much do you know about your uncle Ben?" Cindy said.

Mark hunched his shoulders a little. "Not much I guess. It's been years since Uncle Ben has visited."

"Well, what about your Dad or Aunt? Did they say anything about Ben?" Cindy asked.

Mark turned in his seat to look at Ben's medals. "You see that medal?" Mark said pointing to the biggest medal that had a ribbon and cross on it.

Cindy looked into the rear view mirror. "Yeah, I see it." she said.

"My aunt told me that they just gave that medal to Uncle Ben last week, for leading a 15 man Special Force of commandos in a battle against terrorists in Afghanistan who were holding American hostages. That's the Distinguished Service Cross, the second highest honor you can get."

"Okay." Cindy said, "But that still doesn't explain why he is under a psychiatrist's care."

"Probably because he lost two of his buddies in that battle." Mark said.

"Oh, now I understand." Cindy said.

"Here, put this bottle back before he wakes up. We're almost at the Jukebox Tavern."

Captain Safeway wasn't feeling like being bothered with anybody as he sat in his den in front of the television nursing a bottle of Jack Daniels.

"Tom," Debra said from the doorway. "Drinking that whole bottle of liquor isn't going to make you feel better or make you forget about Ray and Hazel."

Tom looked up at his wife and then to the bottle of Jack. "I know honey but right now it's worth a try," and he took another big gulp from the bottle.

"Oh no you don't, mister!" Debra said striding toward her husband and grabbing the bottle. "Let's get up and get out of this house," she said pulling on Tom. "You need some fresh air buddy boy."

"Where we going?" Tom asked as he was being dragged toward the front door.

"We're going to Maryann O'Bannon's birthday party."

"Oh honey, I was just kidding earlier when I told them we might come. I'm not in the mood to party," he protested.

Prince sat at the bar in the gang's new clubhouse sipping on some gin and juice talking to Hustleman, when his cell phone rang. He recognized Kenya's number. "Yeah, what's up?"

"We took care of that fair exchange," Kenya said.

"Righteous!" Prince said slapping the bar with his other hand. "What you want us to do now?"

"Come to the clubhouse and have a drink. Hold up, that's Street on the other end. Just get here." Prince said to Kenya and clicked over to the other line. "Yo, give me some good news," Prince said to Street.

"Hey cuz, I got good news and bad." Street said.

"Oh shit!" Prince said. "What happened?"

"Ain't nothing bad dogg. We hit the lick, but we couldn't open the safe. So we just took the whole damn thing. It's sitting in our living room right now."

Prince laughed hard. "You niggaz are crazy!"

"Well, all we got left is the James O'Neal hit," Prince told Street over the phone.

"You want us to roll over that way and help Blaze and them out?"

"Yeah, yeah," Prince said into the phone. "That's a good idea. I'm gonna call Blaze and see if everything is ready."

"Alright dog. I'll get at you." Street said and hung up the phone.

Street looked over to Fats and Stickyfingers who were still trying to figure out how they were going to get the safe open." Prince wants us to go backup Blaze and Dino at the Jukebox."

"Let's go then," Fats said jacking a bullet into the chamber of his 9mm.

Sticky was still trying to get that money. "Listen, I'll guard the safe while you two go."

"Man, fuck that!" Street said. "Bring your ass on!" and out the door they went. Ben mumbled something in his sleep as he stirred a little in the back seat. "I see you," he mumbled again, but this time Cindy and Mark heard it and looked at each other.

"You don't think it's time for his medication do you?" Cindy asked Mark.

Mark looked at Ben. "I don't know, but I can wake him up and ask." Mark said playing with Cindy

"Oh no! Let him sleep. We're almost at his drop off." Cindy whispered.

While Ben was mumbling in his sleep in the backseat of Cindy's truck, his mother Maryann O'Bannon was telling all her friends at the bar how this was going to be her best birthday ever because her son Ben was coming.

"Everybody!" James yelled over the loud country tunes coming out of the jukebox. "First round is on me. It's my sister's birthday."

He held his glass up. "Happy Birthday!"

"Wait a minute!" Maryann yelled. "Save some celebrating for Ben."

"I'm gonna peak outside and see if they're here." James said jumping off the bar stool. Across the street sitting in the United Dairy Farmer parking lot was J. Blaze, Dino and Hitman smoking a blunt and drinking to calm their nerves. They watched the front door of the Jukebox Tavern.

James O'Neal was a walking dead man and didn't know it. That was the vote by each gang member for his shooting of one of their own. That was the law of the streets – an eye for an eye, the equal of a fair exchange.

J. Blaze's phone started ringing just as Street's Cadillac pulled up and parked on the street. "It's Prince," he announced. "Yeah, my nigga."

"What's it look like on your end?" Prince asked.

"Just waiting on the word from you. They're in there. I just saw him stick his head out the door."

"Did Sticky and them make it there yet?" Prince asked. "I sent them to back you up."

"Yeah, he's sitting across the street with Street and Fats," Blaze said into the phone.

"Well nigga, handle your business and be safe about it. Make sure you leave that message behind. Call me when the problem is solved." and Prince hung up. Prince looked at Hustleman. "Two down and one to go." and he took a big sip from his gin.

J. Blaze started putting his mask on. "It's a go," he said to his two partners in the black Blazer. He checked his thirty-two clip long handled Uzi, then turned it over to Hitman and started the Blazer. Blaze moved the car forward until he reached the Tavern. Hitman opened the door and jumped out. Hitman, Dino and J. Blaze followed and rolled one by one through the entrance of the Jukebox Tavern. Dino started it off with two shots from his shotgun into the Jukebox, which was playing the Oak Ridge Boys from way back.

"Let me have your attention please," shouted J. Blaze. Everyone held their hands up thinking this was another robbery.

"We don't have any money in here!" Maryann O'Bannon spoke up from across the room, sitting at the bar.

"Bitch, shut up! Didn't nobody ask you shit!" Dino yelled in her direction. She grabbed her brother's arm to calm him before he did something stupid.

"I'm not here to take your money, but I am here to get my fair exchange!" J. Blaze shouted. At that moment James and Ed the bartender simultaneously reached for their firearms, believing they were heroes. Maryann saw the look on her brother's face and squeezed his arm hard to warn him to keep his cool. James' mind was racing with thoughts of things to do and when he felt his sister squeeze his arm, he thought it meant go and reached for his gun. Maryann heard one shot as Dino's shotgun blast tore a hole the size of a bowling ball into James' chest. Maryann leaped towards Dino as her brother hit the floor.

J. Blaze was almost fooled by the double move James and the bartender made at the exact same time, but he recovered as his first shot took Maryann's face off midway through her leap towards Dino. He chambered another round. The trio spun around to cover the rest of the room only to see that Fats already had everyone covered from the front door. J. Blaze stood over James and Maryann's bloody bodies. He looked at Maryann's mouth gaped open in the fear she felt at the time of her death.

"C'mon!" Fats said from the door. "We got to raise up outta here! Like right now!"

J. Blaze reached in his pocket and pulled out a piece of paper that had a message written on it. He bent down and stuck the piece of paper in Maryann's open mouth then he stood up and nodded to Hitman and Dino. "Let's go. Our business is done."

The three slowly backed up, watching everybody in the bar with their guns on ready for any sudden moves. Fats held the door open as they turned and made their way toward the get away ride.

Captain Safeway was a little tipsy from the Jack Daniels. So Debra felt it was best if she drove. She didn't care; she just wanted to get her husband out the house for a while and his mind off his problems, at least before he finished the whole bottle. Tom's speech was starting to slur a bit, but Debra understood what he was saying as he lay back in the passenger seat. "I'm thinking about retiring early," Tom said as his wife drove down Hamilton Avenue. "Now that Ray is gone, working at the precinct just isn't the same anymore." he said.

"Honey," Debra said reaching over to grab her husband's hand. "You're just hurting right now. It's never easy losing someone you were close to, but giving up on yourself isn't the answer or an option. Give yourself some time before you start making hasty decisions that are going to affect your life."

Tom thought about what his wife said and then responded "You're right honey. I'm just a little wounded right now and tired of all of this killing that's going on every day. This police work can beat you down sometime."

"If you let it," Debra said.

Suddenly the police radio in the car came to life breaking the mood of their moment. "Shots fired! Shots fired! 2232 Chase Street, The Jukebox Tavern! Officers are requesting backup and medical assistance!"

"Oh shit, honey!" Tom said instantly alert.

"Shots fired, I repeat! Two homicides and one critically wounded have been reported! 2232 Chase Street, The Jukebox Tavern. The police radio went silent for a few seconds and then another transmitted message came across the airwaves. "This is General Hospital. Three ambulances are now in route to 2232 Chase Street, The Jukebox Tavern. Thank you General." the police dispatcher replied and the radio airwaves went silent again.

Tom just looked at his wife and she just looked at him when they heard The JukeBox tavern. Cindy wasn't far from the Jukebox; maybe a couple of blocks when she told Mark he needed to wake Ben from his deep sleep.

"If I'm not mistaken, this street should take us straight to Chase Street," Cindy said looking out of the window at the names of streets as they passed.

Mark looked back at Ben's sleeping body. "I sure hate to wake a man who's sleeping that good," Mark said calling to his Uncle Ben.

Cindy was watching in the rearview mirror to see if Ben woke up.

"Uncle Ben!" Mark said again shaking his leg this time.

Ben's body didn't move, but his eyelids shot open and you could see his eyes trying to focus. "Are we there yet?" Ben asked sitting up looking out the window.

"Almost," Cindy said. "It's just right around the corner up here."

"I wanna thank you two," Ben said stretching his limbs a bit and trying to straighten his uniform.

Mark pointed to the floor at the pill bottle and asked Ben if that was his medication.

Ben moved his foot and looked down. "I think so." as he reached down to pick up the bottle. As Cindy turned the corner, all the flashing lights on the police cars blocking the street blinded them all. "Something must have happened because they've got the streets blocked off."

"Get as close as you can," Ben said "and just drop me off. If you don't mind, would you drop my suitcase off at my mother's house? That's where I'm staying."

"Sure, Uncle Ben. No problem." Mark said.

As Cindy got closer to the crowd of people, the hair on the back of her neck stood up as she said, " I've got a bad feeling about this."

Ben leaned up and stuck his head between the front seats. "You've got a bad feeling about what?" Ben asked looking at the chaos that was in front of them. "Hold up a minute." Ben said as he started getting out of the truck.

"That's the Jukebox Tavern?" Ben asked as he began running to the tavern. Cindy grabbed Mark's arm. "You stay with me! We've got to find a place to park."

As Debra turned the corner they saw the mob of people standing around the Jukebox. Tom knew it was probably a ugly inside. "Honey, drop me off here and you turn around and go back the way you came. I'll catch a ride with somebody after we clean up this mess."

"Okay honey," and Debra kissed her husband goodbye. "Be careful," she said as she pulled off. Cindy parked at the end of a darkly lighted dead end street facing l the chaos. "Look! It's Uncle Tom. This must be pretty important if it got the Captain out of bed."

Mark sat quietly as he was getting the same funny feeling. He looked at Cindy over the top of his glasses and asked, "Do you think my dad and aunt are hurt in there?"

"Captain Safeway! Captain Safeway!" Officer Tony Ward yelled from the doorway of the Jukebox.

"I'm coming!" Tom yelled back. "Okay everybody step back!" he shouted at the crowd as he crossed the street. Tom spotted Officers Spencer and Adams talking to a witness. "You got anything yet?"

"Nothing yet, Captain," Spencer said. "Nobody seems to have seen anything."

"Damn! Don't these people know we're busting our butts trying to keep the streets safe? We need some cooperation!" Tom just shook his head as he continued to walk towards the entrance of the Jukebox where Officer Ward was waiting.

"Well Captain, we've got a problem," and Officer Ward opened the door to the Jukebox wide enough so the Captain could see in. Captain Safeway peaked in and almost blew a fuse. "Hey! Hey! Get away from there!" he ordered after seeing the bloody mess and then seeing Ben leaning over a body.

Ben was on his knees cradling his mother's lifeless body crying and begging God to bring her back. "Please Lord. Don't take my mother. She's all I got. Please Lord please." Ben's mind wasn't about to accept that his mother was gone and never going to return.

"Hey!" Captain Safeway said again as he turned to Officer Ward. "Who is this guy?"

"I think it's her son, Captain."

"Well son or not, we can't have him disrupting a crime scene. We need this entire area secure right now!" Captain Safeway noticing the shattered glass and blood everywhere.

Ben was still rocking back and forth with his mother's head in his arms when he noticed something bloody stuck to her mouth. He lay her bloody body back down on the floor and pulled what looked like paper from her mouth. "Excuse me," Captain Safeway said. "I understand you're family, but we've got to secure this area so forensics can do their job."

Ben wasn't paying any attention to Captain Safeway, although he felt him standing over his shoulder. He opened the bloody piece of paper and read what seemed to be a message. The words 'Fair Exchange' were scrawled in red ink.

Captain Safeway read the message over Ben's shoulder and instantly understood who was responsible. "That's evidence. Put that down," he said touching Ben on his shoulder.

At that moment, Ben's mind started having violent flashbacks and he let out a scream as he stared at his mother's blood all over him and the floor. He jumped up in a defensive crouch, as if he was a panther about to leap.

The movement caught Captain Safeway off guard and he jumped out of Ben's reach. He ordered the officers around to give him his space because Tom knew the look in Ben's eyes wasn't a look to be messed with. He knew Ben was trained for combat and that made this man very dangerous when provoked.

As Ben began to sense that he wasn't being threatened any longer, he looked down at his mother once more and then took off running with his mother's blood covering his uniform.

Mark sat quietly in the truck as they both watched the activity around the bar. "I think something is wrong. Uncle Ben should've been back by now."

Cindy looked at Mark. "I think you're right. Why don't you go check on Ben and I'll wait here."

Suddenly there were screams outside as the crowd started to move.

Cindy and Mark watched as Ben burst through the crowd running like a mad man covered in blood and then disappear into a wooded area just behind them.

Cindy looked at Mark. "Where's he going?

"I don't know. He looked freaked out. Did you see that look on his face?"

"Something's not right." Cindy said starting up the truck. "We better get out of here fast before the police start asking questions."

J. Blaze called Prince as the stolen Blazer rolled south on I-75.

"What's up Blaze? Everything go okay?" Prince asked.

"It's done my nigga, but we had to knock down two more." Blaze said.

"Was it anybody important we need to worry about?"

Blaze laughed into the phone before answering. "If you consider the vigilante, his sister Ms. O'Bannon and the bartender important."

"You killed Ms. O'Bannon the school hall monitor? Okay, okay we can live with that. Where's Street and his crew?"

"Right behind us," Blaze said. "Everybody made it safely."

"Alright good! Now go pick up that safe so we can bust it open. Make sure you wipe that Blazer clean of any prints and then set it on fire."

CHAPTER 19

The week following the murders of Ray and Hazel was the worst week for Captain Safeway. Two murders and now a premeditated plot of revenge on two well-respected people of the community. He couldn't believe it and for the first week he was torn between grief and his duty. The second week started out about the same until he decided to help out on the investigation by going back to the scene of the crime and talking to whoever wanted to talk. But it was the same old song. No one wanted to get involved. The gangs had instilled fear into the community. He was ready to call it quits and head back to the station, when a little black kid no more than seven years old stopped Tom at his car. "Hey Mister! You the police, ain't cha?"

"Maybe, maybe not," Tom said looking down at the kid who looked like he hadn't had a good haircut in awhile. "Why you wanna know? You scared of the police?"

"Naw man," the kid said taking a step back. "I ain't scared of nuttin'. I just asked 'cause I might know something you don't know," the kid said looking Tom straight in the eye.

"Oh yeah, what's that?" Tom asked taking off his shades and stepping closer to the kid.

"One of my sister's boyfriends and his friends shot those people."

"How you know that?" Tom asked listening very closely now to what the kid was saying.

"Because he parked his Cadillac right there on the corner. Then he got out with a gun in his hand. His friends went in and started shooting.

Captain Safeway's mind screamed "Bingo". He felt a break coming in this case but he had to play it cool and make sure he got all the information this kid had to offer. "Would you happen to know any of these guys' names?" he asked trying to go slow.

"Only the one who drives the Cadillac. My sister calls him Street and he only comes around at night. I got his license plate number too," the kid said while he started searching his pockets.

"Oh yeah," Tom said. "Let me see it."

The kid just looked at Captain Safeway. "Ain't you forgettin' something?" the kid asked sticking out his hand.

"Oh, I see. This is a shake down." Tom slipped his hand in his wallet and pulled out a twenty-dollar bill. He didn't mind being shook down by such a young kid but he did wonder where this kid's mother was. "Now if I give you this twenty dollars, are you going to tell me everything you know about this Street guy?"

"Yup, you got my word," the kid said taking the money. He placed a piece of paper in Tom's hand.

Tom opened the paper and sure enough there was a license plate number DBD 9964, burgundy Cadillac written in black ink. "Who wrote this?"

"I did, last night when he came over."

"And you're sure he was involved that night?" Tom asked.

"Positive," the kid said

"What's your sister's name and where does she live?"

The kid turned, picked up his bike and started to get on. "I told you I would tell you what I knew about Street and that's because he treats my sister real bad, but I'm not rattin' on my sister," the kid said and rode off on his bike.

"Hold up kid! Hey wait a minute!" Tom yelled. "What about your name? Here take my card," Tom yelled after the little boy, but he peddled his bike down the street ignoring him. Tom jumped in his unmarked car and sat there for a second thinking. "It's a shame it took a seven-year-old kid to provide the police with their first lead and a solid piece of evidence."

The third week looked more promising as the information the kid provided turned out to be very valuable. Now Tom had a positive ID on Michael Roberts, aka 'Street', which put his gang directly involved in the O'Bannon/O'Neal murders. "Now is the time to start turning up the heat on the streets and bringing this gang down hard," Tom thought as he looked though all the information gathered on the Ruff Riders from the past few years. He sat back and thought of the best way to approach the situation without fumbling the ball. "It's going to take a team of trustworthy, loyal and dedicated cops to bring this gang down," as he drummed his fingers on the top of his desk. So for the rest of the week, Captain Safeway worked late hours going through police personnel files picking out quality officers for this elite Tactical

Narcotics Team. The war on crime was now about to begin.

Street thought today was a good day as he drove his burgundy Cadillac down Reading Road toward 13th Street, where he knew the majority of the Ruff Riders hung out selling the product to the many dope fiends that lived in the low income housing projects. It was the second day of the month and welfare checks had been cashed. Street wasn't surprised to see all the faces and activity, as he turned the corner onto 13th heading toward the crowd of people he saw hanging in front of the corner store down the block. Slowing his speed to a crawl, he began to closely observe the activity taking place. Crap games here and there, boosters selling name brand clothes stolen the day before and the usual laughter and chatter from adults who were glad to have a few dollars in their pockets for beer and wine. He continued to roll toward the hand- full of Ruff Riders he spotted within the crowd that had started to gather on the corner. Somewhat curious as to what was going on, Street headed straight toward the commotion. Pulling to a stop at the corner, Street let his passenger window down for a better look. "What's up?" Street asked a few familiar faces.

"What's up Street?" was the response from one of the brothers that was busy shooting dice.

"I can't call it my brotha," replied Street. "Just making my rounds."

"Park that shit and lets kick it nigga, you ain't doing shit."

"Alright Playboy. Let me pull around the corner. I see my boy Sticky on the block. "Say Sticky, Street yelled out the window", what's going on at the corner over there?"

"Man you know it's the first of the month and Hustleman is doing his three card molly thing. Red sets you ahead and black sets you back," Sticky Fingers said as he laughed loudly.

Street had to laugh at that one, because Hustleman always found a few suckers to trim every month with his three-card molly game. Although Hustleman was a loyal Ruff Rider, he occasionally freelanced with his own hustle. Prince didn't mind, as long as he found time to sell his share of product for the organization.

Street closed the passenger window, sat there for a second watching Hustleman spit his game and flip cards on a towel that was tossed over an overturned trash can. Looking in all directions to make sure the police weren't lurking around, he pulled off and turned right on onto Broadway. He wanted to park where there was an outlet just in case a fast getaway was in order. He parked and walked back toward the action. He could hear Hustleman clearly now, as he spit his game to the onlookers concentrating on his hand flipping the red and black cards. He would flip one card over another and then one under the other, all the time spitting his rhymes.

I got rocks and powder
Baking soda or flower
Triple beam scales
And ecstasy for sale

What ever you need
Pills, Dro, Columbian weed
Hustleman will treat you right
Customer satisfaction
At an affordable price

Now pick a card
They look the same on the back
Underneath though
One is red and two are black

Remember red sets you ahead
And black will set you back
Place your bets at 2 to 1 odds
I'm paying double, how'd you like that.

Street stood there watching, amazed at how many suckers there were in the crowd dropping their money on top of the trash can searching for a red card that only Hustleman could find. He started across the street toward the corner store and made it halfway across before he noticed the boys in blue turning the corner at 12th Street and creeping down Broadway straight toward him and the rest of the gang. It was Officers Spencer and Adams, but this time they had help, lots of help. Street immediately jumped into action sounding the alarm, warning those who didn't know yet. "One time, one time!" was all he needed to say as he ran toward the trunk of the Cadillac, looking over his shoulder to see if all the Ruff Riders were in motion. He cursed to himself as he saw Hustleman scuffling with some nigga on the corner.

"Nigga let go of my money!" said Hustleman.

Street ran back for Hustleman. "Fuck that nigga and the money!" Street yelled at Hustleman.

Captain Safeway jumped out of his police car screaming and directing his TNT Team over there to grab him. "We've got two running down there. Block off the street!" he yelled. More police officers turned the corner heading toward the spot where Hustleman was scuffling with dude.

"Nigga!" said Hustleman as he twisted the dude's arm behind his back.

"Since you want to snatch and grab my money, why don't you use it to pay your bond?" At that instant, Hustleman shoved ol' boy into the arms of the closest cop running toward them. Street pulled Hustleman toward the Cadillac parked up the street and they took off running, but it was too late. They changed direction by jumping the fence to a yard where they knew a shortcut to an abandoned building. The police were on their tails and gaining ground. After jumping several fences, ducking in and out of alleys along the way, the two finally slowed. They checked over their shoulders to make sure they weren't being followed. When they were convinced they had shaken the police, Street told Hustleman that they had to find somewhere close to lay low. After catching their breath, Street poked his head out of the alley entrance and seeing that the coast was clear, he turned back to Hustleman and told him the plan. "I don't think it's safe enough to try to make it back to the car, so we're gonna try to make it to one of our safe houses a few blocks over on Vine Street. There's a car there for emergency purposes that we can use to get back to the clubhouse. You know where I'm talking about don't you?"

"Yeah, I know, the house next to our house joint."

"There's an old Chevy with tinted windows sitting right out front." If somehow we run into the cops, I'll meet you there," Street said.

"I got you baby! Let's get going!" Hustleman said as he clapped his hands. Street took another peek around the corner and then took off like a rocket toward the safe house with Hustleman in tow. They ran in and out of alleys, through front and back yards, until they reached their destination. Once in front of the house joint and out of harm's way, they got a glass of cold water from a girl in a apartment down stairs. Climbing the steps two at a time, Street knocked twice on the door.

"Who is it?" came a female voice from the other side of the door.

"It's me, Street! Open the damn door!"

Before she had a chance to turn the doorknob, Street and Hustleman were pushing through and cussing her out for taking too long. "What the hell is the door doing locked anyway? Ain't this a place of business?" Street yelled from the kitchen. "And why is it so damn nasty in here bitch? How in the fuck are you living, dirty dishes everywhere, the damn trash smells like shit! You got dirty clothes and shoes all over the damn living room!" The more Street saw the madder he got. "Beeyotch," Street screamed until Gee-Gee cut him off.

"You ain't going to keep calling me out my name Street," Gee-Gee said.

In two steps Street was across the room and landed a backhanded slap that sent Gee-Gee flying over the end table onto the couch. "Nasty ass bitch!" Street started screaming. "As long as I'm running shit in this organization ho and we're paying the rent so your funky ass can live free, I'm gonna be calling the fucking shots and if you don't like it, you and your four bay-bay's can get your shit and get the fuck out! I can put another Ruff Rider chick down here in your place. You ain't been doing shit but fucking our money up anyway!"

Gee-Gee pleaded, "I haven't been messing with the money," she whined with fear in her eyes.

"If you're stealing bitch, what's in the dark will come to light and if you get caught stealing ho, you know what the penalty is. All I know is that your till be short every month I come to collect! And now looking around this joint, I can almost see why. I wouldn't set foot in this motherfucka to gamble, eat or drink either, when I see how foul you're living! Now fuck all that, where's the telephone that we pay the bill for? I got more important things to be talking about!"

"The cordless is right behind you," Gee-Gee said as she sat on the couch holding her head in her hands. Hustleman knew to stay out of it, so he just sat in a chair by the window looking out onto the street, pretending that he couldn't hear the confrontation.

Gee-Gee had been a member of the Ruff Riders for years, but her assistance was very seldom used, so Prince just set her and her kids up in a house and told her to run a house joint for the organization.

Street was calling Prince to explain what had gone down earlier on 13th, when he heard Hustleman holler, "Ah shit!"

"What's up?" Street hollered back, still holding the phone as he walked over to Hustleman's side to look out the window.

"The police just pulled up out front. How'd they find us here?" asked Hustleman getting louder as he spoke. Fear began to leap into his voice.

Street motioned for everyone to be quiet. "Shit!" Street said as he peeked around the sheet covering the window. "It's Adams and Spencer, but Spencer is the only one getting out of the car," he told Prince over the phone.

"Is he coming to the house?"

"Yup, he damn sure is," Street replied.

"I'm sending a car to pick you two up. Now go get ghost somewhere and try to avoid any type of gun play."

Gee-Gee was already up and holding a closet door open for them to hide in. Street threw the phone on the couch and slipped into the dark closet with Hustleman just as the knock came on the door. Gee-Gee tried to straighten herself up a little as she yelled "Who is it?"

"The police," Spencer said playfully.

"Just a minute," Gee-Gee said as she unlocked the door to let Officer Spencer into the apartment.

"Hey, brown sugar," Spencer said reaching for Gee-Gee as if to give her a hug. Nervously stepping back a bit, she instantly became scared, because she knew her secret of tricking with Spencer was now no longer a secret. She silently cursed Spencer for his terrible timing. Now she had to find a way to get rid of him fast.

"What's wrong baby? You act like you're not happy to see me," as he grabbed her in a hug and felt her bottom.

"No baby, it's not like that. You know I'm always happy to see you. It's just that you've caught me at a bad time. I'm somewhat in a hurry. I was on my way over to my mother's to check on her. The kids just called to say she wasn't feeling well."

"Oh, I see. Well I guess my usual quickie is out of the question?" asked Spencer as he reached for one of her firm breasts to squeeze.

"Baby, I'll be back later on this evening, so why don't you stop back by then and I promise to take care of you like I always do."

Spencer paid no attention to what Gee-Gee was saying. He was too busy grabbing, squeezing and pulling all over her. The more she resisted and protested, the more it turned him on. 'No' was not a word he wanted to hear and it showed in his actions as he backed her up until she fell on the couch.

"Spencer stop! Not now baby! I've got to go! Come back later."

"Baby I want you now," Spencer said between kisses and he started pulling on her clothes.

Street was getting very upset at the sounds coming from the living room. "The crooked ass cop is taking advantage of Gee-Gee!" His eyes were spitting fire at the sight of what he was seeing from his hiding place in the closet. He knew he couldn't just watch this cop rape the girl in front of him, so he pulled his 9 mm from his waistband and slid off the safety. The phone rang and Gee-Gee quickly answered thankful for the interruption, which stopped Spencer momentarily.

"What's going on down there Gee-Gee?" came the voice of Prince over the phone.

"Mama, I'm on my way," Gee-Gee said into the phone. "I'm putting on my clothes now."

"Just say yes or no" Prince said into the phone. "Is there a problem down there?"

"Yes mama," she replied.

"Is that crocked ass cop, Spencer the problem?" he asked.

"Yes mama, I know," she replied.

"Are Street and Hustleman safe?" asked Prince.

"Yes mama, I understand. I'll bring a change of clothes for the kids."

"I got some boys on the way. Call me when you get the chance," Prince said and he hung up.

"O.K. mama, I'll be there shortly." She walked to the front door and opened it wide as if telling Spencer it was time to go. He grinned at her as he got the message and stepped in the direction of the door while straightening his clothes. He walked out kissing her lightly on the cheek, "I'll be back." Closing the door and double bolting the locks, she collapsed against the door with relief and slowly slid down to the floor. With her knees pulled closely to her chest, the tears came running down her face. All the built up frustration from dealing with Spencer over the past few months came pouring out of her soul.

Suddenly a strong pair of hands picked her up off the floor and gave her a much-needed hug. Street looked into Gee-Gee's eyes and was touched by the pain he saw. The pain was so intense; he lost a tear himself as he finally spoke. "Baby don't worry. Just pull yourself together, because I'm gonna get that honky if it's the last thing I do. I put my life on that. Now go upstairs and get yourself together, while I call Prince."

"That was Prince on the phone. He picked up on my hint that I was in trouble and we talked in code. He asked if it was Spencer and I said yes, then he asked if you two were safe, then he said he was sending some Riders down here to help."

"That's my nigga, always on time." stated Street.

"And they just pulled up," Hustleman said still watching the street. "Three car loads and a watch dog down the street parked on the corner." We got to roll Street!"

"Hurry up, Gee-Gee," Street said as he picked up the phone and started dialing Prince's number. "Go outside and tell those niggaz to sit tight," he instructed Hustleman. While Hustleman went outside to calm the brothas down, Street peeked out of the window and ran everything down to Prince. When Gee-Gee came back downstairs, Street was just finishing his conversation with Prince. "Alright my nigga I got cha."

"Come on baby we got to ride. It's too damn hot down here. Prince wants to see you personally and plus the Ruff Riders members have a meeting at seven and it's six forty five right now." Street said, as he started moving. Opening the door and stepping out onto the porch, he froze in his tracks, puzzled to see no one outside. But before he could give it a second thought, Hustleman turned the corner burning rubber in Street's Cadillac.

When the passenger window came down, Hustleman yelled, "Get in we got to roll! Its still hot down here!" Street grabbed Gee-Gee by the arm and hurried to the car. Gee-Gee started for the backseat when Street stopped her. "Get in the front Gee. It will look better just in case the man pulls us over." Street jumped in the back seat and Hustleman pulled off turning right on Vine Street heading uptown toward Walnut Hills to the clubhouse.

Back at the precinct, Captain Safeway was briefing the TNT task force he had personally hand picked for this mission. "Alright TNT for the record, I want all twelve men in this room to give me their complete attention as I go over the facts and plans that I know, if properly executed, will bring down this entire gang for good."

Every officer in the room wore bulletproof vests and plain clothes as instructed by the Captain. Now they sat quietly listening to instructions as Captain Safeway stood next to the chalkboard running down the game plan. "This is what I know about the Ruff Riders organization." Captain Safeway said as he pointed to a diagram on the blackboard. "Gentleman, I've got the Chief so far up my ass on this one, I'm personally taking over this investigation. I'm through playing games. If we don't take back the streets now from these gangs, every kid in Cincinnati will be on Ecstasy before the year ends and we can't have that. So listen up." He picked up a stack of folders and started passing them around. "In these folders are photos taken from surveillance cameras at the Withrow game of all the key players of the Ruff Riders that we have to take down if we intend to dismantle this gang. The Ruff Riders we nabbed this afternoon on 13th won't help us much, because they aren't talking and they're easily replaced. We all know how this gang continues to find new recruits in the high schools. This gang is growing and the more they grow, the deadlier they become. So in order to bring them down, we've got to get to these two guys." He pointed at two 8x10 photos taped on the chalkboard. "This guy is Prince. Prince is what they call him on the streets and according to my resources, he's the one calling all the shots. This other guy is Michael Roberts, aka 'Street'. He seems to be Prince's right hand man. Michael Roberts has a warrant out for his arrest. He's armed and dangerous so be careful. Captain Safeway stopped briefly to look around the room. "At this point gentleman we only have one eyewitness, a seven-year-old kid who can place Street at the scene of the O'Bannon/O'Neal murders. I also want to question him in Ray and Hazel's murders as well. Captain Safeway looked at the TNT Team he assembled and said, "It's as simple as that. We've got to bring these two down and the rest will follow."

The clubhouse was full of life when Street, Hustleman and Gee-Gee walked through the door. Every member of the Ruff Rider family was in attendance. The jukebox played and the members danced. The bar was full and weed and cigarette smoke filled the air. Prince, J. Blaze, Hitman, and Street's little brother Fats were all in the back in discussion when Street knocked on the door and walked in.

"Where's Gee-Gee?" asked Prince.

"Here I am Prince," answered Gee-Gee as she stepped into the room.

"How are you feeling baby girl?" asked Prince.

"I'm scared shitless," she said honestly.

"Listen everyone, I need to talk to Gee-Gee in private for a moment. Somebody go get some order out there in the other room. When I get through in here, I'll be coming out there to address the entire family as to what needs to happen next." Prince told the room as he held the door open. After the room emptied, Prince offered Gee-Gee a seat and a glass of brandy to calm her nerves. Before he said anything, he stood there looking at her for a moment trying to get an idea of how well she was really holding up before he told her of his plans to pay Spencer back for the harassment and injustice she had endured at the hands of his dirty law enforcement practices. Prince walked around to the other side of his desk and took a seat in his thinking chair. He looked up across his desk into Gee-Gee's eyes and saw the fear and pain Officer Spencer had instilled. He instantly became upset. "Can you tell me about it?"

Gee-Gee took another sip from her drink and put it down, placing her hands on her lap. She said it started about six months ago, when Spencer and Adams pulled her car over and asked to see her driver's license. "I asked him what was the problem and he said that I fit the description of a suspect they were looking for. That pissed me off because I knew I hadn't done anything, but I knew I couldn't argue with the police. He ran my name, brought my license back, and then he ordered me out of my car. He put cuffs on me and sat me in the back of his police car while he and his partner searched my car. When they finished with my car, Spencer came back to the cruiser and showed me an ounce of powder cocaine that he said came from under the passenger seat. "What could I do, Prince? I knew it was a set up but I also knew it was my word against him and his partner. It looked like a no win situation, so I took his proposition, which was a sexual favor in exchange for not going to jail." Gee-Gee stopped talking momentarily and took a deep breath to control her emotions. "I've got four kids Prince. The day I met Officer Spencer has been one of the unluckiest days of my life and ever since that day he has raped me repeatedly. He's left bite marks on my back and breasts and committed sodomy so forcefully upon my body, that I bled for a month every time I used the restroom. Prince, this man has a very perverted sexual appetite, and I don't know how much more I can take before I reach the end of my rope. I've tried to stay strong... but-but-but and," from there Gee-Gee couldn't hold back any longer as she held her head in her hands and softly cried.

Prince sat there and looked at Gee-Gee, somewhat mesmerized by the story he just heard. He scratched his head a couple of times as he thought, then he ran his fingers through his short curly afro before asking Gee-Gee if she was alright.

"I'll be alright Prince," she said quietly.

"Baby I know you will." Prince replied. "All I wanna know is if you want some get back?" he asked. "Cause if you do, I got a plan that will fix that dirty ass cop for life." Prince said as he got up.

"You can count me in baby because I'm tired of this guy hurting me. Just let me know what you want me to do."

"For right now, I just want you to slide over here on the couch and relax. Fix yourself a drink, turn some jams on and get your mind right. I'll let you know what I want you to do later. Right now, I got to go out and get these Ruff Riders together, 'cause it's time to ride." Prince looked around the room until he found what he was looking for, a lamp with an extension cord. Snatching the cord from the socket, Prince grabbed the lamp and stormed out of the office. In the hallway Prince ran into J. Blaze, who was on his way to tell him that everyone was ready.

"What's the lamp for?" J. Blaze asked as Prince handed it to him.

"It's to prove a point," he answered.

"Are the tables set up with all the captains in their seats?"

"Yeah," answered J. Blaze.

"Good! Now go plug that lamp in and set it right in the middle of our tables," said Prince. "I'll be there in a minute."

"I'll let everybody know," said J. Blaze as he walked toward the clubhouse playroom where everyone was waiting.

When Prince entered the dimly lit, smoke filled room of fifty plus Ruff Riders members, he was wearing a bullet proof vest with an AK assault rifle slung over his shoulder like a true soldier prepared for battle. He slowly turned in a 360-degree circle, evaluating the demeanor of each and every soul that lined the walls of the room. Behind him sat the five loyal friends who helped put the Ruff Riders on the map. They sat in silence as their leader began to address the entire organization for the next turn of events. Prince pulled a table close to him in the middle of the floor. On it he placed the AK, vest, and lamp and then he spoke to the whole room. "If you're part of this family as a means of convenience, then get the hell out now, because your free ride is over!" Prince screamed at the top of his lungs. "I only want to speak to those who are true. If you're not for real, then you're not for me or this organization because I am my brother's keeper." Then he walked over and switched off the light. "Now is the time, because the moment of truth has come. In this moment of darkness, question your heart, find your loyalty and ask yourself, are you willing to defend the honor of what you represent? If your answer is yes, then you too are my brother's keeper. Should you be in doubt, then you should be gone before the lights come back on, because I have no room for cowards in my family." Then he switched on the dim lamp and said, "From this point on, we move, we live, we ride as one. Darkness will be our best friend and we will become and remain what we are right now in this room, shadows of the night."

"Ruff Riders, Ruff Riders, Ruff Riders!" every member chanted until Prince lifted his arms and hands for silence. "Look around you Ruff Riders. What do you see? No one in here can see anything because the light of this lamp only allows everyone to be a shadow. I can hear you, but I can't see you and that's how I want every member to be from this day on. We've got a lot of business to take care of people," Prince said looking around the clubhouse. "We've got money to make. Now that I know everybody in this room is legit, let me show you something. Yo, Blaze bring them party supplies out here," Prince yelled.

"Oh, we about to party up in here?" Kenya said snapping her fingers. "I'm all for that girl," and Kenya slapped high fives with China Doll.

"Hold up for a minute," Prince said. "We gonna party but business before pleasure." J. Blaze carried in a box and set it on the table in front of all the captains. Prince pulled an empty table to one side and tossed a notebook pad on it. "Blaze sit at that table. Sticky you go get the champagne."

"Bet," Sticky said jumping up to get the bottles of bub.

"Alright everybody. Listen up," Prince said holding his hand up for silence. "We've been making good money and my word is my bond. I am my brother's keeper and this family is very important to me. So tonight I'm giving every member a bonus," and he dumped the box over. Rolls of bills wrapped with rubber bands spilled out.

Things got pretty happy around the clubhouse at that point as laughter and high fives were being passed around.

"Wait a minute. I ain't finished yet," Prince said. "Each roll of bills has a stack in it, plus I'm giving each member a weekly raise," Prince said reaching back into the box and pulling out a kilo of cocaine in one hand and a Ziploc bag full of Ecstasy in the other. "We've got more drugs for sale. Everybody get fifty pills each. Sign up with J. Blaze and pick up your pills and money. Its time to party!"

Stickyfingers started passing out bottles of bubbly, and everyone stood in line to get paid. Prince looked at Street who was laughing with his brother Fats. "I got a job for you two," Prince said.

"Oh yeah?" Fats said between laughs.

"What's that?" Street said somewhat serious.

"It really ain't that serious, but I got a debt that needs to be collected."

"No problem," Street said.

Dino overheard the conversation. "I want in on the fun."

"I got something I want you to do too Dino," Prince said. I need that nigga Pretty Tony."

"The pool shark nigga on McMillan?"

"Yeah that's him. Bring him to me." He is, the weakest link.

"What else you got in store for me?" Dino asked leaning across the table.

"Some security," Prince said walking away.

"Security?" Dino asked as Street laughed.

"Don't worry dogg. He might have you guarding the President or something," Street said as everybody started laughing.

Prince was walking around the clubhouse looking for China Doll, but everybody was everywhere dancing and drinking so he could only find Gee-Gee. "Yo Gee," Prince yelled over the music.

"Yeah baby. What's up?" Gee-Gee asked as she sat at the bar looking all sexy in a skintight cat suit.

Prince walked up close enough for Gee-Gee to hear him over the loud music. "Where's China Doll?"

Gee pointed towards the DJ booth and sure enough Kenya and China Doll were over there, probably gossiping as usual.

"Thanks," Prince said grabbing Gee Gee's hand. "Don't forget tomorrow at your place."

"I got cha, baby."

Prince started back toward the dance floor when J. Blaze stopped him.

"Damn," Prince said.

Blaze looked at Prince. "What's wrong dogg?"

"This damn clubhouse is too damn small and crowded."

Blaze laughed, "It's just crowded man. We've got a lot of members now. It's just your first time seeing everybody together at once."

"Yeah I guess. Did everybody get paid?" Prince asked.

Blaze held the notebook up. "Yep, and all the pills are out."

"Good, nigga we're moving on up." Prince said to his long time friend. "Oh yeah, guess what?"

"What nigga?"

"That girl Monica is back in town." Prince said. "I know where she is."

"Ah man, that's good looking out 'cause I'm tired of running from that rape charge."

"Go tell Hitman I'm putting a plan together to solve that problem, but right now I got to find China Doll."

"Girl, I told you Danielle called me an hour ago and said her flight would be in early," Kenya said.

"Well whatever." China Doll said.

"It ain't that deep Kenya. We'll just go to the airport early and if she's not on that plane then that would mean you're wrong and I'm right. We'll both have to wait four hours for the next plane. So you better hope you're right about her flight schedule being changed."

"I'm right, just chill and pick through them damn CD's, so we can turn this party out."

"Sshhh," China said. "Here comes Prince walking this way. Danielle definitely don't want him to know just yet she's flying in for a special visit."

"Well if she don't, then shut the hell up! He might read your lips girl."

"Yo, yo China. Damn girl I've been looking all over for you. I got something for you to do, so get with me before you leave."

"What's up Kenya/" and Prince stepped off.

"I wonder what's going down?" Kenya asked.

"It better not go down while Danielle's here or she will be pissed," China said.

"Shit! "Wait 'til Prince finds out he's got a two year old son that he don't know about. He's gonna be a lot more pissed than Danielle could ever be!" Kenya said.

CHAPTER 20

For Cindy, the past few weeks had been like déjà vu. She was trying to block her pain in order to help Mark deal with his pain of losing his dad and aunt. It was a full time job. Making sure Mark made it through all this was very important to Cindy for a few reasons; he was her friend for one and secondly she felt obligated because she had gotten Mark mixed up in this mess in the first place, but the third reason was just as important as the other two. Cindy needed Mark to help her find Ben who had mysteriously disappeared.

Cindy thought it was rather unusual that Ben had made arrangements with the funeral home to have his mother's and Mark's father's bodies cremated without consulting Mark first. In the back of her mind, she kept wondering what was really on Uncle Ben's mind.

"Mark!" Cindy yelled from the kitchen. "What do you want for dinner?"

Since she moved in with Mark, Cindy had taken on the responsibility of cooking and cleaning, which she didn't mind. It beat staying at the hotel. "Mark!" Cindy yelled again from the kitchen. She closed the refrigerator and walked into the dining room to check on Mark. He was sitting in the darkened living room listening to some music. "Hey," Cindy said walking into the living room. "You okay in here?"

"Yeah, I'm okay I guess," Mark said from his slouched position on the living room couch.

"I guess you're not eating again tonight?" Cindy said taking a seat in one of the sofa chairs. "Well, I'm not cooking another meal in this house, until you start eating."

"I'm sorry Cindy, but I just don't have an appetite," Mark said quietly.

"Listen Mark, you not eating isn't good at all. You're gonna have to snap outta this funk. I can't help you through this, if you're gonna keep looking at that vase with your father's ashes and crying."

Mark looked over at Cindy. "I can't help it Cindy. I didn't tell you, but today was my Dad's sixtieth birthday and I was just sitting here thinking about some of the good times we've shared."

"Well, that's obviously not doing you any good, because at some point and time you've got to eat Mark."

"It isn't that I don't want to. It's just that I can't."

"Would you mind if I moved that vase out of your sight?" Cindy asked. "Maybe that'll help."

"Better yet," Mark said sitting up. "Why don't we just get out of here for awhile, cause I'm tired of being cooped up in this house."

"That sounds like a great idea!" Cindy said getting up out of her chair. She moved the urn to the mantle. "There, that's better," she said stepping back.

"So, what we gonna do, catch a movie?" Mark asked as he began lacing up his gym shoes.

Cindy turned and looked at Mark. "Do you think your Uncle Ben is still in Cincinnati?"

"Your guess is as good as mine," Mark said. "Why do you ask?"

Cindy thought for a minute, "I don't know it just seems strange that he would just disappear at a time like this, without saying goodbye."

"I thought that was strange too," Mark said "but everybody deals with their grief differently."

Cindy walked back over to her chair and sat back down in deep thought. "You think it's possible that he doesn't want to be bothered? That could explain why he doesn't answer the doorbell or the phone when we call."

"Uncle Ben has always been a private person. That's why when he's home, he always stays in his mom's basement."

"You think maybe that's where he is?"

"I don't know. I'm just speculating. But I do know he's probably trippin out by now, because he left all his medication in your truck."

"Did he? Why didn't you tell me?"

"Because I just found the bag of pills under the seat this morning."

"Come on," Cindy said jumping up out of the chair. "Let's cruise by your aunt's house."

"What for?" Mark asked in protest. "We've already been by there a thousand times in the last three weeks ringing the doorbell. If he is there, he obviously doesn't want to be bothered which means, he probably won't answer the door this time."

"Well, Mr. Know-It-All," Cindy said pulling on Mark's arm. "Let's go see."

"Alright, alright," Mark said getting up off the couch. "But I still don't understand the purpose Cindy."

"Here put your jacket on and let's go. We'll talk in the truck on the way." The wheels in Cindy's mind were turning. She had a funny feeling about Ben, but she couldn't put her finger on it. Her intuition was trying to tell her something and if it was what she thought it was, finding out what Ben was up to would prove her suspicions right.

Maryann O'Bannon owned a two-story house on Dale Road in a quite North College Hill neighborhood. Mark showed Cindy how to get there the first time they went, so Cindy had no problem finding the red brick house in the dark as they pulled up and parked.

Mark looked up the two flights of stairs leading to the porch of his Aunt's house. "See I told you he wasn't here," Mark said. "That house is pitch black." Cindy leaned over trying to peek out of Mark's window at the house. "It is kind of dark up there. But that still don't tell me what I wanna know. So let's go."

"Hold up," Mark said seeing how dark it got after Cindy shut off the headlights.

"What's wrong?" Cindy asked looking over at Mark. "Don't tell me you're scared of the dark."

"Well, no I'm not, but I don't see why it takes two of us to ring one doorbell."

"Boy, if you don't come on," Cindy said reaching over Mark and opening his door for him. "You get out first."

"Why? Don't you trust me?"

"No," Cindy said and pushed Mark out the door and locked it so he couldn't open it back up. Then she hopped out and locked her side. She walked around the truck and stood next to Mark on the sidewalk. "What do you think?" Cindy asked looking up at the house. "You think he's in there?" If it hadn't been so dark, Cindy could've gotten the answer to her question by the worried expression on Mark's face.

"What do you think?" Mark said repeating Cindy's statement. "Truthfully Cindy, I think you've lost your marbles. I'll wait down here and watch the truck."

"Oh no you won't mister!" Cindy said locking her arm with Mark's. "You're the man, which means you should be protecting me and not me protecting you. So come on and stop acting scary." Cindy pulled on Mark's arm every step of the way. "I can't believe you're that afraid of the dark! What did you do when you were a child, sleep with the light on at night?"

"No and I beg your pardon," Mark said pulling his arm away from Cindy.

"I'm not scared or afraid of the dark."

"Oh okay," Cindy said giggling to herself. "Suddenly you're not scared anymore. I must have insulted that manly pride of yours."

"Yeah, yeah whatever," Mark said, "but I'm here ain't I, so put that in your pipe and smoke it."

"Alright then, I hear you talking," Cindy whispered as they reached the steps leading to the porch.

"Now that I'm up here and the doorbell is right there," Mark said pointing. "It doesn't take both of us to go on the porch to ring it does it?"

Cindy just shook her head. "Give me the bag of pills," Cindy whispered. "Remember, that's your excuse for snooping just in case he answers the door."

"Sure." Mark said reaching in his pocket and pulling out the plastic bag of pill bottles. "I bet cha he ain't here."

Cindy grabbed the bag. "Well, we're sure gonna find out," she said and stepped on the first of the six steps leading up to the O'Bannon porch.

Creak! Creak! Creak!

"I mean do you have to make so much noise?" Mark whispered.

Cindy turned around. "Shhhhh, I can't help it these old ass steps keep squeaking."

"Well try walking a little lighter."

"Shut up Mark," and Cindy took the last three steps very quickly trying not to make any more squeaking sounds before reaching the doorbell.

Cindy rang the bell and waited. She rang again and listened.

"How many times you gonna ring it?" Mark whispered. "I'm sure everybody in the neighborhood heard that."

Cindy waited to hear if she heard any movement in the house. Then she walked over to the large glass window and tried to peek in, but it was too dark.

"You see anything?" Mark whispered.

"No, not really, it's too dark," Cindy said as she pushed her face to the window again trying to see inside.

"Yeah, tell me about it," Mark said as he nervously looked around.

"Well come on then. We done already rang the bell."

"Hold your horses," Cindy said as she jumped off the porch to keep from stepping on the noisy steps again.

Mark turned to start down the concrete steps leading to the truck when Cindy pulled the back of his jacket. "Not so fast, we're not finished. Come on." Cindy said following the walkway around the side of the house.

"Hold it, wait a minute!" Mark said. "You're doing too much now. I ain't going back..." Before he could finish, Cindy had snatched his jacket and was literally pulling him deeper into the darkness as she started around the house.

"Now be real quiet," she whispered "and look for anything out of the ordinary." Cindy took the lead and Mark followed closely behind. Once they got to the back of the house Cindy noticed a small window was broken out of the back door causing Mark to almost knock her down.

"What you stop for?" Mark whispered.

"Look" Cindy said pointing at the broken window on the back door.

"Somebody's in there Mark or was in there."

"That's all I needed to know," Mark said as he turned to leave.

"Chill out!" she whispered. "What happened to all that I'm not scared stuff? "Come on."

This time Mark snatched Cindy by her jacket and pulled her back. "I'm not going in that house," he said as firmly as he could.

"Alright, alright. Let's check out the other side." and Cindy was gone leaving Mark standing in the darkness. "Mark! Mark! Mark!" Cindy said excitedly from around the side of the house. "Come here, hurry up!"

He flew around the side of the house where Cindy had discovered a basement light that was very dim, but proved that someone was actually in the house. "See, I told you," she whispered to Mark.

Mark didn't know what to say, he just pressed himself up against the house and hoped the darkness of the night kept him hidden. He looked down at Cindy who was getting on her hands and knees. "What are you doing?"

"Shhhhh!" she said. "I'm trying to peek in and see if I see anybody. Just keep a lookout." Cindy quietly slid a trashcan lid that was in her way to the side so she could see better. Mark stood behind her looking nervously from left to right while shuffling his feet. She looked up at Mark from her position on the ground. "Quit moving your feet dummy before you get us busted!" she whispered. "You're making too much noise!"

"I can't help it," Mark whispered back. "I gotta pee."

"Well hold it for a minute! I just wanna get a good look, but I can't see too good because it's a candle burning in there." She shifted her position so she could see better making sure she didn't knock over any of the trashcans. Suddenly Cindy saw movement to her left, but when she looked a little harder after her eyes had focused, she didn't see anything. At least not until she glanced down on the floor at the big metal footlocker that was open in the middle of the floor. "Oh my goodness!" Cindy whispered.

"What you see? What you see?" Mark said still rocking back and forth from foot to foot.

"A whole box full of explosives!" Cindy said in amazement. "You got to see this!"

As soon as Mark took his eyes off the house, the curtains in the first floor window suddenly flew open and Ben banged hard on the window scaring Mark so bad he screamed and tripped over Cindy at the same time coming down hard with a loud crash on top of the trash cans. This caused rats to scatter from behind the cans, which made Cindy start screaming and running leaving Mark behind. "Hey! Hey!" Mark yelled. "Don't leave me," as he rolled over the trashcans trying to get away. He jumped a little fence into the next yard and rolled down the hill of the front lawn.

Ben had scared both of them so bad; Cindy ran to the truck and almost left Mark who was rolling down the hill with garbage still stuck to his clothing. "Come on! Come on!" Cindy yelled starting up the truck.

Mark banged on the window. "Unlock the door!" he yelled looking as though he had been scared out of his mind.

Cindy popped the locks and made a quick u-turn before Mark completely got in. "Oh my God!" Mark said holding his chest as if he was about to have a heart attack. "I told you to leave him alone. I told you!"

Cindy was flying down the street, trying to put as much distance as she could between them and that house. "Oh my God!" Cindy said again holding her chest trying to calm down. Then Cindy looked over at Mark with a strange look on her face and then pulled over and stopped the truck. "Get out!"

"Get out?" Mark repeated.

"Yes, get your butt out!" Cindy said opening the door and getting out herself. Mark opened the passenger door and stepped out of the truck into the grass. "What's the problem?"

"Come around to the front of the truck!" Cindy said and stand in front of the head lights.

Mark walked around to the front of the truck, somewhat confused as to why.

Cindy looked Mark up and down. "Just what I thought!" she said and headed to the back of her truck to get a towel out of her swim bag.

She walked back to the front of the truck where Mark was still standing in the light of the truck.

"What's wrong?" Mark asked somewhat puzzled.

Cindy just shook her head and tossed Mark the towel. "You peed all over yourself stupid and now you've got my truck smelling like pee and day old trash. You're not getting back in my truck until you take those smelly clothes off. So wrap yourself in this towel and toss those clothes, so we can get the hell out of here!"

Mark's entire face turned red with embarrassment as he looked down at the huge wet spot on his jeans. "I'm sorry Cindy," he managed to say as he stepped around to the other side of the truck and began undressing.

"I guess ole Ben scared the piss out of ya!" Cindy said laughing at her own joke.

CHAPTER 21

You know there are some exceptionally fine women in this world that sometimes don't get the big bucks and golden opportunities that might pave the path for a better life. Although China Doll was just as beautiful as any woman you may see on television, she was a prime example of how the worship of money can overrule love for self, especially in today's generation. She had the potential to be somebody, but the street life was all the recognition she wanted. She loved being what most men dreams were made of and she enjoyed the attention she got from the many secret admirers that crossed her path. Tonight was a special occasion and she looked exceptionally fine in a see through lace outfit that didn't leave much to the imagination.

She turned to check herself out in the mirror one last time. "Yeah," she thought as she turned and twisted, "this should most definitely get Officer Spencer's attention tonight." The phone began to ring interrupting her thoughts. She checked her nail polish to see if they were dry before picking up the phone. "Hello," China said in her soft sexy voice.

"Hey girl! You almost ready?" Prince said into the phone

"Yup, sure am. I just got to polish my toes and pick out what shoes I'm wearing."

"Well Dino will be there in about a half to scoop you up. Don't forget your cell phone."

"I got you baby, this is the easiest money I've ever made."

"I told you it was a piece of cake," Prince said laughing into the phone.

"Well let me finish getting things ready and I'll call when Dino is on his way."

"Okay Prince," China said and she hung up.

"So, is she ready?" Dino asked from his seat at Prince's well stocked bar.

Prince walked over to the bar and poured himself a drink. He looked around his new plush apartment and offered a drink to J. Blaze, Street and Fats. "Yeah, she's ready," Prince finally said.

Street sat quietly, slouched down on Prince's new leather couch with his eyes closed, and then he opened them and looked at Prince. "You think she can handle this job?"

Prince took a seat in his favorite Lazy Boy chair and sat his drink down on the glass coffee table. "I hope she can handle it. All she got to do is keep Spencer's attention while Hustleman goes through his pockets and gets the pocketknife Gee-Gee says is there."

"Well, what if the pocket knife isn't there?" J. Blaze asked.

"We ain't going to start thinking negative," Prince said. "You know how I hate that shit. The knife will be there, you just be ready to knock that Monica bitch off," Prince said pointing at J. Blaze. "Before the night is over, we'll have Spencer and Adams in such a tight squeeze they won't know what hit'em."

Dino downed the rest of his drink and put the glass on the bar and turned in his seat after checking his watch. "I'm ready to get this shit started. I'll check you niggaz later."

"Before you drop China off, make sure she's got her cell phone."

"All right my nigga," and Dino threw up the peace sign and was on his way.

"Now," Prince said getting up "is everybody clear on what they got to do tonight?"

"Yeah," Street said. "Me and Fats gotta find Pretty Tony."

"Right and what about you Blaze? All you got to do is hit that strippers spot Kenya said Monica is working at and just keep an eye on her until we get that knife from Spencer."

"I got cha, playa," Blaze said smiling at the thought of being surrounded by strippers all night.

"Just remember nigga, this is business not pleasure. Now you niggaz get outta here, so I can finish getting dressed. And Street, leave the keys to your Cadillac and take my Yukon."

"All right cuz," Street said dropping his keys on the kitchen table and picking up Prince's keys. "We'll catch you later when we locate Pretty Tony."

Prince was in the bedroom going through his large collection of clothes in his walk-in closet when Street and Fats left. After he decided what to wear, he laid everything out on his king size bed and thought for a brief second how good the bachelor lifestyle had been to him and his crew over the years. "New cars, plush cribs and plenty of money was a far cry from the nickel and dime days at Woodward High. Yep, the street fame was good with all the money." he thought as he began to get dressed. But it didn't buy happiness. Prince was starting to think more and more about the one love he had let slip away, Danielle. She was the only girl who had ever owned a place in his heart.

Dino was the most flamboyant of the Ruff Riders. He didn't care that a young poor ass nigga out of the ghetto would look rather suspicious driving a brand new BMW around the 'hood all day. Everybody tried to tell him you're gonna make us hot man, but Dino bought the car anyway. The BMW certainly complimented China Doll's beauty as she stepped out of the car in the middle of the strip where all the playas hung out. She had enough skin showing to get a woman's attention as she closed the door to the BMW and leaned inside to thank Dino.

"You know what you gotta do, right?"

"Sure I do," China said. "Chill out here on the strip until Adams and Spencer show up, then slip into Brandy's and wait."

"Basically, yeah." Dino said. "What about your cell phone?"

"I got it," she said showing it to Dino.

"You pull this off girl, there's plenty of dough in it for you. So take care of your business. When they come to the club, get their attention, walk out and head around the corner to Gee-Gee's. They always stop by Gee-Gee's after they make their last round at the club."

After Dino finished briefing China Doll, she stepped away from the BMW and walked gracefully across the street as heads turned and car horns blew. China stood on the sidewalk when she got to the other side of the street and took a look around. The strip was jumping with people moving up and down the street. She looked up the street to see which neon flashing light belonged to the Brandy's Lounge. After seeing how far away the club was she walked the distance slowly looking around for any signs of Adams' and Spencer's cruiser. As she looked behind her, she noticed that Dino had parked and was watching her back. He flashed his lights to let her know he had her. She continued to walk slowly and her heart jumped when she spotted Adams and Spencer walking down the opposite side of the street. They were a block away and seemed to be harassing everyone. China knew she had plenty of time before they made it down that side of the street and back up her side to Brandy's. She forced herself to relax as she said hello to a few people, chit chatted a little and then continued on her journey toward the club. Taking one more glance across the street at the two cops, she stepped into the club and waited for the moment to make her move.

In the meantime on the other side of town, Pretty Tony was working his pool cue in a game of nine ball at the pool hall.

"Nine ball corner pocket to my left," Pretty Tony said.

"Run it back," said Sonny.

"I ain't running shit back nigga, not until you pay up for the three games I done already kicked your ass on," replied Tony.

"Don't sweat it, how 'bout double or nothing," Sonny said as he racked the balls. Tony stopped what he was doing and looked Sonny straight in the eye from across the pool table and said, "Nigga it sounds like you ain't got my money."

Sonny was trying to find a way out and before he could respond. Tony started around the table, but he was intercepted by another brother who pulled Tony to the side and whispered something to him. Sonny used that moment to slide towards the door. Just as he opened the door to make his escape, Pretty Tony yelled, "Hey nigga, where you going?"

Spider who was trying to talk to Tony, grabbed him by the arm and pulled him back, "Get your head right nigga. Let that chump go with that little money, you got much bigger problems to worry about right now. Street and Fats, and known killers of the Ruff Riders are waiting for your ass right now outside in a dark blue Yukon with tinted windows. Nigga you got about thirty seconds to come up with a plan before one of them haters outside tell'em you're in here."

Pretty Tony was thinking fast and then peeked out of the window to see where they were. When he saw the Yukon double parked, he turned to Spider and told him to go out back and unlock the gate leading to the alley, but to leave the lock on the fence. When Spider left and returned, Pretty Tony grabbed his pool case and hit the front door, slowly stepping into the shadows of the entrance. He stood there for a few seconds letting his eyes adjust to the dimness and tuned his ears in to hear that telltale sound that always warned him that someone was after him. Tony checked his nerves, took a deep breath and stepped into the dim streetlight turning left towards the nearest corner. He figured if they started shooting, he was dead anyway. If he could make it to the corner, he would turn it and run for his life or if all else failed he could run back through the pool hall and out the back. That was his plan if Spider had done his part. Tony listened as he walked slowly and he heard his first warning as the power windows of the Yukon came down. He heard the second warning as the engine came to life. Now that Pretty Tony knew for sure Street and Fats were looking for him, he had to decide which way to run. Watching them out of the corner of his eye, he decided the corner was too far away to chance it. As the Yukon got closer, Tony made his move and took off running back towards the pool hall.

The doors of the Yukon flew open and four Ruff Riders jumped out in hot pursuit of Pretty Tony. He hit the door about six steps ahead of the first Ruff Rider and was through the pool hall and out the back door in a flash. By the time Fats and his crew reached the back fence, Tony had locked the gate and was halfway down the alley. Prince wasn't going to like this news. Street and Fats headed back to the Yukon to tell Prince that Pretty Tony had outsmarted them. Adams and Spencer seemed to be on a serious power trip tonight as they threw everyone up against cars and walls, taking any loose change they could find from the pockets of the dope dealers they felt owed them for one reason or another. "Spread your legs or go downtown, punk," Spencer said.

"I ain't got nothing man!" one of the drug boys said as Spencer was going through his pockets.

"What's this?" Spencer asked holding up a wad of cash.

"That's my money! I got a job and today was payday."

"You got a check stub to back that story up, I assume?" He tossed the money onto the hood of a car. Spencer went through all of the dealer's pockets and didn't find drugs, so he let him rise up from the car.

"Today's your lucky day son, but I'll be watching you!" He picked up the money. "This is an awful lot of money to be carrying around at night. You'd better be careful." He gave the money back, and then grabbed two packaged rubbers off the hood and said, "I think I'll keep these for myself and my partner. We might get lucky tonight," and he walked away laughing.

The dope boy counted his money and cursed out loud as he found that three hundred was missing. He tried to burn holes in Spencer and Adams backs as he watched them walk towards Brandy's. He swore one day he'd get some get back, then got in his car and drove away. Prince was talking to China Doll on her cell phone in the club as Adams and Spencer walked in.

"Here they come baby," China said into the phone.

"Just act as if you are a little tipsy, but out for a good time. Let them make their rounds first, because they're out love shopping. When they spot you and check you out, move towards the door like you're about to leave."

"Okay baby, I got you."

"When you got 'em, call me, I got another call on hold," stated Prince and he clicked over to Fats on the other line. "What's up, Fats?"

"The nigga got away from us."

"Damn, where you at now?" Prince asked.

"We're cruising around in Avondale trying to locate the nigga."

"Listen, don't waste your time. That nigga is probably hiding under a rock by now. He'll surface again and when he does, we'll settle our score then. You and Street catch up with Hitman and J. Blaze over on the North side while I coach Gee-Gee and China on this end."

China Doll was grooving to the funky sounds the DJ was playing but making her move to the door. She stumbled a little and lost her balance. Before she could regain her composure, a pair of strong hands caught her by the arm and held her up. When she turned to thank the gentleman, she realized it was Officer Spencer. China knew she had his attention. "Now for the bait and see if he bites." Thought China to herself. She started pulling on the lace top she was wearing, just enough to expose her large pointed nipples and exclaimed how hot it was in the club. When she looked up and noticed his eyes were focused on her breasts, she handed him her empty glass and thanked him for his hospitality and started for the door.

Spencer suddenly came out of his trance and realized the woman of his dreams was getting away. He motioned for Adams to follow as he headed out after China. When China stepped into the parking lot and started towards Gee-Gee's house, she knew Adams and Spencer were behind her. She started shaking her moneymaker so nasty you couldn't help but become mesmerized. Spencer completely lost his cool and ran after China grabbing her by the arm. "Excuse me, but I don't even know your name."

China laughed a little and shot him a killer smile, displaying her pearly whites. "That's because I never gave it to you, Officer Spencer."

"Well now, you seem to know my name," replied Spencer. "It looks like you're on foot. How about I offer you a ride?"

"That's okay, I'm just around the corner."

"No, I insist really. It's late and it's my job to serve and protect."

At that moment Adams pulled up in the cruiser and Spencer hurried and opened the back door for China. "I insist," said Spencer holding the door open.

"Well let me call my cousin and let her know I'm being personally escorted by two officers to her house." She dialed Prince's number and the phone rang twice before he answered.

"Yeah baby doll, talk to me," Prince said into the phone.

"Girl, are you up? I'm on my way and guess what girl? I'm being escorted by two very handsome police officers."

"I got cha," Prince replied and hung up. He dialed Gee-Gee on speed dial and she answered on the first ring. "Get everybody ready Gee-Gee!" Prince yelled into the phone. "China Doll is on her way around the corner with Adams and Spencer."

She hung up the phone and ran to the window. She turned the lights off and told Sticky and Hustleman, who were waiting. Gee-Gee reached over and turned on the stereo and night lamp. Then she made sure Hustleman was behind the couch and Sticky was under her bed upstairs. When she ran back downstairs, she saw the cruiser do a u-turn and park in front. Gee-Gee laid on the couch in her nightgown and acted as if she were asleep. As they parked out front, Spencer and Adams looked at each other and shared a personal laugh.

China played it cool as she reached for the car door to get out.

"Here let me help you," Spencer said as he got out and opened the door.

"I saw the two of you laughing, what's so funny?" China asked in a sexy voice.

"Oh nothing," Spencer said smiling. "I've got a lady friend that lives in this building."

"Oh yeah? What's her name?"

"Gee-Gee," Spencer replied closing the car door.

"Well, small world. That's my cousin."

"Would you gentleman care to come in and have a drink with a couple of friends before you go back to work?"

Adams said nothing. He was not about to cheat on his wife. He would let Spencer have all the action.

"Sure," replied Spencer. "I'm off the clock and I could use a drink. But before we go in, you still haven't told me your name."

"The name is China Doll, but tonight you can call me whatever you like," she said with a smile as she purposefully brushed past Spencer, lightly touching the obvious bulge in his pants.

Spencer lit up like a Christmas tree as her leaned on the top of the cruiser and watched China seductively stroll up the walk and knock on Gee-Gee's door. He couldn't believe his luck and he was glad his partner had declined the invitation to get with these two hot chicks. "Man, I must be on a roll tonight!" he thought as he leaped to the porch behind China.

Holding the door open and standing there in a long sexy black nightgown was Gee-Gee. Spencer's legs turned to stone as he became stuck in one spot completely in awe of how beautiful Gee-Gee looked when completely made up. A man would be amazed at some of the magic created in a beauty and nail salon. China grabbed Spencer's hand, breaking his trance as she pulled him into the apartment and signaled to Gee-Gee to close the door.

Gee-Gee was confused at the change of plans. She thought Spencer's partner was supposed to be with them. China saw Gee-Gee's split second expression of bewilderment and she immediately took charge so Gee-Gee could pick up on the change of plans. "I love this song," China Doll said as she reached over and turned the stereo up a little. "Hey cuz" said China, "Spencer tells me that the two of you are old friends."

Gee-Gee looked at Spencer and said, "Yeah, we are."

"Well if you don't mind cuz, I'd like to see what all this is made of." At that moment China reached out and grabbed Spencer by his belt and led him toward the stairs. Gee-Gee picked up on the play and thought Adams must be sitting outside in the car. While they walked upstairs, Gee-Gee slid over to the window and peeked out. Sure enough Adams was right there in the car smoking a cigarette.

Once China and Spencer reached the bedroom, she opened the door slowly and silently prayed that the occupant in this room was safely tucked away and in a ready position. She glanced in the direction where the cam recorder was hidden making sure she had Spencer's good side was exposed as they stepped in to the room. "Come on baby," China chided as she pulled Spencer by the hand into the dimly lit room that glowed red from the lamp on the dresser. Spencer couldn't resist reaching out and grabbing that big pretty ass of China's. He squeezed it, caressed it, stuck his whole hand in it, but when he dropped to his knees and tried to bite it, China held him back. "Slow down baby," she laughed. "We've got plenty of time, but you can stay right there on your knees because I've got plans for you."

Hustleman was sweating profusely, lying on his belly under the bed with his head sideways. The space was tight and when Spencer dropped to his knees, it nearly scared the shit out of him. He thought Spencer had figured out the whole plan, so he expected to be staring down the barrel of a police issued 9mm Beretta. But no one pulled the covers back on the bed that draped to the floor hiding him, so he relaxed a little. Suddenly he heard a pair of shoes hit the floor and he thought for a moment that the plan must be in motion, but he swore he heard the cop's knees hit the floor again. Then he heard the sound of a zipper, and he saw China Doll's clothes hit the floor as he peeked out a little from under the covers. Suddenly, China stood up and Hustleman was thankful for that as it gave him more room to maneuver. Then China made Spencer stand and there was another zipper sound, then a loud thud on the floor. Instantly Hustleman realized that China had dropped Spencer's gun belt and had kicked the butt of the gun close to his head. Spencer stopped sucking on China's erect nipples and pushed her to the bed as he continued to rub and caress the length of his hard member. When China hit the bed, she landed directly on the space above Hustleman's head making it hard for him to get his hands free. Then he heard Spencer say, "Shit! Ah bitch what are you doing to me?"

China literally had Spencer by the balls with her right hand and her middle finger pressing at the tight entrance of his manhood bringing Spencer to his toes with every lick and suck she gave. When Spencer moved his feet, he kicked his pants and gun belt closer to Hustleman's hand. Hustleman was able to get his hand in Spencer's pocket and grab the little silver pocketknife. China really had her skills working to perfection as she looked up and watched Spencer's face change expressions. She looked for that one expression that told her Spencer was enjoying his short ride to ecstasy.

Downstairs, Sticky had come from behind the couch thinking Adams might come in and play too. It hadn't worked out that way, so Gee-Gee sat on the other couch having a drink while Sticky talked to Prince on the phone, giving him an update on what was going down. "We didn't get Adams in, but China is doing Spencer," he said into the phone.

"Alright," Prince said, "That's good work. Now get outta there. You got transportation?"

"Yeah," Sticky replied. "I got everything under control but directions, my nigga."

"Alright, get up to Northside and help J. Blaze out with that Monica chick."

"I got cha," Sticky said and hung up the phone. He slowly stood up and looked at Gee-Gee. "When they get done upstairs, make sure my nigga gets outta here safely. Tell him I said I'm on my way to the Northside. Check the camcorder in the bedroom and make sure everything is on tape. Then place the tape, knife and the hair samples in a safe place until Prince says he wants it."

Gee-Gee nodded her head in understanding as Stickyfingers stood at the door ready to leave. He gave her the thumbs up and slid out the door into the shadows of the night.

Things were progressing upstairs as Hustleman got back into action. China stood up again as Spencer went back down on his knees. She placed one smoothly shaven thigh on Spencer's shoulder. "Here baby take this."

Spencer couldn't resist and he didn't hesitate to dive in.

China moaned, "That's it baby." China balanced herself on one leg as Spencer went around the world. "Oh thank you baby." China said as their eyes met, "I love a fair exchange."

Now that China was no longer sitting on his head, Hustleman pushed Spencer's pants back in place and hoped China Doll would hurry. China felt the movement as Spencer's pants slightly brushed her foot. She grabbed Spencer's head tighter as his tongue worked wonders. China started to feel that familiar tingle start to creep into her toes as she felt her climax approaching. Suddenly, she let out a little scream. "Oh don't stop baby! Please don't stop!" China begged as she tightened her legs around Spencer's head. She erupted drowning Spencer with the pure pleasure of her ecstasy.

Hustleman worked his way toward the side of the bed to avoid the area he thought they would use. Suddenly China was thrown to the bed and Spencer's pants and gun belt moved as he stood up while she lay there and he prepared to mount her. Hustleman now had to wait until China and Spencer were finished humping and exchanging fuck faces. It was way to risky to move now that everything was in place and the plan so far was successful. So he lay there and listened while Spencer worked China Doll over.

Prince sat impatiently on his leather sofa having drink after drink and flicking through the cable stations wondering what was taking so long at Gee-Gee's. He grabbed the phone and dialed her number, but the answering machine came on. He took another sip from his drink, thought for a minute, and dialed the number again. Again, the answering machine came on. The recording pissed Prince off. It was some stupid song of some nigga singing about falling in love. "This is Prince....," someone picked up. "Hey yo," Prince screamed into the phone. He could hear Gee-Gee talking loud and someone arguing in the background. "What the hell is going on over there?" Prince asked fearing something had gone wrong.

"That's Hustleman and China acting up," Gee-Gee replied.

"What the hell are they arguing about? Did something go wrong?" Prince asked.

"Everything went alright," answered Gee-Gee. "Hustleman is just upset because he had to lay under the bed for so long. He accused China of screwing Spencer for two hours to make him jealous. We think his little feelings are hurt that's all. He'll get over it."

"Tell Hustleman to rush me that package," Prince said as he visualized Hustleman stuck under the bed for two hours listening to a woman he's tried to get next to for some time now, get laid by somebody else. He had to laugh a little. That must have been torture he thought. Oh well, that's business. Prince hung up the phone and dialed Blaze.

"What's up kid," Blaze spoke into his cell phone after seeing Prince's number pop up.

"Yo, listen up. Is that Monica chick still there?"

"Yup," Blaze said. "I got Sticky inside watching her while me and Hitman are chilling outside so nobody recognizes us.

"Good, smart play. I'm about to send Hustleman your way with all the goods you need to pull this off. Make sure you strangle that bitch and then plant the goods. Do you understand?"

"Yeah, yeah I got you dogg," Blaze said.

"Naw nigga. You got yourself. I didn't rape that bitch; you and Hitman did. If y'all niggaz ain't trying to spend the next ten years behind bars, you better not fuck this up."

"You got my word."

"I hope so partner, because we out here living too good to be missing out," Prince said. "Get at me when it's over. I got another call to make." and Prince hung up. He sat there and took another quick sip from his drink, made sure his nerves were calm before picking up the phone and making his last call.

Outside hidden in the shadows, was a figure that suddenly moved when he spotted his target. "Psshh, psshh." came the sound from the figure that was not recognizable, but clearly visible as he walked toward Spencer and Adams, who were still sitting out in front of Gee-Gee's crib in the cruiser. "Hey Spencer!" came a whisper from the stranger. Somewhat startled, Spencer looked out toward the sound at the same time reaching to unsnap the safety on his holster. "Relax," the shadow said upon approaching the cruiser. The stranger's cell phone rang and he handed it to Spencer. "It's for you," he said handing the phone to Spencer. He grabbed the phone and said 'Hello?"

"Yeah, this is Prince. We've got a deal. You can pick your little extortion money up tomorrow night at Brandy's."

"I'm not taking a payoff in a public place!" Spencer yelled into the phone.

"Relax cop, cause I don't trust you either. Just meet me at Brandy's and I'll tell you where to pick your ten grand up," and the line went dead.

Spencer looked at the phone and then looked around for the stranger, but he had disappeared into the night. Adams looked at Spencer and asked, "What's wrong?"

He flipped the phone shut and stated, "Nothing, that was Prince and he agreed to pay our price. We can pick the money up tomorrow night at Brandy's."

Adams started the cruiser and said, "Smart man that Prince is. He can afford ten grand."

"Hell, he's got the entire city selling dope for him," Spencer said. "He can afford 100 grand I bet."

You might be right partner, Adams said and they both shared a little laugh.

Chapter 22

Ben O'Bannon wasn't one for a lot of words; never had been and never would be. First it was the cops that came knocking, and then detectives, and now his nephew Mark and his girlfriend were snooping around. All this unwanted attention prompted Ben to place several "No Trespassing" signs all over his mother's property hoping to discourage anyone else from violating his personal space. Ben missed his mother everyday that went by and every night he cried. Love one, love another but a mother's love can never be replaced. He swore to himself that he wasn't going anywhere. Uncle Sam's war in the Middle East could wait because he had his own war to fight right here in Cincinnati. His mental state was deteriorating because his wasn't taking his medication and he slipped further away from reality.

During the day, Ben became invisible by staying confined to the basement of his mother's house. He cleaned and admired his most prized possession, a gun collection started eight years ago when he first started traveling from country to country on various missions. As a commander of one of the United States Army's top-secret terrorism units, Ben's unit was considered to be one of the best in the world. By the standards of the United States Army, Lt. Ben O'Bannon was indispensable. So when it was discovered that Lt. O'Bannon was two weeks past his intended return date, the Department of Defense, urged by Ben's commanding officer Major Vince Highland, declared him AWOL. They couldn't afford to have such a valuable and highly trained soldier fighting his own battles at the expense of the United States Army, but Ben didn't care. So every morning that he retrieved the daily paper that was delivered, he ignored the many letters in the mailbox that were embossed with the seal of the United States Army. Ben wasn't about to give up his search for his mother's killers, not for Uncle Sam, not for the Cincinnati Police, not for anyone. Personally he thought he was about to do a lot of people a big favor by getting rid of the scum of the Earth.

Ben peeked out from behind the curtains in the front room, making sure no one was paying attention before he opened the front door and grabbed the newspaper. Everyday he read the morning paper hoping to gather more information on the operations of the Ruff Riders. As a child Ben grew up in Cincinnati, so knowing the territory wasn't a problem. But knowing more about the players was and that was one of Ben's biggest obstacles. Knowing who was directly involved was Ben's primary concern at this point as he headed back down the basement stairs with the Cincinnati Enquirer tucked safely under his arm. Who were the key players or the opposition so to say, was Ben's focus. Once he answered that question, he could begin his process of elimination. Cindy hadn't had a peaceful night's sleep since the night at Maryann O'Bannon's house. Ben had practically scared the daylights out of her and Mark. Although the bed she was sleeping on in the O'Bannon's guest room was really cozy and comfortable, it still wasn't her own. She was lying there wide-awake thinking about the normal life she missed. She missed her sister Gina and her Aunt Debra and Uncle Tom. A jumble of thoughts crowded together as she lay there thinking about the entire mess. The reality of her possibly fighting a losing battle was starting to set in. She was starting to feel like she was in way over her head, when suddenly the alarm clock on the dresser started buzzing startling her as she jumped up and turned the alarm off. "Okay Cindy," she said to herself as she sat down on the edge of the bed. "Think girl, you gotta think!" but she was fresh out of ideas. "Maybe it's time to throw in the towel and let the police do their job," she thought. She thought about Ben and his crazy ass. Maybe Ben wasn't the answer to gain her revenge. He wasn't much help. But she still had a gut feeling that he was up to something. As a matter of fact, she was sure of it after seeing the explosives in the trunk from the basement window.

She missed her Mom and Dad at times like this, and to make matters worse, Cindy was starting to feel lonely as she yearned for somebody to talk to this morning. So she slipped her feet into a pair of slippers and headed downstairs to put on a pot of coffee. The only friend in the world she had to talk to was Mark. She made enough noise going down the stairs to wake him up so they could talk. "Mark, its time to get up!" She tapped on his bedroom door. "Come on Mark, get up."

"For what?" Mark yelled through the door. "It's only eight o'clock Cindy and I don't have no where to go. So let me sleep, will you?"

"No, I won't. Now get up Mark. I'm going downstairs to put on some coffee and I want to talk to you, so please get out that bed or else I'm coming back." The morning sun lightly peeked through the kitchen curtains as she put on a pot of coffee. "My, what a lovely morning!" she thought as she opened the curtains to allow the sunlight to completely engulf the kitchen. She opened the refrigerator and grabbed some milk to set on the kitchen counter top. Then she turned and reached inside the cabinet for the box of 'Captain Crunch' cereal. Mark still hadn't come downstairs so she took the milk and cereal into the dining room and placed them on the table. "Mark, breakfast is ready. Come on Mr. Peebody and eat breakfast!" Cindy knew she would get a response when she called him Mr. Peebody, because he hated it when she teased him about peeing on himself the night his uncle scared the daylights out of him.

"Alright Cindy!" Mark yelled from upstairs. "You promised you wouldn't call me Peebody anymore."

"Well get your butt down here then. If you are not down here by the time I get the newspaper, I'm gonna call you Mr. Peebody all day!" By the time she stepped out on the porch and back in with the paper, Mark was sitting on the bottom step yawning and rubbing the sleep from his eyes. Cindy stopped and started giggling.

"What's so funny?" he said standing up and walking into the dining room. "I was checking out your Scooby-Doo pajamas. They're so cute!" she said smiling at Mark and pulling on his pajama top.

"Get off," Mark said pulling away and having a seat at the table. "I haven't forgot that you just called me Peebody."

"Oh, poor baby," Cindy teased Mark. "I'm sorry, Cindy didn't mean to hurt your little feelings."

"It's nice to know that you're not a woman of your word, because you promised you wouldn't call me that anymore."

"Alright, alright for real. My bad, but you wouldn't get out of the bed and I didn't realize you were so sensitive."

"Well I am," Mark said. "Now where's this breakfast you were saying was ready, because I know you wasn't talking about this cereal and milk." I could've fixed this myself when I got up.

"Well, I hate to disappointed you, but that's the breakfast I was talking about. So get on up with your Scooby-Doo pajamas on and get yourself a bowl and dig in," Cindy said as she pulled the plastic off the Cincinnati Enquirer.

Ben couldn't believe his luck when he looked at the 'Tri-State Most Wanted' in the back of the metro section and discovered photos, names and information on the Ruff Rider gang.

"If you have any information on the whereabouts of any members of this gang, please call Crimestoppers at 711-GOTU. A reward of up to $5,000 could be yours if the information leads to an arrest. All of these suspects are wanted for charges ranging from murder, felonious assault, drug trafficking, and rape. Caution, please do not approach these people as they are considered armed and dangerous."

Ben examined each and every photo closely, as if trying to get to know them. Then he began cutting all the information out, so he could add it to his notebook of gathered information.

"Michael Roberts, aka 'Street'. Wanted: Murder
Last known address 2212 Winton Place
Drives a late model Burgundy Cadillac

Ben looked at Street's photo thinking that he looked vaguely familiar. But it was hard to tell because the few times he had observed the gang in action, it was either too dark to get a good look or all of them were sporting white t-shirts and looked alike. But he had a solution for that problem. He would use his night vision goggles that saved his life on many occasions while hunting down bad boys in unfamiliar terrain on his missions for Uncle Sam. Ben continued cutting and pasting names and photos of each gang member into his personal file.

Jeff Wright, aka 'J. Blaze'. Wanted for rape and drug trafficking
Charles Carter, aka 'Hitman'. Wanted for rape and drug trafficking.
Adressess Unknown...

Ben was upset because the main player who ran this outfit, according to the word on the street, was a cat named Prince and he wasn't one of those listed in today's paper. Ben wanted Prince the most. "Kill the head and the body will die." was what Ben always told the soldiers under his command.

Captain Safeway was grasping at straws hoping for a break when he placed those photos in the paper. All he could hope for is that his plan made somebody nervous enough to run into several well placed TNT officers and FBI agents strategically placed in various areas known for Ruff Rider activity. Captain Safeway didn't have enough men to cover everything owned and operated by the gang and it was all or nothing for the police at this point. So asking for a little assistance from the Feds wasn't above him. After all, the gang was a very ruthless bunch of kids. The extra four thousand the Captain tacked on to the thousand dollar reward came out of his pocket, because he felt like this case was about to bust open and he wanted to encourage anyone with information to come forward. None of the kids at Woodward would talk to the police or the school principal Mr. Brunson. Tom had tried both with no results. All he got was the school photos and a visit from Monica Johnson at the precinct, who finally decided to sign a statement for the rape charges. That had helped to turn up the heat a little, if he could keep Monica from running away again. But Monica's running days were over. The Ruff Riders had made sure of that. Captain Safeway just had not heard the news yet.

"No, I'm not! No, I'm not! No, I'm not!" Mark repeated to Cindy.

Cindy's response was, "Yes, you are! Yes, you are, Mark!"

"No, I'm not!" Mark said and sat back in his chair folding his arms across his chest.

"Mark!" Cindy screamed from across the dining room table. "Yes, you are and I ain't playing with you either boy!"

"But...but, you can't make me," and he sat there with his lip stuck out like a little kid.

"Mark," Cindy said in a quiet voice, "look at it this way. Don't you want to help catch your Dad's and Aunt's killers, plus get paid for it?"

He looked across the table with his arms still folded and said, "I don't care about the money and I done already helped with the investigation by busting you out the hospital and since then we've been on adventure after adventure of yours and I'm not going."

"You're still mad at me about calling you Peebody, ain't you?"

"Yup, and you promised you wouldn't."

"Well what if I told you, I'd never call you Mr. Peebody again and split the five thousand dollar reward money with you. If you just drive me to the club and wait in the car, I'll go in and take the picture of Prince, since I'm the one who remembers what he looks like."

"Well," Mark said rubbing his chin, then pushing his glasses up on his nose, "maybe, but only on one condition."

"Oh boy, and what's that?"

"If we get into any more trouble, you got to promise to tell the Captain it was all your idea and I had nothing to do with it."

Cindy hurried and stuck her hand across the table. "Deal."

Mark got up from the table and said, "Remember you promised. I'll be upstairs watching some tube."

Cindy thought turning in the photo of Prince would help the police in their search for her parent's killers since it was obvious they didn't have a suspect. "So how are they going to catch somebody when they don't even know what he looks like? A photo of Prince should be worth a thousand words and five thousand dollars," she thought. What Cindy didn't know was that Captain Safeway had kept Prince's photo out the paper because he didn't want to spook the gang leader into leaving town. He wanted him to feel safe to move about.

She got up from the dining room table and started toward the kitchen with the dirty bowls and box of cereal. On her way back, she stopped and glanced in the mirror. "If I'm gonna be seen tonight, I need a makeover, bad!" she said as she got closer to the mirror. Her mind was racing with plans and ideas. "I need a camera," she thought as she walked into the living room. She ran her fingers through her long hair.

"I need a haircut. Yeah, a haircut, that's what I need! Something completely different that would change my appearance." Then she thought she should find a beauty salon first and let them worry about her new look. Cindy thought about how women like to talk. She could kill two birds with one stone if she got her hair done and at the same time, get an earful on the latest happenings in the streets. She thought about the Jukebox Tavern and its location on Chase Street. Then it hit her, Hair and Nail Options. "That's where that girl Stephanie works who won the 2002 award for best hairstylist competition. Yeah!" Cindy thought. "Her spot is right on Hamilton Avenue, right around the corner from Chase Street and the Juke Box!" Cindy jumped up and grabbed the white pages off the desk, found the number and called to schedule an appointment.

The phone rang twice before someone answered, "Hair and Nail Options."

"Yes, I would like to know if you have any room for another appointment today?" Cindy asked.

"Stephanie," she could hear the girl ask, "do you have room for another appointment?"

Cindy could hear the voice in the background saying she was booked before the girl came back to the phone. "I'm sorry, but...."

Cindy cut her off by saying, "I know this is short notice and my mistake for calling so late, but I'm willing to pay one hundred dollars for the inconvenience if you can persuade Stephanie to take two hundred dollars for a quick haircut and style. I really would appreciate it."

The phone went silent, as if someone put their hand over the mouthpiece. Then the girl's voice returned, "I think we can fit you in. What time today would you like to come in?"

Cindy thought for a moment and said, "Make it around 5:30 this evening."

And what name should I put your appointment under?"

"Cindy Whitehead, and may I ask who I'm speaking to?"

"I'm the owner, Shonie Carter," replied the voice from the other end.

"Well thank you Ms. Carter," replied Cindy.

"Call me Shonie, baby. We're all family up in here."

"Okay," Cindy laughed and said, I'll be there at 5:30 this evening," and hung up.

While Cindy was making her plans to be part of tonight's festivities at Brandy's, Ben O'Bannon was busy making preparations to crash the party as well. He opened the hidden compartment inside the basement walk-in closet. He flipped on the light and stood there in the small space admiring the many souvenirs he had collected from various places around the world.

Neatly mounted on hooks on one wall was a vast assortment of machine guns, which were his pride and joy. The collection included two German machine guns, a Browning machine gun, one each Chinese and Japanese machine gun, a Winchester and a La France semi-automatic machine gun. None of the weapons had ever been fired. Then Ben turned around to observe what other choices of firepower that rested on several shelves behind him. Let's see, on the top shelf he had two Colt pistols, three Berettas, a sixteen shot Glock pistol and several Rutger revolvers. Below, on the other shelves, he had stored several miscellaneous items like a Mossburg shotgun, two Remington sniper rifles with scopes, a few urban precision silencers and over three thousand rounds of assorted ammunition.

Ben looked over everything, trying to decide which weapon of choice would be appropriate for tonight's mission of revenge. He picked up one of his Berettas off the shelf, then grabbed a silencer and screwed it into place on the barrel. He thought, "Yeah this should be enough." He tested the weight of the Beretta with the silencer in his hands. Stroking the gun as if it were a baby, Ben felt his adrenalin begin to rush and that spelled trouble for somebody. He reached for a clip and loaded the Beretta and clicked the safety on. "One more thing," Ben said to himself, "I need something heavy." He looked around the closet.

"I need something that'll back everybody up if I get in a jam," he thought.

Later that afternoon, Cindy took a shower and threw on jeans and a t-shirt. She started blow-drying her hair, trying not to be late for her hair appointment. She was pretty excited about getting a new look and a chance to be out tonight. Cindy knocked lightly on Mark's door to tell him she was leaving, but he was curled up in a ball and sound asleep. She didn't disturb him; she just quietly closed the door behind her and let herself out the house.

While Cindy was on her way to the North side to catch her appointment at Hair and Nail Options, Ben was searching frantically in his closet for a brown box full of blasting caps and detonators. "Shit!" Ben said to himself. "I know they were in here!" he thought as he looked around the closet and then into his bedroom to look as well. He looked inside the trunk of C4 explosives he pulled from the closet. He moved several bricks of C4 aside searching for the blasting caps. "Nope, not there." he thought as his eyes scanned the room. He had searched everywhere trying to remember, but his memory failed him. "No blasting caps, no explosives." he thought and he loved explosives, He sat down on the bed and tried to remember where in the hell had he hidden the blasting caps and detonators.

Cindy drove past the tavern and stopped at the light on Chase and Hamilton. She turned to her right and there was Hair and Nail Options. She parked in the back of the building and walked to the entrance. Before she could reach for the knob and open the door, it swung open and laughter filled the street as two women were leaving. They were joking with the ladies inside. Someone called to Cindy as she stepped into what looked to be the waiting area. "You must be Cindy," a young lady said.

"Yes, I am," Cindy replied.

"Well hello," she said extending her hand to shake Cindy's. "My name is Shonie. We spoke on the phone and I arranged your appointment with Stephanie." She directed Cindy into the salon.

"Hi Cindy, I'll be with you in a moment."

"Thank you." replied Cindy as she handed Shonie the hundred-dollar bill.

"I love it when money comes this easy!" said Shonie with her biggest smile. "Make yourself at home sweetie. Ladies introduce yourselves. This is Cindy Whitehead." and Shonie disappeared into the other room.

After going through a few quick introductions, Cindy decided on a chair she spotted in a corner. It was perfect for being out of the way, but still within earshot of any conversation.

Stephanie was just finishing with the girl she in her chair. "I just put you on the map with this one!" she stated as she stepped back to admire her work. "Ladies check her out." The other stylist agreed with Stephanie. "Where you going tonight, girl?" she asked.

The girl in the chair stated she was headed to Brandy's.

"You got that right!" Stephanie replied. "I might show my face there tonight."

"Well I'll be there," said the girl as she paid and left.

"Come on Cindy," Stephanie said. "What do you want done today?"

"Something low, something different and something I can sport at Brandy's tonight."

Stephanie and the girls laughed, "I got you girl, don't worry."

Cindy decided that this was as good enough time as any to ask about the shooting around the corner. "It looked like something pretty ugly happened around the corner at that bar."

That brought a response from everyone in the room. Cindy just sat back and listened. One thing about black folks, they stay up on current events. All the girls went on talking until someone mentioned Prince's name.

"Who's Prince?" asked Cindy.

One girl stood up and acted like she was riding a horse and then said, "a Ruff Rider." Then she slapped another girl a high five as everyone laughed at the girl's version of Prince being a Ruff Rider.

"Don't pay her no attention Cindy," said Stephanie. "She just happens to be the only girl in here who has fucked Prince and for some reason she thinks that's something to brag about," and everybody started laughing.

Mia was the girl's name that Stephanie was talking about and even she had to laugh because it seemed to be true. "Don't be jealous, because he offered and I accepted. If it were you Stephanie, you'd be talking shit too!" Mia said. "Not only is that nigga fine, he's rich too, and I'd rather give him some pussy than one of these broke ass niggas you whores been sleeping with."

That struck a nerve with Stephanie because she knew like everyone else, that her man was laid off. But she still loved him because he was an honest man trying to earn a honest living. "Alright bitch!" Stephanie said as she stopped working on Cindy's head to turn and stare at Mia. Tension was in the air, but Mia didn't want any trouble with Stephanie for real, so she walked out of the room. Stephanie put the finishing touches on Cindy's new hairstyle. It was like magic! Her new style was short as requested, but sexy. Cindy was officially fine as hell.

Cindy got up out of the chair and turned to look in the mirror to admire her new self. The other girls in the shop loved it and so did Cindy. She checked her watch, then searched her purse and handed Stephanie two hundred dollars as agreed.

****

Ben finally remembered that the box he was looking for was hidden under his bed. So after he cursed himself for fifteen minutes for being so forgetful, he realized nightfall was creeping up on him and he hadn't made one bomb yet. So he started cursing himself again for another fifteen minutes for just being plain stupid. Ben's mind was gone for real. Insane was an understatement, because he was doing the Jeckle and Hyde thing as his mind continued to flip from one personality to another. Every time he became frustrated, he thought he was cussing out one of his soldiers under his command.

"Didn't I tell you soldier to stay focused?" Ben yelled at himself. The outbursts were beginning to become more frequent for Ben as the sane half of his mind continued to slip farther into the darkness of his insanity. Ben needed his medication because by now he was a walking time bomb.

CHAPTER 23

"Okay gentleman, have a seat. We don't have much time to go over these plans," Captain Safeway yelled from the front of the conference room. "I called this emergency meeting because our hard work has finally started to pay off," Captain Safeway said pacing the front of the room. "We've been working in two shifts for the past week, collecting data on the movements of this gang." Tom stopped at the podium and opened a folder he had there for this briefing. He looked up from the folder and said, "Tonight we go hot gentleman. I moved the timetable up because there is a lot of activity going on in the Ruff Riders organization. It looks like the Ruff Riders are closing up a lot of shops we've been watching for the past few months and they seem to be moving money around was the last report that came in. So, I'm thinking somebody is trying to run. Tonight we touch this gang good and roll with what evidence we've got on these kids. Team One surveillance team has located the burgundy Cadillac and has positively identified the driver as Michael Roberts, aka "Street". That's the break we've been waiting for. We've been trying to bust this gang down for over two years now and we still only have knowledge of just a small portion of what this gang owns and operates, but after Team One gets through watching Mr. Street make his rounds we'll know about everything they own."

"Good call Captain!" an officer shouted as many nodded their approval of Captain Safeway's plan.

"Once Team One has pinned Street and his partner down to one location, that's when we'll bust him and confiscate the money. Plus we will raid every house and place of business he has visited. "Is everybody okay with that?" Captain Safeway asked the group. "Any questions?"

"Sounds good to us," Officer Spencer said catching Captain Safeway's attention.

"Officers Spencer and Adams."

"Yeah Captain," Spencer said from his seat.

"I want you and your partner to monitor any gang activity on the street, then report back to me."

"Sure Captain," Spencer replied.

"Okay gentleman, let's get loose and ready. We've got a few FBI boys coming to help us cover some of this territory, so be nice!" Captain Safeway yelled over the chatter that had started up. "We ride out in an hour. I'll be placing teams where they need to be once we get saddled up and in the garage," Captain Safeway said as he began shoving papers back into the folder at the podium. Out the corner of his eye he watched Officer Spencer's reaction as the room began to empty and as expected Officer Spencer started toward the front of the room.

"Um excuse me Captain," Officer Spencer said stepping towards Tom. "Why are you taking me off the task force team for tonight's operation? Remember, I'm one of the most experienced guys you got," Spencer said blowing his own horn a bit.

As Captain Safeway stood there listening to Spencer, he shifted his eyes to Officer Adams who stood a good distance away not wanting any part of the confrontation. At that moment, Tom decided he made the right decision not to involve Spencer and Adams in tonight's raid. Spencer had never set off good vibes and Adams acted like a cowardly puppet that viewed his partner as his master rather than his equal. These two were worthless and that's just what Captain Safeway was thinking when Spencer got finished whining in his ear.

After Spencer was finished, Captain Safeway politely said, "I'm sorry Officer Spencer if you are not happy with your assignment, but for your peace of mind I'm not taking you off the task force team I'm just expanding it and your assignment is to patrol the strip tonight and observe any gang activity. I want to know every move that is made on Reading Road. Is that clear?"

"Yes sir," Spencer said.

"You can move out at any time," Captain Safeway said walking away. You don't have to wait for everyone else."

Spencer just stood there burning a hole in Captain Safeway's back, when his cell phone began to ring. "Yeah, this is Officer Spencer."

"You got that information I want?" the voice asked.

At first Spencer was puzzled as to who the caller was, then it dawned on him and he started looking around to make sure no one was within earshot. "Do you have the money I asked for?" Spencer whispered back.

"Don't play games! I ain't got time for that," Prince snarled.   "I'll be at the back of Woodward High School in thirty minutes with your money."

Spencer flipped his phone shut. "Cocksucker," he said to himself.

"Who was that?" Adams asked from his seat next to Spencer.

"You know who it was. Come on," Spencer said as he started out the roll call room.

****

Dusk was falling quick over the city, a sure sign that nightfall was only a few hours away.   Street and his brother Fats had just finished making their rounds picking up the money from the house joints and dope houses. They rode with their 9mm's in their laps, ready for whatever, as they turned down 13th Street on their way to Gee-Gee's house joint.   Street pulled up in front of the house and looked at the front window. "Do it look like Gee-Gee's in there?" Street asked his brother.

"You want me to go kick on the door?" Fats asked.

Street put the Cadillac in park and looked at the windows again, then checked his rearview mirror. "I really don't feel like dealing with Gee-Gee," Street said thinking aloud.

"I know her money is funny anyway."

"Fuck it," Street finally said. "Yeah, go kick on the door."

Fats jumped out of the Cadillac leaving his pistol on the seat. He knocked on Gee-Gee's door.

Street rolled down the window.   "Come on bro, she ain't there," and he let the window back up.   He grabbed his cell phone and called Prince.

Prince's cell phone rang twice before he answered. "Yo, my brother. How's it going?" Prince asked.

"Man we getting it, that's for sure. We got over two hundred G's in the trunk now and we still have five more houses to pick up from," Street said turning the burgundy Caddie onto 13th Street.

"Well, what about the ya yo? Are you dropping them packages off too?"

"Of course! We ain't shutting down is we?" Street asked as he cruised and lowered his window. "Ah, yo P Man!" Street yelled out to one of the homie's.

"Nigga talk to me and not at them niggaz on the block!" Prince yelled into the phone.

"I'm listening to ya nigga! Damn, slow down," Street replied as he slowed the Caddie down a bit.

"Listen Street, don't be bullshitting cuz about picking up that money 'cause we got the cops breathing down our backs," Prince said into the cell phone.

Street was listening and about to respond, when he looked into the drivers' side mirror and noticed a car pull over and stop.

"Yeah, I'm listening to ya cuz," Street said quietly as he turned the car stereo down. "Fats, I think we got the cops on our tail," Street said holding the phone up to his ear and watching the car in the mirror.

"You got the police on you man?" Prince asked into the phone.

"I think," Street said.

Street's boy P Man was sitting on the step across the street and he shouted out to Street. "You know the police just pulled up and parked up there nigga. You better watch 'em."

"I got you P Man," Street nodded as he and his brother Fats both laid their pistols on the front seat next to them.

"You hear that?" Cory whispered.

"Yeah, I heard it," Detective Hunter said as he spoke into his radio. "Unit Three to base. I think we've been made. I repeat, I think we've been made," he whispered.

"Get outta there," Captain Safeway said into his radio. "Hurry up, we don't want to spook him."

"I hear you Captain," Cory said. The two detectives pulled their red Taurus with dark tinted windows away from the curb and drove right past Street's Cadillac.

Both Street and Fats grabbed their guns tightly watching the red Taurus as it pulled up the street slowly passing by. "Yeah sucka, I see you," Street said.

P Man laughed at the cops. "Yeah, we see you."

"Damn, that was close," Fats said as he started breathing again. "Shit!"

Street relaxed as he slapped his little brother in the chest and said, "That's why we wear these bullet proof vests, because they just didn't know about the gun battle we were about to have had they stopped us.

"Base to Unit 6. Do you copy?"

"Yeah Captain, we copy."

"Unit 3's cover has been blown. Can you pick that tail up on Street over on 13th?" Captain Safeway asked.

"Sure Captain. We'll pick it up and report back when we're in position."

"Thank you, Unit 6. We can't afford to lose this guy."

Prince rang Street's cell phone right back.

"Yeah cuz," Street said. "Everything's cool. They're gone and we're on the move right now."

"Damn man, watch your back!" Prince screamed into the phone. "You're slipping cuz, again!"

"I got everything under control," Street said starting the Caddie up as he watched the rear view mirror.

"Yeah, I hope so cause you got all our damn money in the trunk of that damn car and you're out there bullshitting acting ghetto fabulous!" Prince yelled into the phone. "Leave them niggaz and hos alone on the block and focus nigga on taking care of your damn business. Fuck!" Prince screamed and hung up in Street's ear. He was super heated at his cousin's carelessness and he let out a barrage of strong curse words. "Damn that nigga can be stupid ass hell some damn time!" Prince said to the rest of the gang.

Kenya was sitting on the bleachers behind Prince eavesdropping.

"Let me take a guess," she said. "Street is slipping again."

Prince slowly sat up on his bike placing his feet on the ground and turning around to give Kenya a look that said, "Wrong time bitch, don't play," then he slowly turned back around on his motorcycle and kicked his feet back up. He slipped back into his train of thought as he watched Blaze and Sticky throw the football.

China Doll, who was polishing her bike as she killed time, caught Kenya's eye and put a finger up to her lips to shush her and to let her know not to play with Prince like that when he's mad. Then China whispered, "He'll flip on your ass."

Kenya got up and walked between China and Prince, getting out the line of fire. "My bad," she said as she joined Blaze, Hitman and Stickyfingers on the football field for a game of catch, as everybody waited for the next move.

Everybody knew Prince was heated with his cousin for a few reasons. Street was taking too many pills, smoking too much weed, and taking too many chances at the wrong damn time.

"Fifty two – Red, Blue – Hut, Hut and J. Blaze dropped back and threw the football way over Sticky's head.

Sticky stepped off the line of scrimmage and just watched the ball sail way over his head. "Damn boy! You done got rusty over the years," as he trotted to get the ball and you thought you could make it in the NFL.

J. Blaze was standing on the fifty-yard line kind of winding his arm up as if trying to get it loose. "My bad dogg. That one got away from me," J. Blaze said as Sticky came back with the ball laughing.

"Yeah, my nigga. I hear ya," tossing him the football. "Nigga, you ain't got it in ya no more," Sticky said smiling showing off his gold grill. "You use to be the best at this shit"!

"Aw nigga, you talking shit now huh," Blaze said flipping the football from hand to hand. Nigga I'm still good enough to play college ball. Call the play chump and I bet you it'll be on the money." J. Blaze said.

Sticky looked over at Hitman, who was just listening and laughing. "You think this nigga still got it?" Sticky asked Hitman. The nigga say he can still play college ball. Our days of playing college ball is over my brother, we gave that dream up when we choose this fast money," Sticky said stepping up to J. Blaze.

"Don't remind me," Blaze said stepping up to the fifty-yard line and placing the ball on the ground. He reached in his pocket and pulled out a few hundred bucks and waved them at Stickyfingers. "If it ain't on the money, you win but if it is on the money I win. At a hundred dollars a pop of course."

"Naw nigga, I ain't going to let you get me like that," Sticky said laughing at Blaze. "If it's on the money and I catch it, don't nobody win playa."

"Oh, it's on," Blaze said shaking his head and coming out of his Timberland boots.

Everybody was gathering around getting in on the fun.

"Damn dogg, you ain't playin' are ya?" Sticky said laughing looking at Blaze. "You're taking your boots off."

"Yep, cause I'm about to light dat ass up," Blaze said pulling his socks up.

"You ready?"

"Like Freddie," Sticky said taking his gold chain off.

Blaze picked the ball up. "Hitman, check this nigga. He ain't going to get it that easy." He held the football out as if he were hiking it. "I hope you remember the plays dogg 'cause I'm throwing like Coach Andrews taught us, to the spot and at the numbers. If you ain't there to catch it, just trot your ass back in here with my hundred dollars. Ready. Set. Red. Green. Sixty-Nine. Slash right. Hut, hut!" He did a three-step drop, held the titty of the football tight and threw a tight spiral down the field.

Sticky put a move on Hitman and streaked down the field looking up over his left shoulder like Coach Andrews taught him and picked the ball out the air. Kenya, Dino and Hustleman started clapping and trash talking.

"Yeah baby boy," Sticky said smiling. "I still got it," as he tossed the ball back to Blaze.

"Alright, come on next play," Blaze said talking trash.

Prince took his eyes off the fun and games on the football field and watched as a pair of headlights appeared over the hill behind the school. He watched as the lights circled the back lot and then came to a halt. He leaned up on his Suzuki bike and looked hard. The headlights blinked at him twice. Prince turned the key and the GSXI 1300 five speed came to life. "We've got company on the hill," Prince said.

"Who dat be?" Sticky and Blaze asked Prince.

Prince looked into the compartment on the back of his Suzuki and grabbed a plastic bag containing a small vial of blood he had Blaze and Hitman get from Monica Johnson's dead body, then he made sure her hair samples where present before he placed the bag in his jacket pocket. "Take a guess," Prince said as he put his driving gloves on and snuggly set the brown bag with the ten grand in it between his legs on the bike. "Everybody sit tight while I go deal with these chumps." He gunned the bike's engine spinning the back wheel. The bike leaped forward in the direction of the car parked on the hill. Suddenly, the moment became serious as the rest of the gang gathered around looking and watching, making sure Officers Spencer and Adams hadn't brought company with them.

Prince sped out of the stadium entrance and up the asphalt hill leading toward the back parking lot of the school. Although it was getting dark and Prince had his tinted visor down on his helmet, he could still see inside the police car as he circled checking the area out. So when he pulled the bike up next to the police cruiser, he watched Officer Spencer very closely as he shut the bike off. "Where's your partner?" he asked from under his visor.

Spencer flicked his cigarette butt out the window and watched the fire bounce on the asphalt parking lot. He looked at Prince and his bike. "The dope game must really be profitable these days for a punk to be able to afford one of those."

Prince dropped the kickstand down and slowly took his helmet off and placed it on the backrest of the bike. Then he relaxed and looked the crooked cop in his face. "That's not what I asked you," Prince said.

"It's none of your business where my partner is. You're not doing business with him; you're doing business with me. So where's the money?"

Prince got off his bike and tossed the brown paper bag of money through the driver's window onto Spencer's lap. "There's ten grand as agreed. Count it!"

As Spencer's eyes became focused on all the cash, Prince jumped in the back seat of the cruiser uninvited and shut the door behind him.

"Now let's talk about what my ten grand is going to do for me." As Prince was having this conversation with officer Spencer, he also was opening the plastic bag containing the vial of Monica's blood and hair samples, spilling it all over the carpet of the cruiser's floor. He planted the evidence while Spencer eagerly counted his riches. When he was finished he noticed Prince sitting in the back.

"First of all," Spencer said looking Prince straight in the eyes through his rearview mirror, "I didn't tell you to get into my car, so get out!"

"Get out," Prince repeated. "Ain't that a bitch? I ain't going nowhere until..."

Click!! Spencer turned in his seat stopping Prince in mid sentence, and Prince suddenly realized he was staring down the barrel of Spencer's gun pointed through the fence in between the front and the back seat of the cruiser. "I'm not playing. Get out now," Spencer said.

"Oh I see, it's like that," Prince said opening the door and getting out while keeping an eye on the cop.

"Now, shut my door," Spencer said still pointing his pistol at Prince. "You must think I'm stupid or something," Spencer said to Prince as he exited the police cruiser. "I don't have private conversations with my clientele," Spencer said laughing. "You'll never set me up. Everything is cool right now, so you don't have to worry about any heat. I'll be at Brandy's tonight and we can talk then." Spencer backed the cruiser away from the spot where Prince was standing. "I'll be in touch when I've got something to tell you. In the meantime, don't call me. I'll call you and thanks for the generous donation," Spencer said laughing as he drove away.

Prince sat there on his bike watching the tail lights disappear at the far end exit of the parking lot. "Right back at cha, Prince said to himself. "One dirty deed in exchange for another sounds fair to me," Prince thought as he put his helmet on and started his bike up. "Them blood and hair samples on that carpet will determine who gets the last laugh," Prince quietly said as he tossed the empty vial that had carried Monica's blood into the bushes.

Unfortunately, Monica had determined her own fate when she decided to sign a statement saying two of the Ruff Riders had raped her at school and wanted to press charges. Had she kept quiet, Prince would've allowed her to live. But she talked and for that Prince had no other choice but to protect his own, so now her lifeless body lay naked in a wooded area of Eden Park strangled to death with all sorts of surprises placed around the body just for the police to find.

****

Cindy had just about finished getting dressed. She looked into the mirror and received her own approval on how she looked. "Damn, I'm fine," she thought as she hurried around the room picking up things she needed to take to the club with her. She grabbed her purse, ID, and two disposable Kodak cameras. Before the night was over she planned to have a few pictures of Prince worth a whopping five thousand dollars she thought happily as she stepped in front of the full length mirror one more time checking out her bare shoulders in the new sexy dress she wore with a split that gave plenty of leg action. Cindy had it going on and she knew it as she closed the door to her bedroom and knocked on Mark's bedroom door. "Mark, I know you're not sleeping so come on out of there."

"Um, um. Hold up Cindy here I come," Mark said scrambling around his room.

Cindy listened to the ruckus and wondered what the hell Mark was up to now. "Mark!" Cindy shouted and she banged on the door. "What are you doing?"

Mark was busy lighting incense and opening windows, cause he didn't want Cindy to know what he had been up to while she was getting dressed. He unlocked the door and cracked it a little bit to tell Cindy he was on his way down, but Cindy wasn't having that. She looked at Mark very suspiciously through the crack in the door and her nose caught the scent of something but she couldn't put her finger on it. She leaned over and started sniffing, and that's when Mark slammed the door shut.

"I'll be out in a minute!" he shouted.

"Oh, no you didn't!" Cindy shouted banging on the door. "Open this door right now Mark O'Neal or I'm going to kick it open."

"You'll have to pay for it!" Mark shouted back through the door. Cindy stepped back and took her heels off. "You've got three seconds or I'm kicking it open!"

"Okay, okay," he said unlocking the door and letting Cindy in his room.

"I knew it," Cindy said sniffing again. "You've been smoking that wacky and you promised you'd quit. Look at you, you're stoned out of your mind!"

Mark just sat there munching on chips. "I'm sorry Cindy, but I needed a toke. My nerves are bad. Would you like some chips?"

"No! So you're not going with me?"

"Yeah, yeah," Mark said putting down the chips and then wiping his hands on his pajamas.

"Look at you! It's time to go and you're not even dressed! I'm pissed at you!" Cindy said storming out of the room.

"You ready right now?" Mark asked following Cindy down the stairs.

"Yes, I am and you Mister, high, in your pajamas or not, are still coming with me," Cindy said pulling Mark on out the front door with her purse and shoes in hand. "You thought you were being slick and thought I was going to let you stay. You play too much."

"No, I wasn't Cindy, honest," Mark protested as Cindy dragged

Mark by his pajamas out the front door.

"You'll just have to wait in the car while I go into Brandy's," she screamed.

****

Nighttime had finally fallen and everybody that was anybody was out for a good time. Ben backed the 1979 Olds Regency slowly out the driveway onto Daly Road. Slowing to a stop, he looked around carefully before putting the big Regency into drive and crept up the street. He had written the address to the Winton Terrace projects down on a piece of paper he put on the front seat. His Berretta was holstered on his hip, the silencer in his pocket and enough ammo and explosives in the trunk of the car to level a city block. Ben quietly said, "The moment of truth as thou should defend thy honor."

"Mark I'm telling you," Cindy screamed. "You're jumping all over my last nerve!"

"What? What did I do?" Mark asked as he continued munching on a fresh can of Pringles. "You're mad cause my chips are loud."

"Oh my, never mind," Cindy said shaking her head. "I hope you have enough junk food in that bag to satisfy your munchies while I'm gone. Pothead!" Mark stopped munching and looked over at Cindy in the driver's seat. "I went from Peebody to Pothead, huh? Okay," and he went back to munching as Cindy pulled into the crowded parking lot. He stopped snacking long enough to check out all the fancy cars parked with their rims still spinning. "Wow Cindy, look at those cars!"

It was pretty fascinating, she thought as she worked her way toward an empty parking spot as security cleared her way. She parked and got out to thank the gentleman.

"That's alright baby. Enjoy yourself," the security guy responded. Once he walked away, Cindy looked at Mark then stuck her head in the truck to whisper something to Mark.

"You like those spinning rims, huh?" Cindy whispered.

"Yeah, they're nice aren't they?"

"I would go ask the guy if he'll let you touch them," she whispered as she stepped out of the truck, "but I won't."

"Why? Come on Cindy, I thought we were tight," Mark whined.

"Cause you wore that damn Scooby Doo outfit," she said and

slammed the truck door. "I hope you gotta go pee," she said laughing as she walked away.

"I'll do it in your truck," Mark yelled out the window.

Cindy gave him the finger and then walked up to the door of Brandy's. She started snapping her fingers as she could hear the DJ jamming on the turntables. While she was checking the flash on her camera, somebody kept saying something to her so she looked up.

"Five dollars miss," the guy at the door said.

Cindy stepped up, paid her five dollars and had to stop so the bouncer could search her purse. She immediately recognized how hot it was inside Brandy's. "My God!" she thought to herself. "It's jam packed in here!" She looked toward the bar for somewhere to sit, but that wasn't happening. It was too crowded to even see, so she started working her way through the crowd. Suddenly, she felt a pair of strong hands rest on her shoulder. She turned and looked up into the face of Steve an ex-boyfriend she once dated. His six foot six frame towered over her.

"I just saw you come in."

"I bet you did as tall as you are. You should be able to see everyone come in!" Cindy said

He laughed and shouted over the music, "I've got a table over here," as he pulled Cindy by the hand through the crowd. They stopped at a table with two empty seats. Steve introduced everybody, pulled out a chair for Cindy and helped her get comfortable. When the waiter came by, Steve ordered drinks for everybody. Cindy turned her seat around a little so she could see the club and dance floor. The girls at the salon weren't lying. Brandy's was definitely off the hook and people were still trying to get in. She sat there sipping on her Long Island Iced Tea and watched everybody party. She stood up to go to the bar for another drink and Steve got up as well and followed her through the crowd. "Oh my God," Cindy thought. "I hope Steve isn't about to ask for a booty call, 'cause now ain't the time!"

"Cindy, hold up. I want to holler at you," Steve yelled over the music.

Ben found the perfect parking spot behind the wooded area of the apartment building on Winton Place. He shut off the lights and engine and sat there quietly listening to the night, feeling his mind, body and soul unite and become whole. Then he ducked down in the front seat listening as a faint sound let him know that the enemy was approaching. Ben got down in a crouch position pulling his Beretta from its holster waiting and listening as the sound became clear. "They're getting closer," Ben thought as he peeked up over the front seat. He could hear lots of motorcycles. He stayed low.

Prince was leading the pack as the Riders turned on Creek Street behind Street's crib. They rode the back way; right past the dark shadows that hid Ben.

Ben waited until the enemy had passed, then he made his move from the car to the bushes. He watched his back, then slipped his backpack of C4 over his shoulders and began creeping through the woods towards his target.

Prince, J. Blaze, Stickyfingers and Hustleman sat quietly at the end of Winton Place behind another project building waiting on China Doll and Kenya to pull up the rear. Prince pulled out his cell phone and pressed Street's number. "Yeah, everything's cool," Prince said into the phone.

"Maybe the white boy was telling the truth and the heat ain't coming until a few days."

"Maybe, maybe not," Street said into the phone but I still don't trust nothing a cop says. I'm coming just make sure everything's cool.

"Chill at that end of the street until we do a drive-by," Prince said. "Dino and P. Funk will be waiting for you at the end of the street."

"Yep, I hear ya," Street said and the line went dead.

"Okay everybody," Prince whispered. "I want Kenya and Hitman to ride past the apartment first. If you don't see nothing then chill at the end of the street with Street and Fats. If you see anybody who looks like a cop, hit your horn and split," Prince said putting his gloves on. "Hustleman and Sticky you two ride after them and me and Blaze will pull up the rear. Alright, let's do it!"

Captain Safeway was trying to be very still as he thought he heard something move in the bushes a few feet away from his unmarked car. He was staked out in the back of the building next to Street's apartment. It was pitch dark, so seeing was impossible, but Tom swore he heard something. "Unit Six to Base. Unit Six to Base." Captain Safeway was startled at the sudden loud sound coming from the radio. "Go Unit Six," Captain Safeway responded turning the volume down. "Suspect is heading home. I repeat suspect is approaching from the south end of Winton Place."

"Back off. Back off now Unit Six. We've got them from here. "Base to Unit One," Captain Safeway whispered.

"Unit One here, I copy Captain. I have two Suzuki bikes approaching from the north. What should I do?

"All units stand by," Captain Safeway said. All units stand by!

At night, sound travels far and Ben instantly picked up Captain Safeway's location and immediately froze in his tracks. He could hear the motorcycles again in the distance and Ben began to move faster, but with caution.

Officer Ward was staked out in an empty apartment in the building across the street on the second floor watching with lights out. "Unit One to Base," Officer Ward whispered.

"Yeah, Tony," Captain Safeway whispered back.

"We've got two more Riders coming down the street on bikes."

"Can you recognize any of them Tony? Do any of them look like they might be Prince?"

"Can't tell Captain. They're all dressed in t-shirts with black helmets and visors sir."

"Just sit tight Tony," Captain Safeway said.

Everything was still quiet and looked normal as Prince and J. Blaze rode down the block making the last sweep looking in cars and windows as they cruised by on their Suzuki's. When Prince and Blaze reached the rest of the gang, everybody was standing around quietly kicking it. Prince pulled up next to Street's Cadillac and took his helmet off. "Everything looks copasetic," Prince said.

Street looked over at Fats. "You still feel like cutting this dope up?"

"How many keys you got left?" Prince asked.

"Two," Street replied.

"Cut'em up into ounces and then call me. We'll be at Brandy's waiting."

"Give me a couple of hours," Street said as he pulled the Caddy away from the curb feeling safe and secure. He rode up the street disturbing the peace with his music banging. 'Only God Can Judge Me', his favorite 2 Pac song.

"Is it a crime,

to fight for what's mine
Everybody's dying,
tell me what's the use of trying
I've been trapped since birth,
I wonder am I really cursed
Why do I have these visions of leaving here in a hearse
And they say it's the white man I should fear
But it's my own kind doing all the killing here

I hear the doctor standing over me
screaming I can make it
Even though my body is full of bullet holes
and I'm bleeding and naked
Still I can't breathe, something's evil in my IV
Lord help me, I think they're killing me
Somebody help me, tell me where to go from here
Cause even thugs cry, but do the Lord really care
I'd rather die like a man, than live like a coward
I know there's a ghetto in heaven
and here I come Black Power
That's what we scream
as we dream in a paranoid state
That's our fate
from a lifetime of hate
Only God Can Judge Me".

That's what Street was jamming to when as his Cadillac rolled up the street. Cindy waited in line at the bar and had another Long Island Iced Tea. As she turned to head back to the table, someone pushed her aside with an "Excuse me", but with enough force to make her spill some of her drink on her hand. When she looked up towards the rude brother that bumped her, she saw at least five other thug-like brothers in tow behind the first rude one. She stepped back as their entourage made their way through the crowded club.

"That's Prince," a voice whispered in her ear. Standing behind Cindy was Shonie, the owner of Hair and Nail Options. Cindy smiled and said hello to Shonie. She turned and hugged Cindy like a sister.

"What's up Cindy? I saw Prince and his crew come through and almost run you over."

"I guess I was in the wrong place at the wrong time."

"Well relax girl and enjoy yourself, I'm about to slide over there where all them fine ass honeys are standing."

"I feel you girl," said Cindy as she watched Shonie quickly disappear. Cindy stood there glaring at her parents' killer from across the room, a little shocked that she was in the same room with him. She pulled the camera from her purse and snapped a few pictures. She couldn't believe how everyone was shaking his hand, giving him hugs and smiles like he was God's gift. He was a murderer and he had to pay for her parents' deaths. "That's a fair exchange," she thought. She just watched the VIP stage where Prince and his crew partied. She could see why all the women fell for him. He was good looking and charming, but beneath the surface she knew he was ruthless. Truthfully, she couldn't stomach the sight of him.

Prince stood in the back of the club talking to another gang member as Cindy watched. She wondered what they were talking about when suddenly they stopped and the Rider Prince was talking too started in Cindy's direction. Cindy ducked back into the crowd and then followed him out the door to the parking lot.

Ben heard the rap music from Street's stereo long before he saw the headlights pulling into the narrow driveway leading to the back parking lot. He pressed himself tightly up against a ten-foot cement wall as the Cadillac parked over his head in the parking lot next door. Hidden completely by the darkness, Ben listened, as his ears became his eyes. A car door slammed.

"Pop the trunk," Fats said as he looked around with his 9mm gripped tightly in his hand. "Hurry up," Fats told his brother after grabbing the last two kilos of cocaine and slamming the trunk closed.

"Nigga, I done told you about slamming my trunk like dat," Street said shutting the driver's door. "This is a Cadillac baby boy and the trunk shuts automatically."

"Yeah, yeah. Big timer I hear ya," Fats said opening the basement door to the apartment building, as they both disappeared inside.

"Base to Unit One," Captain Safeway whispered, "both suspects are inside and they're packing guns."

"Copy that, Captain," Tony said.

"Hold your position until back up arrives."

Ben slowly crawled over the wall and rolled under a car that was in the next building's back lot. He waited until he could tell which apartment they entered before he made another move. Suddenly, the second floor light came on and Ben ducked behind a parked car as the window suddenly open and Street stuck his head out checking the fire escape. That's all Ben needed to see, as he dashed back into the weeds to grab his backpack. He fumbled around in his bag of surprises pulling out wires, duck tape, C4 explosives and his needle nose pliers. He got on his tiptoes and placed everything on top of the wall and quietly pulled himself up and over the wall again, making sure he stayed out of sight. He crawled on his belly until he reached the burgundy Cadillac and then he went to work very carefully taping the bomb under the car and hooking up the positive and negative wires to the starter that would trigger the explosives. After checking to make sure that the car was ready to blow when it was started, Ben quietly placed his tools in the bushes in front of the Cadillac and began crawling on his belly across the small distance of the parking lot toward the apartment building. Making sure he didn't make a sound, the darkness that covered the back lot provided enough cover to keep Captain Safeway's watchful eyes from seeing him make his move.

Once Ben reached the building, he rolled on the ground until he was around the corner. Then he quickly got to his feet and pressed himself against the wall as he stared up at the fire escape that gave him the only access to the second floor apartment where Street and Fats were busy chopping up dope. Taking out his Beretta, Ben began screwing on the silencer for his quiet rendezvous of revenge when the sound of a telephone ringing from an apartment upstairs interrupted the still of the night. Ben didn't move as he quietly listened to the phone continue to ring until Street's voice was heard yelling over the loud sound. "Nigga pick up the damn phone, you know I'm on the damn toilet silly ass nigga!"

"Nigga fuck you!" Fats yelled back as he picked up the phone. "I was in the damn kitchen getting some more baking soda Punk! Yeah who is it?" Fats yelled into the phone.

"Damn Nigga, you can't answer a phone better then that water head boy? Sticky yelled back through the phone. "Prince asked what's takin' you niggaz so damn long?"

"Oh, my bad Sticky but this nigga is getting on my last nerve up in here and I'm about to kick his ass in a minute," Fats said into the phone.

"You ain't going to kick shit!" Sticky heard Street yell in the back ground. "Man you two Niggaz better get it together and cut that dope up, or Prince is going to get in both of your asses!" Sticky said into the phone.

Cindy wasn't more then a few feet away from Sticky as she eavesdropped on their conversation. "Cut up dope," she thought as she touched up her lip-gloss. "How much dope" she wondered "and where's the dope at?"

"Listen, we haven't got time to be bullshittin'," Sticky said into the phone. "If you niggaz can't get along then go in different rooms and cut the dope up! Just get it done and we'll be by the apartment to pick the shit up."

"So they're at an apartment cutting up dope," Cindy said to herself as she continued to eaves drop. "I gotta get these pictures developed and this information to Uncle Tom as soon as possible!" she thought.

"Oh Snap," Sticky said into the phone, "we've got company."

"Who's that?" Fats asked with concern as he tried to listen through the commotion. Who's that Sticky?"

"Man, it's Spencer and his partner pulling into the driveway! Listen I got to go!" Sticky said. "You niggaz just hurry up and we'll call you back," and the line went dead.

Cindy saw the police car pull in at the same time Sticky did. She started to run for the truck but instead she turned and went back inside the club.

The music in the club was deafeningly loud and all the Ruff Riders were drinking and dancing as if they didn't have a care in the world. So no one really paid a lot of attention to Officer Spencer when he came through the door and headed straight for the VIP section to have a word with Prince.

Cindy watched until she had them both in her sights. She took one more picture and headed out the door to find Captain Safeway.

Ben had made plenty of progress during the course of the conversation that was taking place inside the apartment. Instead of using the fire escape stairs which would have made too much noise, Ben jumped and pulled himself up by the braces that held the fire escape in place and now in a crouched position he waited outside of the window where Street and Fats stood talking in the living room.

"Did he say the police were on their way or what?" Street asked his brother as he sat down in front of all the dope on the coffee table.

"Naw man! He said Spencer just rolled up in the club and we needed to hurry up," Fats said. "So that's what I'm about to do." He headed to the kitchen for more baking soda and Ben made his move.

Peeking around the corner of the window, Ben lifted his Beretta as he watched Fats disappear into the other room.

Street sat in front of the window and continued chopping and weighing his share of the dope. Ben's first shot made the back of his head explode all over the couch he was sitting on as his body fell with a crash on top of the coffee table. The noise brought Fats running from the kitchen with gun in hand but all he saw was his brother resting in a pool of blood. Ben aimed from the darkness and shot Fats with two quiet slugs that sent his young body crashing into the front door of the tiny apartment. Ben's mission was only half accomplished and he didn't waste any time making his move to get off the fire escape as he jumped back down to the ground and carefully found his way back towards the bushes where his backpack of goodies was hidden.

"Unit Five to base, Unit Five to base. Come in."

Captain Safeway didn't answer his radio right away because he thought his eyes were playing tricks on him. He could have sworn he saw something move in the darkness in the back parking lot. Just as he was about to check it out, somebody on his stakeout team decided to break his strict orders of radio silence and now he was pissed. Now who's ever out there in the darkness knew exactly where he was at and that didn't sit too well with the Captain. "Got damn it Unit Five!" the Captain whispered hoarsely into the radio, "don't you know what radio silence is? That's why I didn't want you on this team!"

"I'm sorry Captain," Spencer said into the radio. "I was just letting you know that I was back from my bathroom break."

"Oh my God," Captain Safeway said to himself. "Officer Spencer just cover the south end of the street and stay off of the radio please."

Ben sat very still as he listened to the exchange. "Something big is going down." He became more careful but even quicker as he made his way out of the wooded area and back to his 79 Olds Regency.

****

Prince had all the Ruff Riders sitting down in the VIP section as he gave out last minute instructions. "The cop Spencer just told me that the heat was off and he'll let me know if the task force puts our name back on the list," Prince said from his seat by the D.J booth.

"You think he's telling the truth?" Kenya asked.

"It's hard to tell. You know you can't trust a cop. All I know is that I paid him Ten Grand for the real and if he sold me out I'm taking him with me."

"An eye for eye," Dino said.

"Hey Prince, I can't get no answer at the apartment! I done tried three times all ready!" Sticky said

"No answer? But you just talked to them fifteen minutes ago and now you can't get an answer? Prince was getting mad now, "Come on let's go! There's some shit in the game and I know it! China Doll, you and Hustleman stay here," Prince instructed as they all headed out the club. If anything goes wrong, you know what to do."

"Okay Prince," China said.

"Kenya, you ride with J. Blaze!" Prince said as he put on his helmet. The noise of all seven bikes starting simultaneously was deafening and was only sound that filled the night air. Prince, J.Blaze, Kenya, Sticky-yfingers, Hitman, P.Funk, and Dino took off after Prince on their way toward Winton Terrace to check on Street and Fats. Prince knew as he led the way that they might be riding into a set up but he couldn't worry about that because it's all part of the game.

"Unit Four to Base, do you copy?"

Base to Unit Four, I copy you," Captain Safeway said.

"I've got motorcycles coming in my direction Captain."

"I copy that Unit Four. All units on stand by! Unit One, Captain Safeway whispered.

"Unit One here Captain," Officer Tony whispered back.

"Keep a close eye on the front entrance of the apartment Tony."

"I copy that Captain."

"All Units, wait for my signal. I repeat, wait for my signal," the Captain whispered.

The gang took the same back route to the projects they had taken earlier and they passed right by Ben just like earlier who was sitting in his car waiting for the fireworks to begin. Ben wasn't going to miss this show for anything in the world, so he watched the gang of Riders ride past him until they turned right on Winton Place.

Prince stopped and put his hand up, "We go in like we did earlier two at a time. Dino, you and P Funk go first. Ride down to the end of the street and then ride back to the apartment. If everything is cool, then I want you two to lock down the back parking lot."

"No problem," Dino and P Funk said as they started up their bikes and took off.

Prince waited until Dino and P Funk had cleared the way for the next two riders to cruise down the street. "Blaze, you and Kenya go check out the apartment. Call me on the cell phone and tell me what the damage is." Prince leaned back on his bike to wait. Sticky and Hitman waited with him. "If this is a set up, I ain't going down by myself. Somebody's going with me!" He pulled two nickel plated 9mm's from his book bag and strapped them to his sides. "I got a funny feeling Spencer just sold us out and if so, I'm taking a few of his buddies with me." With that said, he placed a hand grenade in his jacket pocket. "It's show and tell now!"

"You see Adams," Spencer was saying as he and his partner were watching from their stake out position at all the Ruff Riders riding into Captain Safeway's drag net. "We made an easy ten grand tax free and now were about to get rid of the evidence. Shake 'em down and then set 'em up," Spencer said from the passenger seat of the cruiser.

"I guess we do make all the rules," Adam said to his partner.

"It's just the fringe benefits that comes along with the badge partner," Spencer smugly said.

"Look!" Adams said, pointing at the two riders parking their bikes and entering the front of the apartment. "That's a girl under that helmet!"

"Well, she's going to get treated like a man tonight!" Spencer said as he began checking the clip on his gun. He wanted to be ready to finish the job whenever Captain Safeway gave the word. "Look for Prince. That's the only one we want."

Suddenly loud screams could be heard coming from the building. "Oh shit!" Adams said sitting straight up and staring out the windshield. "Did you hear that?" he asked Spencer.

"Relax, relax," Spencer whispered to his partner with some concern. "I think it's about to go down so get ready."

"Something's wrong!" Prince said. "That was Kenya screaming. Let's go! Watch the front'" Prince told Hitman. "Sticky you come with me!" and they both ran up the stairs to the sound of Kenya hysterical sobbing.

"They didn't have to kill them! They didn't have to kill them!" was all she could say as she held Fats' bloody body in her arms. "Prince why did they do it?" she yelled when Prince walked through the door.

Prince instantly took charge, "Blaze get Kenya out of here. Take her out back away from this mess. Don't nobody touch nothing!" Prince ran to the back room and opened up the window. He stuck his head out and yelled at Dino and P Funk, "Check the Cadillac to see if our money is missing!" then he turned around and went back into the other room. "What the hell is this shit Sticky!" Prince screamed.

"It looks like a hit," Sticky said looking around the room. "If it was a robbery then they would've taken all the dope that's still laying on the table."

"You got a point," Prince said and he headed to the back window. "Have you opened that damn trunk yet?" Prince asked Dino.

"I need the key," Dino whispered as he stood under the window.

"Here's the keys right here," Sticky said from the door.

"Drop them to Dino and let's get outta here," Prince told Sticky as they started for the front door.

"All units stand by," Captain Safeway whispered into his radio as he watched all the gang members in the back lot from his unmarked car. 'Just open the trunk,' he said to himself "and we got cha! "Come on just open the trunk."

"Damn!" J. Blaze said after he got tired of watching them trying to open the trunk with the key. "Ain't you niggaz ever been in a Cadillac before?" he said snatching the keys from Dino. "The trunk button is right here inside the car!" J. Blaze said as he opened the car door and reached over and hit the button.

Just as the trunk opened, Captain Safeway screamed into the radio, "All units go! All units go!" Suddenly, dark became light, and the projects looked like Christmas Eve as red, white, and blue police lights lit the entire area.

"Aw shit, the cops!" Prince yelled heading down the steps with Stickyfingers on his heels. They reached their bikes just as the first police car came rolling in. "Around the back," Prince yelled to Sticky as both bikes headed down the driveway towards the back of the building.

"It's a trap!" J. Blaze screamed to Prince. "Go back, go back!" he yelled as he started running for cover.

Prince popped a wheelie, turned his bike around and headed up the driveway. Another police car came out of nowhere to block his path. He hit the brakes and turned his bike just in time to duck a bullet that came straight for his head. "Oh shit! That's Spencer shooting at me!" Prince said to himself.

"Damn, I missed him," Spencer mumbled taking aim for a second shot just as Prince took off down the driveway.

The police were coming out the woodwork by now and there was no exit. J. Blaze and Hitman tried running through the basement of the building only to be hit with 50,000 volts of electricity by the police who waited there. Dino, P.Funk, and Kenya jumped in the Cadillac to escape the stun guns of the police.

"Turn around! Turn around!" Prince yelled to Sticky as they popped the clutches on their bikes and started moving at a speed that left them no choice but to jump fifty feet over the edge to the next building's back parking lot. "Come on Sticky!" Prince yelled. "We can make this jump!"

The first explosion came just as Dino turned the ignition and Ben's surprise sent flames ten feet high into the air. Then the second explosion sounded as the gas tank blew. All the near by Ruff Riders burned alive in a ball of flames as the fire lit up the night and the screams from those trapped in the fire filled the air.

Prince's fate wasn't much different as the impact from the explosions sent him flying sideways through the air out of control holding tightly to the handlebars of his Suzuki. He crashed into the brick building next door and a third explosion came from the hand grenade that still rested in his pocket. The remainder of the bike and parts of Prince's torso fell to the ground burning.

"Jumping Jesus!" Captain Safeway said as he shielded his eyes from the brightness of the flames and watching the body of Prince suffer its fate. He took his eyes off the flames long enough to look over at Tony and ask, "Do you think that was Prince who crashed into that building?"

Tony looked at the Captain and pointed to the other twisted body of the Rider who took the daring jump. "Do you think he's any better off than what his partner just got?"

"I think the guy who just exploded was much worse off," the Captain said as he started toward the burning money that littered the ground. "I guess I better call someone to clean this mess up. You know what Tony?" The Captain started to ask. But his cell phone ringing interrupted him and he realized it was his wife. "Yes honey?"

"Tom, are you okay sweetheart?"

"Sure honey, why?"

"We're watching this big fire on the news honey and they said there's this big stake out going on. So Cindy told me to call you," Debra said with a concerned voice.

"CINDY!" Tom yelled. "You've found Cindy?"

"Yes honey, she's right here with a bunch of pictures to show you."

"Tell her I said not to move. I'm on my way!" Tom's heart leaped at the news of hearing that Cindy was okay and at home. "Honey listen, calm down. I'm on my way, don't let Cindy out your sight and tell her not worry. Her daddy's killer is dead."

Ben watched the fireworks with mixed feelings as his thoughts were with his mother. Even though his revenge was successful and the games were over, his mother was still gone and to him that didn't feel like a 'Fair Exchange' as he started the engine to his '79 Olds Regency. An eye for an eye didn't add up this time but then if you think about it, does it ever add up?

CHAPTER 24

After the deadly altercation between the police and Ruff Riders, Cincinnati seemed to be rather quite and very still. The streets were empty from the normal thug activity that usually took place on every street corner, no dope boys or activise with bull horns were seen chasing each other through out the nieborhoods that were once littered with crackheads and every day hussling by dope pushers. Finally, the people who once feared the streets of there community could now walk to the corner store with out worry. "Yes, things were quite finally, rather a little too quite but yet and still quite, and that's all that mattered.

Coach Andrews drove through many of the nieborhoods that were once full of life that seemed deserted now, as his designation this morning was the university hospital to visit a friend that he loved like his very own. He road in complete silence and bewilderment after learning about the unfortunate fate three of his past football stars suffered at the hands of the police and the Ruff Riders deadly altercation. A lot of guilt and pity weighed heavily on Coach Andrew's heart as he continued to blame himself for the failure of three kids who's lifes went astray right before his very eye's. Three kids who had promising futures as football stars one day had they stayed in school but unfortunately now there wanted for rape and murder and Coach Andrews just couldn't understand why these three young black kids choose to throw such promising futures away.

Everybody who had a voice in Cincinnati gave the police a ear full as the press and local church groups expressed their concern about the drastic messures of using explosives to clean up the crime in the streets.

One week had past since the last funeral of all the Ruff Riders who were killed at the results of Bens bomb were buried. All the local charity organizations around Cincinnati who stepped up to help the families who lost their child in the much talked about tragedy were giving Capt. Safeway all kinds of grief, as they screamed bloody murder at the police.

How can you use such drastic messures to deal with these kids, people were screaming! Planting bombs, that's ridiculous, one reporter yelled.

No one knew of Ben's existence, he was something of a phatom that didn't exist to the public but a problem that gave Captain Safeway a nagging headache as the blame fell on him for the mess Ben had made.

It could've been worse the Captain thought to himself as he relaxed in his office this morning ducking reporters and all the news media that's been snooping around the past week trying to get a story out of Tom. "NO COMMENT, NO COMMENT was all Captain Safeway had been saying to the media who kept asking Tom the same old question. "Where did the explosives come from"? "Do you think you've put a end to the Ruff Rider gang"?

What about are your officer's fine, are can we do any thing to help there families, Tom thought as he hid out in his office going over in his mind what his next move should be. Every morning the same damn question and Tom wasn't about to let the media eat him alive on this one, I'll let some body else take the fall for the department this time. So Captain Safeway hid out in his office up stairs at the precinct in deep thought in his big comfortable chair thinking, when his telephone started ringing.

Ring, Ring, Ring. Tom looked at the phone and was tempted not to answer thinking it was another reporter trying to get a story, but he refused to keep hiding and ducking so he yanked the phone off the receiver.

Captain Safeway here, he yelled. How can I help you!

Some what taken back by the tone of the Captains voice, "I'm sorry Captain it sounds as if I caught you at a bad time" Coach Andrews said into the phone. "Oh my goodness, I'm sorry Coach Andrews. I thought you might have been another one of those reports that's been harassing me all morning Captain Safeway said. It's like a circus down here at the station.

I'm sure it is Coach Andrews said, I'm rather curious myself as to what happen and that's why I'm calling. If it's okay with you Captain, I'm on my way to the hospital to visit Jason McNickels and I was wondering if you had any objections the Coach asked.

For you Coach Andrews of course not the Captain responded, I think Stickyfingers could use a friend right about now. But I can only give you a half an hour Coach, as you know he is under police supervision at the hospital and I can only bend the rules so far Captain Safeway said into the phone. I appreciate your kindness Captain, as you know these kids mean a great deal to me and what ever time you give me is greatly appreciated.

Don't sweat it Coach, I know how you feel about them kids the Captain said with sincerity. I wish there were more people like you who cared about these kids futures, but unfortunately there isn't and that's why I like you Coach Andrews and if there is anything else I can do please call the captain said.

Thank you Captain, Coach Andrew said. It's a sad situation but these kids need me now more then ever. It is a sad situation Coach, but we all live and learn. Let's just hope these kids learn the valuable lesson that's there to be learned from this and maybe a happy ending will come about from all of this someday.

I hope so Captain and thanks again Coach Andrews said, I'll be in touch Captain and Coach Andrews hung his cell phone up as he was turning into the hospital parking garage.

Officer Storey, Tom turned and shouted into his phone intercome. Yes Captain, came her response.

Contact the officers at the hospital watching Jason McNickels and inform them that I've given visitation rights to Coach Andrews for no longer then thirty minutes.

Yes Captain, I'll get right on it sir and the intercome went silent.

Do to the police round up of all the gang members who pertisapeted in this long and on going deadly turf war between the Riders and Warriors, the county jail was suddenly over populated with young men who's destiny's in life were about to be determined by the judge and jury of the justice system. Unfortunately for a lot of these young men that meant what ever dreams and goals they once had were now gone and what talents God blessed them with would never be shared with the world, as the only thing that awaited them now was the misery and pain of a long penitentiary life.

"Count Time, lock it up for count time the officer yelled to all the inmates sitting in the day room who were watching T.V. or playing cards. J.Blaze and Hitman were amoung the few the officer was talking too. Man this is some bullshit J.Blaze said as he got up from the chess game him and Hitman were playing. Hitman was still sitting down at the table studing his next move on the chess board.

Yeah Man, I agree with you on that Hitman said as he slowly got up and started towards the small 6x9 cell him and J.Blaze had been sharing since they had been locked up in the county jail.

CLANG, CLANG, CLANG, was all that could be heard as each inmate on cell block 4 north retreated to their cells for count time and locked it up, all though count time was a inconvenience that most inmates disliked as it did disrupt their T.V. time, it also was mail call time which meant a moment of temporary joy that every inmate looked forward to with hopes that somebody on the streets took the time to send a few words of encouragement.

"MAIL CALL, so listen up the officer yelled. "If you hear your name called come out your cell after count clears and pick up your mail at the officer's station. The officer stood up and tossed the dingy grey mail bag on the desk, then he stepped towards the middle of the cell block with a pile of letters in his hand and began yelling names, "Juan Amos, Ray Jones, Charles

Carter", Yeah, Yeah, Hitman yelled as he and Blazed rejoiced in their cell after hearing one of their names called.

"Tyron Smith, Jack Jackson, Jeff Wright", Yeah, here I am J. Blaze shouted with lots of excitement as he slapped high fives with Hitman like they use to do when they were scoring touchdowns.

"I wonder who wrote us J. Blaze said as he waited by the bars of his cell door waiting for count to be cleared, so he could hurry to the officer's desk to pick his mail up.

Hitman just relaxed on his top bunk and started thinking about these bars that had him feeling like a caged animal. Reality was starting to sink in. "Count clear, the officer yelled. Line up to pick up your mail!

Tom sat back in his big chair and looked through all the photo's again that Cindy had taken and he still couldn't believe that officer Spencer was on the take, but here it is in living color him and Prince. My oh my I wonder what the Chief would have to say about his future son in law now, Tom thought.

Suddenly the tap of heals walking across the tile floor outside of Tom's office made the captain look up from the photo's to see a very gorgeous light complected black woman in a business suit talking to his secretary "Fancy".

"Tom waited for his intercome to come to life as he new it would right about now."

"Captain Safeway, Fancy yelled through his intercome"

Tom was right on her as he pushed his intercome reply botton. "Um Yes, officer Storey."

"You have a vistor from the F.B.I. sir," an agent Marcia Dixon.

"Send her in Tom said. F.B.I. agent Tom thought, this beautiful lady...

Knock, Knock.

"Please, come right on in Tom said opening the door for this very fine
woman.

Decked out in a Armani pinstriped suit with black pumps that made her a even 5'10 in height, F.B.I. agent Marcia Dixon strolled pass Tom with a killer smile that could've made any man melt.

"Hi, Captain Safeway. My pleasure to meet your acquaintance she said holding out one of her well manicured hands.

Please call me Tom, and really it's all my pleasure Tom said shaking her hand. Have a seat Tom said as he closed his office door and scooted around to sit behind his desk. "So how can I help you agent Dixon, Tom said as he watched agent Dixon open up her briefcase to remove some folders that she pushed in Tom's direction.

"My superiors sent me here to investigate a murder of a young girl by the name of Monica Johnson", agent Dixon said.

"Monica Johnson has been murdered, Captain Safeway said in disbelief. When? Tom asked.

We haven't determined the time of death as of yet Captain, but what we have deteminded is from the evidence we found by the body, the suspect or suspects could very well be apart of your police force and that's when she handed Tom a plastic bag containing a small silver personalized nickel-plated pocketknife that had the initials JS engraved on the handle.

"Our resources tell us that this knife could belong to this officer" and agent Dixon handed Tom a folder and the name on the folder jumped right on Tom so quick he almost lost his breath. Officer James Spencer, are you sure about this Tom looked up and asked.

The intials on the knife J.S. matched the suspect in question and our resource who provided us with the tip gave us a sworn signed statement that officer Spencer raped and then murdered Monica Johnson to cover up the crime, agent Dixon responded.

Tom couldn't believe it and for a moment he was speechless, but things were starting to make some sense as Captain Safeway did remember a small silver pocket knife he scowled Spencer for cleaning his nails with in his office when he first was transferred to his district that looked just like the the knife in the plastic bag he seen Spencer with. Now things were starting to get a little more interesting. It was mid afternoon and the sun was at it's highest peak, it was to hot to hussle on the block but their was some who hussled inside around some air condition and P's Pool Hall had plenty of A/C, that's why all the pool hustlers shot pool at P's because it was the most popular pool hall in the city. The old folks hung around watching soaps on the old T.V. that had a coat hanger for an antenna while discussing current events, while the younger players like Pretty Tony made their living on the pool tables.

"8 ball in the corner off the rail", Pretty Tony said as he bent over the table to take his shot. Hiting the Q ball with a little left hand english, taping the 8 hard enough to bank it off a rail and watch it roll in the corner pocket.

"That'll be a hundred bucks" my brotha Pretty Tony said, as he flashed his gold tooth pretty boy smile and jacked on the slacks of his tailored Gucci 2 piece linen out fit.

"Now, are there any more "Pool Players" up in this joint waiting to make a generous donation to the Pretty Tony foundation, if so then your moment has arrived Pretty Tony shouted.

"Man well you quit blowin your horn, so we can hear our TV program" one old player screamed at Tony from his seat on a stool in front of the old television.

"Yeah Young Blood, hold it down for a minute another old timer said.

"You old cats and yah soap oprea's, Pretty Tony said laughing while putting his pool stick in it's case. I hope I don't ever grow old and be grumpy like you old niggaz in here Pretty Tony said as he headed towards the door to take on the blistering heat of the afternoon.

Suddenly the front door burst open, making Pretty Tony snatch his hand back as his ol' friend Spider came out the heat and into the air condition.

Hey Pretty Tony, Spider yelled. It's hot and funkier then a fort in a brown paper bag outside."Damn we need some rain".

"Say Pretty Toney", let a brother hold something. Remember you owe me for unlocking the back gate when them Ruff Riders was after your ass, plus I got something you might want to know, Spider said.

Man I'm broke Spider for real Pretty Tony said, but I'm gonna tighten you up later after I hit a few licks.

Well o'kay Spider said, when you get some money I'll tell you what I know.

"Hold up Spider, it aint got to be like that baby" Pretty Tony said as he put his arm around Spiders shoulder. If you tell me I promise to pay you tonite, Pretty Tony told him.

Nope Spider said, if you pay me tonite then I'll tell you tonite.

OKAY Damn Pretty Tony said, reaching into his pocket and handing Spider a fiddy spot. This better be good my nizzle or I want a refund, Pretty Tony said in disgust of having to fork over some of his hard earned cash.

Spider looked around the pool hall and then told Tony, let's go out side so we can have some privacy.

Hitman got his piece of mail first and he looked at it and then turned the white envelope over and looked at the back, then he thought to himself wondering who would send him a letter without leaving a return address.

"Who's it from J Blaze said", as he waited in line to get his letter.

"I don't know Hitman said as he opened the envelope and a pink receipt fell to the floor and landed face up, revealing a stamp from the caishiers office that had the sum of five hundred dollars written on it.

Both Hitman and J Blaze said "Damn" at the same time when they saw the amount on the cashiers receipt. That kind of cash didn't just fall out the sky everyday, especially when your locked up and for got about.

Once outside the pool hall and standing in the blistering heat, Pretty Tony listened to the valuable information Spider had to tell him.

I'm telling you man, she was the finest chick I've ever seen around here and she gave me this message to give to you." She said she's taking over operations of the Ruff Riders and all depts owed to Prince are now owed to her. She said you would know what she's talking about and if by chance you might have forgotten, she'll be back to remind you, Spider said.

That's all Pretty Tony needed to hear and he was gone back inside the pool hall in a dash searchin franticly for his pool stick and case. "Spider", open the back door Pretty Tony yelled as he headed for the back door of the pool hall with his pool stick lifted to crack the first head who tried to stop his escape.

"I got cha" Spider said as he hurried through the back room to take the chain off the back door. "Man, you better hurry" Spider said loudly.

In the mean time parked in a dark blue Ford Exployer a few doors up the street. China Doll and Hustleman watched the conversation take place between Spider and Pretty Tony.

"It looks like he took the bait", China Doll said. Come on it's time to move and the Ford Exployer roared to life and rolled right pass Pretty Tony and Spider running back inside the pool hall. China Doll turned the corner and barely missed another car that didn't see the Ford Explore coming. China Doll whipped the truck to a hault as Hustlman and T Baby jumped out in single file taking off in a dead ran across and down a alley towards the back exit of the pool hall, Hustleman limped with his cain in hand but he was step for step with T Baby until they both found the back door and waited with lifted guns for Pretty Tony to come running out to receive the surprise of his life and a fair exchange he would never forget.

In the mean time at the university hospital in room 303 Jason "Stickyfingers" McNickels unconscious body laid shackled to his hospital bed on the 8th floor prison ward, with a half body cast to help heal the three broken ribs, two broken legs, and fractured left hip that he received from the daring jump he and Prince attempted to elude the police the night Ben's bomb blew them and their bikes to the height of fifty feet in the air.

Coach Andrews had been sitting next to Stickys unconscious body for the past hour watching his chest raise and fall with each breath that he took, thanking God for at least sparing his life and giving him a second chance to live and possibly turn his life around.

Suddenly the door to Stickys room opened and in walked a doctor with a chart board in hand.

"Hi, I'm Dr. Miles.

"Hi, Doc. I'm Glen Andrews, the coach of the Woodward Riders football team the coach said standing and shaking hands with the doctor.

"Ah Yes, Dr. Miles said. I recognize you now the docter said with a smile as he placed his telescope in his ear and began listening to Stickys heart beat.

Jason was one of your star players some years back when the Riders won two state championships, Dr. Miles said as he moved his telescope from Stickys heart to his lungs.

"Yes he was, Coach Andrews said from the other side of Stickys bed as he watched the doctor examin Stickys unconscious body.

"Is he gonna be alright Doc., the coach asked.

Their was a moment of silence before the doctor answered, as he was listening to Stickys lungs and finishing up his examination. He'll be fine Dr. Miles said as he removed his telescope from his ears to place it back snugely around his neck, "this young man is a fighter coach and very lucky to be alive after such a sever crash the doctor said as he began checking Stickys pulse.

He's gonna be a very sore young man once this half body cast comes off Dr. Miles said after finishing up, but at least he's gonna live to tell about it.

I suppose so the coach said looking down at Sticky, unfortunately some of his friends can't say that much the coach said with a sad tone as he remembered how many young lifes were lost the night that bomb went off.

Well coach the doctor said, I think we need to let Jason rest. Why don't you stop by tomorrow and check on his progress, hopefully soon he'll regain consciousness and you can talk to him. "Oh Sure Doc, the coach said jumping up from his chair next to Stickys bed, your right he needs his rest.

Back at the precinct the conversation between F.B.I. Agent Marcia Dixson and Captain Safeway was winding down and coming to a hault, just as the phone on the Captains desk came to life.

"You just don't know agent Dixson how happy I am to hand this investigation over to the Feds, and I wish you all the luck in the world in finding Ben O'Bannon. I swear that son of a gun is invisible if you ask me, Capt. Safeway said as he handed the Ruff Rider file to agent Dixson.

"Yes Captain I must agree, it sounds like you've had your hands full for a while with this investigation agent Dixson said as she began stuffing the Ruff Rider file in her brief case when the phone began ringing on the Captains desk.

(RING, RING,)

"Just great a phone call Tom said, excuse me Ms. Dixson.

Hello, Captain Safeway here.

Hey Captain, Tony Ward here.

Hey Tony, What's up?

Well Captain, I got a little bad news for you Tony said over the phone. We just found Tony Raymond aka "Pretty Tony" shot to death execution style over here in Walnut Hills behind "P"s Pool Hall.

"Say What, Tom said. You've got to be kidding me Tony.

"No Captain I'm not kidding," Tony said.

What about witnesses Tony, the Captain asked? Did anybody see anything Tom wondered even though he already knew the answer before he asked the question. Nobody never see's anything in the hood.

No Captain no witnesses yet, but I did find something rather interesting Tony said.

Oh yeah, what's that Tony.

I found a piece of paper in Pretty Tony's pocket that had officer's Spencer cell phone number on it!

Look Hitman I got a five hundred dollar money order too, J Blaze said happily as he waved his pink money receipt around in the air. Did you get a letter with yours Hitman said is what I want to know, as he pointed at the envelope in J blaze's hand. I think I did J. Blaze said seriously as he forgot about the money long enough to pull a folded piece of paper out the envelope that seemed to have nothing more then just a paragraph or two writtin down on it.

Dear J. Blaze and Hitman,

Here's a few dollars to hold you off, sorry it took so long for me to get it to you. Things have been really hectic lately with all the funerals and everything.

We buried Prince, P Funk, Street, and Fats all in past couple of weeks and it was hard on everybody but the whole gang represented as all the Ruff Riders wore there colors and rode double file on our bikes from the church to the cemetery.

Danielle flew in for the funerals and brought your God son little Prince with her, seeing Prince in his coffin was really hard on everybody but Danielle couldn't take it and she just broke down.

I dropped ten grand off to a lawyer last week for you, Hitman, and Sticky. He's suppose to be the best in Cincinnati and he thinks he can get all of you off with some light sentences, maybe a year or two for the dope charges. You don't have to worry about the rape charges, they should be dropping those charges shortly. Watch the news and you'll understand why, it seems that the F.B.I. thinks a certain Cincinnati police officer is responsible for the rape and murder of Monica. That little ace in the hole Prince had set up came right on time.

I got a girl friend at the hospital checking on Stickyfingers condition everyday, right now he's still unconscious but he's gonna live. So keep him in your prayers.

The gang is still together and Hustleman is running things until you three get out, and if you haven't heard yet they found Pretty Tony shot to death behind "P"s Pool hall. Word on the street he was snitching us out to officer Spencer, so his luck ran out just like officer's spencers luck is about to run out. It's all a Fair Exchange and you know that's all the Ruff Riders deal in.

I'll be in touch, we're family 4 life.
-China Doll

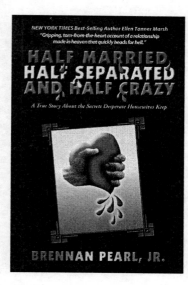

Half Married, Half Separated and Half Crazy
$15.95

Brennan Pearl, Jr.

2006
Booksurge Publishing
Non-Fiction

AVAILABLE ONLINE AT:

www.BPJR.com
www.myspace.com/blog/brennanpearljr
www.amazon.com ✦ www.target.com ✦ www.borders.com

COMING SOON

As I walked through the valley of the shadow of death,
I feared no evil.......*The Autobiography of Brennan Pearl, Jr.*